NIGHTMARE TOWN

Dashiell Hammett was born in St. Mary's County, Maryland, in 1894. He grew up in Philadelphia and Baltimore. He left school at the age of fourteen and held several jobs thereafter – messenger boy, newsboy, clerk, time-keeper, yardman, machine operator, and stevedore. He finally became an operative for the Pinkerton Detective Agency.

World War One, in which he served as a sergeant, interrupted his sleuthing and injured his health. When he was finally discharged from the last of several hospitals, he resumed detective work. Subsequently, he turned to writing, and in the late 1920s he became the unquestioned master of detective story fiction in America. During World War Two, Dashiell Hammett again served in the army, this time for more than two years, most of which he spent in the Aleutians. He died in 1961.

Also by Dashiell Hammett

black & white, shadows
light exploration

NIGHTMARE TOWN
STORIES

DASHIELL HAMMETT

*Edited by Kirby McCauley, Martin H. Greenberg
and Ed Gorman*

crime fiction always describes
the price of this
↓
corruption, dreary & Modernity

PICADOR

First published 1999 as a Borzoi Book by Alfred A. Knopf, Inc.

This edition published 2002 by Picador
an imprint of Pan Macmillan Ltd
Pan Macmillan, 20 New Wharf Road, London N1 9RR
Basingstoke and Oxford
Associated companies throughout the world
www.panmacmillan.com

ISBN 0 330 48110 X

3 5 7 9 8 6 4 2

A CIP catalogue record for this book is available from
the British Library.

Printed and bound in Great Britain by
Mackays of Chatham plc, Chatham, Kent

CONTENTS

INTRODUCTION

From the English-speaking world there are a good many instances of great writers carrying only a few slimmish volumes of their works as they file past St Peter; and just behind Thomas Gray and A.E. Housman we may well spot Samuel Dashiell Hammett in the queue at the 'no-more-than-six-items' counter in the celestial supermarket.

Hammett's six? The five full-length novels written in the brief period 1929–34, including the universally acknowledged masterpieces *The Maltese Falcon* and *The Glass Key*; plus a collection (fairly considerable) of short stories, covering a much longer period. *Nightmare Town* presents the reader with twenty of these stories, most of which have been unavailable in print for some time.

In view then of his comparatively limited output, we may reasonably ask if the high praise bestowed on Hammett by Raymond Chandler and Ross Macdonald – his two most distinguished heirs in the 'hard-boiled' lineage – was perhaps a little over the top. And to put readers' minds at rest (there are enough questions to be sorted out in the stories) the answer is 'decidedly not'.

Each of these three writers was practising his craft in a society that was corrupt – with even some of the private eyes potentially corruptible themselves – and in a world that seemed randomly ordained. The advice to fellow writers who were in some doubt about the continuation of a plot was usually 'Have a man come through the door with a gun!' and the ubiquity of guns then was a match for that of mobile phones today. Furthermore, as Chandler maintained, murder was committed not just to provide a detective-story writer with a plot.

Almost all the sleuths featured in the troubled and often chaotic years between the 20s and the 50s would have been wholly sceptical about solving a case with the aim of putting the universe back to rights, of restoring some semblance of a moral framework to a temporarily blighted planet. No. They were doing the job they were paid to do, as was Hammett himself in his years working for the Pinkerton Detective Agency, with the resolution (if any) of their cases more the result of chance, of hunches, of experience than of some Sherlockian expertise in Eastern European cigar-wrappings.

It is the last mentioned qualification, that of experience, which gives the Hammett stories their distinctive flavour of authenticity. Yet it would be rather misleading to categorize them, in a wholly general sense, as essays in 'realistic' fiction, since Hammett is as liable as most detective-story writers to settle for the reassuringly 'romantic' approach that his gritty and usually fearless sleuths are little short of semi-heroic stature.

Who are these men?

First, we meet the unnamed Continental Op, an operative with the 'Continental Agency', who in spite of his physical appearance, short and fat, is clearly based on the tall and elegant Hammett himself, with the casework based on Hammett's personal experiences as a Pinkerton detective. In this selection, we have seven stories featuring the Op, each narrated in a matter-of-fact style in the first person, and each illustrating some aspect of his tenacity and ruthlessness, but affording virtually no biographical information.

Second (and taking Hammett's first name) is Sam Spade, who features here in 'A Man Called Spade', 'Too Many Have Lived', and 'They Can Only Hang You Once' – the only three stories from the whole corpus in which the memorable hero of *The Maltese Falcon* walks and stalks the streets of San Francisco once again. The narration is in the third person, and as with the Op we are given next to no biographical details that we had not already known. Spade has no wish to solve any erudite riddles; he is a hard and shifty fellow quite capable of looking after himself, thank you; his preoccupation is to do his job and to get the better of the criminals some client has paid him to tangle with.

The third – and for me potentially the most interesting – is a man who appears here, just the once, in 'The Assistant Murderer', introduced as follows in the first sentence:

> Gold on the door, edged with black, said ALEXANDER RUSH, PRIVATE DETECTIVE. Inside, an ugly man sat tilted back in a chair, his feet on a yellow desk.

He is a match for the other two – laconic, sceptical, successful; yet I think that Hammett was striking out in something of a new direction with Alec

Rush, and I wish that he had been more fully developed elsewhere.

The other stories offer considerable range and variety – not only in local-ity, but more interestingly in diction and point of view. Take, for instance, the repetitive, virtually unpunctuated narrative of the young boxer (already punch-drunk, we suspect) at the opening of 'His Brother's Keeper':

> I knew what a lot of people said about Loney but he was always swell to me. Ever since I remember he was swell to me and I guess I would have liked him just as much even if he had been just somebody else instead of my brother; but I was glad he was not somebody else.

Again, take the psychological study, in 'Ruffian's Wife', of a timid woman who suddenly comes to the shocking realization that her husband . . . But readers must read for themselves.

After reading (and greatly enjoying) these stories, what surprised me most was how Hammett has kept the traditional 'puzzle' element alive. The major-ity of the stories end with some cleverly structured surprise, somewhat remi-niscent of O'Henry at his best (see especially, perhaps, 'The Second-Story Angel'). But such surprises are not in the style of a pomaded Poirot shepherd-ing his suspects into the library before finally expounding the truth. Much more likely here is that our investigator happens to be seated amid the ran-domly assembled villains, with a frisson of fear crawling down his back and a loaded revolver pointed at his front.

The secrets of Hammett's huge success as a crime novelist are hardly secrets at all. They comprise his extraordinary talents for story-telling; for char-acterization; and for a literary style that is strikingly innovative.

As a story-teller, he has few equals in the genre. In 'Who Killed Bob Teal?', for example, a suspicious party has flagged down a taxi and the taxi's number has been recorded. The narrative continues:

> Then Dean and I set about tracing the taxi in which Bob Teal had seen the woman ride away. Half an hour in the taxi company's office gave us the information that she had been driven to a number on Greenwich Street. We went to the Greenwich Street address.

Many of us who have been advised by editors to 'Get on with the story!' would have profited greatly from studying such succinct economy of words.

The characterization of Hammett's *dramatis personae* is realized, often vividly, on almost every page here – primarily through the medium of dialogue, secondarily by means of some sharply observed, physical description (especially of the eyes). Such techniques are omnipresent, and require no specific illustration. They are dependent wholly upon the author's writing skills.

Much has been said about Hammett's literary style, and critics have invariably commented on its comparative bareness, with dialogue gritty and terse, and with language pared down to its essentials. But such an assessment may tend to suggest 'barrenness' of style rather than 'bareness' – as if Hammett had been advised that any brief stretch of even palely-purplish prose was suspect, and that almost every adjective and adverb was potentially otiose. Yet we need read only a page or two here to recognize that Hammett knew considerably more about the business of writing than any well-intentioned editor.

Consider, for example, the second paragraph of the major story, 'Nightmare Town':

A small woman – a girl of twenty in tan flannel – stepped into the street. The wavering Ford missed her by inches, missing her at all only because her backward jump was bird-quick. She caught her lower lip between white teeth, dark eyes flashed annoyance at the passing machine, and she essayed the street again.

Immediately we spot the Hammett 'economy' trademark. But something more, too. We may be a little surprised to find such a wealth of happily chosen epithets here (what a splendid coinage is that 'bird-quick'!) as Hammett paints his small but memorably vivid picture.

This story (from which the book takes its title) shows Hammett at the top of his form, and sets the tone for a collection in which we encounter no sentimentality, with not a cliché in sight, and with none of the crudity of language which (at least for me) disfigures a good deal of present-day American crime fiction.

Here, then, is a book to be read with delight; a book in which we pass through a gallery of bizarre characters (most of them crooks) sketched with an almost wistful cynicism by a writer whom even the great Chandler acknowledged as the master.

COLIN DEXTER
January 2001
Oxford

INTRODUCTION

Although he lived into his sixties, Samuel Dashiell Hammett's prose-writing career encompassed just twelve short years, from 1922 into early 1934. But they were richly productive years, during which he wrote more than a hundred stories. Twenty of them have been assembled here in *Nightmare Town*, displaying the full range of Dashiell Hammett's remarkable talent.

In his famous 1944 essay, "The Simple Art of Murder," Raymond Chandler openly acknowledged Hammett's genius. He properly credited him as "the ace performer," the one writer responsible for the creation and development of the hard-boiled school of literature, the genre's revolutionary realist. "He took murder out of the Venetian vase and dropped it into the alley," Chandler declared. "Hammett gave murder back to the kind of people that commit it for reasons, not just to provide a corpse."

And crime novelist Ross Macdonald also granted Hammett the number one position in crime literature: "We all came out from under Hammett's black mask."

Born in 1894 to a tobacco-farming Maryland family, young Samuel grew up in Baltimore and left school at fourteen to work for the railroad. An outspoken nonconformist, he moved restlessly from job to job: yardman, stevedore, nail-machine operator in a box factory, freight handler, cannery worker, stock brokerage clerk. He chafed under authority and was often fired, or else quit out of boredom. He was looking for "something extra" from life.

In 1915 Hammett answered a blind ad which stated that applicants must have "wide work experience and be free to travel and respond to all situations." The job itself was not specified.

Intrigued, Hammett found himself at the Baltimore offices of the Pinkerton Detective Agency. For the next seven years, except during periods of army service or illness, Sam Hammett functioned as an agency operative. Unlike most agency detectives, who worked within a single locale, the Pinkerton detectives, based in a variety of cities, ranged the states from east to west, operating across a wide terrain. Thus, Hammett found himself involved in a varied series of cross-country cases, many of them quite dangerous. Along the way, he was clubbed, shot at, and knifed; but, as he summed it up, "I was never bored."

In 1917 his life changed forever. Working for Pinkerton as a strikebreaker against the International Workers of the World in Butte, Montana, Hammett was offered five thousand dollars to kill union agitator Frank Little. After Hammett bitterly refused, Little was lynched in a crime ascribed to vigilantes. As Lillian Hellman later observed: "This must have been, for Hammett, an abiding horror. I can date [his] belief that he was living in a corrupt society from Little's murder." Hammett's political conscience was formed in Butte. From this point forward, it would permeate his life and work.

In 1918 he left the agency for the first time to enlist in the army, where he was later diagnosed with tuberculosis. ("Guess it runs in the family. My mother had t.b.") Discharged a year later, he was strong enough to rejoin Pinkerton. Unfortunately, the pernicious disease plagued him for many years and took a fearsome toll on his health.

In 1921, with "bad lungs," Hammett was sent to a hospital in Tacoma, Washington, where he was attended by Josephine Dolan, an attractive young ward nurse. This unworldly orphan girl found her new patient "handsome and mature." She admired his military neatness and laughed at all his jokes. Soon they were intimate. Jose (pronounced "Joe's") was very serious about their relationship, but to Hammett it was little more than a casual diversion. At this point in his life he was incapable of love and, in fact, mistrusted the word.

He declared in an unpublished sketch: "Our love seemed dependent on not being phrased. It seemed that if [I] said 'I love you,' the next instant it would have been a lie." Hammett maintained this attitude throughout his life. He could write "with love" in a letter, but he was incapable of verbally declaring it.

Finally, with his illness in remission, Hammett moved to San Francisco, where he received a letter from Jose telling him that she was pregnant. Would Sam marry her? He would.

They became husband and wife in the summer of 1921, with Hammett once again employed by Pinkerton. But by the time daughter Mary Jane was born that October, Hammett was experiencing health problems caused by the cold San Francisco fog, which was affecting his weakened lungs.

In February 1922, at age twenty-seven, he left the agency for the last time. A course at Munson's Business College, a secretarial school, seemed to offer the chance to learn about professional writing. As a Pinkerton agent, Hammett had often been cited for his concise, neatly fashioned case reports. Now it was time to see if he could utilize this latent ability.

By the close of that year he'd made small sales to *The Smart Set* and to a new detective pulp called *The Black Mask*. In December 1922 this magazine printed Hammett's "The Road Home," about a detective named Hagedorn who has been hired to chase down a criminal. After leading Hagedorn halfway around the globe, the fugitive offers the detective a share of "one of the richest gem beds in Asia" if he'll throw in with him. At the story's climax, heading into the jungle in pursuit of his prey, Hagedorn is thinking about the treasure. The reader is led to believe that the detective is tempted by the offer of riches, and that he *will* be corrupted when he sees the jewels. Thus, Hammett's career-long theme of man's basic corruptibility is prefigured here, in his first crime tale.

In 1923 Hammett created the Continental Op for *The Black Mask* and was selling his fiction at a steady rate. In later years, a reporter asked him for his secret. Hammett shrugged. "I was a detective, so I wrote about detectives." He added: "All of my characters were based on people I've known personally, or known about."

A second daughter, Josephine Rebecca, was born in May 1926, and Hammett realized that he could not continue to support his family on *Black Mask* sales. He quit prose writing to take a job as advertising manager for a local jeweler at $350 a month. He quickly learned to appreciate the distinctive features of watches and jeweled rings, and was soon writing the store's weekly newspaper ads. Al Samuels was greatly pleased by his new employee's ability to generate sales with expertly worded advertising copy. Hammett was "a natural."

But his tuberculosis surfaced again, and Hammett was forced to leave his job after just five months. He was now receiving 100 percent disability from the Veterans Bureau. During this flare-up he was nearly bedridden, so weak he had to lean on a line of chairs in order to walk between bed and bathroom.

Because his tuberculosis was highly contagious, his wife and daughters had to live apart from him.

As Hammett's health improved, Joseph T. Shaw, the new editor of *Black Mask*, was able to lure him back to the magazine by promising higher rates (up to six cents a word) and offering him "a free creative hand" in developing novel-length material. "Hammett was the leader in what finally brought the magazine its distinctive form," Shaw declared. "He told his stories with a new kind of compulsion and authenticity. And he was one of the most careful and painstaking workmen I have ever known."

A two-part novella, "The Big Knockover," was followed by the *Black Mask* stories that led to his first four published books: *Red Harvest*, *The Dain Curse*, *The Maltese Falcon*, and *The Glass Key*. They established Hammett as the nation's premier writer of detective fiction.

By 1930 he had separated from his family and moved to New York, where he reviewed books for the *Evening Post*. Later that year, at the age of thirty-six, he journeyed back to the West Coast after *The Maltese Falcon* sold to Hollywood, to develop screen material for Paramount. Hammett cut a dapper figure in the film capital. A sharp, immaculate dresser, he was dubbed "a Hollywood Dream Prince" by one local columnist. Tall, with a trim mustache and a regal bearing, he was also known as a charmer, exuding an air of mature masculinity that made him extremely attractive to women.

It was in Hollywood, late that year, that he met aspiring writer Lillian Hellman and began an intense, volatile, often mutually destructive relationship that lasted, on and off, for the rest of his life. To Hellman, then in her midtwenties, Hammett was nothing short of spectacular. Hugely successful, he was handsome, mature, well-read, and witty—a combination she found irresistible.

Hammett eventually worked with Hellman on nearly all of her original plays (the exception being *The Searching Wind*). He painstakingly supervised structure, scenes, dialogue, and character, guiding Hellman through several productions. His contributions were enormous, and after Hammett's death, Hellman never wrote another original play.

In 1934, the period following the publication of *The Thin Man*, Hammett was at the height of his career. On the surface, his novel featuring Nick and Nora Charles was brisk and humorous, and it inspired a host of imitations. At heart, however, the book was about a disillusioned man who had rejected the detective business and no longer saw value in the pursuit of an investigative career.

The parallel between Nick Charles and Hammett was clear; he was about to reject the genre that had made him famous. He had never been comfortable as a mystery writer. Detective stories no longer held appeal for him. ("This hard-boiled stuff is a menace.")

He wanted to write an original play, followed by what he termed "socially significant novels," but he never indicated exactly what he had in mind. However, after 1934, no new Hammett fiction was printed during his lifetime. He attempted mainstream novels under several titles: "There Was a Young Man" (1938); "My Brother Felix" (1939); "The Valley Sheep Are Fatter" (1944); "The Hunting Boy" (1949); and "December 1" (1950). In each case the work was aborted after a brief start. His only sizable piece of fiction, "Tulip" (1952) — unfinished at 17,000 words — was printed after his death. It was about a man who could no longer write.

Hammett's problems were twofold. Having abandoned detective fiction, he had nothing to put in its place. Even more crippling, he had shut himself down emotionally, erecting an inner wall between himself and his public. He had lost the ability to communicate, to share his emotions. As the years slipped past him, he drank, gambled, womanized, and buried himself in Marxist doctrines. His only creative outlet was his work on Hellman's plays. There is no question that his input was of tremendous value to her, but it did not satisfy his desire to prove himself as a major novelist.

The abiding irony of Hammett's career is that he had already produced at least three major novels: *Red Harvest, The Maltese Falcon,* and *The Glass Key* — all classic works respected around the world.

But here, in this collection, we deal with his shorter tales, many of them novella length. They span a wide range, and some are better than others, but each is pure Hammett, and the least of them is marvelously entertaining.

What makes Dashiell Hammett's work unique in the genre of mystery writing? The answer is: authenticity.

Hammett was able to bring the gritty argot of the streets into print, to realistically portray thugs, hobos, molls, stoolies, gunmen, political bosses, and crooked clients, allowing them to talk and behave on paper as they had talked and behaved during Hammett's manhunting years. His stint as a working operative with Pinkerton provided a rock-solid base for his fiction. He had pursued murderers, investigated bank swindlers, gathered evidence for criminal trials, shadowed jewel thieves, tangled with safecrackers and holdup men, tracked counterfeiters, been involved in street shoot-outs, exposed forgers and blackmailers, uncovered a missing gold shipment, located a stolen Ferris wheel, and performed as guard, hotel detective, and strikebreaker.

When Hammett sent his characters out to work the mean streets of San

Francisco, readers responded to his hard-edged depiction of crime as it actually existed. No other detective-fiction writer of the period could match his kind of reality.

Nightmare Town takes us back to those early years when Hammett's talent burned flame-bright, the years when he was writing with force and vigor in a spare, stripped style that matched the intensity of his material. Working mainly in the pages of *Black Mask* (where ten of these present stories were first printed), Hammett launched a new style of detective fiction in America: bitter, tough, and unsentimental, reflecting the violence of the time. The staid English tradition of the tweedy gentleman detective was shattered, and murder bounced from the tea garden to the back alley. The polite British sleuth gave way to a hard-boiled man of action who didn't mind bending some rules to get the job done, who could hand out punishment and take it, and who often played both sides of the law.

The cynic and the idealist were combined in Hammett's protagonists: their carefully preserved toughness allowed them to survive. Nobody could bluff them or buy them off. They learned to keep themselves under tight control, moving warily through a dark landscape (Melville's "appalling ocean") in which sudden death, duplicity, and corruption were part of the scenery. Nevertheless, they idealistically hoped for a better world and worked toward it. Hammett gave these characters organic life.

Critic Graham McInnes finds that "Hammett's prose . . . has the polish and meat of an essay by Bacon or a poem by Donne, both of whom also lived in an age of violence and transition."

The theme of a corrupt society runs like a dark thread through much of Hammett's work. The title story of this collection, which details a "nightmare" town in which every citizen—from policeman to businessman—is crooked, foreshadows his gangster-ridden saga of Poisonville in *Red Harvest*. (The actual setting for his novel was Butte, Montana, and reflects the corruption Hammett had found there with Frank Little's death in 1917.)

Hammett saw the world around him as chaotic, without form or design. By the mid-1930s he had convinced himself that radical politics could provide a sense of order, and that perhaps an ideal "people's world" was possible. Communism seemed to promise such a world, but he eventually discovered that it was an illusion. In his last years, Hammett realized that there was no apparent solution to world chaos.

Much has been written on the typical "Hammett hero."

Critic John Paterson claims that he "is, in the final analysis, the apotheosis of every man of good will who, alienated by the values of his time, seeks desperately and mournfully to live without shame, to live without compromise to his integrity."

Philip Durham, who wrote the first biography of Raymond Chandler, traces Hammett's hero back to

a tradition that began on the frontier in the early part of the nineteenth century. This American literary hero appeared constantly in the dime novels of the period, and was ready-made for such Western writers of the twentieth century as Owen Wister and Zane Grey. By the time Hammett picked him up in the pages of *Black Mask,* his heroic characteristics were clearly established: courage, physical strength, indestructibility, indifference to danger and death, a knightly attitude, celibacy, a measure of violence, and a sense of justice.

Hammett's most sustained character, the Continental Op (who is featured here in seven stories), reflects the author's dark world view, but he's not overtly political, nor is he knightly. He's a hard-working detective trying to get a job done. The Op describes himself as having a face that is "truthful witness to a life that hasn't been overwhelmed with refinement and gentility," adding that he is "short, middle-aged, and thick-waisted," and stubborn enough to be called "pig-headed."

Hammett claimed to have based the Op on the man who had trained him to be a detective, the Pinkerton Agency's Jimmy Wright of Baltimore. Wright taught young Hammett a basic code: Don't cheat your client. Stay anonymous. Avoid undue physical risks. Be objective. Don't become emotionally involved with a client. And never violate your integrity. This code stayed with Hammett; it not only served him while he was a working detective, but it also gave him a set of personal rules that shaped his actions throughout his life.

Of course, despite his age and physical appearance, the Op is Hammett himself in fictional guise. Told in the first person, many of the Op's adventures are fictionalized versions of actual cases that Hammett worked on during his sporadic years as a detective. When young Hammett first joined the Baltimore branch of the Pinkerton Detective Agency, the headquarters were in the Continental Building—clearly the source for the Op's fictitious agency.

Hammett deliberately kept his character's biographical background to a minimum. As critic Peter Wolfe notes, "he tells us nothing of [the Op's] family, education, or religious beliefs." Of course the Op *has* no religion in any traditional sense of the term; his religion is the always dangerous game of manhunting, a trade he pursues with near-sacred zeal.

If one sifts carefully through the canon (some three dozen stories), it is revealed that the Op joined Continental as "a young sprout of twenty" (Hammett's age when he became a Pinkerton operative), that he held a captain's commission in wartime military intelligence, that he speaks some French and German, eats all his meals out, smokes Fatima cigarettes, enjoys poker and prizefights, and avoids romantic entanglements ("They don't go with the job"). Pragmatic, hard-souled, and tenacious, he resorts to physical violence when necessary and uses a gun when he has to, but prefers using his wits. He is as close to an actual working detective as Hammett could make him.

Hammett featured the Op in his earlier long works, *Blood Money* (also known as *The Big Knockover*), *Red Harvest*, and *The Dain Curse*, all of which were revised from *Black Mask* novellas.

His next major fictional creation was San Francisco private eye Samuel Spade, to whom Hammett gave his first name. (As a Pinkerton, he had always been called Sam. When he turned to writing, he became simply Dashiell Hammett.) Spade made his debut in "The Maltese Falcon," a five-part *Black Mask* serial that Hammett carefully reworked for book publication by Alfred A. Knopf. Most critics rate this "saga of a private detective" as the finest crime novel written in this century. Describing his character for a Modern Library edition of *Falcon*, Hammett stated:

> Spade had no original. He is a dream man in the sense that he is what most of the private detectives I worked with would like to have been and what quite a few of them, in their cockier moments, thought they approached. For your private detective does not . . . want to be an erudite solver of riddles in the Sherlock Holmes manner; he wants to be a hard and shifty fellow, able to take care of himself in any situation, able to get the best of anybody he comes in contact with, whether criminal, innocent bystander, or client.

Indeed, this was precisely the way Hammett wrote Spade in *The Maltese Falcon*—able to match wits with the crafty fat man, Casper Gutman, in tracking down the fabled bird of the title; able to handle the intrusive police; and able to fend off the advances of seductive Brigid O'Shaughnessy in solving the murder of his partner, Miles Archer.

Hammett never intended to make Spade a continuing character; in completing *The Maltese Falcon* he was "done with him." Yet he had not foreseen the book's wide and lasting popularity, nor that it would become a supremely successful radio series, nor that no less than three motion pictures would be produced based on the published novel.

The public demanded more Spade stories, and Hammett's literary agent pleaded with the author to come up with new adventures. Hammett was reluctant, but he was also short of money. He made vast sums in Hollywood as a scriptwriter, but he squandered every dollar as quickly as he earned it. Money was for spending and Hammett always felt that more of it would magically appear as needed. Finally, he sat down to rap out three new Spade stories, placing two of them with *The American Magazine* and the final one with *Collier's*.

All three are in the present collection: "A Man Called Spade," "Too Many Have Lived," and "They Can Only Hang You Once." The tales are crisp, efficient, and swift-moving.

The other stories assembled here demonstrate Hammett's bold experimentation with language and viewpoint. Compare the fussy, ornate narration in "A Man Named Thin" (featuring a poet-detective) with the crude, uneducated narration of the young boxer in "His Brother's Keeper." Both are told first-person, but they are leagues apart. Hammett tackles a female point of view in the superbly written "Ruffian's Wife," and brings off a neat twist ending in "The Second-Story Angel" (note the understated humor in this one).

Both "Afraid of a Gun" and "The Man Who Killed Dan Odams" are set far from his usual San Francisco locale and demonstrate the wide range of Hammett's fiction. "Gun" takes place in the high mountain country, and "Dan Odams" is a semimodern Western set in Montana. They represent Hammett in top form.

While the majority of pulp writers in the twenties and thirties were grinding out stories for money, Hammett worked as a dedicated artist. He gave each story the best of himself, laboring over each sentence, each turn of phrase. And he was constantly seeking new ideas and new characters. His protagonist in "The Assistant Murderer" is a prime example. With Alec Rush, the author created a detective described as incredibly ugly, a radical departure from the usual magazine hero. Hammett was striking out in a fresh direction with this story, which involves a complex case solved not by Rush but by the killer's confession.

"The Assistant Murderer" was written just before Hammett temporarily left *Black Mask* for his unsuccessful attempt at a career in advertising. One feels that had he remained with the magazine, Hammett might well have written more stories featuring this offbeat detective.

During the pulp era, editors constantly called for "Action! More action!" Hammett decided to see just how much action he could pack into a single novella. Originally printed in *Argosy All-Story Weekly*, the title story of this collection, "Nightmare Town," is a tour de force in sustained violence. The hero wields an ebony walking stick with devastating effectiveness, cracking skulls and breaking bones in the finest pulp tradition.

An important contribution in *Nightmare Town* is "The First Thin Man," which here achieves its first book printing. This early version of 1930 stands in sharp contrast to the novel Hammett eventually finished for Alfred A. Knopf three years later, with vast differences in basic approach, mood, plot, and tone. A call from Hollywood and the promise of substantial film money had caused Hammett to abandon the original manuscript at sixty-five typed pages. When he returned to it three years later, John Guild, the Op-like working detective—dedicated, stoic, close-mouthed—was replaced by Nick Charles, a hard-drinking, party-loving cynic, an ex–crime solver with no desire to solve more crimes; he just wanted another martini. It was Nick's wife, Nora (modeled directly on Lillian Hellman), who badgered him into becoming a detective again to solve the case of the missing thin man.

Dashiell Hammett had undergone a major life change between 1930 and 1933, and Nick Charles marked the end of Hammett's career as a novelist. He had written himself into a blind corner and no longer believed that the criminal ills of society could be dealt with on a one-to-one basis. In Hammett's view, a lone detective (such as Sam Spade or John Guild) could do nothing to stem the mounting tide of societal corruption. The detective's code of personal honor could have no effect on a dishonorable world. Hammett's core bitterness and cynicism, reflected in a less obvious form in his earlier work, had now taken center stage. He was no longer able to believe in heroes. Even plainspoken, down-to-earth, working heroes.

In 1951, after he was sentenced for contempt because he refused to name names before a federal judge in New York, Hammett spent five months in jail in defense of his political beliefs. But he never believed in political violence and had been shocked when Senator Joseph McCarthy asked him if he had ever engaged in an act of sabotage against the United States. Having served his country in two world wars as an enlisted soldier, he loved America, even as he despised its capitalist politics.

Hammett's final years, following his release from prison, were sad ones. His name was removed from a film based on one of his characters; his radio shows were canceled; and a scheduled collection of his fiction was dropped by the publisher. He spent most of his last decade isolated in a small gatekeeper's cottage in Katonah, New York. On two occasions shots were fired through his front windows, but Hammett bore his exile with stoic acceptance.

Sick and frail, blacklisted as a political pariah, unable to write, and hounded by the IRS for taxes on money he no longer earned, Samuel Dashiell Hammett died of lung cancer in 1961, at the age of sixty-six.

He considered himself a literary failure, but, as this book helps prove, he was anything but that. No other writer since Edgar Allan Poe has exerted a greater influence on mystery fiction. His art was timeless and his work has not dated. In the genre of detective fiction, he was a master.

That mastery is evident in *Nightmare Town*, the largest collection of his shorter works and by far the most comprehensive.

WILLIAM F. NOLAN
West Hills, California
1999

NIGHTMARE TOWN

NIGHTMARE
TOWN

AFord—whitened by desert travel until it was almost indistinguishable from the dust-clouds that swirled around it—came down Izzard's Main Street. Like the dust, it came swiftly, erratically, zigzagging the breadth of the roadway.

A small woman—a girl of twenty in tan flannel—stepped into the street. The wavering Ford missed her by inches, missing her at all only because her backward jump was bird-quick. She caught her lower lip between white teeth, dark eyes flashed annoyance at the rear of the passing machine, and she essayed the street again.

Near the opposite curb the Ford charged down upon her once more. But turning had taken some of its speed. She escaped it this time by scampering the few feet between her and the sidewalk ahead.

Out of the moving automobile a man stepped. Miraculously he kept his feet, stumbling, sliding, until an arm crooked around an iron awning-post jerked him into an abrupt halt. He was a large man in bleached khaki, tall, broad, and thick-armed; his gray eyes were bloodshot; face and clothing were powdered heavily with dust. One of his hands clutched a thick, black stick, the other swept off his hat, and he bowed with exaggerated lowness before the girl's angry gaze.

The bow completed, he tossed his hat carelessly into the street, and grinned grotesquely through the dirt that masked his face—a grin that accented the heaviness of a begrimed and hair-roughened jaw.

"I *beg* y'r par'on," he said. "'F I hadn't been careful I believe I'd a'most hit you. 'S unreli'ble, tha' wagon. Borr'ed it from an engi—eng'neer. Don't ever borrow one from eng'neer. They're unreli'ble."

The girl looked at the place where he stood as if no one stood there, as if, in fact, no one had ever stood there, turned her small back on him, and walked very precisely down the street.

He stared after her with stupid surprise in his eyes until she had vanished through a doorway in the middle of the block. Then he scratched his head, shrugged, and turned to look across the street, where his machine had pushed its nose into the red-brick side wall of the Bank of Izzard and now shook and clattered as if in panic at finding itself masterless.

"Look at the son-of-a-gun," he exclaimed.

A hand fastened upon his arm. He turned his head, and then, though he stood a good six feet himself, had to look up to meet the eyes of the giant who held his arm.

"We'll take a little walk," the giant said.

The man in bleached khaki examined the other from the tips of his broad-toed shoes to the creased crown of his black hat, examined him with a whole-hearted admiration that was unmistakable in his red-rimmed eyes. There were nearly seven massive feet of the speaker. Legs like pillars held up a great hogshead of a body, with wide shoulders that sagged a little, as if with their own excessive weight. He was a man of perhaps forty-five, and his face was thick-featured, phlegmatic, with sunlines around small light eyes—the face of a deliberate man.

"My God, you're big!" the man in khaki exclaimed when he had finished his examination; and then his eyes brightened. "Let's wrestle. Bet you ten bucks against fifteen I can throw you. Come on!"

The giant chuckled deep in his heavy chest, took the man in khaki by the nape of the neck and an arm, and walked down the street with him.

STEVE THREEFALL awakened without undue surprise at the unfamiliarity of his surroundings as one who has awakened in strange places before. Before his eyes were well open he knew the essentials of his position. The feel of the shelf-bunk on which he lay and the sharp smell of disinfectant in his nostrils told him that he was in jail. His head and his mouth told him that he had been drunk; and the three-day growth of beard on his face told him he had been very drunk.

As he sat up and swung his feet down to the floor details came back to him. The two days of steady drinking in Whitetufts on the other side of the Nevada-California line, with Harris, the hotel proprietor, and Whiting, an irrigation engineer. The boisterous arguing over desert travel, with his own Gobi experience matched against the American experiences of the others.

The bet that he could drive from Whitetufts to Izzard in daylight with nothing to drink but the especially bitter white liquor they were drinking at the time. The start in the grayness of imminent dawn, in Whiting's Ford, with Whiting and Harris staggering down the street after him, waking the town with their drunken shouts and roared-out mocking advice, until he had reached the desert's edge. Then the drive through the desert, along the road that was hotter than the rest of the desert, with— He chose not to think of the ride. He had made it, though—had won the bet. He couldn't remember the amount of the latter.

"So you've come out of it at last?" a rumbling voice inquired.

The steel-slatted door swung open and a man filled the cell's door. Steve grinned up at him. This was the giant who would not wrestle. He was coatless and vestless now, and loomed larger than before. One suspender strap was decorated with a shiny badge that said MARSHAL.

"Feel like breakfast?" he asked.

"I could do things to a can of black coffee," Steve admitted.

"All right. But you'll have to gulp it. Judge Denvir is waiting to get a crack at you, and the longer you keep him waiting, the tougher it'll be for you."

The room in which Tobin Denvir, J.P., dealt justice was a large one on the third floor of a wooden building. It was scantily furnished with a table, an ancient desk, a steel engraving of Daniel Webster, a shelf of books sleeping under the dust of weeks, a dozen uncomfortable chairs, and half as many cracked and chipped china cuspidors.

The judge sat between desk and table, with his feet on the latter. They were small feet, and he was a small man. His face was filled with little irritable lines, his lips were thin and tight, and he had the bright, lidless eyes of a bird.

"Well, what's he charged with?" His voice was thin, harshly metallic. He kept his feet on the table.

The marshal drew a deep breath, and recited:

"Driving on the wrong side of the street, exceeding the speed limit, driving while under the influence of liquor, driving without a driver's license, endangering the lives of pedestrians by taking his hands off the wheel, and parking improperly—on the sidewalk up against the bank."

The marshal took another breath, and added, with manifest regret:

"There was a charge of attempted assault, too, but that Vallance girl won't appear, so that'll have to be dropped."

The justice's bright eyes turned upon Steve.

"What's your name?" he growled.

"Steve Threefall."

"Is that your real name?" the marshal asked.

"Of course it is," the justice snapped. "You don't think anybody'd be damn fool enough to give a name like that unless it was his, do you?" Then to Steve: "What have you got to say—guilty or not?"

"I was a little—"

"Are you guilty or not?"

"Oh, I suppose I did—"

"That's enough! You're fined a hundred and fifty dollars and costs. The costs are fifteen dollars and eighty cents, making a total of a hundred and sixty-five dollars and eighty cents. Will you pay it or will you go to jail?"

"I'll pay it if I've got it," Steve said, turning to the marshal. "You took my money. Have I got that much?"

The marshal nodded his massive head.

"You have," he said, "exactly—to the nickel. Funny it should have come out like that—huh?"

"Yes—funny," Steve repeated.

While the justice of the peace was making out a receipt for the fine, the marshal restored Steve's watch, tobacco and matches, pocket-knife, keys, and last of all the black walking-stick. The big man weighed the stick in his hand and examined it closely before he gave it up. It was thick and of ebony, but heavy even for that wood, with a balanced weight that hinted at loaded ferrule and knob. Except for a space the breadth of a man's hand in its middle, the stick was roughened, cut and notched with the marks of hard use— marks that much careful polishing had failed to remove or conceal. The unscarred hand's-breadth was of a softer black than the rest—as soft a black as the knob—as if it had known much contact with a human palm.

"Not a bad weapon in a pinch," the marshal said meaningly as he handed the stick to its owner. Steve took it with the grasp a man reserves for a favorite and constant companion.

"Not bad," he agreed. "What happened to the flivver?"

"It's in the garage around the corner on Main Street. Pete said it wasn't altogether ruined, and he thinks he can patch it up if you want."

The justice held out the receipt.

"Am I all through here now?" Steve asked.

"I hope so," Judge Denvir said sourly.

"Both of us," Steve echoed. He put on his hat, tucked the black stick under his arm, nodded to the big marshal, and left the room.

Steve Threefall went down the wooden stairs toward the street in as cheerful a frame of mind as his body—burned out inwardly with white liquor and outwardly by a day's scorching desert-riding—would permit. That justice had emptied his pockets of every last cent disturbed him little. That, he knew, was the way of justice everywhere with the stranger, and he had left the greater part of his money with the hotel proprietor in White-tufts. He had escaped a jail sentence, and he counted himself lucky. He would wire Harris to send him some of his money, wait here until the Ford was repaired, and then drive back to Whitetufts—but not on a whisky ration this time.

"You will not!" a voice cried in his ear.

He jumped, and then laughed at his alcohol-jangled nerves. The words had not been meant for him. Beside him, at a turning of the stairs, was an open window, and opposite it, across a narrow alley, a window in another building was open. This window belonged to an office in which two men stood facing each other across a flat-topped desk.

One of them was middle-aged and beefy, in a black broadcloth suit out of which a white-vested stomach protruded. His face was purple with rage. The man who faced him was younger—a man of perhaps thirty, with a small dark mustache, finely chiseled features, and satiny brown hair. His slender athlete's body was immaculately clothed in gray suit, gray shirt, gray and silver tie, and on the desk before him lay a Panama hat with gray band. His face was as white as the other's was purple.

The beefy man spoke—a dozen words pitched too low to catch.

The younger man slapped the speaker viciously across the face with an open hand—a hand that then flashed back to its owner's coat and flicked out a snub-nosed automatic pistol.

"You big lard-can," the younger man cried, his voice sibilant; "you'll lay off or I'll spoil your vest for you!"

He stabbed the protuberant vest with the automatic, and laughed into the scared fat face of the beefy man—laughed with a menacing flash of even teeth and dark slitted eyes. Then he picked up his hat, pocketed the pistol, and vanished from Steve's sight. The fat man sat down.

Steve went on down to the street.

STEVE UNEARTHED the garage to which the Ford had been taken, found a greasy mechanic who answered to the name of Pete, and was told that Whiting's automobile would be in condition to move under its own power within two days.

"A beautiful snootful you had yesterday," Pete grinned.

Steve grinned back and went on out. He went down to the telegraph office, next door to the Izzard Hotel, pausing for a moment on the sidewalk to look at a glowing, cream-colored Vauxhall-Velox roadster that stood at the curb—as out of place in this grimy factory town as a harlequin opal in a grocer's window.

In the doorway of the telegraph office Steve paused again, abruptly.

Behind the counter was a girl in tan flannel—the girl he had nearly run down twice the previous afternoon—the "Vallance girl" who had refrained from adding to justice's account against Steve Threefall. In front of the counter, leaning over it, talking to her with every appearance of intimacy, was one of the two men he had seen from the staircase window half an hour before—the slender dandy in gray who had slapped the other's face and threatened him with an automatic.

The girl looked up, recognized Steve, and stood very erect. He took off his hat, and advanced smiling.

"I'm awfully sorry about yesterday," he said. "I'm a crazy fool when I—"

"Do you wish to send a telegram?" she asked frigidly.

"Yes," Steve said; "I also wish to—"

"There are blanks and pencils on the desk near the window," and she turned her back on him.

Steve felt himself coloring, and since he was one of the men who habitually grin when at a loss, he grinned now, and found himself looking into the dark eyes of the man in gray.

That one smiled back under his little brown mustache, and said:

"Quite a time you had yesterday."

"Quite," Steve agreed, and went to the table the girl had indicated. He wrote his telegram:

> Henry Harris
> Harris Hotel, Whitetufts:
> Arrived right side up, but am in hock. Wire me two
> hundred dollars. Will be back Saturday.
> > Threefall. T.

But he did not immediately get up from the desk. He sat there holding the piece of paper in his fingers, studying the man and girl, who were again engaged in confidential conversation over the counter. Steve studied the girl most.

She was quite a small girl, no more than five feet in height, if that; and she had that peculiar rounded slenderness which gives a deceptively fragile appearance. Her face was an oval of skin whose fine whiteness had thus far withstood the grimy winds of Izzard; her nose just missed being upturned, her violet-black eyes just missed being too theatrically large, and her black-brown hair just missed being too bulky for the small head it crowned; but in no respect did she miss being as beautiful as a figure from a Monticelli canvas.

All these things Steve Threefall, twiddling his telegram in sun-brown fingers, considered and as he considered them he came to see the pressing necessity of having his apologies accepted. Explain it as you will—he carefully avoided trying to explain it to himself—the thing was there. One moment there was nothing, in the four continents he knew, of any bothersome importance to Steve Threefall; the next moment he was under an unescapable compulsion to gain the favor of this small person in tan flannel with brown ribbons at wrists and throat.

At this point the man in gray leaned farther over the counter, to whisper something to the girl. She flushed, and her eyes flinched. The pencil in her hand fell to the counter, and she picked it up with small fingers that were suddenly incongruously awkward. She made a smiling reply, and went on with her writing, but the smile seemed forced.

Steve tore up his telegram and composed another:

> I made it, slept it off in the cooler, and I am going to
> settle here a while. There are things about the place
> I like. Wire my money and send my clothes to hotel
> here. Buy Whiting's Ford from him as cheap as you
> can for me.

He carried the blank to the counter and laid it down.

The girl ran her pencil over it, counting the words.

"Forty-seven," she said, in a tone that involuntarily rebuked the absence of proper telegraphic brevity.

"Long, but it's all right," Steve assured her. "I'm sending it collect."

She regarded him icily.

"I can't accept a collect message unless I know that the sender can pay for it if the addressee refuses it. It's against the rules."

"You'd better make an exception this time," Steve told her solemnly, "because if you don't you'll have to lend me the money to pay for it."

"I'll have—?"

"You will," he insisted. "You got me into this jam, and it's up to you to help me get out. The Lord knows you've cost me enough as it is—nearly two hundred dollars! The whole thing was your fault."

"*My fault?*"

"It was! Now I'm giving you a chance to square yourself. Hurry it off, please, because I'm hungry and I need a shave. I'll be waiting on the bench outside." And he spun on his heel and left the office.

ONE END of the bench in front of the telegraph office was occupied when Steve, paying no attention to the man who sat there, made himself comfortable on the other. He put his black stick between his legs and rolled a cigarette with thoughtful slowness, his mind upon the just completed scene in the office.

Why, he wondered, whenever there was some special reason for gravity, did he always find himself becoming flippant? Why, whenever he found himself face to face with a situation that was important, that meant something to him, did he slip uncontrollably into banter—play the clown? He lit his cigarette and decided scornfully—as he had decided a dozen times before—that it all came from a childish attempt to conceal his self-consciousness; that for all his thirty-three years of life and his eighteen years of rubbing shoulders with the world—its rough corners as well as its polished—he was still a green boy underneath—a big kid.

"A neat package you had yesterday," the man who sat on the other end of the bench remarked.

"Yeah," Steve admitted without turning his head. He supposed he'd be hearing about his crazy arrival as long as he stayed in Izzard.

"I reckon old man Denvir took you to the cleaner's as usual?"

"Uh-huh!" Steve said, turning now for a look at the other.

He saw a very tall and very lean man in rusty brown, slouched down on the small of his back, angular legs thrust out across the sidewalk. A man past forty, whose gaunt, melancholy face was marked with lines so deep that they were folds in the skin rather than wrinkles. His eyes were the mournful chestnut eyes of a basset hound, and his nose was as long and sharp as a paper-knife. He puffed on a black cigar, getting from it a surprising amount of smoke, which he exhaled upward, his thin nose splitting the smoke into two gray plumes.

"Ever been to our fair young city before?" this melancholy individual asked next. His voice held a monotonous rhythm that was not unpleasant to the ear.

"No, this is my first time."

The thin man nodded ironically.

"You'll like it if you stay," he said. "It's very interesting."

"What's it all about?" Steve asked, finding himself mildly intrigued by his benchmate.

"Soda niter. You scoop it up off the desert, and boil and otherwise cook it, and sell it to fertilizer manufacturers, and nitric acid manufacturers, and any other kind of manufacturers who can manufacture something out of soda niter. The factory in which, for which, and from which you do all this lies yonder, beyond the railroad tracks."

He waved a lazy arm down the street, to where a group of square concrete buildings shut out the desert at the end of the thoroughfare.

"Suppose you don't play with this soda?" Steve asked, more to keep the thin man talking than to satisfy any thirst for local knowledge. "What do you do then?"

The thin man shrugged his sharp shoulders.

"That depends," he said, "on who you are. If you're Dave Brackett"—he wiggled a finger at the red bank across the street—"you gloat over your mortgages, or whatever it is a banker does; if you're Grant Fernie, and too big for a man without being quite big enough for a horse, you pin a badge on your bosom and throw rough-riding strangers into the can until they sober up; or if you're Larry Ormsby, and your old man owns the soda works, then you drive trick cars from across the pond"—nodding at the cream Vauxhall—"and spend your days pursuing beautiful telegraph operators. But I take it that you're broke, and have just wired for money, and are waiting for the more or less doubtful results. Is that it?"

"It is," Steve answered absent-mindedly. So the dandy in gray was named Larry Ormsby and was the factory owner's son.

The thin man drew in his feet and stood up on them.

"In that case it's lunchtime, and my name is Roy Kamp, and I'm hungry, and I don't like to eat alone, and I'd be glad to have you face the greasy dangers of a meal at the Finn's with me."

Steve got up and held out his hand.

"I'll be glad to," he said. "The coffee I had for breakfast could stand company. My name's Steve Threefall."

They shook hands, and started up the street together. Coming toward them were two men in earnest conversation; one of them was the beefy man whose face Larry Ormsby had slapped. Steve waited until they had passed, and then questioned Kamp casually:

"And who are those prominent-looking folks?"

"The little round one in the checkered college-boy suit is Conan Elder, real estate, insurance, and securities. The Wallingford-looking personage at his side is W. W. himself—the town's founder, owner, and whatnot—W. W. Ormsby, the Hon. Larry's papa."

The scene in the office, with its slapping of a face and flourish of a pistol, had been a family affair, then; a matter between father and son, with the son in the more forcible rôle. Steve, walking along with scant attention just now for the words Kamp's baritone voice was saying, felt a growing dissatisfaction in the memory of the girl and Larry Ormsby talking over the counter with their heads close together.

The Finn's lunchroom was little more than a corridor squeezed in between a poolroom and a hardware store, of barely sufficient width for a counter and a row of revolving stools. Only one customer was there when the two men entered. "Hello, Mr. Rymer," said Kamp.

"How are you, Mr. Kamp?" the man at the counter said, and as he turned his head toward them, Steve saw that he was blind. His large blue eyes were filmed over with a gray curtain which gave him the appearance of having dark hollows instead of eyes.

He was a medium-sized man who looked seventy, but there was a suggestion of fewer years in the suppleness of his slender white hands. He had a thick mane of white hair about a face that was crisscrossed with wrinkles, but it was a calm face, the face of a man at peace with his world. He was just finishing his meal, and left shortly, moving to the door with the slow accuracy of the blind man in familiar surroundings.

"Old man Rymer," Kamp told Steve, "lives in a shack behind where the new fire house is going to be, all alone. Supposed to have tons of gold coins under his floor—thus local gossip. Some day we're going to find him all momicked up. But he won't listen to reason. Says nobody would hurt him. Says that in a town as heavy with assorted thugs as this!"

"A tough town, is it?" Steve asked.

"Couldn't help being! It's only three years old—and a desert boom town draws the tough boys."

Kamp left Steve after their meal, saying he probably would run across him later in the evening, and suggesting that there were games of a sort to be found in the next-door poolroom.

"I'll see you there then," Steve said, and went back to the telegraph office. The girl was alone. "Anything for me?" he asked her.

She put a green check and a telegram on the counter and returned to her desk. The telegram read:

> Collected bet. Paid Whiting two hundred for Ford.
> Sending balance six hundred forty. Shipping clothes.
> Watch your step.   Harris.

"Did you send the wire collect, or do I owe—"

"Collect." She did not look up.

Steve put his elbows on the counter and leaned over; his jaw, still exaggerated by its growth of hair, although he had washed the dirt from it, jutted forward with his determination to maintain a properly serious attitude until he had done this thing that had to be done.

"Now listen, Miss Vallance," he said deliberately. "I was all kinds of a damned fool yesterday, and I'm sorrier than I can say. But, after all, nothing terrible happened, and—"

"Nothing terrible!" she exploded. "Is it nothing to be humiliated by being chased up and down the street like a rabbit by a drunken man with a dirty face in a worse car?"

"I wasn't chasing you. I came back that second time to apologize. But, anyway"—in the uncomfortable face of her uncompromising hostility his determination to be serious went for nothing, and he relapsed into his accustomed defensive mockery—"no matter how scared you were you ought to accept my apology now and let bygones be bygones."

"Scared? Why—"

"I wish you wouldn't repeat words after me," he complained. "This morning you did it, and now you're at it again. Don't you ever think of anything to say on your own account?"

She glared at him, opened her mouth, shut it with a little click. Her angry face bent sharply over the papers on the desk, and she began to add a column of figures.

Steve nodded with pretended approval, and took his check across the street to the bank.

The only man in sight in the bank when Steve came in was a little plump fellow with carefully trimmed salt-and-pepper whiskers hiding nearly all of a jovial round face except the eyes—shrewd, friendly eyes.

This man came to the window in the grille, and said: "Good afternoon. Can I do something for you?"

Steve laid down the telegraph company's check. "I want to open an account."

The banker picked up the slip of green paper and flicked it with a fat finger. "You are the gentleman who assaulted my wall with an automobile yesterday?"

Steve grinned. The banker's eyes twinkled, and a smile ruffled his whiskers. "Are you going to stay in Izzard?"

"For a while."

"Can you give me references?" the banker asked.

"Maybe Judge Denvir or Marshal Fernie will put in a word for me," Steve said. "But if you'll write the Seaman's Bank in San Francisco they'll tell you that so far as they know I'm all right."

The banker stuck a plump hand through the window in the grille.

"I'm very glad to make your acquaintance. My name is David Brackett, and anything I can do to help you get established—call on me."

Outside of the bank ten minutes later, Steve met the huge marshal, who stopped in front of him. "You still here?" Fernie asked.

"I'm an Izzardite now," Steve said. "For a while, anyhow. I like your hospitality."

"Don't let old man Denvir see you coming out of a bank," Fernie advised him, "or he'll soak you plenty next time."

"There isn't going to be any next time."

"There always is—in Izzard," the marshal said enigmatically as he got his bulk in motion again.

THAT NIGHT, shaved and bathed, though still wearing his bleached khaki, Steve, with his black stick beside him, played stud poker with Roy Kamp and four factory workers. They played in the poolroom next door to the Finn's lunchroom. Izzard apparently was a wide-open town. Twelve tables given to craps, poker, red dog, and twenty-one occupied half of the poolroom, and white-hot liquor was to be had at the cost of fifty cents and a raised finger. There was nothing surreptitious about the establishment; obviously its proprietor—a bullet-headed Italian whose customers called him "Gyp"—was in favor with the legal powers of Izzard.

The game in which Steve sat went on smoothly and swiftly, as play does when adepts participate. Though, as most games are, always potentially crooked, it was, in practice, honest. The six men at the table were, without exception, men who knew their way around—men who played quietly and watchfully, winning and losing without excitement or inattention. Not one of the six—except Steve, and perhaps Kamp—would have hesitated to favor himself at the expense of honesty had the opportunity come to him; but where knowledge of trickery is evenly distributed honesty not infrequently prevails.

Larry Ormsby came into the poolroom at a little after eleven and sat at a table some distance from Steve. Faces he had seen in the street during the day were visible through the smoke. At five minutes to twelve the four factory men at Steve's table left for work—they were in the "graveyard" shift— and the game broke up with their departure. Steve, who had kept about even throughout the play, found that he had won something less than ten dollars; Kamp had won fifty-some.

Declining invitations to sit in another game, Steve and Kamp left together, going out into the dark and night-cool street, where the air was sweet after the smoke and alcohol of the poolroom. They walked slowly down the dim thoroughfare toward the Izzard Hotel, neither in a hurry to end their first evening together; for each knew by now that the unpainted bench in front of the telegraph office had given him a comrade. Not a thousand words had passed between the two men, but they had as surely become brothers-in-arms as if they had tracked a continent together.

Strolling thus, a dark doorway suddenly vomited men upon them.

Steve rocked back against a building front from a blow on his head, arms were around him, the burning edge of a knife blade ran down his left arm. He chopped his black stick up into a body, freeing himself from encircling grip. He used the moment's respite this gave him to change his grasp on the stick; so that he held it now horizontal, his right hand grasping its middle, its lower half flat against his forearm, its upper half extending to the left.

He put his left side against the wall, and the black stick became a whirling black arm of the night. The knob darted down at a man's head. The man threw an arm up to fend the blow. Spinning back on its axis, the stick reversed—the ferruled end darted up under warding arm, hit jaw-bone with a click, and no sooner struck than slid forward, jabbing deep into throat. The owner of that jaw and throat turned his broad, thick-featured face to the sky, went backward out of the fight, and was lost to sight beneath the curbing.

Kamp, struggling with two men in the middle of the sidewalk, broke loose from them, whipped out a gun; but before he could use it his assailants were on him again.

Lower half of stick against forearm once more, Steve whirled in time to take the impact of a blackjack-swinging arm upon it. The stick spun sidewise with thud of knob on temple—spun back with loaded ferrule that missed opposite temple only because the first blow had brought its target down on knees. Steve saw suddenly that Kamp had gone down. He spun his stick and battered a passage to the thin man, kicked a head that bent over the prone, thin form, straddled it; and the ebony stick whirled swifter in his hand—spun as quarter-staves once spun in Sherwood Forest. Spun to the clicking tune of wood on bone, on metal weapons; to the duller rhythm of wood on flesh. Spun never in full circles, but always in short arcs—one end's recovery from a blow adding velocity to the other's stroke. Where an instant ago knob had swished from left to right, now weighted ferrule struck from right to left—struck under upthrown arms, over low-thrown arms—put into space a forty-inch sphere, whose radii were whirling black flails.

Behind his stick that had become a living part of him, Steve Threefall knew happiness—that rare happiness which only the expert ever finds—the joy in doing a thing that he can do supremely well. Blows he took—blows that shook him, staggered him—but he scarcely noticed them. His whole consciousness was in his right arm and the stick it spun. A revolver, tossed from a smashed hand, exploded ten feet over his head, a knife tinkled like a bell on the brick sidewalk, a man screamed as a stricken horse screams.

As abruptly as it had started, the fight stopped. Feet thudded away, forms vanished into the more complete darkness of a side street; and Steve was standing alone—alone except for the man stretched out between his feet and the other man who lay still in the gutter.

Kamp crawled from beneath Steve's legs and scrambled briskly to his feet.

"Your work with a bat is what you might call adequate," he drawled.

Steve stared at the thin man. This was the man he had accepted on an evening's acquaintance as a comrade! A man who lay on the street and let his companion do the fighting for both. Hot words formed in Steve's throat.

"You—"

The thin man's face twisted into a queer grimace, as if he were listening to faint, far-off sounds. He caught his hands to his chest, pressing the sides together. Then he turned half around, went down on one knee, went over backward with a leg bent over him.

"Get—word—to—"

The fourth word was blurred beyond recognition. Steve knelt beside Kamp, lifted his head from the bricks, and saw that Kamp's thin body was ripped open from throat to waistline.

"Get—word—to—" The thin man tried desperately to make the last word audible.

A hand gripped Steve's shoulder.

"What the hell's all this?" The roaring voice of Marshal Grant Fernie blotted out Kamp's words.

"Shut up a minute!" Steve snapped, and put his ear again close to Kamp's mouth.

But now the dying man could achieve no articulate sound. He tried with an effort that bulged his eyes; then he shuddered horribly, coughed, the slit in his chest gaped open, and he died.

"What's all this?" the marshal repeated.

"Another reception committee," Steve said bitterly, easing the dead body to the sidewalk, and standing up. "There's one of them in the street; the others beat it around the corner."

He tried to point with his left hand, then let it drop to his side. Looking at it, he saw that his sleeve was black with blood.

The marshal bent to examine Kamp, grunted, "He's dead, all right," and moved over to where the man Steve had knocked into the gutter lay.

"Knocked out," the marshal said, straightening up; "but he'll be coming around in a while. How'd you make out?"

"My arm's slashed, and I've got some sore spots, but I'll live through it."

Fernie took hold of the wounded arm.

"Not bleeding so bad," he decided. "But you better get it patched up. Doc MacPhail's is only a little way up the street. Can you make it, or do you want me to give you a lift?"

"I can make it. How do I find the place?"

"Two blocks up this street, and four to the left. You can't miss it—it's the only house in town with flowers in front of it. I'll get in touch with you when I want you."

STEVE THREEFALL found Dr. MacPhail's house without difficulty— a two-story building set back from the street, behind a garden that did its best to make up a floral profusion for Izzard's general barrenness. The fence was hidden under twining virgin's bower, clustered now with white blossoms, and the narrow walk wound through roses, trillium, poppies, tulips, and geraniums that were ghosts in the starlight. The air was heavily sweet with the fragrance of saucerlike moon flowers, whose vines covered the doctor's porch.

Two steps from the latter Steve stopped, and his right hand slid to the middle of his stick. From one end of the porch had come a rustling, faint but not of the wind, and a spot that was black between vines had an instant before been paler, as if framing a peeping face.

"Who is—" Steve began, and went staggering back.

From the vine-blackened porch a figure had flung itself on his chest.

"Mr. Threefall," the figure cried in the voice of the girl of the telegraph office, "there's somebody in the house!"

"You mean a burglar?" he asked stupidly, staring down into the small white face that was upturned just beneath his chin.

"Yes! He's upstairs—in Dr. MacPhail's room!"

"Is the doctor up there?"

"No, no! He and Mrs. MacPhail haven't come home yet."

He patted her soothingly on a velvet-coated shoulder, selecting a far shoulder, so that he had to put his arm completely around her to do the patting.

"We'll fix that," he promised. "You stick here in the shadows, and I'll be back as soon as I have taken care of our friend."

"No, no!" She clung to his shoulder with both hands. "I'll go with you. I couldn't stay here alone; but I won't be afraid with you."

He bent his head to look into her face, and cold metal struck his chin, clicking his teeth together. The cold metal was the muzzle of a big nickel-plated revolver in one of the hands that clung to his shoulder.

"Here, give me that thing," he exclaimed; "and I'll let you come with me."

She gave him the gun and he put it in his pocket.

"Hold on to my coat-tails," he ordered; "keep as close to me as you can, and when I say 'Down,' let go, drop flat to the floor, and stay there."

Thus, the girl whispering guidance to him, they went through the door she had left open, into the house, and mounted to the second floor. From their right, as they stood at the head of the stairs, came cautious rustlings.

Steve put his face down until the girl's hair was on his lips.

"How do you get to that room?" he whispered.

"Straight down the hall. It ends there."

They crept down the hall. Steve's outstretched hand touched a door-frame.

"Down!" he whispered to the girl.

Her fingers released his coat. He flung the door open, jumped through, slammed it behind him. A head-sized oval was black against the gray of a window. He spun his stick at it. Something caught the stick overhead;

glass crashed, showering him with fragments. The oval was no longer visible against the window. He wheeled to the left, flung out an arm toward a sound of motion. His fingers found a neck—a thin neck with skin as dry and brittle as paper.

A kicking foot drove into his shin just below the knee. The paperish neck slid out of his hand. He dug at it with desperate fingers, but his fingers, weakened by the wound in his forearm, failed to hold. He dropped his stick and flashed his right hand to the left's assistance. Too late. The weakened hand had fallen away from the paperish neck, and there was nothing for the right to clutch.

A misshapen blot darkened the center of an open window, vanished with a thud of feet on the roof of the rear porch. Steve sprang to the window in time to see the burglar scramble up from the ground, where he had slid from the porch roof, and make for the low back fence. One of Steve's legs was over the sill when the girl's arms came around his neck.

"No, no!" she pleaded. "Don't leave me! Let him go!"

"All right," he said reluctantly, and then brightened.

He remembered the gun he had taken from the girl, got it out of his pocket as the fleeing shadow in the yard reached the fence; and as the shadow, one hand on the fence top, vaulted high over it, Steve squeezed the trigger. The revolver clicked. Again—another click. Six clicks, and the burglar was gone into the night.

Steve broke the revolver in the dark, and ran his fingers over the back of the cylinder—six empty chambers.

"Turn on the lights," he said brusquely.

WHEN THE GIRL had obeyed, Steve stepped back into the room and looked first for his ebony stick. That in his hand, he faced the girl. Her eyes were jet-black with excitement and pale lines of strain were around her mouth. As they stood looking into each other's eyes something of a bewilderment began to show through her fright. He turned away abruptly and gazed around the room.

The place had been ransacked thoroughly if not expertly. Drawers stood out, their contents strewn on the floor; the bed had been stripped of clothing, and pillows had been dumped out of their cases. Near the door a broken wall-light—the obstruction that had checked Steve's stick—hung crookedly. In the center of the floor lay a gold watch and half a length of gold chain. He picked them up and held them out to the girl.

"Dr. MacPhail's?"

She shook her head in denial before she took the watch, and then, examining it closely, she gave a little gasp. "It's Mr. Rymer's!"

"Rymer?" Steve repeated, and then he remembered. Rymer was the blind man who had been in the Finn's lunchroom, and for whom Kamp had prophesied trouble.

"Yes! Oh, I know something has happened to him!"

She put a hand on Steve's left arm.

"We've got to go see! He lives all alone, and if any harm has—"

She broke off, and looked down at the arm under her hand.

"Your arm! You're hurt!"

"Not as bad as it looks," Steve said. "That's what brought me here. But it has stopped bleeding. Maybe by the time we get back from Rymer's the doctor will be home."

They left the house by the back door, and the girl led him through dark streets and across darker lots. Neither of them spoke during the five-minute walk. The girl hurried at a pace that left her little breath for conversation, and Steve was occupied with uncomfortable thinking.

The blind man's cabin was dark when they reached it, but the front door was ajar. Steve knocked his stick against the frame, got no answer, and struck a match. Rymer lay on the floor, sprawled on his back, his arms outflung.

The cabin's one room was topsy-turvy. Furniture lay in upended confusion, clothing was scattered here and there, and boards had been torn from the floor. The girl knelt beside the unconscious man while Steve hunted for a light. Presently he found an oil lamp that had escaped injury, and got it burning just as Rymer's filmed eyes opened and he sat up. Steve righted an overthrown rocking-chair and, with the girl, assisted the blind man to it, where he sat panting. He had recognized the girl's voice at once, and he smiled bravely in her direction.

"I'm all right, Nova," he said; "not hurt a bit. Someone knocked at the door, and when I opened it I heard a swishing sound in my ear—and that was all I knew until I came to to find you here."

He frowned with sudden anxiety, got to his feet, and moved across the room. Steve pulled a chair and an upset table from his path, and the blind man dropped on his knees in a corner, fumbling beneath the loosened floor boards. His hands came out empty, and he stood up with a tired droop to his shoulders. "Gone," he said softly.

Steve remembered the watch then, took it from his pocket, and put it into one of the blind man's hands.

"There was a burglar at our house," the girl explained. "After he had gone we found that on the floor. This is Mr. Threefall."

The blind man groped for Steve's hand, pressed it, then his flexible fingers caressed the watch, his face lighting up happily.

"I'm glad," he said, "to have this back—gladder than I can say. The money wasn't so much—less than three hundred dollars. I'm not the Midas I'm said to be. But this watch was my father's."

He tucked it carefully into his vest, and then, as the girl started to straighten up the room, he remonstrated.

"You'd better run along home, Nova; it's late, and I'm all right. I'll go to bed now, and let the place go as it is until to-morrow."

The girl demurred, but presently she and Steve were walking back to the MacPhails' house, through the black streets; but they did not hurry now. They walked two blocks in silence, Steve looking ahead into dark space with glum thoughtfulness, the girl eyeing him covertly.

"What is the matter?" she asked abruptly.

Steve smiled pleasantly down at her.

"Nothing. Why?"

"There is," she contradicted him. "You're thinking of something unpleasant, something to do with me."

He shook his head.

"That's wrong, wrong on the face of it—they don't go together."

But she was not to be put off with compliments. "You're—you're—" She stood still in the dim street, searching for the right word.

"You're on your guard—you don't trust me—that's what it is!"

Steve smiled again, but with narrowed eyes. This reading of his mind might have been intuitive, or it might have been something else.

He tried a little of the truth:

"Not distrustful—just wondering. You know you *did* give me an empty gun to go after the burglar with, and you know you *wouldn't* let me chase him."

Her eyes flashed, and she drew herself up to the last inch of her slender five feet.

"So you think—" she began indignantly. Then she drooped toward him, her hands fastening upon the lapels of his coat. "Please, please, Mr. Threefall, you've got to believe that I didn't know the revolver was empty. It was

Dr. MacPhail's. I took it when I ran out of the house, never dreaming that it wasn't loaded. And as for not letting you chase the burglar—I was afraid to be left alone again. I'm a little coward. I—I— Please believe in me, Mr. Threefall. Be friends with me. I need friends. I—"

Womanhood had dropped from her. She pleaded with the small white face of a child of twelve—a lonely, frightened child. And because his suspicions would not capitulate immediately to her appeal, Steve felt dumbly miserable, with an obscure shame in himself, as if he were lacking in some quality he should have had.

She went on talking, very softly, so that he had to bend his head to catch the words. She talked about herself, as a child would talk.

"It's been terrible! I came here three months ago because there was a vacancy in the telegraph office. I was suddenly alone in the world, with very little money, and telegraphy was all I knew that could be capitalized. It's been terrible here! The town—I can't get accustomed to it. It's so bleak. No children play in the streets. The people are different from those I've known—cruder, more brutal. Even the houses—street after street of them without curtains in the windows, without flowers. No grass in the yards, no trees.

"But I had to stay—there was nowhere else to go. I thought I could stay until I had saved a little money—enough to take me away. But saving money takes so long. Dr. MacPhail's garden has been like a piece of paradise to me. If it hadn't been for that I don't think I could have—I'd have gone crazy! The doctor and his wife have been nice to me; some people have been nice to me, but most of them are people I can't understand. And not all have been nice. At first it was awful. Men would say things, and women would say things, and when I was afraid of them they thought I was stuck up. Larry—Mr. Ormsby—saved me from that. He made them let me alone, and he persuaded the MacPhails to let me live with them. Mr. Rymer has helped me, too, given me courage; but I lose it again as soon as I'm away from the sight of his face and the sound of his voice.

"I'm scared—scared of everything! Of Larry Ormsby especially! And he's been wonderfully helpful to me. But I can't help it. I'm afraid of him—of the way he looks at me sometimes, of things he says when he has been drinking. It's as if there was something inside of him waiting for something. I shouldn't say that—because I owe him gratitude for— But I'm so afraid! I'm afraid of every person, of every house, of every doorstep even. It's a nightmare!"

Steve found that one of his hands was cupped over the white cheek that was not flat against his chest, and that his other arm was around her shoulders, holding her close.

"New towns are always like this, or worse," he began to tell her. "You should have seen Hopewell, Virginia, when the Du Ponts first opened it. It takes time for the undesirables who come with the first rush to be weeded out. And, stuck out here in the desert, Izzard would naturally fare a little worse than the average new town. As for being friends with you—that's why I stayed here instead of going back to Whitetufts. We'll be great friends. We'll—"

He never knew how long he talked, or what he said; though he imagined afterward that he must have made a very long-winded and very stupid speech. But he was not talking for the purpose of saying anything; he was talking to soothe the girl, and to keep her small face between his hand and chest, and her small body close against his for as long a time as possible.

So, he talked on and on and on—

THE MacPHAILS were at home when Nova Vallance and Steve came through the flowered yard again, and they welcomed the girl with evident relief. The doctor was a short man with a round bald head, and a round jovial face, shiny and rosy except where a sandy mustache drooped over his mouth. His wife was perhaps ten years younger than he, a slender blond woman with much of the feline in the set of her blue eyes and the easy grace of her movements.

"The car broke down with us about twenty miles out," the doctor explained in a mellow rumbling voice with a hint of a burr lingering around the r's. "I had to perform a major operation on it before we could get going again. When we got home we found you gone, and were just about to rouse the town."

The girl introduced Steve to the MacPhails, and then told them about the burglar, and of what they had found in the blind man's cabin.

Dr. MacPhail shook his round naked head and clicked his tongue on teeth. "Seems to me Fernie doesn't do all that could be done to tone Izzard down," he said.

Then the girl remembered Steve's wounded arm, and the doctor examined, washed, and bandaged it.

"You won't have to wear the arm in a sling," he said, "if you take a reasonable amount of care of it. It isn't a deep cut, and fortunately it went between the supinator longus and the great palmar without injury to either. Get it from our burglar?"

"No. Got it in the street. A man named Kamp and I were walking toward the hotel to-night and were jumped. Kamp was killed. I got this."

An asthmatic clock somewhere up the street was striking three as Steve passed through the MacPhails' front gate and set out for the hotel again. He felt tired and sore in every muscle, and he walked close to the curb.

"If anything else happens to-night," he told himself, "I'm going to run like hell from it. I've had enough for one evening."

At the first cross-street he had to pause to let an automobile race by. As it passed him he recognized it—Larry Ormsby's cream Vauxhall. In its wake sped five big trucks, with a speed that testified to readjusted gears. In a roar of engines, a cloud of dust, and a rattling of windows, the caravan vanished toward the desert.

Steve went on toward the hotel, thinking. The factory worked twenty-four hours a day, he knew; but surely no necessity of niter manufacturing would call for such excessive speed in its trucks—if they were factory trucks. He turned into Main Street and faced another surprise. The cream Vauxhall stood near the corner, its owner at the wheel. As Steve came abreast of it Larry Ormsby let its near door swing open, and held out an inviting hand.

Steve stopped and stood by the door.

"Jump in and I'll give you a lift as far as the hotel."

"Thanks."

Steve looked quizzically from the man's handsome, reckless face to the now dimly lighted hotel, less than two blocks away. Then he looked at the man again, and got into the automobile beside him.

"I hear you're a more or less permanent fixture among us," Ormsby said, proffering Steve cigarettes in a lacquered leather case, and shutting off his idling engine.

"For a while."

Steve declined the cigarettes and brought out tobacco and papers from his pocket, adding, "There are things about the place I like."

"I also hear you had a little excitement to-night."

"Some," Steve admitted, wondering whether the other meant the fight in which Kamp had been killed, the burglary at the MacPhails', or both.

"If you keep up the pace you've set," the factory owner's son went on, "it won't take you long to nose me out of my position as Izzard's brightest light."

Tautening nerves tickled the nape of Steve's neck. Larry Ormsby's words and tones seemed idle enough, but underneath them was a suggestion that they were not aimless—that they were leading to some definite place. It was not likely that he had circled around to intercept Steve merely to exchange meaningless chatter with him. Steve, lighting his cigarette, grinned and waited.

"The only thing I ever got from the old man, besides money," Larry Ormsby was saying, "is a deep-rooted proprietary love for my own property. I'm a regular burgher for insisting that my property is mine and must stay mine. I don't know exactly how to feel about a stranger coming in and making himself the outstanding black sheep of the town in two days. A reputation—even for recklessness—is property, you know; and I don't feel that I should give it up—or any other rights—without a struggle."

There it was. Steve's mind cleared. He disliked subtleties. But now he knew what the talk was about. He was being warned to keep away from Nova Vallance.

"I knew a fellow once in Onehunga," he drawled, "who thought he owned all of the Pacific south of the Tropic of Capricorn—and had papers to prove it. He'd been that way ever since a Maori bashed in his head with a stone mele. Used to accuse us of stealing our drinking water from his ocean."

Larry Ormsby flicked his cigarette into the street and started the engine.

"But the point is"—he was smiling pleasantly—"that a man is moved to protect what he thinks belongs to him. He may be wrong, of course, but that wouldn't affect the—ah—vigor of his protecting efforts."

Steve felt himself growing warm and angry.

"Maybe you're right," he said slowly, with deliberate intent to bring this thing between them to a crisis, "but I've never had enough experience with property to know how I'd feel about being deprived of it. But suppose I had a—well, say—a white vest that I treasured. And suppose a man slapped my face and threatened to spoil the vest. I reckon I'd forget all about protecting the vest in my hurry to tangle with him."

Larry laughed sharply.

Steve caught the wrist that flashed up, and pinned it to Ormsby's side with a hand that much spinning of a heavy stick had muscled with steel.

"Easy," he said into the slitted, dancing eyes; "easy now."

Larry Ormsby's white teeth flashed under his mustache.

"Righto," he smiled. "If you'll turn my wrist loose, I'd like to shake hands with you—a sort of ante-bellum gesture. I like you, Threefall; you're going to add materially to the pleasures of Izzard."

In his room on the third floor of the Izzard Hotel, Steve Threefall undressed slowly, hampered by a stiff left arm and much thinking. Matter for thought he had in abundance. Larry Ormsby slapping his father's face and threatening him with an automatic; Larry Ormsby and the girl in confidential conversation; Kamp dying in a dark street, his last words lost in the noise of the marshal's arrival; Nova Vallance giving him an empty revolver, and persuading him to let a burglar escape; the watch on the floor and the looting of the blind man's savings; the caravan Larry Ormsby had led toward the desert; the talk in the Vauxhall, with its exchange of threats.

Was there any connection between each of these things and the others? Or were they simply disconnected happenings? If there was a connection — and the whole of that quality in mankind which strives toward simplification of life's phenomena, unification, urged him to belief in a connection — just what was it? Still puzzling, he got into bed; and then out again quickly. An uneasiness that had been vague until now suddenly thrust itself into his consciousness. He went to the door, opened and closed it. It was a cheaply carpentered door, but it moved easily and silently on well-oiled hinges.

"I reckon I'm getting to be an old woman," he growled to himself; "but I've had all I want to-night."

He blocked the door with the dresser, put his stick where he could reach it quickly, got into bed again, and went to sleep.

A POUNDING on the door awakened Steve at nine o'clock the next morning. The pounder was one of Fernie's subordinates, and he told Steve that he was expected to be present at the inquest into Kamp's death within an hour. Steve found that his wounded arm bothered him little; not so much as a bruised area on one shoulder — another souvenir of the fight in the street.

He dressed, ate breakfast in the hotel café, and went up to Ross Amthor's "undertaking parlor," where the inquest was to be held.

The coroner was a tall man with high, narrow shoulders and a sallow, puffy face, who sped proceedings along regardless of the finer points of legal technicality. Steve told his story; the marshal told his, and then produced a prisoner — a thick-set Austrian who seemingly neither spoke nor understood English. His throat and lower face were swathed in white bandages.

"Is this the one you knocked down?" the coroner asked.

Steve looked at as much of the Austrian's face as was visible above the bandages.

"I don't know. I can't see enough of him."

"This is the one I picked out of the gutter," Grant Fernie volunteered; "whether you knocked him there or not. I don't suppose you got a good look at him. But this is he all right."

Steve frowned doubtfully. "I'd know him," he said, "if he turned his face up and I got a good look at him."

"Take off some of his bandages so the witness can see him," the coroner ordered. Fernie unwound the Austrian's bandages, baring a bruised and swollen jaw.

Steve stared at the man. This fellow may have been one of his assailants, but he most certainly wasn't the one he had knocked into the street. He hesitated. Could he have confused faces in the fight?

"Do you identify him?" the coroner asked impatiently.

Steve shook his head.

"I don't remember ever seeing him."

"Look here, Threefall"—the giant marshal scowled down at Steve—"this is the man I hauled out of the gutter—one of the men you said jumped you and Kamp. Now what's the game? What's the idea of forgetting?"

Steve answered slowly, stubbornly:

"I don't know. All I know is that this isn't the first one I hit, the one I knocked out. He was an American—had an American face. He was about this fellow's size, but this isn't he."

The coroner exposed broken yellow teeth in a snarl, the marshal glowered at Steve, the jurors regarded him with frank suspicion. The marshal and the coroner withdrew to a far corner of the room, where they whispered together, casting frequent glances at Steve.

"All right," the coroner told Steve when this conference was over; "that's all."

From the inquest Steve walked slowly back to the hotel, his mind puzzled by this newest addition to Izzard's mysteries. What was the explanation of the certain fact that the man the marshal had produced at the inquest was not the man he had taken from the gutter the previous night? Another thought: the marshal had arrived immediately after the fight with the men who had attacked him and Kamp, had arrived noisily, drowning the dying man's last words. That opportune arrival and the accompanying noise— were they accidental? Steve didn't know; and because he didn't know he strode back to the hotel in frowning meditation.

At the hotel he found that his bag had arrived from Whitetufts. He took it up to his room and changed his clothes. Then he carried his perplexity to the window, where he sat smoking cigarette after cigarette, staring into the alley below, his forehead knotted beneath his tawny hair. Was it possible that so many things should explode around one man in so short a time, in a small city of Izzard's size, without there being a connection between

Deputation of city

them—and between them and him? And if he was being involved in a vicious maze of crime and intrigue, what was it all about? What had started it? What was the key to it? The girl?

Confused thoughts fell away from him. He sprang to his feet.

Down the other side of the alley a man was walking—a thick-set man in soiled blue—a man with bandaged throat and chin. What was visible of his face was the face Steve had seen turned skyward in the fight—the face of the man he had knocked out.

Steve sprang to the door, out of the room, down three flights of stairs, past the desk, and out of the hotel's back door. He gained the alley in time to see a blue trouser-leg disappearing into a doorway in the block below. Thither he went.

The doorway opened into an office building. He searched the corridors, upstairs and down, and did not find the bandaged man. He returned to the ground floor and discovered a sheltered corner near the back door, near the foot of the stairs. The corner was shielded from the stairs and from most of the corridor by a wooden closet in which brooms and mops were kept. The man had entered through the rear of the building; he would probably leave that way; Steve waited.

Fifteen minutes passed, bringing no one within sight of his hiding-place. Then from the front of the building came a woman's soft laugh, and foot-steps moved toward him. He shrank back in his dusky corner. The footsteps passed—a man and a woman laughing and talking together as they walked. They mounted the stairs. Steve peeped out at them, and then drew back suddenly, more in surprise than in fear of detection, for the two who mounted the stairs were completely engrossed in each other.

The man was Elder, the insurance and real-estate agent. Steve did not see his face, but the checkered suit on his round figure was unmistakable—"college-boy suit," Kamp had called it. Elder's arm was around the woman's waist as they went up the stairs, and her cheek leaned against his shoulder as she looked coquettishly into his face. The woman was Dr. MacPhail's feline wife.

"What next?" Steve asked himself, when they had passed from his sight. "Is the whole town wrong? What next, I wonder?"

The answer came immediately—the pounding of crazy footsteps directly over Steve's head—footsteps that might have belonged to a drunken man, or to a man fighting a phantom. Above the noise of heels on wooden floor, a scream rose—a scream that blended horror and pain into a sound that was all the more unearthly because it was unmistakably of human origin.

Steve bolted out of his corner and up the steps three at a time, pivoted into the second-floor corridor on the newel, and came face to face with David Brackett, the banker.

Brackett's thick legs were far apart, and he swayed on them. His face was a pallid agony above his beard. Big spots of beard were gone, as if torn out or burned away. From his writhing lips thin wisps of vapor issued.

"They've poisoned me, the damned—"

He came suddenly up on the tips of his toes, his body arched, and he fell stiffly backward, as dead things fall.

Steve dropped on a knee beside him, but he knew nothing could be done—knew Brackett had died while still on his feet. For a moment, as he crouched there over the dead man, something akin to panic swept Steve Threefall's mind clean of reason. Was there never to be an end to this piling of mystery upon mystery, of violence upon violence? He had the sensation of being caught in a monstrous net—a net without beginning or end, and whose meshes were slimy with blood. Nausea—spiritual and physical—gripped him, held him impotent. Then a shot crashed.

He jerked erect—sprang down the corridor toward the sound; seeking in a frenzy of physical activity escape from the sickness that had filled him.

At the end of the corridor a door was labeled ORMSBY NITER COR-PORATION, W. W. ORMSBY, PRESIDENT. There was no need for hesitancy before deciding that the shot had come from behind that label. Even as he dashed toward it, another shot rattled the door and a falling body thudded behind it.

Steve flung the door open—and jumped aside to avoid stepping on the man who lay just inside. Over by a window, Larry Ormsby stood facing the door, a black automatic in his hand. His eyes danced with wild merriment, and his lips curled in a tight-lipped smile. "Hello, Threefall," he said. "I see you're still keeping close to the storm centers."

Steve looked down at the man on the floor—W. W. Ormsby. Two bullet-holes were in the upper left-hand pocket of his vest. The holes, less than an inch apart, had been placed with a precision that left no room for doubting that the man was dead. Steve remembered Larry's threat to his father: "I'll spoil your vest!"

He looked up from killed to killer. Larry Ormsby's eyes were hard and bright; the pistol in his hand was held lightly, with the loose alertness peculiar to professional gunmen.

"This isn't a—ah—personal matter with you, is it?" he asked.

Steve shook his head; and heard the trampling of feet and a confusion of excited voices in the corridor behind him.

"That's nice," the killer was saying; "and I'd suggest that you—"

He broke off as men came into the office. Grant Fernie, the marshal, was one of them.

"Dead?" he asked, with a bare glance at the man on the floor.

"Rather," Larry replied.

"How come?"

Larry Ormsby moistened his lips, not nervously, but thoughtfully. Then he smiled at Steve, and told his story.

"Threefall and I were standing down near the front door talking, when we heard a shot. I thought it had been fired up here, but he said it came from across the street. Anyhow, we came up here to make sure—making a bet on it first; so Threefall owes me a dollar. We came up here, and just as we got to the head of the steps we heard another shot, and Brackett came running out of here with this gun in his hand."

He gave the automatic to the marshal, and went on: "He took a few steps from the door, yelled, and fell down. Did you see him out there?"

"I did," Fernie said.

"Well, Threefall stopped to look at him while I came on in here to see if my father was all right—and found him dead. That's all there is to it."

STEVE WENT slowly down to the street after the gathering in the dead man's office had broken up, without having either contradicted or corroborated Larry Ormsby's fiction. No one had questioned him. At first he had been too astonished by the killer's boldness to say anything; and when his wits had resumed their functions, he had decided to hold his tongue for a while.

Suppose he had told the truth? Would it have helped justice? Would anything help justice in Izzard? If he had known what lay behind this piling-up of crime, he could have decided what to do; but he did not know—did not even know that there was anything behind it. So he had kept silent. The inquest would not be held until the following day—time enough to talk then, after a night's consideration.

He could not grasp more than a fragment of the affair at a time now; disconnected memories made a whirl of meaningless images in his brain. Elder and Mrs. MacPhail going up the stairs—to where? What had become of them? What had become of the man with the bandages on throat and jaw? Had those three any part in the double murder? Had Larry killed the banker as well as his father? By what chance did the marshal appear on the scene immediately after murder had been done?

Steve carried his jumbled thoughts back to the hotel, and lay across his bed for perhaps an hour. Then he got up and went to the Bank of Izzard, drew out the money he had there, put it carefully in his pocket, and returned to his hotel room to lie across the bed again.

Nova Vallance, nebulous in yellow crêpe, was sitting on the lower step of the MacPhails' porch when Steve went up the flowered walk that evening. She welcomed him warmly, concealing none of the impatience with which she had been waiting for him. He sat on the step beside her, twisting around a little for a better view of the dusky oval of her face.

"How is your arm?" she asked.

"Fine!" He opened and shut his left hand briskly. "I suppose you heard all about to-day's excitement?"

"Oh, yes! About Mr. Brackett's shooting Mr. Ormsby, and then dying with one of his heart attacks."

"Huh?" Steve demanded.

"But weren't you there?" she asked in surprise.

"I was, but suppose you tell me just what you heard."

"Oh, I've heard all sorts of things about it! But all I really know is what Dr. MacPhail, who examined both of them, said."

"And what was that?"

"That Mr. Brackett killed Mr. Ormsby—shot him—though nobody seems to know why; and then, before he could get out of the building, his heart failed him and he died."

"And he was supposed to have a bad heart?"

"Yes. Dr. MacPhail told him a year ago that he would have to be careful, that the least excitement might be fatal."

Steve caught her wrist in his hand.

"Think now," he commanded. "Did you ever hear Dr. MacPhail speak of Brackett's heart trouble until to-day?"

She looked curiously into his face, and a little pucker of bewilderment came between her eyes.

"No," she replied slowly. "I don't think so; but, of course, there was never any reason why he should have mentioned it. Why do you ask?"

"Because," he told her, "Brackett did *not* shoot Ormsby; and any heart attack that killed Brackett was caused by poison—some poison that burned his face and beard."

She gave a little cry of horror.

"You think—" She stopped, glanced furtively over her shoulder at the front door of the house, and leaned close to him to whisper: "Didn't—didn't you say that the man who was killed in the fight last night was named Kamp?"

"Yes."

"Well, the report, or whatever it was that Dr. MacPhail made of his examination, reads Henry Cumberpatch."

"You sure? Sure it's the same man?"

"Yes. The wind blew it off the doctor's desk, and when I handed it back to him, he made some joke"—she colored with a little laugh—"some joke about it nearly being your death certificate instead of your companion's. I glanced down at it then, and saw that it was for a man named Henry Cumberpatch. What does it all mean? What is—"

The front gate clattered open, and a man swayed up the walk. Steve got up, picked up his black stick, and stepped between the girl and the advancing man. The man's face came out of the dark. It was Larry Ormsby; and when he spoke his words had a drunken thickness to match the unsteadiness—not quite a stagger, but nearly so—of his walk.

"Lis'en," he said; "I'm dam' near—"

Steve moved toward him. "If Miss Vallance will excuse us," he said, "we'll stroll to the gate and talk."

Without waiting for a reply from either of them, Steve linked an arm through one of Ormsby's and urged him down the path. At the gate Larry broke away, pulling his arm loose and confronting Steve.

"No time for foolishness," he snarled. "Y' got to get out! Get out o' Izzard!"

"Yes?" Steve asked. "And why?"

Larry leaned back against the fence and raised one hand in an impatient gesture.

"Your lives are not worth a nickel—neither of you."

He swayed and coughed. Steve grasped him by the shoulder and peered into his face.

"What's the matter with you?"

Larry coughed again and clapped a hand to his chest, up near the shoulder.

"Bullet—up high—Fernie's. But I got him—the big tramp. Toppled him out a window—down like a kid divin' for pennies." He laughed shrilly, and then became earnest again. "Get the girl—beat it—now! Now! Now! Ten minutes'll be too late. They're comin'!"

"Who? What? Why?" Steve snapped. "Talk turkey! I don't trust you. I've got to have reasons."

"Reasons, my God!" the wounded man cried. "You'll get your reasons. You think I'm trying to scare you out o' town b'fore th' inquest." He laughed insanely. "Inquest! You fool! There won't be any inquest! There won't be any to-morrow—for Izzard! And you—"

He pulled himself sharply together and caught one of Steve's hands in both of his.

"Listen," he said. "I'll give it to you, but we're wasting time! But if you've got to have it—listen.

"**IZZARD IS** a plant! The whole damned town is queer. Booze—that's the answer. The man I knocked off this afternoon—the one you thought was my father—originated the scheme. You make soda niter by boiling the nitrate in tanks with heated coils. He got the idea that a niter plant would make a good front for a moonshine factory. And he got the idea that if you had a whole town working together it'd be impossible for the game ever to fall down.

"You can guess how much money there is in this country in the hands of men who'd be glad to invest it in a booze game that was air-tight. Not only crooks, I mean, but men who consider themselves honest. Take your guess, whatever it is, and double it, and you still won't be within millions of the right answer. There are men with— But anyway, Ormsby took his scheme east and got his backing—a syndicate that could have raised enough money to build a dozen cities.

"Ormsby, Elder, and Brackett were the boys who managed the game. I was here to see that they didn't double-cross the syndicate; and then there's a flock of trusty lieutenants, like Fernie, and MacPhail, and Heman—he's postmaster—and Harker—another doctor, who got his last week—and Leslie, who posed as a minister. There was no trouble to getting the population we wanted. The word went around that the new town was a place where a crook would be safe so long as he did what he was told. The slums of all the cities of America, and half of 'em out of it, emptied themselves here. Every crook that was less than a step ahead of the police, and had car fare here, came and got cover.

"Of course, with every thug in the world blowing in here we had a lot of sleuths coming, too; but they weren't hard to handle, and if worse came to worst, we could let the law take an occasional man; but usually it wasn't hard to take care of the gumshoes. We have bankers, and ministers, and doctors, and postmasters, and prominent men of all sorts either to tangle the sleuths up with bum leads, or, if necessary, to frame them. You'll find a flock of men in the state pen who came here—most of them as narcotics agents or prohibition agents—and got themselves tied up before they knew what it was all about.

"God, there never was a bigger game! It couldn't flop—unless we spoiled it for ourselves. And that's what we've done. It was too big for us! There was too much money in it—it went to our heads! At first we played square with the syndicate. We made booze and shipped it out—shipped it in carload lots, in trucks, did everything but pipe it out, and we made money for the syndicate and for ourselves. Then we got the real idea—the big one! We kept on making the hooch; but we got the big idea going for our own profit. The syndicate wasn't in on that.

"First, we got the insurance racket under way. Elder managed that, with three or four assistants. Between them they became agents of half the insurance companies in the country, and they began to plaster Izzard with policies. Men who had never lived were examined, insured, and then killed—sometimes they were killed on paper, sometimes a real man who died was substituted, and there were times when a man or two was killed to order. It was soft! We had the insurance agents, the doctors, the coroner, the undertaker, and all the city officials. We had the machinery to swing any deal we wanted! You were with Kamp the night he was killed! That was a good one. He was an insurance company sleuth—the companies were getting suspicious. He came here and was foolish enough to trust his reports to the mail. There aren't many letters from strangers that get through the post office without being read. We read his reports, kept them, and sent phony ones out in their places. Then we nailed Mr. Kamp, and changed his name on the records to fit a policy in the very company he represented. A rare joke, eh?

"The insurance racket wasn't confined to men—cars, houses, furniture, everything you can insure was plastered. In the last census—by distributing the people we could count on, one in a house, with a list of five or six names—we got a population on the records of at least five times as many as are really here. That gave us room for plenty of policies, plenty of deaths, plenty of property insurance, plenty of everything. It gave us enough political influence in the county and state to strengthen our hands a hundred per cent, make the game safer.

"You'll find street after street of houses with nothing in them out of sight of the front windows. They cost money to put up, but we've made the money right along, and they'll show a wonderful profit when the clean-up comes.

"Then, after the insurance stunt was on its feet, we got the promotion game going. There's a hundred corporations in Izzard that are nothing but addresses on letterheads—but stock certificates and bonds have been sold in them from one end of these United States to the other. And they have bought goods, paid for them, shipped them out to be got rid of—maybe at a loss—and put in larger and larger orders until they've built up a credit with the manufacturers that would make you dizzy to total. Easy! Wasn't Brackett's bank here to give them all the financial references they needed? There was nothing to it; a careful building-up of credit until they reached the highest possible point. Then, the goods shipped out to be sold through fences, and—bingo! The town is wiped out by fire. The stocks of goods are presumably burned; the expensive buildings that the out-of-town investors were told about are presumably destroyed; the books and records are burned.

"What a killing! I've had a hell of a time stalling off the syndicate, trying to keep them in the dark about the surprise we're going to give them. They're too suspicious as it is for us to linger much longer. But things are about ripe for the blow-off—the fire that's to start in the factory and wipe out the whole dirty town—and next Saturday was the day we picked. That's the day when Izzard becomes nothing but a pile of ashes—and a pile of collectable insurance policies.

"The rank and file in town won't know anything about the finer points of the game. Those that suspect anything take their money and keep quiet. When the town goes up in smoke there will be hundreds of bodies found in the ruins—all insured—and there will be proof of the death of hundreds of others—likewise insured—whose bodies can't be found.

"There never was a bigger game! But it was too big for us! My fault—some of it—but it would have burst anyway. We always weeded out those who came to town looking too honest or too wise, and we made doubly sure that nobody who was doubtful got into the post office, railroad depot, telegraph office, or telephone exchange. If the railroad company or the telegraph or telephone company sent somebody here to work, and we couldn't make them see things the way we wanted them seen, we managed to make the place disagreeable for them—and they usually flitted elsewhere in a hurry.

"Then the telegraph company sent Nova here and I flopped for her. At first it was just that I liked her looks. We had all sorts of women here—but they were mostly all sorts—and Nova was something different. I've done my share of dirtiness in this world, but I've never been able to get rid of a certain fastidiousness in my taste for women. I— Well, the rest of them— Brackett, Ormsby, Elder, and the lot—were all for giving Nova the works. But I talked them out of it. I told them to let her alone and I'd have her on the inside in no time. I really thought I could do it. She liked me, or seemed to, but I couldn't get any further than that. I didn't make any headway. The others got impatient, but I kept putting them off, telling them that everything would be fine, that if necessary I'd marry her, and shut her up that way. They didn't like it. It wasn't easy to keep her from learning what was going on—working in the telegraph office—but we managed it somehow.

"Next Saturday was the day we'd picked for the big fireworks. Ormsby gave me the call yesterday—told me flatly that if I didn't sew Nova up at once they were going to pop her. They didn't know how much she had found out, and they were taking no chances. I told him I'd kill him if he touched her, but I knew I couldn't talk them out of it. To-day the break came. I heard he had given the word that she was to be put out of the way to-night. I went to his office for a showdown. Brackett was there. Ormsby salved me along, denied he had given any order affecting the girl, and poured out drinks for the three of us. The drink looked wrong. I waited to see what was going to happen next. Brackett gulped his down. It was poisoned. He went outside to die, and I nailed Ormsby.

"The game has blown up! It was too rich for us. Everybody is trying to slit everybody else's throat. I couldn't find Elder—but Fernie tried to pot me from a window; and he's Elder's right-hand man. Or he was—he's a stiff now. I think this thing in my chest is the big one—I'm about— But you can get the girl out. You've got to! Elder will go through with the play—try to make the killing for himself. He'll have the town touched off to-night. It's now or never with him. He'll try to—"

A shriek cut through the darkness.

"Steve! *Steve!! Steve!!!*"

STEVE WHIRLED away from the gate, leaped through flower-beds, crossed the porch in a bound, and was in the house. Behind him Larry Ormsby's feet clattered. An empty hallway, an empty room, another. Nobody was in sight on the ground floor. Steve went up the stairs. A strip of golden light lay under a door. He went through the door, not knowing or caring whether it was locked or not. He simply hurled himself shoulder-first at it, and was in the room. Leaning back against a table in the center of the room, Dr. MacPhail was struggling with the girl. He was behind her, his arms around her, trying to hold her head still. The girl twisted and squirmed like a cat gone mad. In front of her Mrs. MacPhail poised an uplifted blackjack.

Steve flung his stick at the woman's white arm, flung it instinctively, without skill or aim. The heavy ebony struck arm and shoulder, and she staggered back. Dr. MacPhail, releasing the girl, dived at Steve's legs, got them, and carried him to the floor. Steve's fumbling fingers slid off the doctor's bald head, could get no grip on the back of his thick neck, found an ear, and gouged into the flesh under it.

The doctor grunted and twisted away from the digging fingers. Steve got a knee free—drove it at the doctor's face. Mrs. MacPhail bent over his head, raising the black leather billy she still held. He dashed an arm at her ankles, missed—but the down-crashing blackjack fell obliquely on his shoulder. He twisted away, scrambled to his knees and hands—and sprawled headlong under the impact of the doctor's weight on his back.

He rolled over, got the doctor under him, felt his hot breath on his neck. Steve raised his head and snapped it back—hard. Raised it again, and snapped it down, hammering MacPhail's face with the back of his skull. The doctor's arms fell away and Steve lurched upright to find the fight over.

Larry Ormsby stood in the doorway grinning evilly over his pistol at Mrs. MacPhail, who stood sullenly by the table. The blackjack was on the floor at Larry's feet.

Against the other side of the table the girl leaned weakly, one hand on her bruised throat, her eyes dazed and blank with fear. Steve went around to her.

"Get going, Steve! There's no time for playing. You got a car?" Larry Ormsby's voice was rasping.

"No," Steve said.

Larry cursed bitterly—an explosion of foul blasphemies. Then:

"We'll go in mine—it can outrun anything in the state. But you can't wait here for me to get it. Take Nova over to blind Rymer's shack. I'll pick you up there. He's the only one in town you can trust. Go ahead, damn you!" he yelled.

Steve glanced at the sullen MacPhail woman, and at her husband, now getting up slowly from the floor, his face blood-smeared and battered.

"How about them?"

"Don't worry about them," Larry said. "Take the girl and make Rymer's place. I'll take care of this pair and be over there with the car in fifteen minutes. Get going!"

Steve's eyes narrowed and he studied the man in the doorway. He didn't trust him, but since all Izzard seemed equally dangerous, one place would be as safe as another—and Larry Ormsby might be honest this time.

"All right," he said, and turned to the girl. "Get a heavy coat."

Five minutes later they were hurrying through the same dark streets they had gone through on the previous night. Less than a block from the house, a muffled shot came to their ears, and then another. The girl glanced quickly at Steve but did not speak. He hoped she had not understood what the two shots meant.

They met nobody. Rymer had heard and recognized the girl's footsteps on the sidewalk, and he opened the door before they could knock.

"Come in, Nova," he welcomed her heartily, and then fumbled for Steve's hand. "This is Mr. Threefall, isn't it?"

He led them into the dark cabin, and then lighted the oil lamp on the table. Steve launched at once into a hurried summarizing of what Larry Ormsby had told him. The girl listened with wide eyes and wan face; the blind man's face lost its serenity, and he seemed to grow older and tired as he listened.

"Ormsby said he would come after us with his car," Steve wound up. "If he does, you will go with us, of course, Mr. Rymer. If you'll tell us what you want to take with you we'll get it ready; so that there will be no delay when he comes—if he comes." He turned to the girl. "What do you think, Nova? Will he come? And can we trust him if he does?"

"I—I hope so—he's not all bad, I think."

The blind man went to a wardrobe in the room's other end.

"I've got nothing to take," he said, "but I'll get into warmer clothes."

He pulled the wardrobe door open, so that it screened a corner of the room for him to change in. Steve went to a window, and stood there looking between blind and frame, into the dark street where nothing moved. The girl stood close to him, between his arm and side, her fingers twined in his sleeve.

"Will we—? Will we—?"

He drew her closer and answered the whispered question she could not finish.

"We'll make it," he said, "if Larry plays square, or if he doesn't. We'll make it."

A rifle cracked somewhere in the direction of Main Street. A volley of pistol shots. The cream-colored Vauxhall came out of nowhere to settle on the sidewalk, two steps from the door. Larry Ormsby, hatless and with his shirt torn loose to expose a hole under one of his collar-bones, tumbled out of the car and through the door that Steve threw open for him.

Larry kicked the door shut behind him, and laughed.

"Izzard's frying nicely!" he cried, and clapped his hands together. "Come, come! The desert awaits!"

Steve turned to call the blind man. Rymer stepped out from behind his screening door. In each of Rymer's hands was a heavy revolver. The film was gone from Rymer's eyes.

His eyes, cool and sharp now, held the two men and the girl.

"Put your hands up, all of you," he ordered curtly.

Larry Ormsby laughed insanely.

"Did you ever see a damned fool do his stuff, Rymer?" he asked.

"Put your hands up!"

"Rymer," Larry said, "I'm dying now. To hell with you!"

And without haste he took a black automatic pistol from an inside coat pocket.

The guns in Rymer's hands rocked the cabin with explosion after explosion.

Knocked into a sitting position on the floor by the heavy bullets that literally tore him apart, Larry steadied his back against the wall, and the crisp, sharp reports of his lighter weapon began to punctuate the roars of the erstwhile blind man's guns.

Instinctively jumping aside, pulling the girl with him, at the first shot, Steve now hurled himself upon Rymer's flank. But just as he reached him the shooting stopped. Rymer swayed, the very revolvers in his hands seemed to go limp. He slid out of Steve's clutching hands—his neck scraping one hand with the brittle dryness of paper—and became a lifeless pile on the floor.

Steve kicked the dead man's guns across the floor a way, and then went over to where the girl knelt beside Larry Ormsby. Larry smiled up at Steve with a flash of white teeth.

"I'm gone, Steve," he said. "That Rymer—fooled us all—phony films on eyes—painted on—spy for rum syndicate."

He writhed, and his smile grew stiff and strained.

"Mind shaking hands, Steve?" he asked a moment later.

"You're a good guy, Larry," was the only thing he could think to say.

The dying man seemed to like that. His smile became real again.

"Luck to you—you can get a hundred and ten out of the Vauxhall," he managed to say.

And then, apparently having forgotten the girl for whom he had given up his life, he flashed another smile at Steve and died.

The front door slammed open—two heads looked in. The heads' owners came in.

Steve bounded upright, swung his stick. A bone cracked like a whip, a man reeled back holding a hand to his temple.

"Behind me—close!" Steve cried to the girl, and felt her hands on his back.

Men filled the doorway. An invisible gun roared and a piece of the ceiling flaked down. Steve spun his stick and charged the door. The light from the lamp behind him glittered and glowed on the whirling wood. The stick whipped backward and forward, from left to right, from right to left. It writhed like a live thing—seemed to fold upon its grasped middle as if spring-hinged with steel. Flashing half-circles merged into a sphere of deadliness. The rhythm of incessant thudding against flesh and clicking on bone became a tune that sang through the grunts of fighting men, the groans and oaths of stricken men. Steve and the girl went through the door.

Between moving arms and legs and bodies the cream of the Vauxhall showed. Men stood upon the automobile, using its height for vantage in the fight. Steve threw himself forward, swinging his stick against shin and thigh, toppling men from the machine. With his left hand he swept the girl around to his side. His body shook and rocked under the weight of blows from men who were packed too closely for any effectiveness except the smothering power of sheer weight.

His stick was suddenly gone from him. One instant he held and spun it; the next, he was holding up a clenched fist that was empty—the ebony had vanished as if in a puff of smoke. He swung the girl up over the car door, hammered her down into the car—jammed her down upon the legs of a man who stood there—heard a bone break, and saw the man go down. Hands gripped him everywhere; hands pounded him. He cried aloud with joy when he saw the girl, huddled on the floor of the car, working with ridiculously small hands at the car's mechanism.

The machine began to move. Holding with his hands, he lashed both feet out behind. Got them back on the step. Struck over the girl's head with a hand that had neither thought nor time to make a fist—struck stiff-fingered into a broad red face.

The car moved. One of the girl's hands came up to grasp the wheel, holding the car straight along a street she could not see. A man fell on her. Steve pulled him off—tore pieces from him—tore hair and flesh. The car swerved, scraped a building; scraped one side clear of men. The hands that held Steve fell away from him, taking most of his clothing with them. He picked a man off the back of the seat, and pushed him down into the street that was flowing past them. Then he fell into the car beside the girl.

Pistols exploded behind them. From a house a little ahead a bitter-voiced rifle emptied itself at them, sieving a mudguard. Then the desert—white and smooth as a gigantic hospital bed—was around them. Whatever pursuit there had been was left far behind.

Presently the girl slowed down, stopped.

"Are you all right?" Steve asked.

"Yes; but you're—"

"All in one piece," he assured her. "Let me take the wheel."

"No! No!" she protested. "You're bleeding. You're—"

"No! No!" he mocked her. "We'd better keep going until we hit something. We're not far enough from Izzard yet to call ourselves safe."

He was afraid that if she tried to patch him up he would fall apart in her hands. He felt like that.

She started the car, and they went on. A great sleepiness came to him. What a fight! What a fight!

"Look at the sky!" she exclaimed.

He opened his heavy eyes. Ahead of them, above them, the sky was lightening—from blue-black to violet, to mauve, to rose. He turned his head and looked back. Where they had left Izzard, a monstrous bonfire was burning, painting the sky with jeweled radiance.

"Goodbye, Izzard," he said drowsily, and settled himself more comfortably in the seat.

He looked again at the glowing pink in the sky ahead.

"My mother has primroses in her garden in Delaware that look like that sometimes," he said dreamily. "You'll like 'em."

His head slid over against her shoulder, and he went to sleep.

HOUSE
DICK

The Montgomery Hotel's regular detective had taken his last week's rake-off from the hotel bootlegger in merchandise instead of cash, had drunk it down, had fallen asleep in the lobby, and had been fired. I happened to be the only idle operative in the Continental Detective Agency's San Francisco branch at the time, and thus it came about that I had three days of hotel-coppering while a man was being found to take the job permanently.

The Montgomery is a quiet hotel of the better sort, and so I had a very restful time of it — until the third and last day. Then things changed.

I came down into the lobby that afternoon to find Stacey, the assistant manager, hunting for me.

"One of the maids just phoned that there's something wrong up in 906," he said.

We went up to that room together. The door was open. In the center of the floor stood a maid, staring goggle-eyed at the closed door of the clothes-press. From under it, extending perhaps a foot across the floor toward us, was a snake-shaped ribbon of blood.

I stepped past the maid and tried the door. It was unlocked. I opened it. Slowly, rigidly, a man pitched out into my arms — pitched out backward — and there was a six-inch slit down the back of his coat, and the coat was wet and sticky.

That wasn't altogether a surprise: the blood on the floor had prepared me for something of the sort. But when another followed him — facing me, this one, with a dark, distorted face — I dropped the one I had caught and jumped back.

And as I jumped a third man came tumbling out after the others.

From behind me came a scream and a thud as the maid fainted. I wasn't feeling any too steady myself. I'm no sensitive plant, and I've looked at a lot of unlovely sights in my time, but for weeks afterward I could see those three dead men coming out of that clothespress to pile up at my feet: coming out slowly—almost deliberately—in a ghastly game of "follow your leader."

Seeing them, you couldn't doubt that they were really dead. Every detail of their falling, every detail of the heap in which they now lay, had a horrible certainty of lifelessness in it.

I turned to Stacey, who, deathly white himself, was keeping on his feet only by clinging to the foot of the brass bed.

"Get the woman out! Get doctors—police!"

I pulled the three dead bodies apart, laying them out in a grim row, faces up. Then I made a hasty examination of the room.

A soft hat, which fitted one of the dead men, lay in the center of the unruffled bed. The room key was in the door, on the inside. There was no blood in the room except what had leaked out of the clothespress, and the room showed no signs of having been the scene of a struggle.

The door to the bathroom was open. In the bottom of the bathtub was a shattered gin bottle, which, from the strength of the odor and the dampness of the tub, had been nearly full when broken. In one corner of the bathroom I found a small whisky glass, and another under the tub. Both were dry, clean, and odorless.

The inside of the clothespress door was stained with blood from the height of my shoulder to the floor, and two hats lay in the puddle of blood on the closet floor. Each of the hats fitted one of the dead men.

That was all. Three dead men, a broken gin bottle, blood.

Stacey returned presently with a doctor, and while the doctor was examining the dead men, the police detectives arrived.

The doctor's work was soon done.

"This man," he said, pointing to one of them, "was struck on the back of the head with a small blunt instrument, and then strangled. This one"—pointing to another—"was simply strangled. And the third was stabbed in the back with a blade perhaps five inches long. They have been dead for about two hours—since noon or a little after."

The assistant manager identified two of the bodies. The man who had been stabbed—the first to fall out of the clothespress—had arrived at the hotel three days before, registering as Tudor Ingraham of Washington, D.C., and had occupied room 915, three doors away.

The last man to fall out—the one who had been simply choked—was the occupant of this room. His name was Vincent Develyn. He was an insurance broker and had made the hotel his home since his wife's death, some four years before.

The third man had been seen in Develyn's company frequently, and one of the clerks remembered that they had come into the hotel together at about five minutes after twelve this day. Cards and letters in his pockets told us that he was Homer Ansley, a member of the law firm of Lankershim and Ansley, whose offices were in the Miles Building—next door to Develyn's office.

Develyn's pockets held between $150 and $200; Ansley's wallet contained more than $100; Ingraham's pockets yielded nearly $300, and in a money-belt around his waist we found $2,200 and two medium-sized unset diamonds. All three had watches—Develyn's was a valuable one—in their pockets, and Ingraham wore two rings, both of which were expensive ones. Ingraham's room key was in his pocket.

Beyond this money—whose presence would seem to indicate that robbery hadn't been the motive behind the three killings—we found nothing on any of the persons to throw the slightest light on the crime. Nor did the most thorough examination of both Ingraham's and Develyn's rooms teach us anything.

In Ingraham's room we found a dozen or more packs of carefully marked cards, some crooked dice, and an immense amount of data on race-horses. Also we found that he had a wife who lived on East Delavan Avenue in Buffalo, and a brother on Crutcher Street in Dallas; as well as a list of names and addresses that we carried off to investigate later. But nothing in either room pointed, even indirectly, at murder.

Phels, the Police Department Bertillon man, found a number of finger-prints in Develyn's room, but we couldn't tell whether they would be of any value or not until he had worked them up. Though Develyn and Ansley had apparently been strangled by hands, Phels was unable to get prints from either their necks or their collars.

The maid who had discovered the blood said that she had straightened up Develyn's room between ten and eleven that morning, but had not put fresh towels in the bathroom. It was for this purpose that she had gone to the room in the afternoon. She had gone there earlier—between 10:20 and 10:45—for that purpose, but Ingraham had not then left it.

The elevator man who had carried Ansley and Develyn up from the lobby at a few minutes after twelve remembered that they had been laugh-ingly discussing their golf scores of the previous day during the ride. No one had seen anything suspicious in the hotel around the time at which the doc-tor had placed the murders. But that was to be expected.

The murderer could have left the room, closing the door behind him, and walked away secure in the knowledge that at noon a man in the corri-dors of the Montgomery would attract little attention. If he was staying at the hotel he would simply have gone to his room; if not, he would have either walked all the way down to the street, or down a floor or two and then caught an elevator.

None of the hotel employees had ever seen Ingraham and Develyn together. There was nothing to show that they had even the slightest acquaintance. Ingraham habitually stayed in his room until noon, and did not return to it until late at night. Nothing was known of his affairs.

At the Miles Building we—that is, Marty O'Hara and George Dean of the Police Department Homicide Detail, and I—questioned Ansley's part-ner and Develyn's employees. Both Develyn and Ansley, it seemed, were ordinary men who led ordinary lives: lives that held neither dark spots nor queer kinks. Ansley was married and had two children; he lived on Lake Street. Both men had a sprinkling of relatives and friends scattered here and there through the country; and, so far as we could learn, their affairs were in perfect order.

They had left their offices this day to go to luncheon together, intending to visit Develyn's room first for a drink apiece from a bottle of gin someone coming from Australia had smuggled in to him.

"Well," O'Hara said, when we were on the street again, "this much is clear. If they went up to Develyn's room for a drink, it's a cinch that they were killed almost as soon as they got in the room. Those whisky glasses you found were dry and clean. Whoever turned the trick must have been wait-ing for them. I wonder about this fellow Ingraham."

"I'm wondering, too," I said. "Figuring it out from the positions I found them in when I opened the closet door, Ingraham sizes up as the key to the whole thing. Develyn was back against the wall, with Ansley in front of him, both facing the door. Ingraham was facing them, with his back to the door. The clothespress was just large enough for them to be packed in it—too small for them to slip down while the door was closed.

"Then there was no blood in the room except what had come from the clothespress. Ingraham, with that gaping slit in his back, couldn't have been stabbed until he was inside the closet, or he'd have bled elsewhere. He was standing close to the other men when he was knifed, and whoever knifed him closed the door quickly afterward.

"Now, why should he have been standing in such a position? Do you dope it out that he and another killed the two friends, and that while he was stowing their bodies in the closet his accomplice finished him off?"

"Maybe," Dean said.

And that "maybe" was still as far as we had gone three days later.

We had sent and received bales of telegrams, having relatives and acquaintances of the dead men interviewed; and we had found nothing that seemed to have any bearing upon their deaths. Nor had we found the slightest connecting link between Ingraham and the other two. We had traced those other two back step by step almost to their cradles. We had accounted for every minute of their time since Ingraham had arrived in San Francisco—thoroughly enough to convince us that neither of them had met Ingraham.

Ingraham, we had learned, was a bookmaker and all around crooked gambler. His wife and he had separated, but were on good terms. Some fifteen years before, he had been convicted of "assault with intent to kill" in Newark, N.J., and had served two years in the state prison. But the man he had assaulted had died of pneumonia in Omaha in 1914.

Ingraham had come to San Francisco for the purpose of opening a gambling club, and all our investigations had tended to show that his activities while in the city had been toward that end alone.

The fingerprints Phels had secured had all turned out to belong to Stacey, the maid, the police detectives, or myself. In short, we had found nothing!

So much for our attempts to learn the motive behind the three murders.

We now dropped that angle and settled down to the detail-studying, patience-taxing grind of picking up the murderer's trail. From any crime to its author there is a trail. It may be—as in this case—obscure; but, since matter cannot move without disturbing other matter along its path, there always is—there must be—a trail of some sort. And finding and following such trails is what a detective is paid to do.

In the case of a murder it is possible sometimes to take a short-cut to the end of the trail, by first finding the motive. A knowledge of the motive often reduces the field of possibilities; sometimes points directly to the guilty one.

So far, all we knew about the motive in the particular case we were dealing with was that it hadn't been robbery; unless something we didn't know about had been stolen—something of sufficient value to make the murderer scorn the money in his victims' pockets.

We hadn't altogether neglected the search for the murderer's trail, of course, but—being human—we had devoted most of our attention to trying to find a short-cut. Now we set out to find our man, or men, regardless of what had urged him or them to commit the crimes.

Of the people who had been registered at the hotel on the day of the killing there were nine men of whose innocence we hadn't found a reasonable amount of proof. Four of these were still at the hotel, and only one of that four interested us very strongly. That one—a big raw-boned man of forty-five or fifty, who had registered as J. J. Cooper of Anaconda, Montana—wasn't, we had definitely established, really a mining man, as he pretended to be. And our telegraphic communications with Anaconda failed to show that he was known there. Therefore we were having him shadowed—with few results.

Five men of the nine had departed since the murders; three of them leaving forwarding addresses with the mail clerk. Gilbert Jacquemart had occupied room 946 and had ordered his mail forwarded to him at a Los Angeles hotel. W. F. Salway, who had occupied room 1022, had given instructions that his mail be readdressed to a number on Clark Street in Chicago. Ross Orrett, room 609, had asked to have his mail sent to him care of General Delivery at the local post office.

Jacquemart had arrived at the hotel two days before, and had left on the afternoon of the murders. Salway had arrived the day before the murders and had left the day after them. Orrett had arrived the day of the murders and had left the following day.

Sending telegrams to have the first two found and investigated, I went after Orrett myself. A musical comedy named *"What For?"* was being widely advertised just then with gaily printed plum-colored handbills. I got one of them and, at a stationery store, an envelope to match, and mailed it to Orrett at the Montgomery Hotel. There are concerns that make a practice of securing the names of arrivals at the principal hotels and mailing them advertisements. I trusted that Orrett, knowing this, wouldn't be suspicious when my gaudy envelope, forwarded from the hotel, reached him through the General Delivery window.

Dick Foley—the Agency's shadow specialist—planted himself in the post office, to loiter around with an eye on the "O" window until he saw my plum-colored enveloped passed out, and then to shadow the receiver.

I spent the next day trying to solve the mysterious J. J. Cooper's game, but he was still a puzzle when I knocked off that night.

At a little before five the following morning Dick Foley dropped into my room on his way home to wake me up and tell me what he had done.

"This Orrett baby is our meat!" he said. "Picked him up when he got his mail yesterday afternoon. Got another letter besides yours. Got an apartment on Van Ness Avenue. Took it the day after the killing, under the name of B. T. Quinn. Packing a gun under his left arm—there's that sort of a bulge there. Just went home to bed. Been visiting all the dives in North Beach. Who do you think he's hunting for?"

"Who?"

"Guy Cudner."

That was news! This Guy Cudner, alias "The Darkman," was the most dangerous bird on the Coast, if not in the country. He had only been nailed once, but if he had been convicted of all the crimes that everybody knew he had committed he'd have needed half a dozen lives to crowd his sentences into, besides another half-dozen to carry to the gallows. However, he had decidedly the right sort of backing—enough to buy him everything he needed in the way of witnesses, alibis, even juries and an occasional judge.

I don't know what went wrong with his support that one time he was convicted up North and sent over for a one-to-fourteen-year hitch; but it adjusted itself promptly, for the ink was hardly dry on the press notices of his conviction before he was loose again on parole.

"Is Cudner in town?"

"Don't know," Dick said, "but this Orrett, or Quinn, or whatever his name is, is surely hunting for him. In Rick's place, at 'Wop' Healey's, and at Pigatti's. 'Porky' Grout tipped me off. Says Orrett doesn't know Cudner by sight, but is trying to find him. Porky didn't know what he wants with him."

This Porky Grout was a dirty little rat who would sell out his family—if he ever had one—for the price of a flop. But with these lads who play both sides of the game it's always a question of which side they're playing when you think they're playing yours.

"Think Porky was coming clean?" I asked.

"Chances are—but you can't gamble on him."

"Is Orrett acquainted here?"

"Doesn't seem to be. Knows where he wants to go but has to ask how to get there. Hasn't spoken to anybody that seemed to know him."

"What's he like?"

"Not the kind of egg you'd want to tangle with offhand, if you ask me. He and Cudner would make a good pair. They don't look alike. This egg is tall and slim, but he's built right—those fast, smooth muscles. Face is sharp without being thin, if you get me. I mean all the lines in it are straight. No curves. Chin, nose, mouth, eyes—all straight, sharp lines and angles. Looks like the kind of egg we know Cudner is. Make a good pair. Dresses well and doesn't look like a rowdy—but harder than hell! A big-game hunter! Our meat, I bet you!"

"It doesn't look bad," I agreed. "He came to the hotel the morning of the day the men were killed, and checked out the next morning. He packs a rod, and changed his name after he left. And now he's paired off with The Dark-man. It doesn't look bad at all!"

"I'm telling you," Dick said, "this fellow looks like three killings wouldn't disturb his rest any. I wonder where Cudner fits in."

"I can't guess. But, if he and Orrett haven't connected yet, then Cudner wasn't in on the murders; but he may give us the answer."

Then I jumped out of bed. "I'm going to gamble on Porky's dope being on the level! How would you describe Cudner?"

"You know him better than I do."

"Yes, but how would you describe him to me if I didn't know him?"

"A little fat guy with a red forked scar on his left cheek. What's the idea?"

"It's a good one," I admitted. "That scar makes all the difference in the world. If he didn't have it and you were to describe him you'd go into all the details of his appearance. But he has it, so you simply say, 'A little fat guy with a red forked scar on his left cheek.' It's a ten to one that that's just how he has been described to Orrett. I don't look like Cudner, but I'm his size and build, and with a scar on my face Orrett will fall for me."

"What then?"

"There's no telling; but I ought to be able to learn a lot if I can get Orrett talking to me as Cudner. It's worth a try anyway."

"You can't get away with it—not in San Francisco. Cudner is too well-known."

"What difference does that make, Dick? Orrett is the only one I want to fool. If he takes me for Cudner, well and good. If he doesn't, still well and good. I won't force myself on him."

"How are you going to fake the scar?"

"Easy! We have pictures of Cudner, showing the scar, in the criminal gallery. I'll get some collodion—it's sold in drug stores under several trade names for putting on cuts and scratches—color it, and imitate Cudner's scar on my cheek. It dries with a shiny surface and, put on thick, will stand out enough to look like an old scar."

It was a little after eleven the following night when Dick telephoned me that Orrett was in Pigatti's place, on Pacific Street, and apparently settled there for some little while. My scar already painted on, I jumped into a taxi and within a few minutes was talking to Dick, around the corner from Pigatti's.

"He's sitting at the last table back on the left side. And he was alone when I came out. You can't miss him. He's the only egg in the joint with a clean collar."

"You better stick outside — half a block or so away — with the taxi," I told Dick. "Maybe brother Orrett and I will leave together and I'd just as leave have you standing by in case things break wrong."

Pigatti's place is a long, narrow, low-ceilinged cellar, always dim with smoke. Down the middle runs a narrow strip of bare floor for dancing. The rest of the floor is covered with closely packed tables, whose cloths are always soiled.

Most of the tables were occupied when I came in, and half a dozen couples were dancing. Few of the faces to be seen were strangers to the morning "line-up" at police headquarters.

Peering through the smoke, I saw Orrett at once, seated alone in a far corner, looking at the dancers with the set blank face of one who masks an all-seeing watchfulness. I walked down the other side of the room and crossed the strip of dance-floor directly under a light, so that the scar might be clearly visible to him. Then I selected a vacant table not far from his, and sat down facing him.

Ten minutes passed while he pretended an interest in the dancers and I affected a thoughtful stare at the dirty cloth on my table; but neither of us missed so much as a flicker of the other's lids.

His eyes — gray eyes that were pale without being shallow, with black needle-point pupils — met mine after a while in a cold, steady, inscrutable stare; and, very slowly, he got to his feet. One hand — his right — in a side pocket of his dark coat, he walked straight across to my table and sat down.

"Cudner?"

"Looking for me, I hear," I replied, trying to match the icy smoothness of his voice, as I was matching the steadiness of his gaze.

He had sat down with his left side turned slightly toward me, which put his right arm in not too cramped a position for straight shooting from the pocket that still held his hand.

"You were looking for me, too."

I didn't know what the correct answer to that would be, so I just grinned. But the grin didn't come from my heart. I had, I realized, made a mistake — one that might cost me something before we were done. This bird wasn't hunting for Cudner as a friend, as I had carelessly assumed, but was on the war path.

I saw those three dead men falling out of the closet in room 906!

My gun was inside the waist-band of my trousers, where I could get it quickly, but his was in his hand. So I was careful to keep my own hands motionless on the edge of the table, while I widened my grin.

His eyes were changing now, and the more I looked at them the less I liked them. The gray in them had darkened and grown duller, and the pupils were larger, and white crescents were showing beneath the gray. Twice before I had looked into eyes such as these — and I hadn't forgotten what they meant — the eyes of the congenital killer!

"Suppose you speak your piece," I suggested after a while.

But he wasn't to be beguiled into conversation. He shook his head a mere fraction of an inch and the corners of his compressed mouth dropped down a trifle. The white crescents of eyeballs were growing broader, pushing the gray circles up under the upper lids.

It was coming! And there was no use waiting for it!

I drove a foot at his shins under the table, and at the same time pushed the table into his lap and threw myself across it. The bullet from his gun went off to one side. Another bullet — not from his gun — thudded into the table that was upended between us.

I had him by the shoulders when the second shot from behind took him in the left arm, just below my hand. I let go then and fell away, rolling over against the wall and twisting around to face the direction from which the bullets were coming.

I twisted around just in time to see — jerking out of sight behind a corner of the passage that gave to a small dining-room — Guy Cudner's scarred face. And as it disappeared a bullet from Orrett's gun splattered the plaster from the wall where it had been.

I grinned at the thought of what must be going on in Orrett's head as he lay sprawled out on the floor confronted by two Cudners. But he took a shot at me just then and I stopped grinning. Luckily, he had to twist around to fire at me, putting his weight on his wounded arm, and the pain made him wince, spoiling his aim.

Before he had adjusted himself more comfortably I had scrambled on hands and knees to Pigatti's kitchen door—only a few feet away—and had myself safely tucked out of range around an angle in the wall; all but my eyes and the top of my head, which I risked so that I might see what went on.

Orrett was now ten or twelve feet from me, lying flat on the floor, facing Cudner, with a gun in his hand and another on the floor beside him.

Across the room, perhaps thirty feet away, Cudner was showing himself around his protecting corner at brief intervals to exchange shots with the man on the floor, occasionally sending one my way. We had the place to ourselves. There were four exits, and the rest of Pigatti's customers had used them all.

I had my gun out, but I was playing a waiting game. Cudner, I figured, had been tipped off to Orrett's search for him and had arrived on the scene with no mistaken idea of the other's attitude. Just what there was between them and what bearing it had on the Montgomery murders was a mystery to me, but I didn't try to solve it now.

They were firing in unison. Cudner would show around his corner, both men's weapons would spit, and he would duck out of sight again. Orrett was bleeding about the head now and one of his legs sprawled crookedly behind him. I couldn't determine whether Cudner had been hit or not.

Each had fired eight, or perhaps nine, shots when Cudner suddenly jumped out into full view, pumping the gun in his left hand as fast as its mechanism would go, the gun in his right hand hanging at his side. Orrett had changed guns, and was on his knees now, his fresh weapon keeping pace with his enemy's.

That couldn't last!

Cudner dropped his left-hand gun, and, as he raised the other, he sagged forward and went down on one knee. Orrett stopped firing abruptly and fell over on his back—spread out full-length. Cudner fired once more—wildly, into the ceiling—and pitched down on his face.

I sprang to Orrett's side and kicked both of his guns away. He was lying still but his eyes were open.

"Are you Cudner, or was he?"

"He."

"Good!" he said, and closed his eyes.

I crossed to where Cudner lay and turned him over on his back. His chest was literally shot to pieces.

His thick lips worked, and I put my ear down to them. "I get him?"

"Yes," I lied, "he's already cold."

His dying face twisted into a grin.

"Sorry . . . three in hotel . . . ," he gasped hoarsely. "Mistake . . . wrong room . . . got one . . . had to . . . other two . . . protect myself . . . I . . ." He shuddered and died.

A week later the hospital people let me talk to Orrett. I told him what Cudner had said before he died.

"That's the way I doped it out," Orrett said from out of the depths of the bandages in which he was swathed. "That's why I moved and changed my name the next day.

"I suppose you've got it nearly figured out by now," he said after a while.

"No," I confessed, "I haven't. I've an idea what it was all about but I could stand having a few details cleared up."

"I'm sorry I can't clear them up for you, but I've got to cover myself up. I'll tell you a story, though, and it may help you. Once upon a time there was a high-class crook—what the newspapers call a master-mind. Came a day when he found he had accumulated enough money to give up the game and settle down as an honest man.

"But he had two lieutenants—one in New York and one in San Francisco—and they were the only men in the world who knew he was a crook. And, besides that, he was afraid of both of them. So he thought he'd rest easier if they were out of the way. And it happened that neither of these lieutenants had ever seen the other.

"So this master-mind convinced each of them that the other was double-crossing him and would have to be bumped off for the safety of all concerned. And both of them fell for it. The New Yorker went to San Francisco to get the other, and the San Franciscan was told that the New Yorker would arrive on such-and-such a day and would stay at such-and-such a hotel.

"The master-mind figured that there was an even chance of both men passing out when they met—and he was nearly right at that. But he was sure that one would die, and then, even if the other missed hanging, there would only be one man left for him to dispose of later."

There weren't as many details in the story as I would have liked to have, but it explained a lot.

"How do you figure out Cudner's getting the wrong room?" I asked.

"That was funny! Maybe it happened like this: My room was 609 and the killing was done in 906. Suppose Cudner went to the hotel on the day he knew I was due and took a quick slant at the register. He wouldn't want to be seen looking at it if he could avoid it, so he didn't turn it around, but flashed a look at it as it lay—facing the desk.

"When you read numbers of three figures upside-down you have to transpose them in your head to get them straight. Like 123. You'd get that 321, and then turn them around in your head. That's what Cudner did with mine. He was keyed up, of course, thinking of the job ahead of him, and he overlooked the fact that 609 upside-down still reads 609 just the same. So he turned it around and made it 906 — Develyn's room."

"That's how I doped it," I said, "and I reckon it's about right. And then he looked at the key-rack and saw that 906 wasn't there. So he thought he might just as well get his job done right then, when he could roam the hotel corridors without attracting attention. Of course, he may have gone up to the room before Ansley and Develyn came in and waited for them, but I doubt it.

"I think it more likely that he simply happened to arrive at the hotel a few minutes after they had come in. Ansley was probably alone in the room when Cudner opened the unlocked door and came in — Develyn being in the bathroom getting the glasses.

"Ansley was about your size and age, and close enough in appearance to fit a rough description of you. Cudner went for him, and then Develyn, hearing the scuffle, dropped the bottle and glasses, rushed out, and got his.

"Cudner, being the sort he was, would figure that two murders were not worse than one, and he wouldn't want to leave any witnesses around.

"And that is probably how Ingraham got into it. He was passing on his way from his room to the elevator and perhaps heard the racket and investigated. And Cudner put a gun in his face and made him stow the two bodies in the clothespress. And then he stuck his knife in Ingraham's back and slammed the door on him. That's about the —"

An indignant nurse descended on me from behind and ordered me out of the room, accusing me of getting her patient excited.

Orrett stopped me as I turned to go.

"Keep your eye on the New York dispatches," he said, "and maybe you'll get the rest of the story. It's not over yet. Nobody has anything on me out here. That shooting in Pigatti's was self-defense so far as I'm concerned. And as soon as I'm on my feet again and can get back East there's going to be a master-mind holding a lot of lead. That's a promise!"

I believed him.

RUFFIAN'S
WIFE

Margaret Tharp habitually passed from slumber to clear-eyed live-
liness without intermediate languor. This morning nothing was
unusual in her awakening save the absence of the eight o'clock
San Francisco boat's sad hooting. Across the room the clock's
hands pointed like one long hand to a few minutes past seven. Margaret
rolled over beneath the covers, putting her back to the sunpainted west wall,
and closed her eyes again.

But drowsiness would not come. She was definitely awake to the morning excitement of the next-door chickens, the hum of an automobile going
toward the ferry, the unfamiliar fragrance of magnolia in the breeze tickling
her cheek with loose hair-ends. She got up, slid feet into soft slippers, shoulders into bathrobe, and went downstairs to start toast and coffee before
dressing.

A fat man in black was on the point of leaving the kitchen.

Margaret cried out, catching the robe to her throat with both hands.

Red and crystal glinted on the hand with which the fat man took off his
black derby. Holding the doorknob, he turned to face Margaret. He turned
slowly, with the smooth precision of a globe revolving on a fixed axis, and
he managed his head with care, as if it balanced an invisible burden.

"You—are—Mrs.—Tharp."

Sighing puffs of breath spaced his words, cushioned them, gave them the
semblance of gems nested separately in raw cotton. He was a man past forty,
with opaquely glistening eyes whose blackness was repeated with variety of
finish in mustache and hair, freshly ironed suit, and enameled shoes. The
dark skin of his face—ball-round over a tight stiff collar—was peculiarly

coarse, firm-grained, as if it had been baked. Against this background his tie was half a foot of scarlet flame.

"Your—husband—is—not—home."

It was no more a question than his naming her had been, but he paused expectantly. Margaret, standing where she had stopped in the passageway between stairs and kitchen, was still too startled not to say "No."

"You're—expecting—him."

There was nothing immediately threatening in the attitude of this man who should not have been in her kitchen but who seemed nowise disconcerted by her finding him there. Margaret's words came almost easily. "Not just—I expect him, yes, but I don't know exactly when he will come."

Black hat and black shoulders, moving together, achieved every appearance of a bow without disturbing round head's poise.

"You—will—so—kindly—tell—him—when—he—comes—I—am—waiting. I—await—him—at—the—hotel." The spacing puffs prolonged his sentences interminably, made of his phrases thin-spread word-groups whose meanings were elusive. "You—will—tell—him—Leonidas—Doucas—is—waiting. He—will—know. We—are—friends—very—good—friends. You—will—not—forget—the—name—Leonidas—Doucas."

"Certainly I shall tell him. But I really do not know when he will come."

The man who called himself Leonidas Doucas nodded frugally beneath the unseen something his head supported. Darkness of mustache and skin exaggerated whiteness of teeth. His smile went away as stiffly as it came, with as little elasticity.

"You—may—expect—him. He—comes—now."

He revolved slowly away from her and went out of the kitchen, shutting the door behind him.

Margaret ran tiptoe across the room to twist the key in the door. The lock's inner mechanism rattled loosely, the bolt would not click home. The warmly sweet fragrance of magnolia enveloped her. She gave up the struggle with the broken lock and dropped down on a chair beside the door. Points of dampness were on her back. Under gown and robe her legs were cold. Doucas, not the breeze, had brought the breath of magnolia to her in bed. His unguessed presence in the bedroom had wakened her. He had been up there looking with his surface-shining eyes for Guy. If Guy had been home, asleep beside her? A picture came of Doucas bending over the bed, his head still stiffly upright, a bright blade in his jeweled fist. She shivered.

Then she laughed. Little silly! How conceivably could Guy—her hard-bodied, hard-nerved Guy, to whom violence was no more than addition to a bookkeeper—be harmed by a perfumed, asthmatic fat man? Whether Guy slept or Guy woke, if Doucas came as an enemy, then so much the worse for Doucas—a fleshbound house dog growling at her red wolf of a husband!

She jumped up from her chair and began to bustle with toaster and coffeepot. Leonidas Doucas was put out of her mind by the news he had brought. Guy was coming home. The fat man in black had said so, speaking with assurance. Guy was coming home to fill the house with boisterous laughter, shouted blasphemies, tales of lawlessness in strangely named places; with the odors of tobacco and liquor; with odds and ends of rover's equipment that never could be confined to closet or room, but overflowed to litter the house from roof to cellar. Cartridges would roll underfoot; boots and belts would turn up in unexpected places; cigars, cigar ends, cigar ashes would be everywhere; empty bottles, likely as not, would get to the front porch to scandalize the neighbors.

Guy was coming home and there were so many things to be done in so small a house; windows and pictures and woodwork to be washed, furniture and floors to be polished, curtains to be hung, rugs to be cleaned. If only he did not come for two days, or even three.

The rubber gloves she had put aside as nuisances—had she put them in the hall closet or upstairs? She must find them. So much scrubbing to do, and her hands must not be rough for Guy. She frowned at the small hand raising toast to her mouth, accused it of roughness. She would have to get another bottle of lotion. If there was time after she finished her work, she might run over to the city for an afternoon. But first the house must be made bright and tidy, so Guy could tweak a stiff curtain and laugh, "A damned dainty nest for a bull like me to be stabled in!"

And perhaps tell of the month he had shared a Rat Island hut with two vermin-live Siwashes, sleeping three abed because their blankets were too few for division.

The two days Margaret had desired went by without Guy, another, others. Her habit of sleeping until the eight o'clock boat whistled up the hill was broken. She was dressed and moving around the house by seven, six, five-thirty one morning, repolishing already glowing fixtures, laundering some thing slightly soiled by yesterday's use, fussing through her rooms ceaselessly, meticulously, happily.

Whenever she passed the hotel on her way to the stores in lower Water Street she saw Doucas. Usually he was in the glass-fronted lobby, upright in the largest chair, facing the street, round, black-clothed, motionless.

Once he came out of the hotel as she passed.

He looked neither at her nor away from her, neither claimed recognition nor avoided it. Margaret smiled pleasantly, nodded pleasantly, and went on down the street away from his hat raised in a jeweled hand, her small head high. The fragrance of magnolia, going a dozen steps with her, deepened her feeling of somewhat amused, though lenient, graciousness.

The same high-held kindliness went with her through the streets, into the shops, to call on Dora Milner, to her own street door to welcome Agnes Peppler and Helen Chase. She made proud sentences for herself while she spoke other sentences, or listened to them. *Guy moves among continents as easily as Tom Milner from drug counter to soda fountain,* she thought while Dora talked of guest-room linen. *He carries his life as carelessly in his hands as Ned Peppler his brief case,* she boasted to the tea she poured for Agnes and Helen, *and sells his daring as Paul Chase sells high-grade corner lots.*

These people, friends and neighbors, talked among themselves of "poor Margaret," "poor little Mrs. Tharp," whose husband was notoriously a ruffian, always off some distant where, up to any imaginable sort of scoundrelism. They pitied her, or pretended to pity her, these owners of docile pets, because her man was a ranging beast who could not be penned, because he did not wear the dull uniform of respectability, did not walk along smooth, safe ways. Poor little Mrs. Tharp! She put her cup to her mouth to check the giggle that threatened to break in rudely on Helen's interpretation of a disputed bridge point.

"It really doesn't matter, so long as everyone knows what rule is to be followed before the game starts," she said into a pause that asked words of her, and went on with her secret thinking.

What, she wondered with smug assurance that it never could have happened to her, would it be like to have for husband a tame, housebroken male who came regularly to meals and bed, whose wildest flying could attain no giddier height than an occasional game of cards, a suburbanite's holiday in San Francisco, or, at very most, a dreary adventure with some stray stenographer, manicurist, milliner?

Late on the sixth day that Margaret expected him, Guy came.

Preparing her evening meal in the kitchen, she heard the creaking halt of an automobile in front of the house. She ran to the door and peeped through the curtained glass. Guy stood on the sidewalk, his broad back to her, taking leather traveling bags out of the car that had brought him up from the ferry. She smoothed her hair with cold hands, smoothed her apron, and opened the door.

Guy turned from the machine, a bag in each hand, one under his arm. He grinned through a two-day stubble of florid beard and waved a bag as you would wave a handkerchief.

A torn cap was crooked on his tangled red hair, his chest bulged a corduroy jacket of dilapidated age, grimy khaki trousers were tight around knotted thighs and calves, once-white canvas shoes tried to enclose feet meant for larger shoes, and failed to the extent of a brown-stockinged big toe. A ruddy viking in beggar's misfits. There would be other clothes in his bags. Rags were his homecoming affectation, a laborer-home-from-the-fields gesture. He strode up the walk, careless bags brushing geraniums and nasturtiums back.

Margaret's throat had some swollen thing in it. Fog blurred everything but the charging red face. An unvoiced whimper shook her breast. She wanted to run to him as to a lover. She wanted to run from him as from a ravisher. She stood very still in her doorway, smiling demurely with dry, hot mouth.

His feet padded on steps, on porch. Bags fell away from him. Thick arms reached for her.

The odors of alcohol, sweat, brine, tobacco cut her nostrils. Bearded flesh scrubbed her cheek. She lost foothold, breath, was folded into him, crushed, bruised, bludgeoned by hard lips. Eyes clenched against the pain in them, she clung hard to him who alone was firmly planted in a whirling universe. Foul endearments, profane love names rumbled in her ear. Another sound was even nearer—a throaty cooing. She was laughing.

Guy was home.

THE EVENING was old before Margaret remembered Leonidas Doucas.

She was sitting on her husband's knees, leaning forward to look at the trinkets, Ceylonese spoils, heaped on the table before her. Cockleshell earrings half hid her ears, heavy gold incongruities above the starched primness of her housedress.

Guy—bathed, shaved, and all in fresh white—tugged beneath his shirt with his one free hand. A moneybelt came sluggishly away from his body, thudded on the table, and lay there thick and apathetic as an overfed snake.

Guy's freckled fingers worked at the belt's pockets. Green banknotes slid out, coins rolled out to be bogged by the paper, green notes rustled out to bury the coins.

"Oh, Guy!" she gasped. "All that?"

He chuckled, jiggling her on his knees, and fluttered the green notes up from the table like a child playing with fallen leaves.

"All that. And every one of 'em cost a pint of somebody's pink blood. Maybe they look cool and green to you, but I'm telling you every last one of 'em is as hot a red as the streets of Colombo, if you could only see it."

She refused to shudder under the laugh in his red-veined eyes, laughed, and stretched a tentative finger to the nearest note.

"How much is there, Guy?"

"I don't know. I took 'em moving," he boasted. "No time for bookkeeping. It was bing, bang, get clear and step in again. We dyed the Yoda-ela red that one night. Mud under, darkness over, rain everywhere, with a brown devil for every raindrop. A pith helmet hunting for us with a flashlight that never found anything but a stiff-necked Buddha up on a rock before we put it out of business."

The "stiff-necked Buddha" brought Doucas's face to Margaret.

"Oh! There was a man here to see you last week. He's waiting to see you at the hotel. His name is Doucas, a very stout man with—"

"The Greek!"

Guy Tharp put his wife off his knees. He put her off neither hastily nor roughly, but with that deliberate withdrawal of attention which is the toy's lot when serious work is at hand.

"What else did he have to say?"

"That was all, except that he was a friend of yours. It was early in the morning, and I found him in the kitchen, and I know he had been upstairs. Who is he, Guy?"

"A fellow," her husband said vaguely around the knuckle he bit. He seemed to attach no importance to, not even be interested by, the news that Doucas had come furtively into his house. "Seen him since then?"

"Not to talk to, but I see him every time I pass the hotel."

Guy took the knuckle from between his teeth, rubbed his chin with a thumb, hunched his thick shoulders, let them fall lax, and reached for Margaret. Slumped comfortably in his chair, holding her tight to him with hard arms, he fell to laughing, teasing, boasting again, his voice a mellow, deep-bodied rumble under her head. But his eyes did not pale to their normal sapphire. Behind jest and chuckle an aloof thoughtfulness seemed to stand.

Asleep that night, he slept with the soundness of child or animal, but she knew he had been long going to sleep.

Just before daylight she crept out of bed and carried the money into another room to count it. Twelve thousand dollars were there.

In the morning Guy was merry, full of laughter and words that had no alien seriousness behind them. He had stories to tell of a brawl in a Madras street, or another in a gaming house in Saigon; of a Finn, met in the Queen's Hotel in Kandy, who was having a giant raft towed to a spot in mid-Pacific where he thought he could live with least annoyance from the noise of the earth's spinning.

Guy talked, laughed, and ate breakfast with the heartiness of one who does not ordinarily know when he will eat again. The meal done, he lit a black cigar and stood up. "Reckon I'll trot down the hill for a visit with your friend Leonidas, and see what's on his mind."

When he mauled her to his chest to kiss her, she felt the bulk of a revolver holstered under his coat. She went to a front window to watch him go away from the house. He swaggered carelessly down the hill, shoulders swinging, whistling, "Bang Away, My Lulu."

Back in the kitchen, Margaret made a great to-do with the breakfast dishes, setting about cleaning them as if it were a difficult task attempted for the first time. Water splashed on her apron, twice the soap slipped from her hand to the floor, a cup's handle came away in her fingers. Then dishwashing became accustomed work, no longer an occupation to banish unwanted thoughts. The thoughts came, of Guy's uneasiness last night, of his laughter that had lacked honesty.

She fashioned a song that compared a fleshbound house dog with a red wolf; a man to whom violence was no more than addition to a bookkeeper, with a perfumed, asthmatic fat man. Repetition gave the unspoken chant rhythm, rhythm soothed her, took her mind from what might be happening in the hotel down the hill.

She had finished the dishes and was scouring the sink when Guy came back. She looked a brief smile up at him and bent her face to her work again, to hide the questions she knew her eyes held.

He stood in the doorway watching her.

"Changed my mind," he said presently. "I'll let him write his own ticket. If he wants to see me, he knows the way. It's up to him."

He moved away from the door. She heard him going upstairs.

Her hands rested on idle palms in the sink. The white porcelain of the sink was white ice. Its chill went through her arms into her body.

An hour later, when Margaret went upstairs, Guy was sitting on the side of the bed running a cloth through the barrel of his black revolver. She fidgeted around the room, pretending to be busy with this and that, hoping he would answer the questions she could not ask. But he talked of unrelated things. He cleaned and greased the revolver with the slow, fondling thoroughness of a chronic whittler sharpening his knife, and talked of matters that had no bearing on Leonidas Doucas.

The rest of the day he spent indoors, smoking and drinking the afternoon through in the living-room. When he leaned back, the revolver made a lump under his left armpit. He was merry and profane and boastful. For the first time Margaret saw his thirty-five years in his eyes, and in the individual clearness of each thick facial muscle.

After dinner they sat in the dining-room with no illumination but the light of fading day. When that was gone neither of them got up to press the electric button beside the portiered hall door. He was as garrulous as ever. She found speech difficult, but he did not seem to notice that. She was never especially articulate with him.

They were sitting in complete darkness when the doorbell rang.

"If that's Doucas, show him in," Guy said. "And then you'd better get upstairs out of the way."

Margaret turned on the lights before she left the room, and looked back at her husband. He was putting down the cold cigar stub he had been chewing. He grinned mockingly at her.

"And if you hear a racket," he suggested, "you'd better stick your head under the covers and think up the best way to get blood out of rugs."

She held herself very erect going to the door and opening it.

Doucas's round black hat came off to move with his shoulders in a counterfeit bow that swept the odor of magnolia to her.

"Your—husband—is—in."

"Yes." Her chin was uptilted so she could seem to smile on him, though he stood a head taller than she, and she tried to make her smile very sweetly gentle. "Come in. He is expecting you."

Guy, sitting where she had left him, fresh cigar alight, did not get up to greet Doucas. He took the cigar from his mouth and let smoke leak between his teeth to garnish the good-natured insolence of his smile.

"Welcome to our side of the world," he said.

The Greek said nothing, standing just inside the portiere.

Margaret left them thus, going through the room and up the back stairs. Her husband's voice came up the steps behind her in a rumble of which she could pick no words. If Doucas spoke she did not hear him.

She stood in her dark bedroom, clutching the foot of the bed with both hands, the trembling of her body making the bed tremble. Out of the night questions came to torment her, shadowy questions, tangling, knotting, raveling in too swiftly shifting a profusion for any to be clearly seen, but all having something to do with a pride that in eight years had become a very dear thing.

They had to do with a pride in a man's courage and hardihood, courage and hardihood that could make of thefts, of murder, of crimes dimly guessed, wrongs no more reprehensible than a boy's apple-stealing. They had to do with the existence or nonexistence of this gilding courage, without which a rover might be no more than a shoplifter on a geographically larger scale, a sneak thief who crept into strangers' lands instead of houses, a furtive, skulking figure with an aptitude for glamorous autobiography. Then pride would be silliness.

Out of the floor came a murmur, all that distance and intervening carpentry left of words that were being said down in her tan-papered dining-room. The murmur drew her toward the dining-room, drew her physically, as the questions drove her.

She left her slippers on the bedroom floor. Very softly, stockinged feet carried her down the dark front stairs, tread by tread. Skirts held high and tight against rustling, she crept down the black stairs toward the room where two men—equally strangers for the time—sat trafficking.

Beneath the portiere, and from either side, yellow light came to lay a pale, crooked U on the hall floor. Guy's voice came through.

". . . not there. We turned the island upside down from Dambulla all the way to the Kala-wewa, and got nothing. I told you it was a bust. Catch those limeys leaving that much sugar lay round under their noses!"

"Dahl—said—it—was—there."

Doucas's voice was soft with the infinitely patient softness of one whose patience is nearly at end.

Creeping to the doorway, Margaret peeped around the curtain. The two men and the table between them came into the opening. Doucas's overcoated shoulder was to her. He sat straight up, hands inert on fat thighs, cocked profile inert. Guy's white-sleeved forearms were on the table. He leaned over them, veins showing in forehead and throat, smaller and more vivid around the blue-black of his eyes. The glass in front of him was empty; the one before Doucas still brimmed with dark liquor.

"I don't give a damn what Dahl says." Guy's voice was blunt, but somehow missed finality. "I'm telling you the stuff wasn't there."

Doucas smiled. His lips bared white teeth and covered them again in a cumbersome grimace that held as little of humor as of spontaneity.

"But—you—came—from—Ceylon—no—poorer—than—you—went."

Guy's tongue-tip showed flat between his lips, vanished. He looked at his freckled hands on the table. He looked up at Doucas.

"I didn't. I brought fifteen thousand hard roundmen away with me, if it's any of your business," he said, and then robbed his statement of sincerity, made a weak blustering of it, with an explanation. "I did a thing a man needed done. It had nothing to do with our game. It was after that blew up."

"Yes. I—choose—to—doubt—it."

Soft, sigh-cushioned, the words had a concussive violence no shouted *You lie!* could have matched.

Guy's shoulders bunched up, teeth clicked, blood pulsed in the veins that welted his face. His eyes flared purplishly at the dark baked mask before him, flared until the held breath in Margaret's chest became an agony.

The flare went down in the purple eyes. The eyes went down. Guy scowled at his hands, at his knuckles that were round white knobs.

"Suit yourself, brother," he said, not distinctly.

Margaret swayed behind her shielding curtain, reason barely checking the instinctive hand with which she clutched for steadiness at it. Her body was a cold damp shell around a vacancy that had been until to-day—until, despite awakening doubts, this very instant—eight years' accumulation of pride. Tears wet her face, tears for the high-held pride that was now a ridiculous thing. She saw herself as a child going among adults, flaunting a Manila-paper bandeau, crying shrilly, "See my gold crown!"

"We—waste—time. Dahl—said—half—a—million—rupees. Doubtless—it—was—less. But—most—surely—half—that—amount—would—be—there." The pad of breath before and after each word became by never-varying repetition an altogether unnatural thing. Each word lost association with each other word, became a threatening symbol hung up in the room. "Not—regarding—odd—amounts—my—portion—would—be—say—seventy-five—thousand—dollars. I—will—take—that."

Guy did not look up from his hard white knuckles. His voice was sullen. "Where do you expect to find it?"

The Greek's shoulders moved the least fraction of an inch. Because he had for so long not moved at all that slight motion became a pronounced shrug.

"You—will—give—it—to—me. You—would—not—have—a—word— dropped—to—the—British—consul—of—one—who—was—Tom— Berkey—in—Cairo—not—many—yesterdays—back."

Guy's chair spun back from him. He lunged across the table.

Margaret clapped a palm to her mouth to stop the cry her throat had no strength to voice.

The Greek's right hand danced jewels in Guy's face. The Greek's left hand materialized a compact pistol out of nothing.

"Sit—down—my—friend."

Hanging over the table, Guy seemed to become abruptly smaller, as oncoming bodies do when stopped. For a moment he hung there. Then he grunted, regained his balance, picked up his chair, and sat down. His chest swelled and shrank slowly.

"Listen, Doucas," he said with great earnestness, "you're all wrong. I've got maybe ten thousand dollars left. I got it myself, but if you think you've got a kick coming, I'll do what's right. You can have half of the ten thousand."

Margaret's tears were gone. Pity for self had turned to hatred of the two men who sat in her dining-room making a foolish thing of her pride. She still trembled, but with anger now, and contempt for her boasted red wolf of a husband, trying to buy off the fat man who threatened him. The contempt she felt for her husband was great enough to include Doucas. She had a desire to step through the doorway, to show them that contempt. But nothing came of the impulse. She would not have known what to do, what to say to them. She was not of their world.

Only her pride had been in her husband's place in that world.

"Five—thousand—dollars—is—nothing. Twenty—thousand—rupees— I—spent—preparing—Ceylon—for—you."

Margaret's helplessness turned contempt in on herself. The very bitterness of that contempt drove her to attempt to justify, recapture some fragment of, her pride in Guy. After all, what knowledge had she of his world? What standards had she with which to compute its values? Could any man win every encounter? What else could Guy do under Doucas's pistol?

The futility of the self-posed questions angered her. The plain truth was she had never seen Guy as a man, but always as a half-fabulous being. The weakness of any defense she could contrive for him lay in his needing a defense. Not to be ashamed of him was a sorry substitute for her exultance in him. To convince herself that he was not a coward still would leave vacant the place lately occupied by her joy in his daring.

Beyond the curtain the two men bargained on across the table.

". . . every—cent. Men—do—not—profitably—betray—me."

She glared through the gap between portiere and frame, at fat Doucas with his pistol level on tabletop, at red Guy pretending to ignore the pistol. Rage filled her—weaponless, impotent rage. Or was it weaponless? The light-button was beside the door. Doucas and Guy were occupied with one another—

Her hand moved before the motive impulse was full-formed inside her. The situation was intolerable; darkness would change the situation, however slightly, therefore darkness was desirable. Her hand moved between portiere and doorframe, bent to the side as if gifted with sight, drove her finger into the button.

Roaring blackness was streaked by a thin bronze flame. Guy bellowed out, an animal noise without meaning. A chair slammed to the floor. Feet shuffled, stamped, scuffled. Grunts punctuated snarls.

Concealed by night, the two men and what they did became for the first time real to Margaret, physically actual. They were no longer figures whose substance was in what they did to her pride. One was her husband, a man who could be maimed, killed. Doucas was a man who could be killed. They could die, either or both, because of a woman's vanity. A woman, she, had flung them toward death rather than confess she could be less than a giant's wife.

Sobbing, she pushed past the portiere and with both hands hunted for the switch that had come so readily to her finger a moment ago. Her hands fumbled across a wall that shuddered when bodies crashed into it. Behind her, fleshed bone smacked on fleshed bone. Feet shuffled in time with hoarse breathing. Guy cursed. Her fingers fluttered back and forth, to and fro across wallpaper that was unbroken by electric fixture.

The scuffling of feet stopped. Guy's cursing stopped in mid-syllable. A purring gurgle had come into the room, swallowing every other sound, giving density, smothering weight to the darkness, driving Margaret's frenzied fingers faster across the wall.

Her right hand found the doorframe. She held it there, pressed it there until the edge of the wood cut into her hand, holding it from frantic search while she made herself form a picture of the wall. The light-switch was a little below her shoulder, she decided.

"Just below my shoulder," she whispered harshly, trying to make herself hear the words above the purring gurgle. Her shoulder against the frame, she flattened both hands on the wall, moved them across it.

The purring gurgle died, leaving a more oppressive silence, the silence of wide emptiness.

Cold metal came under sliding palm. A finger found the button, fumbled too eagerly atop it, slid off. She clutched at the button with both hands. Light came. She whirled her back to the wall.

Across the room Guy straddled Doucas, holding his head up from the floor with thick hands that hid the Greek's white collar. Doucas's tongue was a bluish pendant from a bluish mouth. His eyes stood out, dull. The end of a red silk garter hung from one trouser-leg, across his shoe.

Guy turned his head toward Margaret, blinking in the light.

"Good girl," he commended her. "This Greek was no baby to jump at in daylight."

One side of Guy's face was wet red under a red furrow. She sought escape in his wound from the implication of *was*.

"You're hurt!"

He took his hands away from the Greek's neck and rubbed one of them across the cheek. It came away dyed red. Doucas's head hit the floor hollowly and did not quiver.

"Only nicked me," Guy said. "I need it to show self-defense."

The reiterated implication drove Margaret's gaze to the man on the floor, and quickly away.

"He is—?"

"Deader than hell," Guy assured her.

His voice was light, tinged faintly with satisfaction.

She stared at him in horror, her back pressed against the wall, sick with her own part in this death, sick with Guy's callous brutality of voice and mien. Guy did not see these things. He was looking thoughtfully at the dead man.

"I told you I'd give him a bellyful if he wanted it," he boasted. "I told *him* the same thing five years ago, in Malta."

He stirred the dead Doucas gently with one foot. Margaret cringed against the wall, feeling as if she were going to vomit.

Guy's foot nudged the dead man slowly, reflectively. Guy's eyes were dull with distant things, things that might have happened five years ago in a place that to her was only a name on a map, vaguely associated with Crusades and kittens. Blood trickled down his cheek, hung momentarily in fattening drops, dripped down on the dead man's coat.

The poking foot stopped its ghoulish play. Guy's eyes grew wide and bright, his face lean with eagerness. He snapped fist into palm and jerked around to Margaret.

"By God! This fellow has got a pearl concession down in La Paz! If I can get down there ahead of the news of the killing, I can— Why, what's the matter?"

He stared at her, puzzlement wiping animation from his face.

Margaret's gaze faltered away from him. She looked at the overturned table, across the room, at the floor. She could not hold up her eyes for him to see what was in them. If understanding had come to him at once—but she could not stand there and look at him and wait for the thing in her eyes to burn into his consciousness.

She tried to keep that thing out of her voice.

"I'll bandage your cheek before we phone the police," she said.

THE MAN WHO KILLED
DAN ODAMS

When the light that came through the barred square foot of the cell's one high window had dwindled until he could no longer clearly make out the symbols and initials his predecessors had scratched and penciled on the opposite wall, the man who had killed Dan Odams got up from the cot and went to the steel-slatted door.

"Hey, chief!" he called, his voice rumbling within the narrow walls.

A chair scraped across a floor in the front of the building, deliberate footsteps approached, and the marshal of Jingo came into the passage between his office and the cell.

"I got something I want to tell you," the man in the cell said.

Then the marshal was near enough to see in the dim light the shiny muzzle of a short, heavy revolver threatening him from just in front of the prisoner's right hip.

Without waiting for the time-honored order the marshal raised his hands until their palms were level with his ears.

The man behind the bars spoke in a curt whisper.

"Turn around! Push your back against the door!"

When the marshal's back pressed against the bars a hand came up under his left armpit, pulled aside his unbuttoned vest, and plucked his revolver from its holster. "Now unlock this here door!"

The prisoner's own weapon had disappeared and the captured one had taken its place. The marshal turned around, lowered one hand, keys jingled in it, and the cell door swung open.

The prisoner backed across the cell, inviting the other in with a beckoning flip of the gun in his hand. "Flop on the bunk, face-down."

In silence the marshal obeyed. The man who had killed Dan Odams bent over him. The long black revolver swept down in a swift arc that ended at the base of the prone official's head.

His legs jerked once, and he lay still.

With unhurried deftness the prisoner's fingers explored the other's pockets, appropriating money, tobacco, and cigarette papers. He removed the holster from the marshal's shoulder and adjusted it to his own. He locked the cell door behind him when he left.

The marshal's office was unoccupied. Its desk gave up two sacks of tobacco, matches, an automatic pistol, and a double handful of cartridges. The wall yielded a hat that sat far down on the prisoner's ears, and a too-tight, too-long, black rubber slicker.

Wearing them, he essayed the street.

The rain, after three days of uninterrupted sovereignty, had stopped for the time. But Jingo's principal thoroughfare was deserted—Jingo ate between five and six in the evening.

His deep-set maroon eyes—their animality emphasized by the absence of lashes—scanned the four blocks of wooden-sidewalked street. A dozen automobiles were to be seen, but no horses.

At the first corner he left the street and half a block below turned into a muddy alley that paralleled it. Under a shed in the rear of a poolroom he found four horses, their saddles and bridles hanging near by. He selected a chunky, well-muscled roan—the race is not to the swift through the mud of Montana—saddled it, and led it to the end of the alley.

Then he climbed into the saddle and turned his back on the awakening lights of Jingo.

Presently he fumbled beneath the slicker and took from his hip pocket the weapon with which he had held up the marshal: a dummy pistol of molded soap, covered with tinfoil from cigarette packages. He tore off the wrapping, squeezed the soap into a shapeless handful, and threw it away.

The sky cleared after a while and the stars came out. He found that the road he was traveling led south. He rode all night, pushing the roan unrelentingly through the soft, viscid footing.

At daylight the horse could go no farther without rest. The man led it up a coulee—safely away from the road—and hobbled it beneath a clump of cottonwoods.

Then he climbed a hill and sprawled on the soggy ground, his lashless red eyes on the country through which he had come: rolling hills of black and green and gray, where wet soil, young grass, and dirty snow divided dominion—the triple rule trespassed here and there by the sepia ribbon of county road winding into and out of sight.

He saw no man while he lay there, but the landscape was too filled with the marks of man's proximity to bring any feeling of security. Shoulder-high wire fencing edged the road, a footpath cut the side of a near-by hill, telephone poles held their short arms stiffly against the gray sky.

At noon he saddled the roan again and rode on along the coulee. Several miles on he came to a row of small poles bearing a line of telephone wire. He left the coulee bottom, found the ranch house to which the wire ran, circled it, and went on.

Late in the afternoon he was not so fortunate.

With lessening caution—he had seen no wires for more than an hour—he rode across a hill to stumble almost into the center of a cluster of buildings. Into the group, from the other side, ran a line of wire.

The man who had killed Dan Odams retreated, crossed to another hill, and as he dropped down, on the far side, a rifle snapped from the slope he had just quit.

He bent forward until his nose was deep in the roan's mane, and worked upon the horse with hand and foot. The rifle snapped again.

He rolled clear of the horse as it fell, and continued to roll until bunch grass and sagebrush screened him from behind. Then he crawled straight away, rounded the flank of a hill, and went on.

The rifle did not snap again. He did not try to find it.

He turned from the south now, toward the west, his short, heavy legs pushing him on toward where Tiger Butte bulked against the leaden sky like a great crouching cat of black and green, with dirty white stripes where snow lay in coulee and fissure.

His left shoulder was numb for a while, and then the numbness was replaced by a searing ache. Blood trickled down his arm, staining his mud-caked hand. He stopped to open coat and shirt and readjust the bandage over the wound in his shoulder—the fall from the horse had broken it open and started it bleeding again. Then he went on.

The first road he came to bent up toward Tiger Butte. He followed it, plowing heavily through the sticky, clinging mud.

Only once did he break the silence he had maintained since his escape from the Jingo jail. He stopped in the middle of the road and stood with legs far apart, turned his bloodshot eyes from right to left and from ground to sky, and without emotion but with utter finality cursed the mud, the fence, the telephone wires, the man whose rifle had set him afoot, and the meadow larks whose taunting flutelike notes mocked him always from just ahead.

Then he went on, pausing after each few miles to scrape the ever-accumulating mud from his boots, using each hilltop to search the country behind for signs of pursuit.

The rain came down again, matting his thin, clay-plastered hair—his hat had gone with his mount. The ill-fitting slicker restricted his body and flapped about his ankles, impeding his progress, but his wounded shoulder needed its protection from the rain.

Twice he left the road to let vehicles pass—once a steaming Ford, once a half-load of hay creeping along behind four straining horses.

His way was still through fenced land that offered scant concealment. Houses dotted the country, with few miles between them; and the loss of his horse was ample evidence that the telephone wires had not been idle. He had not eaten since noon of the previous day but—notwithstanding the absence of visible pursuit—he could not forage here.

Night was falling as he left the road for the slope of Tiger Butte. When it was quite dark he stopped. The rain kept up all night. He sat through it—his back against a boulder, the slicker over his head.

THE SHACK, unpainted and ramshackle, groveled in a fork of the coulee. Smoke hung soddenly, lifelessly above its roof, not trying to rise, until beaten into nothingness by the rain. The structures around the chimneyed shack were even less lovely. The group seemed asprawl in utter terror of the great cat upon whose flank it found itself.

But to the red eyes of the man who had killed Dan Odams—he lay on his belly on the crest of the hill around which the coulee split—the lack of telephone wires gave this shabby homestead a wealth of beauty beyond reach of architect or painter.

Twice within the morning hour that he lay there a woman came into view. Once she left the shack, went to one of the other sheds, and then returned. The other time she came to the door, to stand a while looking down the coulee. She was a small woman, of age and complexion indeterminable through the rain, in a limp, grayish dress.

Later, a boy of ten or twelve came from the rear of the house, his arms piled high with kindling, and passed out of sight.

Presently the watcher withdrew from his hill, swung off in a circle, and came within sight of the shack again from the rear.

art ≠ beauty

Half an hour passed. He saw the boy carrying water from a spring below, but he did not see the woman again.

The fugitive approached the building stealthily, his legs carrying him stiffly, their elasticity gone. Now and then his feet faltered under him. But under its layers of clay and three-day beard his jaw jutted with nothing of weakness.

Keeping beyond them, he explored the outbuildings—wretched, flimsy structures, offering insincere pretenses of protection to an abject sorrel mare and a miscellaneous assortment of farm implements, all of which had come off second-best in their struggle with the earth. Only the generous, though not especially skillful, application of the material which has given to establishments of this sort the local sobriquet "hay-wire outfit" held the tools from frank admission of defeat.

Nowhere did the ground hold the impression of feet larger than a small woman's or a ten- or twelve-year-old boy's.

The fugitive crossed the yard to the dwelling, moving with wide-spread legs to offset the unsteadiness of his gait. With the unhurried, unresting spacing of clock-ticks, fat drops of blood fell from the fingers of his limp left hand to be hammered by the rain into the soggy earth.

Through the dirty pane of a window he saw the woman and boy, sitting together on a cot, facing the door.

The boy's face was white when the man threw the door open and came into the unpartitioned interior, and his mouth trembled; but the woman's thin, sallow face showed nothing—except, by its lack of surprise, that she had seen him approaching. She sat stiffly on the cot, her hands empty and motionless in her lap, neither fear nor interest in her faded eyes.

The man stood for a time where he had halted—just within the door to one side—a grotesque statue modeled of mud. Short, sturdy-bodied, with massive sagging shoulders. Nothing of clothing or hair showed through his husk of clay, and little of face and hands. The marshal's revolver in his hand, clean and dry, took on by virtue of that discordant immaculateness an exaggerated deadliness.

His eyes swept the room: two cots against the undressed board side walls, a plain deal table in the center, rickety kitchen chairs here and there, a battered and scratched bureau, a trunk, a row of hooks holding an indiscriminate assembly of masculine and feminine clothing, a pile of shoes in a corner, an open door giving access to a lean-to kitchen.

He crossed to the kitchen door, the woman's face turning to follow.

The lean-to was empty. He confronted the woman.

"Where's your man?"

"Gone."

"When'll he be back?"

"Ain't coming back."

The flat, expressionless voice of the woman seemed to puzzle the fugitive, as had her lack of emotion at his entrance. He scowled, and turned his eyes—now redder than ever with flecks of blood—from her face to the boy's and back to hers.

"Meaning what?" he demanded.

"Meaning he got tired of homesteading."

He pursed his lips thoughtfully. Then he went to the corner where the shoes were piled. Two pairs of men's worn shoes were there—dry and without fresh mud.

He straightened, slipped the revolver back into its holster, and awkwardly took off the slicker. "Get me some grub."

The woman left the cot without a word and went into the kitchen. The fugitive pushed the boy after her, and stood in the doorway while she cooked coffee, flapjacks, and bacon. Then they returned to the living-room. She put the food on the table and with the boy beside her resumed her seat on the cot.

The man wolfed the meal without looking at it—his eyes busy upon door, window, woman, and boy, his revolver beside his plate. Blood still dripped from his left hand, staining table and floor. Bits of earth were dislodged from his hair and face and hands and fell into his plate, but he did not notice them.

His hunger appeased, he rolled and lit a cigarette, his left hand fumbling stiffly through its part.

For the first time the woman seemed to notice the blood. She came around to his side. "You're bleeding. Let me fix it."

His eyes—heavy now with the weights of fatigue and satisfied hunger—studied her face suspiciously. Then he leaned back in his chair and loosened his clothes, exposing the week-old bullet-hole.

She brought water and cloths, and bathed and bandaged the wound. Neither of them spoke again until she had returned to the cot.

Then: "Had any visitors lately?"

"Ain't seen nobody for six or seven weeks."

"How far's the nearest phone?"

"Nobel's—eight miles up the coulee."

"Got any horses besides the one in the shed?"

"No."

He got up wearily and went to the bureau, pulling the drawers out and plunging his hands into them. In the top one he found a revolver, and pocketed it. In the trunk he found nothing. Behind the clothes on the wall he found a rifle. The cots concealed no weapons.

He took two blankets from one of the cots, the rifle, and his slicker. He staggered as he walked to the door.

"I'm going to sleep a while," he said thickly, "out in the shed where the horse is at. I'll be turning out every now and then for a look around, and I don't want to find nobody missing. Understand?"

She nodded, and made a suggestion.

"If any strangers show up, I guess you want to be woke up before they see you?"

His sleep-dull eyes became alive again, and he came unsteadily back to thrust his face close to hers, trying to peer behind the faded surfaces of her eyes.

"I killed a fellow in Jingo last week," he said after a while, talking slowly, deliberately, in a monotone that was both cautioning and menacing. "It was fair shooting. He got me in the shoulder before I downed him. But he belonged in Jingo and I don't. The best I could expect is the worst of it. I got a chance to get away before they took me to Great Falls, and I took it. And I ain't figuring on being took back there and hung. I ain't going to be here long, but while I am—"

The woman nodded again.

He scowled at her and left the shack.

He tied the horse in one corner of the hut with shortened rope and spread his blankets between it and the door. Then, with the marshal's revolver in his hand, he lay down and slept.

The afternoon was far gone when he woke, and the rain was still falling. He studied the bare yard carefully, and reconnoitered the house before re-entering it.

The woman had swept and tidied the room; had put on a fresh dress, which much washing had toned down to a soft pink; had brushed and fluffed her hair. She looked up at his entrance from the sewing that occupied her, and her face, still young in spite of the harshness that work had laid upon it, was less sallow than before.

"Where's the kid?" the man snapped.

She jerked a thumb over her shoulder.

"Up on the hill. I sent him up to watch the coulee."

His eyes narrowed and he left the building. Studying the hill through the rain, he discerned the outline of the boy, lying face-down under a stunted red cedar, looking toward the east. The man returned indoors.

"How's the shoulder?" she asked.

He raised an experimental arm.

"Better. Pack me some grub. I'm moving on."

"You're a fool," she said without spirit as she went into the kitchen. "You'd do better to stay here until your shoulder's fit to travel."

"Too close to Jingo."

"Ain't nobody going to fight all that mud to come after you. A horse couldn't get through, let alone a car. And you don't think they'd foot it after you even if they knew where to find you, do you? And this rain ain't going to do your shoulder no good."

She bent to pick up a sack from the floor. Under the thin pink dress the line of back and hips and legs stood out sharply against the wall.

As she straightened she met his gaze, her lids dropped, her face flushed, her lips parted a little.

The man leaned against the jamb of the door and caressed the muddy stubble of his chin with a thick thumb.

"Maybe you're right," he said.

She put away the food she had been bundling, took a galvanized pail from the corner, and made three trips to the spring, filling an iron tub that she had set on the stove. He stood in the doorway watching.

She stirred the fire, went into the living-room, and took a suit of underwear, a blue shirt, and a pair of socks from the bureau, a pair of gray trousers from one of the hooks, and a pair of carpet slippers from the pile of footwear. She put the clothing on a chair in the kitchen.

Then she returned to the living-room, closing the connecting door.

As the man undressed and bathed, he heard her humming softly. Twice he tiptoed to the connecting door and put an eye to the crack between it and the jamb. Each time he saw her sitting on the cot, bending over her sewing, her face still flushed.

He had one leg in the trousers she had given him when the humming stopped suddenly.

His right hand swept up the revolver from a convenient chair, and he moved to the door, the trousers trailing across the floor behind the ankle he had thrust through them. Flattening himself against the wall, he put an eye to the crack.

In the front door of the shack stood a tall youth in a slicker that was glistening with water. In the youth's hands was a double-barreled shotgun, the twin muzzles of which, like dull, malignant eyes, were focused on the center of the connecting door.

The man in the kitchen swung his revolver up, his thumb drawing back the hammer with the mechanical precision of the man who is accustomed to single-action pistols.

The lean-to's rear door slammed open. "Drop it!"

The fugitive, wheeling with the sound of the door's opening, was facing this new enemy before the order was out.

Two guns roared together.

But the fugitive's feet, as he wheeled, had become entangled in the trailing trousers. The trousers had tripped him. He had gone to his knees at the very instant of the two guns' roaring.

His bullet had gone out into space over the shoulder of the man in the doorway. That one's bullet had driven through the wall a scant inch over the falling fugitive's head.

Floundering on his knees, the fugitive fired again.

The man in the door swayed and spun half around.

As he righted himself, the fugitive's forefinger tightened again around the trigger—

From the connecting doorway a shotgun thundered.

The fugitive came straight up on his feet, his face filled with surprise, stood bolt upright for a moment, and wilted to the floor.

The youth with the shotgun crossed to the man who leaned against the door with a hand clapped to his side. "Did he get you, Dick?"

"Just through the flesh, I reckon—don't amount to nothing. Reckon you killed him, Bob?"

"I reckon I did. I hit him fair!"

The woman was in the lean-to. "Where's Buddy?"

"The kid's all right, Mrs. Odams," Bob assured her. "But he was all in from running through the mud, so Ma put him to bed."

The man who lay still on the floor made a sound then, and they saw that his eyes were open.

Mrs. Odams and Bob knelt beside him, but he stopped them when they tried to move him to examine the wreckage the shotgun had made of his back.

"No use," he protested, blood trickling thinly from the corners of his mouth as he spoke. "Let me alone."

Then his eyes—their red savageness glazed—sought the woman's.

"You—Dan—Odams's—woman?" he managed.

There was something of defiance—a hint that she felt the need of justification—in her answer. "Yes."

His face—thick-featured and deep-lined without the mud—told nothing of what was going on in his mind.

"Dummy," he murmured to himself presently, his eyes flickering toward the hill on whose top he had seen what he had believed to be a reclining boy.

She nodded.

The man who had killed Dan Odams turned his head away and spat his mouth empty of blood. Then his eyes returned to hers.

"Good girl," he said clearly—and died.

NIGHT
SHOTS

The house was of red brick, large and square, with a green slate roof whose wide overhang gave the building an appearance of being too squat for its two stories; and it stood on a grassy hill, well away from the country road upon which it turned its back to look down on the Mokelumne River.

The Ford that I had hired to bring me out from Knownburg carried me into the grounds through a high steel-meshed gate, followed the circling gravel drive, and set me down within a foot of the screened porch that ran all the way around the house's first floor.

"There's Exon's son-in-law now," the driver told me as he pocketed the bill I had given him and prepared to drive away.

I turned to see a tall, loose-jointed man of thirty or so coming across the porch toward me—a carelessly dressed man with a mop of rumpled brown hair over a handsome sunburned face. There was a hint of cruelty in the lips that were smiling lazily just now, and more than a hint of recklessness in his narrow gray eyes.

"Mr. Gallaway?" I asked as he came down the steps.

"Yes." His voice was a drawling baritone. "You are—"

"From the Continental Detective Agency's San Francisco branch," I finished for him.

He nodded, and held the screen door open for me.

"Just leave your bag there. I'll have it taken up to your room."

He guided me into the house and—after I had assured him that I had already eaten luncheon—gave me a soft chair and an excellent cigar. He sprawled on his spine in an armchair opposite me—all loose-jointed angles sticking out of it in every direction—and blew smoke at the ceiling.

"First off," he began presently, his words coming out languidly, "I may as well tell you that I don't expect very much in the way of results. I sent for you more for the soothing effect of your presence on the household than because I expect you to do anything. I don't believe there's anything to do. However, I'm not a detective. I may be wrong. You may find out all sorts of more or less important things. If you do—fine! But I don't insist upon it."

I didn't say anything, though this beginning wasn't much to my taste. He smoked in silence for a moment, and then went on, "My father-in-law, Talbert Exon, is a man of fifty-seven, and ordinarily a tough, hard, active, and fiery old devil. But just now he's recovering from a rather serious attack of pneumonia, which has taken most of the starch out of him. He hasn't been able to leave his bed yet, and Dr. Rench hopes to keep him on his back for at least another week.

"The old man has a room on the second floor—the front, right-hand corner room—just over where we are sitting. His nurse, Miss Caywood, occupies the next room, and there is a connecting door between. My room is the other front one, just across the hall from the old man's; and my wife's bedroom is next to mine—across the hall from the nurse's. I'll show you around later. I just want to make the situation clear.

"Last night, or rather this morning at about half-past one, somebody shot at Exon while he was sleeping—and missed. The bullet went into the frame of the door that leads to the nurse's room, about six inches above his body as he lay in bed. The course the bullet took in the woodwork would indicate that it had been fired from one of the windows—either through it or from just inside.

"Exon woke up, of course, but he saw nobody. The rest of us—my wife, Miss Caywood, the Figgs, and myself—were also awakened by the shot. We all rushed into his room, and we saw nothing either. There's no doubt that whoever fired it left by the window. Otherwise some of us would have seen him—we came from every other direction. However, we found nobody on the grounds, and no traces of anybody."

"Who are the Figgs, and who else is there on the place besides you and your wife, Mr. Exon, and his nurse?"

"The Figgs are Adam and Emma—she is the housekeeper and he is a sort of handy man about the place. Their room is in the extreme rear, on the second floor. Besides them, there is Gong Lim, the cook, who sleeps in a little room near the kitchen, and the three farm hands. Joe Natara and Felipe

Fadelia are Italians, and have been here for more than two years; Jesus Mesa, a Mexican, has been here a year or longer. The farm hands sleep in a little house near the barns. I think—if my opinion is of any value—that none of these people had anything to do with the shooting."

"Did you dig the bullet out of the doorframe?"

"Yes. Shand, the deputy sheriff at Knownburg, dug it out. He says it is a thirty-eight-caliber bullet."

"Any guns of that caliber in the house?"

"No. A twenty-two and my forty-four—which I keep in the car—are the only pistols on the place. Then there are two shotguns and a thirty-thirty rifle. Shand made a thorough search, and found nothing else in the way of firearms."

"What does Mr. Exon say?"

"Not much of anything, except that if we'll put a gun in bed with him he'll manage to take care of himself without bothering any policemen or detectives. I don't know whether he knows who shot at him or not—he's a close-mouthed old devil. From what I know of him, I imagine there are quite a few men who would think themselves justified in killing him. He was, I understand, far from being a lily in his youth—or in his mature years either, for that matter."

"Anything definite you know, or are you guessing?"

Gallaway grinned at me—a mocking grin that I was to see often before I was through with this Exon affair.

"Both," he drawled. "I know that his life has been rather more than sprinkled with swindled partners and betrayed friends, and that he saved himself from prison at least once by turning state's evidence and sending his associates there. And I know that his wife died under rather peculiar circumstances while heavily insured, and that he was for some time held on suspicion of having murdered her, but was finally released because of a lack of evidence against him. Those, I understand, are fair samples of the old boy's normal behavior, so there may be any number of people gunning for him."

"Suppose you give me a list of all the names you know of enemies he's made, and I'll have them checked up."

"The names I could give you would be only a few of many, and it might take you months to check up those few. It isn't my intention to go to all that trouble and expense. As I told you, I'm not insisting upon results. My wife is very nervous, and for some peculiar reason she seems to like the old man. So, to soothe her, I agreed to employ a private detective when she asked me to. My idea is that you hang around for a couple of days, until things quiet down and she feels safe again. Meanwhile, if you should stumble upon any-thing—go to it! If you don't—well and good."

My face must have shown something of what I was thinking, for his eyes twinkled and he chuckled.

"Don't, please," he drawled, "get the idea that you aren't to find my father-in-law's would-be assassin if you wish to. You're to have a free hand. Go as far as you like, except that I want you to be around the place as much as possible, so my wife will see you and feel that we are being adequately protected. Beyond that, I don't care what you do. You can apprehend crim-inals by the carload. As you may have gathered by now, I'm not exactly in love with my wife's father, and he's no more fond of me. To be frank, if hat-ing weren't such an effort—I think I should hate the old devil. But if you want to, and can, catch the man who shot at him, I'd be glad to have you do it. But—"

"All right," I said. "I don't like this job much, but since I'm up here I'll take it on. But, remember, I'm trying all the time."

"Sincerity and earnestness"—he showed his teeth in a sardonic smile as we got to our feet—"are very praiseworthy traits."

"So I hear," I growled shortly. "Now let's take a look at Mr. Exon's room."

Gallaway's wife and the nurse were with the invalid, but I examined the room before I asked the occupants any questions.

It was a large room, with three wide windows opening over the porch, and two doors, one of which gave to the hall and the other to the adjoining room occupied by the nurse. This door stood open, with a green Japanese screen across it, and, I was told, was left that way at night, so that the nurse could hear readily if her patient was restless or if he wanted attention.

A man standing on the slate roof of the porch, I found, could have easily leaned across one of the window-sills (if he did not care to step over it into the room) and fired at the man in his bed. To get from the ground to the porch roof would have required but little effort, and the descent would be still easier—he could slide down the roof, let himself go feet-first over the edge, checking his speed with hands and arms spread out on the slate, and drop down to the gravel drive. No trick at all, either coming or going. The windows were unscreened.

The sick man's bed stood just beside the connecting doorway between his room and the nurse's, which, when he was lying down, placed him between the doorway and the window from which the shot had been fired. Outside, within long rifle range, there was no building, tree, or eminence of any character from which the bullet that had been dug out of the door-frame could have been fired.

I turned from the room to the occupants, questioning the invalid first. He had been a raw-boned man of considerable size in his health, but now he was wasted and stringy and dead-white. His face was thin and hollow; small beady eyes crowded together against the thin bridge of his nose; his mouth was a colorless gash above a bony projecting chin.

His statement was a marvel of petulant conciseness.

"The shot woke me. I didn't see anything. I don't know anything. I've got a million enemies, most of whose names I can't remember."

He jerked this out crossly, turned his face away, closed his eyes, and refused to speak again.

Mrs. Gallaway and the nurse followed me into the latter's room, where I questioned them. They were of as opposite types as you could find anywhere, and between them there was a certain coolness, an unmistakable hostility which I was able to account for later in the day.

Mrs. Gallaway was perhaps five years older than her husband; dark, strikingly beautiful in a statuesque way, with a worried look in her dark eyes that was particularly noticeable when those eyes rested on her husband. There was no doubt that she was very much in love with him, and the anxiety that showed in her eyes at times—the pains she took to please him in each slight thing during my stay at the Exon house—convinced me that she struggled always with a fear that she was about to lose him.

Mrs. Gallaway could add nothing to what her husband had told me. She had been awakened by the shot, had run to her father's room, had seen nothing—knew nothing—suspected nothing.

The nurse—Barbra Caywood was her name—told the same story, in almost the same words. She had jumped out of bed when awakened by the shot, pushed the screen away from the connecting doorway, and rushed into her patient's room. She was the first one to arrive there, and she had seen nothing but the old man sitting up in bed, shaking his feeble fists at the window.

This Barbra Caywood was a girl of twenty-one or -two, and just the sort that a man would pick to help him get well—a girl of little under the average height, with an erect figure wherein slimness and roundness got an even break under the stiff white of her uniform; with soft golden hair above a face that was certainly made to be looked at. But she was businesslike and had an air of efficiency, for all her prettiness.

From the nurse's room, Gallaway led me to the kitchen, where I questioned the Chinese cook. Gong Lim was a sad-faced Oriental whose ever-present smile somehow made him look more gloomy than ever; and he bowed and smiled and yes-yes'd me from start to finish, and told me nothing.

Adam and Emma Figg—thin and stout, respectively, and both rheumatic—entertained a wide variety of suspicions, directed at the cook and the farm hands, individually and collectively, flitting momentarily from one to the other. They had nothing upon which to base these suspicions, however, except their firm belief that nearly all crimes of violence were committed by foreigners.

The farm hands—two smiling, middle-aged, and heavily mustached Italians, and a soft-eyed Mexican youth—I found in one of the fields. I talked to them for nearly two hours, and I left with a reasonable amount of assurance that none of the three had had any part in the shooting.

DR. RENCH had just come down from a visit to his patient when Gallaway and I returned from the fields. He was a little, wizened old man with mild manners and eyes, and a wonderful growth of hair on head, brows, cheeks, lips, chin, and nostrils.

The excitement, he said, had retarded Exon's recovery somewhat, but he did not think the setback would be serious. The invalid's temperature had gone up a little, but he seemed to be improving now.

I followed Dr. Rench out to his car after he left the others, for a few questions I wanted to put to him in privacy, but the questions might as well have gone unasked for all the good they did me. He could tell nothing of any value. The nurse, Barbra Caywood, had been secured, he said, from San Francisco, through the usual channels, which made it seem unlikely that she had worked her way into the Exon house for any hidden purpose which might have some connection with the attempt upon Exon's life.

Returning from my talk with the doctor, I came upon Hilary Gallaway and the nurse in the hall, near the foot of the stairs. His arm was resting lightly across her shoulders, and he was smiling down at her. Just as I came through the door, she twisted away so that his arm slid off, laughed elfishly up into his face, and went on up the stairs.

I did not know whether she had seen me approaching before she eluded the encircling arm or not, nor did I know how long the arm had been there; and both of those questions would make a difference in how their positions were to be construed.

Hilary Gallaway was certainly not a man to allow a girl as pretty as the nurse to lack attention, and he was just as certainly attractive enough in himself to make his advances not too unflattering. Nor did Barbra Caywood impress me as being a girl who would dislike his admiration. But, at that, it was more than likely that there was nothing very serious between them, nothing more than a playful sort of flirtation.

But, no matter what the situation might be in that quarter, it didn't have any direct bearing upon the shooting—none that I could see, anyway. But I understood now the strained relations between the nurse and Gallaway's wife.

Gallaway was grinning quizzically at me while I was chasing these thoughts around in my head.

"Nobody's safe with a detective around," he complained.

I grinned back at him. That was the only sort of answer you could give this bird.

After dinner, Gallaway drove me to Knownburg in his roadster, and set me down on the doorstep of the deputy sheriff's house. He offered to drive me back to the Exon house when I had finished my investigations in town, but I did not know how long those investigations would take, so I told him I would hire a car when I was ready to return.

Shand, the deputy sheriff, was a big, slow-spoken, slow-thinking, blond man of thirty or so—just the type best fitted for a deputy sheriff job in a San Joaquin County town.

"I went out to Exon's as soon as Gallaway called me up," he said. "About four-thirty in the morning, I reckon it was when I got there. I didn't find nothing. There weren't no marks on the porch roof, but that don't mean nothing. I tried climbing up and down it myself, and I didn't leave no marks neither. The ground around the house is too firm for footprints to be followed. I found a few, but they didn't lead nowhere; and everybody had run all over the place before I got there, so I couldn't tell who they belonged to.

"Far's I can learn, there ain't been no suspicious characters in the neighborhood lately. The only folks around here who have got any grudge against the old man are the Deemses—Exon beat 'em in a law suit a couple years back—but all of them—the father and both the boys—were at home when the shooting was done."

"How long has Exon been living here?"

"Four-five years, I reckon."

"Nothing at all to work on, then?"

"Nothing I know about."

"What do you know about the Exon family?" I asked.

Shand scratched his head thoughtfully and frowned.

"I reckon it's Hilary Gallaway you're meaning," he said slowly. "I thought of that. The Gallaways showed up here a couple of years after her father had bought the place, and Hilary seems to spend most of his evenings up in Ady's back room, teaching the boys how to play poker. I hear he's fitted to teach them a lot. I don't know, myself. Ady runs a quiet game, so I let 'em alone. But naturally I don't never set in, myself.

"Outside of being a cardhound, and drinking pretty heavy, and making a lot of trips to the city, where he's supposed to have a girl on the string, I don't know nothing much about Hilary. But it's no secret that him and the old man don't hit it off together very well. And then Hilary's room is just across the hall from Exon's, and their windows open out on the porch roof just a little apart. But I don't know—"

Shand confirmed what Gallaway had told me about the bullet being .38 caliber, about the absence of any pistol of that caliber on the premises, and about the lack of any reason for suspecting the farm hands or servants.

I put in the next couple of hours talking to whomever I could find to talk to in Knownburg, and I learned nothing worth putting down on paper. Then I got a car and driver from the garage, and was driven out to Exon's.

Gallaway had not yet returned from town. His wife and Barbra Caywood were just about to sit down to a light dinner before retiring, so I joined them. Exon, the nurse said, was asleep, and had spent a quiet evening. We talked for a while—until about half-past twelve—and then went to our rooms.

My room was next to the nurse's, on the same side of the hall that divided the second story in half. I sat down and wrote my report for the day, smoked a cigar, and then, the house being quiet by this time, put a gun and a flashlight in my pockets, went downstairs, and out the kitchen door.

The moon was just coming up, lighting the grounds vaguely, except for the shadows cast by house, outbuildings, and the several clumps of shrubbery. Keeping in these shadows as much as possible, I explored the grounds, finding everything as it should be.

The lack of any evidence to the contrary pointed to last night's shot having been fired—either accidentally, or in fright at some fancied move of Exon's—by a burglar, who had been entering the sick man's room through a window. If that were so, then there wasn't one chance in a thousand of anything happening to-night. But I felt restless and ill at ease, nevertheless.

Gallaway's roadster was not in the garage. He had not returned from

Knownburg. Beneath the farm hands' window I paused until snores in three distinct keys told me that they were all safely abed.

After an hour of this snooping around, I returned to the house. The luminous dial of my watch registered 2:35 as I stopped outside the Chinese cook's door to listen to his regular breathing.

Upstairs, I paused at the door of the Figgs's room, until my ear told me that they were sleeping. At Mrs. Gallaway's door I had to wait several minutes before she sighed and turned in bed. Barbra Caywood was breathing deeply and strongly, with the regularity of a young animal whose sleep is without disturbing dreams. The invalid's breath came to me with the evenness of slumber and the rasping of the pneumonia convalescent.

This listening tour completed, I returned to my room.

Still feeling wide-awake and restless, I pulled a chair up to a window, and sat looking at the moonlight on the river which twisted just below the house so as to be visible from this side, smoking another cigar, and turning things over in my mind—to no great advantage.

Outside there was no sound.

Suddenly down the hall came the heavy explosion of a gun being fired indoors! I threw myself across the room, out into the hall.

A woman's voice filled the house with its shriek—high, frenzied.

Barbra Caywood's door was unlocked when I reached it. I slammed it open. By the light of the moonbeams that slanted past her window, I saw her sitting upright in the center of her bed. She wasn't beautiful now. Her face was twisted with terror. The scream was just dying in her throat.

All this I got in the flash of time that it took me to put a running foot across her sill.

Then another shot crashed out—in Exon's room.

The girl's face jerked up—so abruptly that it seemed her neck must snap—she clutched both hands to her breast—and fell face-down among the bedclothes.

I don't know whether I went through, over, or around the screen that stood in the connecting doorway. I was circling Exon's bed. He lay on the floor on his side, facing a window. I jumped over him—leaned out the window.

In the yard that was bright now under the moon, nothing moved. There was no sound of flight. Presently, while my eyes still searched the surrounding country, the farm hands, in their underwear, came running barefooted from the direction of their quarters. I called down to them, stationing them at points of vantage.

Meanwhile, behind me, Gong Lim and Adam Figg had put Exon back in his bed, while Mrs. Gallaway and Emma Figg tried to check the blood that spurted from a hole in Barbra Caywood's side.

I sent Adam Figg to the telephone, to wake the doctor and the deputy sheriff, and then I hurried down to the grounds.

Stepping out of the door, I came face to face with Hilary Gallaway coming from the direction of the garage. His face was flushed, and his breath was eloquent of the refreshments that had accompanied the game in Ady's back room, but his step was steady enough, and his smile was as lazy as ever.

"What's the excitement?" he asked.

"Same as last night! Meet anybody on the road? Or see anybody leaving here?"

"No."

"All right. Get in that bus of yours, and burn up the road in the other direction. Stop anybody you meet going away from here or who looks wrong! Got a gun?"

He spun on his heel with nothing of indolence.

"One in my car," he called as he broke into a run.

The farm hands still at their posts, I combed the grounds from east to west and from north to south. I realized that I was spoiling my chance of finding footprints when it would be light enough to see them, but I was banking on the man I wanted still being close at hand. And then Shand had told me that the ground was unfavorable for tracing prints, anyway.

On the gravel drive in front of the house I found the pistol from which the shots had been fired—a cheap .38-caliber revolver, slightly rusty, smelling freshly of burned powder, with three empty shells and three that had not been fired in it.

Besides that I found nothing. The murderer—from what I had seen of the hole in the girl's side, I called him that—had vanished.

Shand and Dr. Rench arrived together, just as I was finishing my fruitless search. A little later, Hilary Gallaway came back—empty-handed.

BREAKFAST THAT morning was a melancholy meal, except to Hilary Gallaway. He refrained from jesting openly about the night's excitement, but his eyes twinkled whenever they met mine, and I knew he thought it a tremendously good joke for the shooting to have taken place right under my nose. During his wife's presence at the table, however, he was almost grave, as if not to offend her.

Mrs. Gallaway left the table shortly, and Dr. Rench joined us. He said that both of his patients were in as good shape as could be expected, and he thought both would recover.

The bullet had barely grazed the girl's ribs and breast-bone, going through the flesh and muscles of her chest, in on the right side and out again, on the left. Except for the shock and the loss of blood, she was not in danger, although unconscious.

Exon was sleeping, the doctor said, so Shand and I crept up into his room to examine it. The first bullet had gone into the doorframe, about four inches above the one that had been fired the night before. The second bullet had pierced the Japanese screen, and, after passing through the girl, had lodged in the plaster of the wall. We dug out both bullets—they were of .38 caliber. Both had apparently been fired from the vicinity of one of the windows—either just inside or just outside.

Shand and I grilled the Chinese cook, the farm hands, and the Figgs unmercifully that day. But they came through it standing up—there was nothing to fix the shooting on any of them.

And all day long that damned Hilary Gallaway followed me from pillar to post, with a mocking glint in his eyes that said plainer than words, "I'm the logical suspect. Why don't you put me through your little third degree?" But I grinned back, and asked him nothing.

Shand had to go to town that afternoon. He called me up on the telephone later, and told me that Gallaway had left Knownburg early enough that morning to have arrived home fully half an hour before the shooting, if he had driven at his usual fast pace.

The day passed—too rapidly—and I found myself dreading the coming of night. Two nights in succession Exon's life had been attempted—and now the third night was coming.

At dinner Hilary Gallaway announced that he was going to stay home this evening. Knownburg, he said, was tame in comparison; and he grinned at me.

Dr. Rench left after the meal, saying that he would return as soon as possible, but that he had two patients on the other side of town whom he must visit. Barbra Caywood had returned to consciousness, but had been extremely hysterical, and the doctor had given her an opiate. She was asleep now. Exon was resting easily except for a high temperature.

I went up to Exon's room for a few minutes after the meal and tried him out with a gentle question or two, but he refused to answer them, and he was too sick for me to press him.

He asked how the girl was.

"The doc says she's in no particular danger. Just loss of blood and shock. If she doesn't rip her bandages off and bleed to death in one of her hysterical spells, he says, he'll have her on her feet in a couple of weeks."

Mrs. Gallaway came in then, and I went downstairs again, where I was seized by Gallaway, who insisted with bantering gravity that I tell him about some of the mysteries I had solved. He was enjoying my discomfort to the limit. He kidded me for about an hour, and had me burning up inside; but I managed to grin back with a fair pretense of indifference.

When his wife joined us presently—saying that both of the invalids were sleeping—I made my escape from her tormenting husband, saying that I had some writing to do. But I didn't go to my room.

Instead, I crept stealthily into the girl's room, crossed to a clothespress that I had noted earlier in the day, and planted myself in it. By leaving the door open the least fraction of an inch, I could see through the connecting doorway—from which the screen had been removed—across Exon's bed, and out of the window from which three bullets had already come, and the Lord only knew what else might come.

Time passed, and I was stiff from standing still. But I had expected that.

Twice Mrs. Gallaway came up to look at her father and the nurse. Each time I shut my closet door entirely as soon as I heard her tiptoeing steps in the hall. I was hiding from *everybody.*

She had just gone from her second visit, when, before I had time to open my door again, I heard a faint rustling, and a soft padding on the floor. Not knowing what it was or where it was, I was afraid to push the door open. In my narrow hiding place I stood still and waited.

The padding was recognizable now—quiet footsteps, coming nearer. They passed not far from my clothespress door.

I waited.

An almost inaudible rustling. A pause. The softest and faintest of tearing sounds.

I came out of the closet—my gun in my hand.

Standing beside the girl's bed, leaning over her unconscious form, was old Talbert Exon, his face flushed with fever, his nightshirt hanging limply around his wasted legs. One of his hands still rested upon the bedclothes he had turned down from her body. The other hand held a narrow strip of adhesive tape, with which her bandages had been fixed in place, and which he had just torn off.

He snarled at me, and both his hands went toward the girl's bandages.

The crazy, feverish glare of his eyes told me that the threat of the gun in my hand meant nothing to him. I jumped to his side, plucked his hands aside, picked him up in my arms, and carried him—kicking, clawing, and swearing—back to his bed.

Then I called the others.

HILARY GALLAWAY, Shand—who had come out from town again— and I sat over coffee and cigarettes in the kitchen, while the rest of the household helped Dr. Rench battle for Exon's life. The old man had gone through enough excitement in the last three days to kill a healthy man, let alone a pneumonia convalescent.

"But why should the old devil want to kill her?" Gallaway asked me.

"Search me," I confessed, a little testily perhaps. "I don't know why he wanted to kill her, but it's a cinch that he did. The gun was found just about where he could have thrown it when he heard me coming. I was in the girl's room when she was shot, and I got to Exon's window without wasting much time, and I saw nothing. You, yourself, driving home from Knownburg, and arriving here right after the shooting, didn't see anybody leave by the road; and I'll take an oath that nobody could have left in any other direction without either one of the farm hands or me seeing them.

"And then, to-night, I told Exon that the girl would recover if she didn't tear off her bandages, which, while true enough, gave him the idea that she had been trying to tear them off. And from that he built up a plan of tearing them off himself—knowing that she had been given an opiate, perhaps— and thinking that everybody would believe she had torn them off herself. And he was putting that plan into execution—had torn off one piece of tape—when I stopped him. He shot her intentionally, and that's flat. Maybe I couldn't prove it in court without knowing why, but I know he did. But the doc says he'll hardly live to be tried; he killed himself trying to kill the girl."

"Maybe you're right"—Gallaway's mocking grin flashed at me—"but you're a hell of a detective. Why didn't you suspect me?"

"I did," I grinned back, "but not enough."

"Why not? You may be making a mistake," he drawled. "You know my room is just across the hall from his, and I could have left my window, crept across the porch, fired at him, and then run back to my room, on that first night.

"And on the second night—when you were here—you ought to know that I left Knownburg in plenty of time to have come out here, parked my car down the road a bit, fired those two shots, crept around in the shadow of the house, run back to my car, and then come driving innocently up to the garage. You should know also that my reputation isn't any too good—that I'm supposed to be a bad egg; and you do know that I don't like the old man. And for a motive, there is the fact that my wife is Exon's only heir. I hope"—he raised his eyebrows in burlesqued pain—"that you don't think I have any moral scruples against a well-placed murder now and then."

I laughed. "I don't."

"Well, then?"

"If Exon had been killed that first night, and I had come up here, you'd be doing your joking behind bars long before this. And if he'd been killed the second night, even, I might have grabbed you. But I don't figure you as a man who'd bungle so easy a job—not twice, anyway. You wouldn't have missed, and then run away, leaving him alive."

He shook my hand gravely.

"It is comforting to have one's few virtues appreciated."

Before Talbert Exon died he sent for me. He wanted to die, he said, with his curiosity appeased; and so we traded information. I told him how I had come to suspect him and he told me why he had tried to kill Barbra Caywood.

Fourteen years ago he had killed his wife, not for the insurance, as he had been suspected of doing, but in a fit of jealousy. However, he had so thoroughly covered up the proofs of his guilt that he had never been brought to trial; but the murder had weighed upon him, to the extent of becoming an obsession.

He knew that he would never give himself away consciously—he was too shrewd for that—and he knew that proof of his guilt could never be found. But there was always the chance that some time, in delirium, in his sleep, or when drunk, he might tell enough to bring him to the gallows.

He thought upon this angle too often, until it became a morbid fear that always hounded him. He had given up drinking—that was easy—but there was no way of guarding against the other things.

And one of them, he said, had finally happened. He had got pneumonia, and for a week he had been out of his head, and he had talked. Coming out of that week's delirium, he had questioned the nurse. She had given him vague answers, would not tell him what he had talked about, what he had said. And then, in unguarded moments, he had discovered that her eyes rested upon him with loathing—with intense repulsion.

He knew then that he had babbled of his wife's murder; and he set about laying plans for removing the nurse before she repeated what she had heard.

For so long as she remained in his house, he counted himself safe. She would not tell strangers, and it might be that for a while she would not tell anyone. Professional ethics would keep her quiet, perhaps; but he could not let her leave his house with her knowledge of his secret.

Daily and in secret, he had tested his strength until he knew himself strong enough to walk about the room a little, and to hold a revolver steady. His bed was fortunately placed for his purpose—directly in line with one of the windows, the connecting door, and the girl's bed. In an old bond box in his closet—and nobody but he had ever seen the things in that box—was a revolver; a revolver that could not possibly be traced to him.

On the first night, he had taken this gun out, stepped back from his bed a little, and fired a bullet into the doorframe. Then he had jumped back into bed, concealing the gun under the blankets—where none thought to look for it—until he could return it to its box.

That was all the preparation he had needed. He had established an attempted murder directed against himself, and he had shown that a bullet fired at him could easily go near—and therefore through—the connecting doorway.

On the second night, he had waited until the house had seemed quiet. Then he had peeped through one of the cracks in the Japanese screen at the girl, whom he could see in the reflected light from the moon. He had found, though, that when he stepped far enough back from the screen for it to escape powder marks, he could not see the girl, not while she was lying down. So he had fired first into the doorframe—near the previous night's bullet—to awaken her.

She had sat up in bed immediately, screaming, and he had shot her. He had intended firing another shot into her body—to make sure of her death—but my approach had made that impossible, and had made concealment of the gun impossible; so, with what strength he had left, he had thrown the revolver out of the window.

He died that afternoon, and I returned to San Francisco.

But that was not quite the end of the story.

In the ordinary course of business, the Agency's bookkeeping department sent Gallaway a bill for my services. With the check that he sent by return mail, he enclosed a letter to me, from which I quote a paragraph:

I don't want to let you miss the cream of the whole affair. The lovely Caywood, when she recovered, denied that Exon had talked of murder or any other crime during his delirium. The cause of the distaste with which she might have looked at him afterward, and the reason she would not tell him what he had said, was that his entire conversation during that week of delirium had consisted of an uninterrupted stream of obscenities and blasphemies, which seem to have shocked the girl through and through.

ZIGZAGS OF
TREACHERY

I

All I know about Dr. Estep's death," I said, "is the stuff in the papers."

Vance Richmond's lean gray face took on an expression of distaste.

"The newspapers aren't always either thorough or accurate. I'll give you the salient points as I know them; though I suppose you'll want to go over the ground for yourself, and get your information first-hand."

I nodded, and the attorney went on, shaping each word precisely with his thin lips before giving it sound.

"Dr. Estep came to San Francisco in '98 or '99—a young man of twenty-five, just through qualifying for his license. He opened an office here, and, as you probably know, became in time a rather excellent surgeon. He married two or three years after he came here. There were no children. He and his wife seem to have been a bit happier together than the average.

"Of his life before coming to San Francisco, nothing is known. He told his wife briefly that he had been born and raised in Parkersburg, W. Va., but that his home life had been so unpleasant that he was trying to forget it, and that he did not like to talk—or even think—about it. Bear that in mind.

"Two weeks ago—on the third of the month—a woman came to his office, in the afternoon. His office was in his residence on Pine Street. Lucy Coe, who was Dr. Estep's nurse and assistant, showed the woman into his office, and then went back to her own desk in the reception room.

"She didn't hear anything the doctor said to the woman, but through the closed door she heard the woman's voice now and then—a high and anguished voice, apparently pleading. Most of the words were lost upon the nurse, but she heard one coherent sentence. 'Please! Please!' she heard the woman cry. 'Don't turn me away!' The woman was with Dr. Estep for about fifteen minutes, and left sobbing into a handkerchief. Dr. Estep said nothing about the caller either to his nurse or to his wife, who didn't learn of it until after his death.

"The next day, toward evening, while the nurse was putting on her hat and coat preparatory to leaving for home, Dr. Estep came out of his office, with his hat on and a letter in his hand. The nurse saw that his face was pale—'white as my uniform,' she says—and he walked with the care of one who takes pains to keep from staggering.

"She asked him if he was ill. 'Oh, it's nothing!' he told her. 'I'll be all right in a very few minutes.' Then he went on out. The nurse left the house just behind him, and saw him drop the letter he had carried into the mailbox on the corner, after which he returned to the house.

"Mrs. Estep, coming downstairs ten minutes later—it couldn't have been any later than that—heard, just as she reached the first floor, the sound of a shot from her husband's office. She rushed into it, meeting nobody. Her husband stood by his desk, swaying, with a hole in his right temple and a smoking revolver in his hand. Just as she reached him and put her arms around him, he fell across the desk—dead."

"Anybody else—any of the servants, for instance—able to say that Mrs. Estep didn't go to the office until after the shot?" I asked.

The attorney shook his head sharply.

"No, damn it! That's where the rub comes in!"

His voice, after this one flare of feeling, resumed its level, incisive tone, and he went on with his tale.

"The next day's papers had accounts of Dr. Estep's death, and late that morning the woman who had called upon him the day before his death came to the house. She is Dr. Estep's first wife—which is to say, his legal wife! There seems to be no reason—not the slightest—for doubting it, as much as I'd like to. They were married in Philadelphia in '96. She has a certified copy of the marriage record. I had the matter investigated in Philadelphia, and it's a certain fact that Dr. Estep and this woman—Edna Fife was her maiden name—were really married.

"She says that Estep, after living with her in Philadelphia for two years, deserted her. That would have been in '98, or just before he came to San

Francisco. She has sufficient proof of her identity—that she really is the Edna Fife who married him; and my agents in the East found positive proof that Estep had practiced for two years in Philadelphia.

"And here is another point. I told you that Estep had said he was born and raised in Parkersburg. I had inquiries made there, but found nothing to show that he had ever lived there, and found ample evidence to show that he had never lived at the address he had given his wife. There is, then, nothing for us to believe except that his talk of an unhappy early life was a ruse to ward off embarrassing questions."

"Did you do anything toward finding out whether the doctor and his first wife had ever been divorced?" I asked.

"I'm having that taken care of now, but I hardly expect to learn that they had. That would be too crude. To get on with my story: This woman—the first Mrs. Estep—said that she had just recently learned her husband's whereabouts, and had come to see him in an attempt to effect a reconciliation. When she called upon him the afternoon before his death, he asked for a little time to make up his mind what he should do. He promised to give her his decision in two days. My personal opinion, after talking to the woman several times, is that she had learned that he had accumulated some money, and that her interest was more in getting the money than in getting him. But that, of course, is neither here nor there.

"At first the authorities accepted the natural explanation of the doctor's death—suicide. But after the first wife's appearance, the second wife—my client—was arrested and charged with murder.

"The police theory is that after his first wife's visit, Dr. Estep told his second wife the whole story; and that she, brooding over the knowledge that he had deceived her, that she was not his wife at all, finally worked herself up into a rage, went to the office after his nurse had left for the day, and shot him with the revolver that she knew he always kept in his desk.

"I don't know, of course, just what evidence the prosecution has, but from the newspapers I gather that the case against her will be built upon her fingerprints on the revolver with which he was killed; an upset inkwell on his desk; splashes of ink on the dress she wore; and an inky print of her hand on a torn newspaper on his desk.

"Unfortunately, but perfectly naturally, one of the first things she did was to take the revolver out of her husband's hand. That accounts for her prints on it. He fell—as I told you—just as she put her arms around him, and, though her memory isn't very clear on this point, the probabilities are that he dragged her with him when he fell across the desk. That accounts for the upset inkwell, the torn paper, and the splashes of ink. But the prosecution will try to persuade the jury that those things all happened before the shooting—that they are proofs of a struggle."

"Not so bad," I gave my opinion.

"Or pretty damned bad—depending on how you look at it. And this is the worst time imaginable for a thing like this to come up! Within the past few months there have been no less than five widely advertised murders of men by women who were supposed to have been betrayed, or deceived, or one thing or another.

"Not one of those five women was convicted. As a result, we have the press, the public, and even the pulpit, howling for a stricter enforcement of justice. The newspapers are lined up against Mrs. Estep as strongly as their fear of libel suits will permit. The women's clubs are lined up against her. Everybody is clamoring for an example to be made of her.

"Then, as if all that isn't enough, the prosecuting attorney has lost his last two big cases, and he'll be out for blood this time—election day isn't far off."

The calm, even, precise voice was gone now. In its place was a passionate eloquence.

"I don't know what you think," Richmond cried. "You're a detective. This is an old story to you. You're more or less callous, I suppose, and skeptical of innocence in general. But I *know* that Mrs. Estep didn't kill her husband. I don't say it because she's my client! I was Dr. Estep's attorney, and his friend, and if I thought Mrs. Estep guilty, I'd do everything in my power to help convict her. But I know as well as I know anything that she didn't kill him—couldn't have killed him.

"She's innocent. But I know too that if I go into court with no defense beyond what I now have, she'll be convicted! There has been too much leniency shown feminine criminals, public sentiment says. The pendulum will swing the other way—Mrs. Estep, if convicted, will get the limit. I'm putting it up to you! Can you save her?"

"Our best mark is the letter he mailed just before he died," I said, ignoring everything he said that didn't have to do with the facts of the case. "It's good betting that when a man writes and mails a letter and then shoots himself, that the letter isn't altogether unconnected with the suicide. Did you ask the wife about the letter?"

"I did, and she denies having received one."

"That wasn't right. If the doctor had been driven to suicide by her appearance, then according to all the rules there are, the letter should have been addressed to her. He might have written one to his second wife, but he would hardly have mailed it. Would she have any reason for lying about it?"

"Yes," the lawyer said slowly, "I think she would. His will leaves everything to the second wife. The first wife, being the only legal wife, will have no difficulty in breaking that will, of course; but if it is shown that the second wife had no knowledge of the first one's existence—that she really believed herself to be Dr. Estep's legal wife—then I think that she will receive at least a portion of the estate. I don't think any court would, under the circumstances, take everything away from her. But if she should be found guilty of murdering Dr. Estep, then no consideration will be shown her, and the first wife will get every penny."

"Did he leave enough to make half of it, say, worth sending an innocent person to the gallows for?"

"He left about half a million, roughly; two hundred and fifty thousand dollars isn't a mean inducement."

"Do you think it would be enough for the first wife—from what you have seen of her?"

"Candidly, I do. She didn't impress me as being a person of many very active scruples."

"Where does this first wife live?" I asked.

"She's staying at the Montgomery Hotel now. Her home is in Louisville, I believe. I don't think you will gain anything by talking to her, however. She has retained Somerset, Somerset and Quill to represent her—a very reputable firm, by the way—and she'll refer you to them. They will tell you nothing. But if there's anything dishonest about her affairs—such as the concealing of Dr. Estep's letter—I'm confident that Somerset, Somerset and Quill know nothing of it."

"Can I talk to the second Mrs. Estep—your client?"

"Not at present, I'm afraid; though perhaps in a day or two. She is on the verge of collapse just now. She has always been delicate; and the shock of her husband's death, followed by her own arrest and imprisonment, has been too much for her. She's in the city jail, you know, held without bail. I've tried to have her transferred to the prisoner's ward of the City Hospital, even; but the authorities seem to think that her illness is simply a ruse. I'm worried about her. She's really in a critical condition."

His voice was losing its calmness again, so I picked up my hat, said something about starting to work at once, and went out. I don't like eloquence: if it isn't effective enough to pierce your hide, it's tiresome; and if it is effective enough, then it muddles your thoughts.

11

I spent the next couple of hours questioning the Estep servants, to no great advantage. None of them had been near the front of the house at the time of the shooting, and none had seen Mrs. Estep immediately prior to her husband's death.

After a lot of hunting, I located Lucy Coe, the nurse, in an apartment on Vallejo Street. She was a small, brisk, businesslike woman of thirty or so. She repeated what Vance Richmond had told me, and could add nothing to it.

That cleaned up the Estep end of the job; and I set out for the Montgomery Hotel, satisfied that my only hope for success—barring miracles, which usually don't happen—lay in finding the letter that I believed Dr. Estep had written to his first wife.

My drag with the Montgomery Hotel management was pretty strong—strong enough to get me anything I wanted that wasn't too far outside the law. So as soon as I got there, I hunted up Stacey, one of the assistant managers.

"This Mrs. Estep who's registered here," I asked, "what do you know about her?"

"Nothing, myself, but if you'll wait a few minutes I'll see what I can learn."

The assistant manager was gone about ten minutes.

"No one seems to know much about her," he told me when he came back. "I've questioned the telephone girls, bellboys, maids, clerks, and the house detective; but none of them could tell me much.

"She registered from Louisville, on the second of the month. She has never stopped here before, and she seems unfamiliar with the city—asks quite a few questions about how to get around. The mail clerks don't remember handling any mail for her, nor do the girls on the switchboard have any record of phone calls for her.

"She keeps regular hours—usually goes out at ten or later in the morning, and gets in before midnight. She doesn't seem to have any callers or friends."

"Will you have her mail watched—let me know what postmarks and return addresses are on any letters she gets?"

"Certainly."

"And have the girls on the switchboard put their ears up against any talking she does over the wire?"

"Yes."

"Is she in her room now?"

"No, she went out a little while ago."

"Fine! I'd like to go up and take a look at her stuff."

Stacey looked sharply at me, and cleared his throat.

"Is it as—ah—important as all that? I want to give you all the assistance I can, but—"

"It's this important," I assured him, "that another woman's life depends on what I can learn about this one."

"All right!" he said. "I'll tell the clerk to let us know if she comes in before we are through; and we'll go right up."

The woman's room held two valises and a trunk, all unlocked, and containing not the least thing of importance—no letters—nothing. So little, in fact, that I was more than half convinced that she had expected her things to be searched.

Downstairs again, I planted myself in a comfortable chair within sight of the key-rack, and waited for a view of this first Mrs. Estep.

She came in at 11:15 that night. A large woman of forty-five or fifty, well-dressed, and carrying herself with an air of assurance. Her face was a little too hard as to mouth and chin, but not enough to be ugly. A capable-looking woman—a woman who would get what she went after.

I I I

Eight o'clock was striking as I went into the Montgomery lobby the next morning and picked out a chair, this time within eye-range of the elevators.

At 10:30 Mrs. Estep left the hotel, with me in her wake. Her denial that a letter from her husband, written immediately before his death, had come to her didn't fit in with the possibilities as I saw them. And a good motto for the detective business is, "When in doubt—shadow 'em."

After eating breakfast at a restaurant on O'Farrell Street, she turned toward the shopping district; and for a long, long time—though I suppose it was a lot shorter than it seemed to me—she led me through the most densely packed portions of the most crowded department stores she could find.

She didn't buy anything, but she did a lot of thorough looking, with me muddling along behind her, trying to act like a little fat guy on an errand for his wife, while stout women bumped me and thin ones prodded me and all sorts got in my way and walked on my feet.

Finally, after I had sweated off a couple of pounds, she left the shopping district, and cut up through Union Square, walking along casually, as if out for a stroll.

Three-quarters way through, she turned abruptly, and retraced her steps, looking sharply at everyone she passed. I was on a bench, reading a stray page from a day-old newspaper, when she went by. She walked on down Post Street to Kearney, stopping every now and then to look—or to pretend to look—in store windows, while I ambled along sometimes behind her, sometimes almost by her side, and sometimes in front.

She was trying to check up the people around her, trying to determine whether she was being followed or not. But here, in the busy part of town, that gave me no cause for worry. On a less crowded street it might have been different, though not necessarily so.

There are four rules for shadowing: Keep behind your subject as much as possible; never try to hide from him; act in a natural manner no matter what happens; and never meet his eye. Obey them, and, except in unusual circumstances, shadowing is the easiest thing that a sleuth has to do.

Assured, after a while, that no one was following her, Mrs. Estep turned back toward Powell Street, and got into a taxicab at the St. Francis stand. I picked out a modest touring car from the rank of hire-cars along the Geary Street side of Union Square, and set out after her.

Our route was out Post Street to Laguna, where the taxi presently swung into the curb and stopped. The woman got out, paid the driver, and went up the steps of an apartment building. With idling engine my own car had come to rest against the opposite curb in the block above.

As the taxicab disappeared around a corner, Mrs. Estep came out of the apartment-building doorway, went back to the sidewalk, and started down Laguna Street.

"Pass her," I told my chauffeur, and we drew down upon her.

As we came abreast, she went up the front steps of another building, and this time she rang a bell. These steps belonged to a building apparently occupied by four flats, each with its separate door, and the button she had pressed belonged to the right-hand second-story flat.

Under cover of my car's rear curtains, I kept my eye on the doorway while my driver found a convenient place to park in the next block.

I kept my eye on the vestibule until 5:35 p.m., when she came out, walked to the Sutter Street car line, returned to the Montgomery, and went to her room.

I called up the Old Man—the Continental Detective Agency's San Francisco manager—and asked him to detail an operative to learn who and what were the occupants of the Laguna Street flat.

That night Mrs. Estep ate dinner at her hotel, and went to a show afterward, and she displayed no interest in possible shadowers. She went to her room at a little after eleven, and I knocked off for the day.

I V

The following morning I turned the woman over to Dick Foley, and went back to the Agency to wait for Bob Teal, the operative who had investigated the Laguna Street flat. He came in at a little after ten.

"A guy named Jacob Ledwich lives there," Bob said. "He's a crook of some sort, but I don't know just what. He and 'Wop' Healey are friendly, so he must be a crook! 'Porky' Grout says he's an ex–bunko man who is in with a gambling ring now; but Porky would tell you a bishop was a safe-ripper if he thought it would mean five bucks for himself.

"This Ledwich goes out mostly at night, and he seems to be pretty prosperous. Probably a high-class worker of some sort. He's got a Buick—license number 645-221—that he keeps in a garage around the corner from his flat. But he doesn't seem to use the car much."

"What sort of looking fellow is he?"

"A big guy—six feet or better—and he'll weigh a couple hundred easy. He's got a funny mug on him. It's broad and heavy around the cheeks and jaw, but his mouth is a little one that looks like it was made for a smaller man. He's no youngster—middle-aged."

"Suppose you tail him around for a day or two, Bob, and see what he's up to. Try to get a room or apartment in the neighborhood—a place that you can cover his front door from."

V

Vance Richmond's lean face lighted up as soon as I mentioned Ledwich's name to him.

"Yes!" he exclaimed. "He was a friend, or at least an acquaintance, of Dr. Estep's. I met him once—a large man with a peculiarly inadequate mouth. I dropped in to see the doctor one day, and Ledwich was in the office. Dr. Estep introduced us."

"What do you know about him?"

"Nothing."

"Don't you know whether he was intimate with the doctor, or just a casual acquaintance?"

"No. For all I know, he might have been a friend, a patient, or almost anything. The doctor never spoke of him to me, and nothing passed between them while I was there that afternoon. I simply gave the doctor some information he had asked for and left. Why?"

"Dr. Estep's first wife—after going to a lot of trouble to see that she wasn't followed—connected with Ledwich yesterday afternoon. And from what we can learn he seems to be a crook of some sort."

"What would that indicate?"

"I'm not sure what it means, but I can do a lot of guessing. Ledwich knew both the doctor and the doctor's first wife; then it's not a bad bet that *she* knew where her husband was all the time. If she did, then it's another good bet that she was getting money from him right along. Can you check up his accounts and see whether he was passing out any money that can't be otherwise accounted for?"

The attorney shook his head.

"No, his accounts are in rather bad shape, carelessly kept. He must have had more than a little difficulty with his income-tax statements."

"I see. To get back to my guesses: If she knew where he was all the time, and was getting money from him, then why did his first wife finally come to see her husband? Perhaps because—"

"I think I can help you there," Richmond interrupted. "A fortunate investment in lumber nearly doubled Dr. Estep's wealth two or three months ago."

"That's it, then! She learned of it through Ledwich. She demanded, either through Ledwich, or by letter, a rather large share of it—more than the doctor was willing to give. When he refused, she came to see him in person, to demand the money under threat—we'll say—of instant exposure. He thought she was in earnest. Either he couldn't raise the money she demanded, or he was tired of leading a double life. Anyway, he thought it all over, and decided to commit suicide. This is all a guess, or a series of guesses—but it sounds reasonable to me."

"To me, too," the attorney said. "What are you going to do now?"

"I'm still having both of them shadowed—there's no other way of tackling them just now. I'm having the woman looked up in Louisville. But, you understand, I might dig up a whole flock of things on them, and when I got through still be as far as ever from finding the letter Dr. Estep wrote before he died.

"There are plenty of reasons for thinking that the woman destroyed the letter—that would have been her wisest play. But if I can get enough on her, even at that, I can squeeze her into admitting that the letter was written, and that it said something about suicide—if it did. And that will be enough to spring your client. How is she to-day—any better?"

His thin face lost the animation that had come to it during our discussion of Ledwich, and became bleak.

"She went completely to pieces last night, and was removed to the hospital, where she should have been taken in the first place. To tell you the truth, if she isn't liberated soon, she won't need our help. I've done my utmost to have her released on bail—pulled every wire I know—but there's little likelihood of success in that direction.

"Knowing that she is a prisoner—charged with murdering her husband—is killing her. She isn't young, and she has always been subject to nervous disorders. The bare shock of her husband's death was enough to prostrate her—but now— You've *got* to get her out—and quickly!"

He was striding up and down his office, his voice throbbing with feeling. I left quickly.

V I

From the attorney's office, I returned to the Agency, where I was told that Bob Teal had phoned in the address of a furnished apartment he had rented on Laguna Street. I hopped on a street car, and went up to take a look at it.

But I didn't get that far.

Walking down Laguna Street, after leaving the car, I spied Bob Teal coming toward me. Between Bob and me—also coming toward me—was a big man whom I recognized as Jacob Ledwich: a big man with a big red face around a tiny mouth.

I walked on down the street, passing both Ledwich and Bob, without paying any apparent attention to either. At the next corner I stopped to roll a cigarette, and steal a look at the pair.

And then I came to life!

Ledwich had stopped at a vestibule cigar stand up the street to make a purchase. Bob Teal, knowing his stuff, had passed him and was walking steadily up the street.

He was figuring that Ledwich had either come out for the purpose of buying cigars or cigarettes, and would return to his flat with them; or that after making his purchase the big man would proceed to the car line, where, in either event, Bob would wait.

But as Ledwich had stopped before the cigar stand, a man across the street had stepped suddenly into a doorway, and stood there, back in the shadows. This man, I now remembered, had been on the opposite side of the street from Bob and Ledwich, and walking in the same direction.

He, too, was following Ledwich.

By the time Ledwich had finished his business at the stand, Bob had reached Sutter Street, the nearest car line. Ledwich started up the street in that direction. The man in the doorway stepped out and went after him. I followed that one.

A ferry-bound car came down Sutter Street just as I reached the corner. Ledwich and I got aboard together. The mysterious stranger fumbled with a shoe-string several pavements from the corner until the car was moving again, and then he likewise made a dash for it.

He stood beside me on the rear platform, hiding behind a large man in overalls, past whose shoulder he now and then peeped at Ledwich. Bob had gone to the corner above, and was already seated when Ledwich, this amateur detective—there was no doubting his amateur status—and I got on the car.

I sized up the amateur while he strained his neck peeping at Ledwich. He was small, this sleuth, and scrawny and frail. His most noticeable feature was his nose—a limp organ that twitched nervously all the time. His clothes were old and shabby, and he himself was somewhere in his fifties.

After studying him for a few minutes, I decided that he hadn't tumbled to Bob Teal's part in the game. His attention had been too firmly fixed upon Ledwich, and the distance had been too short thus far for him to discover that Bob was also tailing the big man.

So when the seat beside Bob was vacated presently, I chucked my cigarette away, went into the car, and sat down, my back toward the little man with the twitching nose.

"Drop off after a couple of blocks and go back to the apartment. Don't shadow Ledwich any more until I tell you. Just watch his place. There's a bird following him, and I want to see what he's up to," I told Bob in an undertone.

He grunted that he understood, and, after a few minutes, left the car.

At Stockton Street, Ledwich got off, the man with the twitching nose behind him and me in the rear. In that formation we paraded around town all afternoon.

The big man had business in a number of poolrooms, cigar stores, and soft-drink parlors—most of which I knew for places where you can get a bet down on any horse that's running in North America, whether at Tanforan, Tijuana, or Timonium.

Just what Ledwich did in these places, I didn't learn. I was bringing up the rear of the procession, and my interest was centered upon the mysterious little stranger. He didn't enter any of the places behind Ledwich, but loitered in their neighborhoods until Ledwich reappeared.

He had a rather strenuous time of it—laboring mightily to keep out of Ledwich's sight, and only succeeding because we were downtown, where you can get away with almost any sort of shadowing. He certainly made a lot of work for himself, dodging here and there.

After a while, Ledwich shook him.

The big man came out of a cigar store with another man. They got into an automobile that was standing beside the curb and drove away, leaving my man standing on the edge of the sidewalk twitching his nose in chagrin. There was a taxi stand just around the corner, but he either didn't know it or didn't have enough money to pay the fare.

I expected him to return to Laguna Street then, but he didn't. He led me down Kearny Street to Portsmouth, where he stretched himself out on the grass face-down, lit a black pipe, and lay looking dejectedly at the Stevenson Monument, probably without seeing it.

I sprawled on a comfortable piece of sod some distance away—between a Chinese woman with two perfectly round children and an ancient Portuguese in a gaily checkered suit—and we let the afternoon go by.

When the sun had gone low enough for the ground to become chilly, the little man got up, shook himself, and went back up Kearny Street to a cheap lunchroom, where he ate meagerly. Then he entered a hotel a few doors away, took a key from the row of hooks, and vanished down a dark corridor. Running through the register, I found that the key he had taken belonged to a room whose occupant was "John Boyd, St. Louis, Mo.," and that he had arrived the day before.

This hotel wasn't of the sort where it is safe to make inquiries, so I went down to the street again, and came to rest on the least conspicuous near-by corner.

Twilight came, and the street- and shop-lights were turned on. It got dark. The night traffic of Kearny Street went up and down past me: Filipino boys in their too-dapper clothes, bound for the inevitable blackjack game; gaudy women still heavy-eyed from their day's sleep; plain-clothes men on their way to headquarters, to report before going off duty; Chinese going to or from Chinatown; sailors in pairs, looking for action of any sort; hungry people making for the Italian and French restaurants; worried people going into the bail-bond broker's office on the corner to arrange for the release of friends and relatives whom the police had nabbed; Italians on their homeward journeys from work; odds and ends of furtive-looking citizens on various shady errands.

Midnight came, and no John Boyd, and I called it a day, and went home.

Before going to bed, I talked with Dick Foley over the wire. He said that Mrs. Estep had done nothing of any importance all day, and had received neither mail nor phone calls. I told him to stop shadowing her until I solved John Boyd's game.

I was afraid Boyd might turn his attention to the woman, and I didn't want him to discover that she was being shadowed. I had already instructed Bob Teal to simply watch Ledwich's flat—to see when he came in and went out, and with whom—and now I told Dick to do the same with the woman.

My guess on this Boyd person was that he and the woman were working together—that she had him watching Ledwich for her, so that the big man couldn't double-cross her. But that was only a guess—and I don't gamble too much on my guesses.

VII

The next morning I dressed myself up in an army shirt and shoes, an old faded cap, and a suit that wasn't downright ragged, but was shabby enough not to stand out too noticeably beside John Boyd's old clothes.

It was a little after nine o'clock when Boyd left his hotel and had breakfast at the grease-joint where he had eaten the night before. Then he went up to Laguna Street, picked himself a corner, and waited for Jacob Ledwich.

He did a lot of waiting. He waited all day, because Ledwich didn't show until after dark. But the little man was well-stocked with patience—I'll say that for him. He fidgeted, and stood on one foot and then the other, and even tried sitting on the curb for a while, but he stuck it out.

I took it easy, myself. The furnished apartment Bob Teal had rented to watch Ledwich's flat from was a ground-floor one, across the street and just a little above the corner where Boyd waited. So we could watch him and the flat with one eye.

Bob and I sat and smoked and talked all day, taking turns watching the fidgeting man on the corner and Ledwich's door.

Night had just definitely settled when Ledwich came out and started up toward the car line. I slid out into the street, and our parade was under way again—Ledwich leading, Boyd following him, and we following *him*.

Half a block of this, and I got an idea!

I'm not what you'd call a brilliant thinker—such results as I get are usually the fruits of patience, industry, and unimaginative plugging, helped out now and then, maybe, by a little luck—but I do have my flashes of intelligence. And this was one of them.

Ledwich was about a block ahead of me; Boyd half that distance. Speeding up, I passed Boyd, and caught up with Ledwich. Then I slackened my pace so as to walk beside him, though with no appearance from the rear of having any interest in him.

"Jake," I said, without turning my head, "there's a guy following you!"

The big man almost spoiled my little scheme by stopping dead still, but he caught himself in time, and, taking his cue from me, kept walking.

"Who the hell are you?" he growled.

"Don't get funny!" I snapped back, still looking and walking ahead. "It ain't my funeral. But I was coming up the street when you came out, and I seen this guy duck behind a pole until you was past, and then follow you up."

That got him.

"You sure?"

"Sure! All you got to do to prove it is turn the next corner and wait."

I was two or three steps ahead of him by this time. I turned the corner, and halted, with my back against the brick building front. Ledwich took up the same position at my side.

"Want any help?" I grinned at him—a reckless sort of grin, unless my acting was poor.

"No."

His little lumpy mouth was set ugly, and his blue eyes were hard as pebbles.

I flicked the tail of my coat aside to show him the butt of my gun.

"Want to borrow the rod?" I asked.

"No."

He was trying to figure me out, and small wonder.

"Don't mind if I stick around to see the fun, do you?" I asked mockingly.

There wasn't time for him to answer that. Boyd had quickened his steps, and now he came hurrying around the corner, his nose twitching like a tracking dog's.

Ledwich stepped into the middle of the sidewalk, so suddenly that the little man thudded into him with a grunt. For a moment they stared at each other, and there was recognition between them.

Ledwich shot one big hand out and clamped the other by a shoulder.

"What are you snooping around me for, you rat? Didn't I tell you to keep away from 'Frisco?"

"Aw, Jake!" Boyd begged. "I didn't mean no harm. I just thought that—"

Ledwich silenced him with a shake that clicked his mouth shut, and turned to me.

"A friend of mine," he sneered.

His eyes grew suspicious and hard again and ran up and down me from cap to shoes.

"How'd you know my name?" he demanded.

"A famous man like you?" I asked, in burlesque astonishment.

"Never mind the comedy!" He took a threatening step toward me. "How'd you know my name?"

"None of your damned business," I snapped.

My attitude seemed to reassure him. His face became less suspicious.

"Well," he said slowly, "I owe you something for this trick, and— How are you fixed?"

"I have been dirtier." Dirty is Pacific Coast argot for prosperous.

He looked speculatively from me to Boyd, and back.

"Know The Circle?" he asked me.

I nodded. The underworld calls Wop Healey's joint The Circle.

"If you'll meet me there to-morrow night, maybe I can put a piece of change your way."

"Nothing stirring!" I shook my head with emphasis. "I ain't circulating that prominent these days."

A fat chance I'd have of meeting him there! Wop Healey and half his customers knew me as a detective. So there was nothing to do but to try to get the impression over that I was a crook who had reasons for wanting to keep away from the more notorious hang-outs for a while. Apparently it got over. He thought a while, and then gave me his Laguna Street number.

"Drop in this time to-morrow and maybe I'll have a proposition to make you—if you've got the guts."

"I'll think it over," I said noncommittally, and turned as if to go down the street.

"Just a minute," he called, and I faced him again. "What's your name?"

"Wisher," I said. "Shine, if you want a front one."

"Shine Wisher," he repeated. "I don't remember ever hearing it before."

It would have surprised me if he had—I had made it up only about fifteen minutes before.

"You needn't yell it," I said sourly, "so that everybody in the burg *will* remember hearing it."

And with that I left him, not at all dissatisfied with myself. By tipping him off to Boyd, I had put him under obligations to me, and had led him to accept me, at least tentatively, as a fellow crook. And by making no apparent effort to gain his good graces, I had strengthened my hand that much more.

I had a date with him for the next day, when I was to be given a chance to earn—illegally, no doubt—"a piece of change."

There was a chance that this proposition he had in view for me had nothing to do with the Estep affair, but then again it might; and whether it did or not, I had my entering wedge at least a little way into Jake Ledwich's business.

I strolled around for about half an hour, and then went back to Bob Teal's apartment.

"Ledwich come back?"

"Yes," Bob said, "with that little guy of yours. They went in about half an hour ago."

"Good! Haven't seen a woman go in?"

"No."

I expected to see the first Mrs. Estep arrive sometime during the evening, but she didn't. Bob and I sat around and talked and watched Ledwich's doorway, and the hours passed.

At one o'clock Ledwich came out alone.

"I'm going to tail him, just for luck," Bob said, and caught up his cap.

Ledwich vanished around a corner, and then Bob passed out of sight behind him.

Five minutes later Bob was with me again.

"He's getting his machine out of the garage."

I jumped for the telephone and put in a rush order for a fast touring car.

Bob, at the window, called out, "Here he is!"

I joined Bob in time to see Ledwich going into his vestibule. His car stood in front of the house. A very few minutes, and Boyd and Ledwich came out together. Boyd was leaning heavily on Ledwich, who was supporting the little man with an arm across his back. We couldn't see their faces in the dark, but the little man was plainly either sick, drunk, or drugged!

Ledwich helped his companion into the touring car. The red tail-light laughed back at us for a few blocks, and then disappeared. The automobile I had ordered arrived twenty minutes later, so we sent it back unused.

At a little after three that morning, Ledwich, alone and afoot, returned from the direction of his garage. He had been gone exactly two hours.

V I I I

Neither Bob nor I went home that night, but slept in the Laguna Street apartment.

Bob went down to the corner grocer's to get what we needed for breakfast in the morning, and he brought a morning paper back with him.

I cooked breakfast while he divided his attention between Ledwich's front door and the newspaper.

"Hey!" he called suddenly, "look here!"

I ran out of the kitchen with a handful of bacon.

"What is it?"

"Listen! 'Park Murder Mystery!'" he read. "'Early this morning the body of an unidentified man was found near a driveway in Golden Gate Park. His neck had been broken, according to the police, who say that the absence of any considerable bruises on the body, as well as the orderly condition of the clothes and the ground near by, show that he did not come to his death through falling, or being struck by an automobile. It is believed that he was killed and then carried to the park in an automobile, to be left there.'"

"Boyd!" I said.

"I bet you!" Bob agreed.

And at the morgue a very little while later, we learned that we were correct. The dead man was John Boyd.

"He was dead when Ledwich brought him out of the house," Bob said. I nodded.

"He was! He was a little man, and it wouldn't have been much of a stunt for a big bruiser like Ledwich to have dragged him along with one arm the short distance from the door to the curb, pretending to be holding him up, like you do with a drunk. Let's go over to the Hall of Justice and see what the police have got on it—if anything."

At the detective bureau we hunted up O'Gar, the detective-sergeant in charge of the Homicide Detail, and a good man to work with.

"This dead man found in the park," I asked, "know anything about him?"

O'Gar pushed back his village constable's hat—a big black hat with a floppy brim that belonged in vaudeville—scratched his bullet-head, and scowled at me as if he thought I had a joke up my sleeve.

"Not a damned thing except that he's dead!" he said at last.

"How'd you like to know who he was last seen with?"

"It wouldn't hinder me any in finding out who bumped him off, and that's a fact."

"How do you like the sound of this?" I asked. "His name was John Boyd and he was living at a hotel down in the next block. The last person he was seen with was a guy who is tied up with Dr. Estep's first wife. You know—the Dr. Estep whose second wife is the woman you people are trying to prove a murder on. Does that sound interesting?"

"It does," he said. "Where do we go first?"

"This Ledwich—he's the fellow who was last seen with Boyd—is going to be a hard bird to shake down. We better try to crack the woman first—the first Mrs. Estep. There's a chance that Boyd was a pal of hers, and in that case when she finds out that Ledwich rubbed him out, she may open up and spill the works to us.

"On the other hand, if she and Ledwich are stacked up against Boyd together, then we might as well get her safely placed before we tie into him. I don't want to pull him before night, anyway. I got a date with him, and I want to try to rope him first."

Bob Teal made for the door.

"I'm going up and keep my eye on him until you're ready for him," he called over his shoulder.

"Good," I said. "Don't let him get out of town on us. If he tries to blow, have him chucked in the can."

In the lobby of the Montgomery Hotel, O'Gar and I talked to Dick Foley first. He told us that the woman was still in her room—had had her breakfast sent up. She had received neither letters, telegrams, nor phone calls since we began to watch her.

I got hold of Stacey again.

"We're going up to talk to this Estep woman, and maybe we'll take her away with us. Will you send up a maid to find out whether she's up and dressed yet? We don't want to announce ourselves ahead of time, and we don't want to burst in on her while she's in bed, or only partly dressed."

He kept us waiting about fifteen minutes, and then told us that Mrs. Estep was up and dressed.

We went up to her room, taking the maid with us.

The maid rapped on the door.

"What is it?" an irritable voice demanded.

"The maid; I want to—"

The key turned on the inside, and an angry Mrs. Estep jerked the door open. O'Gar and I advanced, O'Gar flashing his "buzzer."

"From headquarters," he said. "We want to talk to you."

O'Gar's foot was where she couldn't slam the door on us, and we were both walking ahead, so there was nothing for her to do but to retreat into the room, admitting us—which she did with no pretense of graciousness.

We closed the door, and then I threw our big load at her.

"Mrs. Estep, why did Jake Ledwich kill John Boyd?"

The expressions ran over her face like this: Alarm at Ledwich's name, fear at the word "kill," but the name John Boyd brought only bewilderment.

"Why did what?" she stammered meaninglessly, to gain time.

"Exactly," I said. "Why did Jake kill him last night in his flat, and then take him in the park and leave him?"

Another set of expressions: Increased bewilderment until I had almost finished the sentence, and then the sudden understanding of something, followed by the inevitable groping for poise. These things weren't as plain as billboards, you understand, but they were there to be read by anyone who had ever played poker—either with cards or people.

What I got out of them was that Boyd hadn't been working with or for her, and that, though she knew Ledwich had killed somebody at some time, it wasn't Boyd and it wasn't last night. Who, then? And when? Dr. Estep? Hardly! There wasn't a chance in the world that—if he had been murdered—anybody except his wife had done it—his second wife. No possible reading of the evidence could bring any other answer.

Who, then, had Ledwich killed before Boyd? Was he a wholesale murderer?

These things were flitting through my head in flashes and odd scraps while Mrs. Estep was saying:

"This is absurd! The idea of your coming up here and—"

She talked for five minutes straight, the words fairly sizzling from between her hard lips; but the words themselves didn't mean anything. She was talking for time—talking while she tried to hit upon the safest attitude to assume.

And before we could head her off, she had hit upon it—silence!

We got not another word out of her; and that is the only way in the world to beat the grilling game. The average suspect tries to talk himself out of being arrested; and it doesn't matter how shrewd a man is, or how good a liar, if he'll talk to you, and you play your cards right, you can hook him— can make him help you convict him. But if he won't talk you can't do a thing with him.

And that's how it was with this woman. She refused to pay any attention to our questions—she wouldn't speak, nod, grunt, or wave an arm in reply. She gave us a fine assortment of facial expressions, true enough, but we wanted verbal information—and we got none.

We weren't easily licked, however. Three beautiful hours of it we gave her without rest. We stormed, cajoled, threatened, and at times I think we danced; but it was no go. So in the end we took her away with us. We didn't have anything on her, but we couldn't afford to have her running around loose until we nailed Ledwich.

At the Hall of Justice we didn't book her; but simply held her as a material witness, putting her in an office with a matron and one of O'Gar's men, who were to see what they could do with her while we went after Ledwich. We had had her frisked as soon as she reached the Hall, of course; and, as we expected, she hadn't a thing of importance on her.

O'Gar and I went back to the Montgomery and gave her room a thorough overhauling—and found nothing.

"Are you sure you know what you're talking about?" the detective-sergeant asked as we left the hotel. "It's going to be a pretty joke on somebody if you're mistaken."

I let that go by without an answer.

"I'll meet you at six-thirty," I said, "and we'll go up against Ledwich."

He grunted an approval, and I set out for Vance Richmond's office.

I X

The attorney sprang up from his desk as soon as his stenographer admitted me. His face was leaner and grayer than ever; its lines had deepened, and there was a hollowness around his eyes.

"You've *got* to do something!" he cried huskily. "I have just come from the hospital. Mrs. Estep is on the point of death! A day more of this—two days at the most—and she will—"

I interrupted him, and swiftly gave him an account of the day's happenings, and what I expected, or hoped, to make out of them. But he received the news without brightening, and shook his head hopelessly.

"But don't you see," he exclaimed when I had finished, "that that won't do? I know you can find proof of her innocence in time. I'm not complaining—you've done all that could be expected, and more! But all that's no good! I've got to have—well—a miracle, perhaps.

"Suppose that you do finally get the truth out of Ledwich and the first Mrs. Estep or it comes out during their trials for Boyd's murder? Or that you even get to the bottom of the matter in three or four days? That will be too late! If I can go to Mrs. Estep and tell her she's free now, she may pull herself together, and come through. But another day of imprisonment—two days, or perhaps even two hours—and she won't need anybody to clear her. Death will have done it! I tell you, she's—"

I left Vance Richmond abruptly again. This lawyer was bound upon getting me worked up; and I like my jobs to be simply jobs—emotions are nuisances during business hours.

X

At a quarter to seven that evening, while O'Gar remained down the street, I rang Jacob Ledwich's bell. As I had stayed with Bob Teal in our apartment the previous night, I was still wearing the clothes in which I had made Ledwich's acquaintance as Shine Wisher.

Ledwich opened the door.

"Hello, Wisher!" he said without enthusiasm, and led me upstairs.

His flat consisted of four rooms, I found, running the full length and half the breadth of the building, with both front and rear exits. It was furnished with the ordinary none-too-spotless appointments of the typical moderately priced furnished flat—alike the world over.

In his front room we sat down and talked and smoked and sized one another up. He seemed a little nervous. I thought he would have been just as well satisfied if I had forgotten to show up.

"About this job you mentioned?" I asked presently.

"Sorry," he said, moistening his little lumpy mouth, "but it's all off." And then he added, obviously as an afterthought, "For the present, at least."

I guessed from that that my job was to have taken care of Boyd—but Boyd had been taken care of for good.

He brought out some whisky after a while, and we talked over it for some time, to no purpose whatever. He was trying not to appear too anxious to get rid of me, and I was cautiously feeling him out.

Piecing together things he let fall here and there, I came to the conclusion that he was a former con man who had fallen into an easier game of late years. That was in line, too, with what Porky Grout had told Bob Teal.

I talked about myself with the evasiveness that would have been natural to a crook in my situation; and made one or two carefully planned slips that would lead him to believe that I had been tied up with the "Jimmy the Riveter" hold-up mob, most of whom were doing long hitches at Walla Walla then.

He offered to lend me enough money to tide me over until I could get on my feet again. I told him I didn't need chicken feed so much as a chance to pick up some real jack.

The evening was going along, and we were getting nowhere.

"Jake," I said casually — outwardly casual, that is — "you took a big chance putting that guy out of the way like you did last night."

I meant to stir things up, and I succeeded.

His face went crazy.

A gun came out of his coat.

Firing from my pocket, I shot it out of his hand.

"Now behave!" I ordered.

He sat rubbing his benumbed hand and staring with wide eyes at the smoldering hole in my coat.

Looks like a great stunt, this shooting a gun out of a man's hand, but it's a thing that happens now and then. A man who is a fair shot (and that is exactly what I am — no more, no less) naturally and automatically shoots pretty close to the spot upon which his eyes are focused. When a man goes for his gun in front of you, you shoot at *him* — not at any particular part of him. There isn't time for that — you shoot at *him*. However, you are more than likely to be looking at his gun, and in that case it isn't altogether surprising if your bullet should hit his gun — as mine had done. But it looks impressive.

I beat out the fire around the bullet-hole in my coat, crossed the room to where his revolver had been knocked, and picked it up. I started to eject the bullets from it, but, instead, I snapped it shut again and stuck it in my pocket. Then I returned to my chair, opposite him.

"A man oughtn't to act like that," I kidded him; "he's likely to hurt somebody."

His little mouth curled up at me.

"An elbow, huh?" putting all the contempt he could in his voice; and somehow any synonym for detective seems able to hold a lot of contempt.

I might have tried to talk myself back into the Wisher role. It could have been done, but I doubted that it would be worth it; so I nodded my confession.

His brain was working now, and the passion left his face, while he sat rubbing his right hand, and his little mouth and eyes began to screw themselves up calculatingly.

I kept quiet, waiting to see what the outcome of his thinking would be. I knew he was trying to figure out just what my place in this game was. Since, to his knowledge, I had come into it no later than the previous evening, then the Boyd murder hadn't brought me in. That would leave the Estep affair — unless he was tied up in a lot of other crooked stuff that I didn't know anything about.

"You're not a city dick, are you?" he asked finally, and his voice was on the verge of friendliness now: the voice of one who wants to persuade you of something, or sell you something.

The truth, I thought, wouldn't hurt.

"No," I said, "I'm with the Continental."

He hitched his chair a little closer to the muzzle of my automatic.

"What are you after, then? Where do you come in on it?"

I tried the truth again.

"The second Mrs. Estep. She didn't kill her husband."

"You're trying to dig up enough dope to spring her?"

"Yes."

I waved him back as he tried to hitch his chair still nearer.

"How do you expect to do it?" he asked, his voice going lower and more confidential with each word.

I took still another flier at the truth.

"He wrote a letter before he died."

"Well?"

But I called a halt for the time.

"Just that," I said.

He leaned back in his chair, and his eyes and mouth grew small in thought again.

"What's your interest in the man who died last night?" he asked slowly.

"It's something on you," I said, truthfully again. "It doesn't do the second Mrs. Estep any direct good, maybe; but you and the first wife are stacked up together against her. Anything, therefore, that hurts you two will help her, somehow. I admit I'm wandering around in the dark; but I'm going ahead wherever I see a point of light—and I'll come through to daylight in the end. Nailing you for Boyd's murder is one point of light."

He leaned forward suddenly, his eyes and mouth popping open as far as they would go.

"You'll come out all right," he said very softly, "if you use a little judgment."

"What's that supposed to mean?"

"Do you think," he asked, still very softly, "that you can nail me for Boyd's murder—that you can convict me of murder?"

"I do."

But I wasn't any too sure. In the first place, though we were morally certain of it, neither Bob Teal nor I could swear that the man who had got in the machine with Ledwich was John Boyd.

We knew it was, of course, but the point is that it had been too dark for us to see his face. And, again, in the dark, we had thought him alive; it wasn't until later that we knew he had been dead when he came down the steps.

Little things, those, but a private detective on the witness stand—unless he is absolutely sure of every detail—has an unpleasant and ineffectual time of it.

"I do," I repeated, thinking these things over, "and I'm satisfied to go to the bat with what I've got on you and what I can collect between now and the time you and your accomplice go to trial."

"Accomplice?" he said, not very surprised. "That would be Edna. I suppose you've already grabbed her?"

"Yes."

He laughed.

"You'll have one sweet time getting anything out of her. In the first place, she doesn't know much, and in the second—well, I suppose you've tried, and have found out what a helpful sort she is! So don't try the old gag of pretending that she has talked!"

"I'm not pretending anything."

Silence between us for a few seconds, and then—

"I'm going to make you a proposition," he said. "You can take it or leave it. The note Dr. Estep wrote before he died was to me, and it is positive proof that he committed suicide. Give me a chance to get away—just a chance— a half-hour start—and I'll give you my word of honor to send you the letter."

"I know I can trust you," I said sarcastically.

"I'll trust you, then!" he shot back at me. "I'll turn the note over to you if you'll give me your word that I'm to have half an hour's start."

"For what?" I demanded. "Why shouldn't I take both you and the note?"

"If you can get them! But do I look like the kind of sap who would leave the note where it would be found? Do you think it's here in the room maybe?"

I didn't, but neither did I think that because he had hidden it, it couldn't be found.

"I can't think of any reason why I should bargain with you," I told him. "I've got you cold, and that's enough."

"If I can show you that your only chance of freeing the second Mrs. Estep is through my voluntary assistance, will you bargain with me?"

"Maybe—I'll listen to your persuasion, anyway."

"All right," he said, "I'm going to come clean with you. But most of the things I'm going to tell you can't be proven in court without my help; and if you turn my offer down I'll have plenty of evidence to convince the jury that these things are all false, that I never said them, and that you are trying to frame me."

That part was plausible enough. I've testified before juries all the way from the city of Washington to the state of Washington, and I've never seen one yet that wasn't anxious to believe that a private detective is a double-crossing specialist who goes around with a cold deck in one pocket, a complete forger's outfit in another, and who counts that day lost in which he railroads no innocent to the hoosegow.

X I

"There was once a young doctor in a town a long way from here," Ledwich began. "He got mixed up in a scandal—a pretty rotten one—and escaped the pen only by the skin of his teeth. The state medical board revoked his license.

"In a large city not far away, this young doc, one night when he was drunk—as he usually was in those days—told his troubles to a man he had met in a dive. The friend was a resourceful sort; and he offered, for a price, to fix the doc up with a fake diploma, so he could set up in practice in some other state.

"The young doctor took him up, and the friend got the diploma for him. The doc was the man you know as Dr. Estep, and I was the friend. The real Dr. Estep was found dead in the park this morning!"

That was news—if true!

"You see," the big man went on, "when I offered to get the phony diploma for the young doc—whose real name doesn't matter—I had in mind a forged one. Nowadays they're easy to get—there's a regular business in them—but twenty-five years ago, while you could manage it, they were hard to get. While I was trying to get one, I ran across a woman I used to work with—Edna Fife. That's the woman you know as the first Mrs. Estep.

"Edna had married a doctor—the real Dr. Humbert Estep. He was a hell of a doctor, though; and after starving with him in Philadelphia for a couple of years, she made him close up his office, and she went back to the bunko game, taking him with her. She was good at it, I'm telling you—a real cleaner—and, keeping him under her thumb all the time, she made him a pretty good worker himself.

"It was shortly after that that I met her, and when she told me all this, I offered to buy her husband's medical diploma and other credentials. I don't know whether he wanted to sell them or not—but he did what she told him, and I got the papers.

"I turned them over to the young doc, who came to San Francisco and opened an office under the name of Humbert Estep. The real Esteps promised not to use that name any more—not much of an inconvenience for them, as they changed names every time they changed addresses.

"I kept in touch with the young doctor, of course, getting my regular rake-off from him. I had him by the neck, and I wasn't foolish enough to pass up any easy money. After a year or so, I learned that he had pulled himself together and was making good. So I jumped on a train and came to San Francisco. He was doing fine; so I camped here, where I could keep my eye on him and watch out for my own interests.

"He got married about then, and, between his practice and his investments, he began to accumulate a roll. But he tightened up on me—damn him! He wouldn't be bled. I got a regular percentage of what he made, and that was all.

"For nearly twenty-five years I got it—but not a nickel over the percentage. He knew I wouldn't kill the goose that laid the golden eggs, so no matter how much I threatened to expose him, he sat tight, and I couldn't budge him. I got my regular cut, and not a nickel more.'

"That went along, as I say, for years. I was getting a living out of him, but I wasn't getting any big money. A few months ago I learned that he had cleaned up heavily in a lumber deal so I made up my mind to take him for what he had.

"During all these years I had got to know the doc pretty well. You do when you're bleeding a man—you get a pretty fair idea of what goes on in his head, and what he's most likely to do if certain things should happen. So I knew the doc pretty well.

"I knew, for instance, that he had never told his wife the truth about his past; that he had stalled her with some lie about being born in West Virginia. That was fine—for me! Then I knew that he kept a gun in his desk, and I knew why. It was kept there for the purpose of killing himself if the truth ever came out about his diploma. He figured that if, at the first hint of exposure, he wiped himself out, the authorities, out of respect for the good reputation he had built up, would hush things up.

"And his wife—even if she herself learned the truth—would be spared the shame of a public scandal. I can't see myself dying just to spare some woman's feelings, but the doc was a funny guy in some ways—and he was nutty about his wife.

"That's the way I had him figured out, and that's the way things turned out.

"My plan might sound complicated, but it was simple enough. I got hold of the real Esteps—it took a lot of hunting, but I found them at last. I brought the woman to San Francisco, and told the man to stay away.

"Everything would have gone fine if he had done what I told him; but he was afraid that Edna and I were going to double-cross him, so he came here to keep an eye on us. But I didn't know that until you put the finger on him for me.

"I brought Edna here and, without telling her any more than she had to know, drilled her until she was letter-perfect in her part.

"A couple days before she came I had gone to see the doc, and had demanded a hundred thousand cool smacks. He laughed at me, and I left, pretending to be as hot as hell.

"As soon as Edna arrived, I sent her to call on him. She asked him to perform an illegal operation on her daughter. He, of course, refused. Then she pleaded with him, loud enough for the nurse or whoever else was in the reception room to hear. And when she raised her voice she was careful to stick to words that could be interpreted the way we wanted them to. She ran off her end to perfection, leaving in tears.

"Then I sprung my other trick! I had a fellow—a fellow who's a whiz at that kind of stuff—make me a plate: an imitation of newspaper printing. It was all worded like the real article, and said that the state authorities were investigating information that a prominent surgeon in San Francisco was practicing under a license secured by false credentials. This plate measured four and an eighth by six and three-quarter inches. If you'll look at the first inside page of the *Evening Times* any day in the week you'll see a photograph just that size.

"On the day after Edna's call, I bought a copy of the first edition of the *Times*—on the street at ten in the morning. I had this scratcher friend of mine remove the photograph with acid, and print this fake article in its place.

"That evening I substituted a 'home edition' outer sheet for the one that had come with the paper we had cooked up, and made a switch as soon as the doc's newsboy made his delivery. There was nothing to that part of it. The kid just tossed the paper into the vestibule. It's simply a case of duck into the doorway, trade papers, and go on, leaving the loaded one for the doc to read."

I was trying not to look too interested, but my ears were cocked for every word. At the start, I had been prepared for a string of lies. But I knew now that he was telling me the truth! Every syllable was a boast; he was half-drunk with appreciation of his own cleverness—the cleverness with which he had planned and carried out his program of treachery and murder.

I knew that he was telling the truth, and I suspected that he was telling more of it than he had intended. He was fairly bloated with vanity—the vanity that fills the crook almost invariably after a little success, and makes him ripe for the pen.

His eyes glistened, and his little mouth smiled triumphantly around the words that continued to roll out of it.

"The doc read the paper, all right—and shot himself. But first he wrote and mailed a note—to me. I didn't figure on his wife's being accused of killing him. That was plain luck.

"I figured that the fake piece in the paper would be overlooked in the excitement. Edna would then go forward, claiming to be his first wife; and his shooting himself after her first call, with what the nurse had overheard, would make his death seem a confession that Edna *was* his wife.

"I was sure that she would stand up under any sort of an investigation. Nobody knew anything about the doc's real past; except what he had told them, which would be found false.

"Edna had really married a Dr. Humbert Estep in Philadelphia in '96; and the twenty-seven years that had passed since then would do a lot to hide the fact that that Dr. Humbert Estep wasn't this Dr. Humbert Estep.

"All I wanted to do was convince the doc's real wife and her lawyers that she wasn't really his wife at all. And we did that! Everybody took it for granted that Edna was the legal wife.

"The next play would have been for Edna and the real wife to have reached some sort of an agreement about the estate, whereby Edna would have got the bulk—or at least half—of it; and nothing would have been made public.

"If worse came to worst, we were prepared to go to court. We were sitting pretty! But I'd have been satisfied with half the estate. It would have come to a few hundred thousand at the least, and that would have been plenty for me—even deducting the twenty thousand I had promised Edna.

"But when the police grabbed the doc's wife and charged her with his murder, I saw my way into the whole roll. All I had to do was sit tight and wait until they convicted her. Then the court would turn the entire pile over to Edna.

"I had the only evidence that would free the doc's wife: the note he had written me. But I couldn't—even if I had wanted to—have turned it in without exposing my hand. When he read that fake piece in the paper, he tore it out, wrote his message to me across the face of it, and sent it to me. So the note is a dead give-away. However, I didn't have any intention of publishing it, anyhow.

"Up to this point everything had gone like a dream. All I had to do was wait until it was time to cash in on my brains. And that's the time that the real Humbert Estep picked out to mess up the works.

"He shaved his mustache off, put on some old clothes, and came snooping around to see that Edna and I didn't run out on him. As if he could have stopped us! After you put the finger on him for me, I brought him up here.

"I intended salving him along until I could find a place to keep him until all the cards had been played. That's what I was going to hire you for—to take care of him.

"But we got to talking, and wrangling, and I had to knock him down. He didn't get up, and I found that he was dead. His neck was broken. There was nothing to do but take him out to the park and leave him.

"I didn't tell Edna. She didn't have a lot of use for him, as far as I could see, but you can't tell how women will take things. Anyhow, she'll stick, now that it's done. She's on the up and up all the time. And if she should talk, she can't do a lot of damage. She only knows her own part of the lay.

"All this long-winded story is so you'll know just exactly what you're up against. Maybe you think you can dig up the proof of these things I have told you. You can this far. You can prove that Edna wasn't the doc's wife. You can prove that I've been blackmailing him. But you can't prove that the doc's wife didn't *believe* that Edna was his real wife! It's her word against Edna's and mine.

"We'll swear that we had convinced her of it, which will give her a motive. You can't prove that the phony news article I told you about ever existed. It'll sound like a hophead's dream to a jury.

"You can't tie last night's murder on me—I've got an alibi that will knock your hat off! I can prove that I left here with a friend of mine who was drunk, and that I took him to his hotel and put him to bed, with the help of a night clerk and a bellboy. And what have you got against that? The word of two private detectives. Who'll believe you?

"You can convict me of conspiracy to defraud, or something—maybe. But, regardless of that, you can't free Mrs. Estep without my help.

"Turn me loose and I'll give you the letter the doc wrote me. It's the goods, right enough! In his own handwriting, written across the face of the fake newspaper story—which ought to fit the torn place in the paper that the police are supposed to be holding—and he wrote that he was going to kill himself, in words almost that plain."

That would turn the trick—there was no doubt of it. And I believed Ledwich's story. The more I thought it over the better I liked it. It fitted into the facts everywhere. But I wasn't enthusiastic about giving this big crook his liberty.

"Don't make me laugh!" I said. "I'm going to put you away and free Mrs. Estep—both."

"Go ahead and try it! You're up against it without the letter; and you don't think a man with brains enough to plan a job like this one would be foolish enough to leave the note where it could be found, do you?"

I wasn't especially impressed with the difficulty of convicting this Ledwich and freeing the dead man's widow. His scheme—that cold-blooded zigzag of treachery for everybody he had dealt with, including his latest accomplice, Edna Estep—wasn't as air-tight as he thought it. A week in which to run out a few lines in the East, and— But a week was just what I didn't have!

Vance Richmond's words were running through my head: "But another day of imprisonment—two days, or perhaps even two hours—and she won't need anybody to clear her. Death will have done it!"

If I was going to do Mrs. Estep any good, I had to move quick. Law or no law, her life was in my fat hands. This man before me—his eyes bright and hopeful now and his mouth anxiously pursed—was thief, blackmailer, double-crosser, and at least twice a murderer. I hated to let him walk out. But there was the woman dying in a hospital. . . .

X I I

Keeping my eye on Ledwich, I went to the telephone, and got Vance Richmond on the wire at his residence.

"How is Mrs. Estep?" I asked.

"Weaker! I talked with the doctor half an hour ago, and he says—"

I cut in on him; I didn't want to listen to the details.

"Get over to the hospital, and be where I can reach you by phone. I may have news for you before the night is over."

"What— Is there a chance? Are you—"

I didn't promise him anything. I hung up the receiver and spoke to Ledwich. "I'll do this much for you. Slip me the note, and I'll give you your gun and put you out the back door. There's a bull on the corner out front, and I can't take you past him."

He was on his feet, beaming.

"Your word on it?" he demanded.

"Yes—get going!"

He went past me to the phone, gave a number (which I made a note of), and then spoke hurriedly into the instrument.

"This is Shuler. Put a boy in a taxi with that envelope I gave you to hold for me, and send him out here right away."

He gave his address, said "Yes" twice, and hung up.

There was nothing surprising about his unquestioning acceptance of my word. He couldn't afford to doubt that I'd play fair with him. And, also, all successful bunko men come in time to believe that the world—except for themselves—is populated by a race of human sheep who may be trusted to conduct themselves with true sheeplike docility.

Ten minutes later the doorbell rang. We answered it together, and Ledwich took a large envelope from a messenger boy, while I memorized the number on the boy's cap. Then we went back to the front room.

Ledwich slit the envelope and passed its contents to me: a piece of rough-torn newspaper. Across the face of the fake article he had told me about was written a message in a jerky hand.

I wouldn't have suspected you, Ledwich, of such profound stupidity. My last thought will be—this bullet that ends my life also ends your years of leisure. You'll have to go to work now.　　　　　　　　*Estep.*

The doctor had died game!

I took the envelope from the big man, put the death note in it, and put them in my pocket. Then I went to a front window, flattening a cheek against the glass until I could see O'Gar, dimly outlined in the night, patiently standing where I had left him hours before.

"The city dick is still on the corner," I told Ledwich. "Here's your gat"—holding out the gun I had shot from his fingers a little while back—"take it, and blow through the back door. Remember, that's all I'm offering you—the gun and a fair start. If you play square with me, I'll not do anything to help find you—unless I have to keep myself in the clear."

"Fair enough!"

He grabbed the gun, broke it to see that it was still loaded, and wheeled toward the rear of the flat. At the door he pulled up, hesitated, and faced me again. I kept him covered with my automatic.

"Will you do me one favor I didn't put in the bargain?" he asked.

"What is it?"

"That note of the doc's is in an envelope with my handwriting and maybe my fingerprints on it. Let me put it in a fresh envelope, will you? I don't want to leave any broader trail behind than I have to."

With my left hand—my right being busy with the gun—I fumbled for the envelope and tossed it to him. He took a plain envelope from the table, wiped it carefully with his handkerchief, put the note in it, taking care not to touch it with the balls of his fingers, and passed it back to me; and I put it in my pocket.

I had a hard time to keep from grinning in his face.

That fumbling with the handkerchief told me that the envelope in my pocket was empty, that the death note was in Ledwich's possession—though I hadn't seen it pass there. He had worked one of his bunko tricks upon me.

"Beat it!" I snapped, to keep from laughing in his face.

He spun on his heel. His feet pounded against the floor. A door slammed in the rear.

I tore into the envelope he had given me. I needed to be sure he had double-crossed me.

The envelope was empty.

Our agreement was wiped out.

I sprang to the front window, threw it wide open, and leaned out. O'Gar saw me immediately—clearer than I could see him. I swung my arm in a wide gesture toward the rear of the house. O'Gar set out for the alley on the run. I dashed back through Ledwich's flat to the kitchen, and stuck my head out of an already open window.

I could see Ledwich against the white-washed fence—throwing the back gate open, plunging through it into the alley.

O'Gar's squat bulk appeared under a light at the end of the alley.

Ledwich's revolver was in his hand. O'Gar's wasn't—not quite.

Ledwich's gun swung up—the hammer clicked.

O'Gar's gun coughed fire.

Ledwich fell with a slow, revolving motion over against the white fence, gasped once or twice, and went down in a pile.

I walked slowly down the stairs to join O'Gar; slowly, because it isn't a nice thing to look at a man you've deliberately sent to his death. Not even if it's the surest way of saving an innocent life, and if the man who dies is a Jake Ledwich—altogether treacherous.

"How come?" O'Gar asked, when I came into the alley, where he stood looking down at the dead man.

"He got out on me," I said simply.

"He must've."

I stooped and searched the dead man's pockets until I found the suicide note, still crumpled in the handkerchief. O'Gar was examining the dead man's revolver.

"Lookit!" he exclaimed. "Maybe this ain't my lucky day! He snapped at me once, and his gun missed fire. No wonder! Somebody must've been using an ax on it—the firing pin's broke clean off!"

"Is that so?" I asked; just as if I hadn't discovered, when I first picked the revolver up, that the bullet which had knocked it out of Ledwich's hand had made it harmless.

THE ASSISTANT
MURDERER

Gold on the door, edged with black, said ALEXANDER RUSH, PRIVATE DETECTIVE. Inside, an ugly man sat tilted back in a chair, his feet on a yellow desk.

The office was in no way lovely. Its furnishings were few and old with the shabby age of second-handdom. A shredding square of dun carpet covered the floor. On one buff wall hung a framed certificate that licensed Alexander Rush to pursue the calling of private detective in the city of Baltimore in accordance with certain red-numbered regulations. A map of the city hung on another wall. Beneath the map a frail bookcase, small as it was, gaped emptily around its contents: a yellowish railway guide, a smaller hotel directory, and street and telephone directories for Baltimore, Washington, and Philadelphia. An insecure oaken clothes-tree held up a black derby and a black overcoat beside a white sink in one corner. The four chairs in the room were unrelated to one another in everything except age. The desk's scarred top held, in addition to the proprietor's feet, a telephone, a black-clotted inkwell, a disarray of papers having generally to do with criminals who had escaped from one prison or another, and a grayed ashtray that held as much ash and as many black cigar stumps as a tray of its size could expect to hold.

An ugly office—the proprietor was uglier.

His head was squatly pear-shaped. Excessively heavy, wide, blunt at the jaw, it narrowed as it rose to the close-cropped, erect grizzled hair that sprouted above a low, slanting forehead. His complexion was of a rich dark-ish red, his skin tough in texture and rounded over thick cushions of fat.

These fundamental inelegancies were by no means all his ugliness. Things had been done to his features.

One way you looked at his nose, you said it was crooked. Another way, you said it could not be crooked; it had no shape at all. Whatever your opinion of its form, you could not deny its color. Veins had broken to pencil its already florid surface with brilliant red stars and curls and puzzling scrawls that looked as if they must have some secret meanings. His lips were thick, tough-skinned. Between them showed the brassy glint of two solid rows of gold teeth, the lower row lapping the upper, so undershot was the bulging jaw. His eyes—small, deep-set, and pale blue of iris—were bloodshot to a degree that made you think he had a heavy cold. His ears accounted for some of his earlier years: they were the thickened, twisted cauliflower ears of the pugilist.

A man of forty-something, ugly, sitting tilted back in his chair, feet on desk.

The gilt-labeled door opened and another man came into the office. Perhaps ten years younger than the man at the desk, he was, roughly speaking, everything that one was not. Fairly tall, slender, fair-skinned, brown-eyed, he would have been as little likely to catch your eye in a gambling-house as in an art gallery. His clothes—suit and hat were gray—were fresh and properly pressed, and even fashionable in that inconspicuous manner which is one sort of taste. His face was likewise unobtrusive, which was surprising when you considered how narrowly it missed handsomeness through the least meagerness of mouth—a mark of the too-cautious man.

Two steps into the office he hesitated, brown eyes glancing from shabby furnishings to ill-visaged proprietor. So much ugliness seemed to disconcert the man in gray. An apologetic smile began on his lips, as if he were about to murmur, "I beg your pardon, I'm in the wrong office."

But when he finally spoke it was otherwise. He took another step forward, asking uncertainly:

"You are Mr. Rush?"

"Yeah." The detective's voice was hoarse with a choking harshness that seemed to corroborate the heavy-cold testimony of his eyes. He put his feet down on the floor and jerked a fat, red hand at a chair. "Sit down, sir."

The man in gray sat down, tentatively upright on the chair's front edge.

"Now what can I do for you?" Alec Rush croaked amiably.

"I want—I wish—I would like—" and further than that the man in gray said nothing.

"Maybe you'd better just tell me what's wrong," the detective suggested. "Then I'll know what you want of me." He smiled.

There was kindliness in Alec Rush's smile, and it was not easily resisted. True, his smile was a horrible grimace out of a nightmare, but that was its charm. When your gentle-countenanced man smiles there is small gain: his smile expresses little more than his reposed face. But when Alec Rush distorted his ogre's mask so that jovial friendliness peeped incongruously from his savage red eyes, from his brutal metal-studded mouth—then that was a heartening, a winning thing.

"Yes, I daresay that would be better." The man in gray sat back in his chair, more comfortably, less transiently. "Yesterday on Fayette Street, I met a—a young woman I know. I hadn't—we hadn't met for several months. That isn't really pertinent, however. But after we separated—we had talked for a few minutes—I saw a man. That is, he came out of a doorway and went down the street in the same direction she had taken, and I got the idea he was following her. She turned into Liberty Street and he did likewise. Countless people walk along that same route, and the idea that he was following her seemed fantastic, so much so that I dismissed it and went on about my business.

"But I couldn't get the notion out of my head. It seemed to me there had been something peculiarly intent in his carriage, and no matter how much I told myself the notion was absurd, it persisted in worrying me. So last night, having nothing especial to do, I drove out to the neighborhood of— of the young woman's house. And I saw the same man again. He was standing on a corner two blocks from her house. It was the same man—I'm certain of it. I tried to watch him, but while I was finding a place for my car he disappeared and I did not see him again. Those are the circumstances. Now will you look into it, learn if he is actually following her, and why?"

"Sure," the detective agreed hoarsely, "but didn't you say anything to the lady or to any of her family?"

The man in gray fidgeted in his chair and looked at the stringy dun carpet.

"No, I didn't. I didn't want to disturb her, frighten her, and still don't. After all, it may be no more than a meaningless coincidence, and—and— well—I don't— That's impossible! What I had in mind was for you to find out what is wrong, if anything, and remedy it without my appearing in the matter at all."

"Maybe, but, mind you, I'm not saying I will. I'd want to know more first."

"More? You mean more—"

"More about you and her."

"But there is nothing about us!" the man in gray protested. "It is exactly as I have told you. I might add that the young woman is—is married, and that until yesterday I had not seen her since her marriage."

"Then your interest in her is—?" The detective let the husky interrogation hang incompleted in the air.

"Of friendship—past friendship."

"Yeah. Now who is this young woman?"

The man in gray fidgeted again.

"See here, Rush," he said, coloring, "I'm perfectly willing to tell you, and shall, of course, but I don't want to tell you unless you are going to handle this thing for me. I mean I don't want to be bringing her name into it if—if you aren't. Will you?"

Alec Rush scratched his grizzled head with a stubby forefinger.

"I don't know," he growled. "That's what I'm trying to find out. I can't take a hold of a job that might be anything. I've got to know that you're on the up-and-up."

Puzzlement disturbed the clarity of the younger man's brown eyes.

"But I didn't think you'd be—" He broke off and looked away from the ugly man.

"Of course you didn't." A chuckle rasped in the detective's burly throat, the chuckle of a man touched in a once-sore spot that is no longer tender. He raised a big hand to arrest his prospective client in the act of rising from his chair. "What you did, on a guess, was to go to one of the big agencies and tell 'em your story. They wouldn't touch it unless you cleared up the fishy points. Then you ran across my name, remembered I was chucked out of the department a couple of years ago. 'There's my man,' you said to yourself, 'a baby who won't be so choicy!'"

The man in gray protested with head and gesture and voice that this was not so. But his eyes were sheepish.

Alec Rush laughed harshly again and said, "No matter. I ain't sensitive about it. I can talk about politics, and being made the goat, and all that, but the records show the Board of Police Commissioners gave me the air for a list of crimes that would stretch from here to Canton Hollow. All right, sir! I'll take your job. It sounds phony, but maybe it ain't. It'll cost you fifteen a day and expenses."

"I can see that it sounds peculiar," the younger man assured the detective, "but you'll find that it's quite all right. You'll want a retainer, of course."

"Yes, say fifty."

The man in gray took five new ten-dollar bills from a pigskin billfold and put them on the desk. With a thick pen Alec Rush began to make muddy ink-marks on a receipt blank.

"Your name?" he asked.

"I would rather not. I'm not to appear in it, you know. My name would not be of importance, would it?"

Alec Rush put down his pen and frowned at his client.

"Now! Now!" he grumbled good-naturedly. "How am I going to do business with a man like you?"

The man in gray was sorry, even apologetic, but he was stubborn in his reticence. He would not give his name. Alec Rush growled and complained, but pocketed the five ten-dollar bills.

"It's in your favor, maybe," the detective admitted as he surrendered, "though it ain't to your credit. But if you were off-color I guess you'd have sense enough to fake a name. Now this young woman—who is she?"

"Mrs. Hubert Landow."

"Well, well, we've got a name at last! And where does Mrs. Landow live?"

"On Charles-Street Avenue," the man in gray said, and gave a number.

"Her description?"

"She is twenty-two or -three years old, rather tall, slender in an athletic way, with auburn hair, blue eyes, and very white skin."

"And her husband? You know him?"

"I have seen him. He is about my age—thirty—but larger than I, a tall, broad-shouldered man of the clean-cut blond type."

"And your mystery man? What does he look like?"

"He's quite young, not more than twenty-two at the most, and not very large—medium size, perhaps, or a little under. He's very dark, with high cheek-bones and a large nose. High, straight shoulders, too, but not broad. He walks with small, almost mincing, steps."

"Clothes?"

"He was wearing a brown suit and a tan cap when I saw him on Fayette Street yesterday afternoon. I suppose he wore the same last night, but I'm not positive."

"I suppose you'll drop in here for my reports," the detective wound up, "since I won't know where to send them to you?"

"Yes." The man in gray stood up and held out his hand. "I'm very grateful to you for undertaking this, Mr. Rush."

Alec Rush said that was all right. They shook hands, and the man in gray went out.

The ugly man waited until his client had had time to turn off into the corridor that led to the elevators. Then the detective said, "Now, Mr. Man!" got up from his chair, took his hat from the clothes-tree in the corner, locked his office door behind him, and ran down the back stairs.

like Spade

He ran with the deceptive heavy agility of a bear. There was something bearlike, too, in the looseness with which his blue suit hung on his stout body, and in the set of his heavy shoulders—sloping, limber-jointed shoulders whose droop concealed much of their bulk.

He gained the ground floor in time to see the gray back of his client issuing into the street. In his wake Alec Rush sauntered. Two blocks, a turn to the left, another block, and a turn to the right. The man in gray went into the office of a trust company that occupied the ground floor of a large office building.

The rest was the mere turning of a hand. Half a dollar to a porter: the man in gray was Ralph Millar, assistant cashier.

Darkness was settling in Charles-Street Avenue when Alec Rush, in a modest black coupé, drove past the address Ralph Millar had given him. The house was large in the dusk, spaced from its fellows as from the paving by moderate expanses of fenced lawn.

Alec Rush drove on, turned to the left at the first crossing, again to the left at the next, and at the next. For half an hour he guided his car along a many-angled turning and returning route until, when finally he stopped beside the curb at some distance from, but within sight of, the Landow house, he had driven through every piece of thoroughfare in the vicinity of that house.

He had not seen Millar's dark, high-shouldered young man.

Lights burned brightly in Charles-Street Avenue, and the night traffic began to purr southward into the city. Alec Rush's heavy body slumped against the wheel of his coupé while he filled its interior with pungent fog from a black cigar, and held patient, bloodshot eyes on what he could see of the Landow residence.

Three-quarters of an hour passed, and there was motion in the house. A limousine left the garage in the rear for the front door. A man and a woman, faintly distinguishable at that distance, left the house for the limousine. The limousine moved out into the cityward current. The third car behind it was Alec Rush's modest coupé.

Except for a perilous moment at North Avenue, when the interfering cross-stream of traffic threatened to separate him from his quarry, Alec Rush followed the limousine without difficulty. In front of a Howard Street theater it discharged its freight: a youngish man and a young woman, both tall, evening-clad, and assuringly in agreement with the descriptions the detective had got from his client.

The Landows went into the already dark theater while Alec Rush was buying his ticket. In the light of the first intermission he discovered them again. Leaving his seat for the rear of the auditorium, he found an angle from which he could study them for the remaining five minutes of illumination.

Hubert Landow's head was rather small for his stature, and the blond hair with which it was covered threatened each moment to escape from its imposed smoothness into crisp curls. His face, healthily ruddy, was handsome in a muscular, very masculine way, not indicative of any great mental nimbleness. His wife had that beauty which needs no cataloguing. However, her hair was auburn, her eyes blue, her skin white, and she looked a year or two older than the maximum twenty-three Millar had allowed her.

While the intermission lasted Hubert Landow talked to his wife eagerly, and his bright eyes were the eyes of a lover. Alec Rush could not see Mrs. Landow's eyes. He saw her replying now and again to her husband's words. Her profile showed no answering eagerness. She did not show she was bored.

Midway through the last act, Alec Rush left the theater to maneuver his coupé into a handy position from which to cover the Landows' departure. But their limousine did not pick them up when they left the theater. They turned down Howard Street afoot, going to a rather garish second-class restaurant, where an abbreviated orchestra succeeded by main strength in concealing its smallness from the ear.

His coupé conveniently parked, Alec Rush found a table from which he could watch his subjects without being himself noticeable. Husband still wooed wife with incessant, eager talking. Wife was listless, polite, unkindled. Neither more than touched the food before them. They danced once, the woman's face as little touched by immediate interest as when she listened to her husband's words. A beautiful face, but empty.

The minute hand of Alec Rush's nickel-plated watch had scarcely begun its last climb of the day from where VI is inferred to XII when the Landows left the restaurant. The limousine—against its side a young Norfolk-jacketed Negro smoking—was two doors away. It bore them back to their house. The detective having seen them into the house, having seen the limousine into the garage, drove his coupé again around and around through the neighboring thoroughfares. And saw nothing of Millar's dark young man.

Then Alec Rush went home and to bed.

At eight o'clock the next morning ugly man and modest coupé were stationary in Charles-Street Avenue again. Male Charles-Street Avenue went with the sun on its left toward its offices. As the morning aged and the shadows grew shorter and thicker, so, generally, did the individuals who composed this morning procession. Eight o'clock was frequently young and slender and brisk, Eight-thirty less so, Nine still less, and rear-guard Ten o'clock was preponderantly neither young nor slender, and more often sluggish than brisk.

Into this rear guard, though physically he belonged to no later period than eight-thirty, a blue roadster carried Hubert Landow. His broad shoulders were blue-coated, his blond hair gray-capped, and he was alone in the roadster. With a glance around to make sure Millar's dark young man was not in sight, Alec Rush turned his coupé in the blue car's wake.

They rode swiftly into the city, down into its financial center, where Hubert Landow deserted his roadster before a Redwood Street stockbroker's office. The morning had become noon before Landow was in the street again, turning his roadster northward.

When shadowed and shadower came to rest again they were in Mount Royal Avenue. Landow got out of his car and strode briskly into a large apartment building. A block distant, Alec Rush lighted a black cigar and sat still in his coupé. Half an hour passed. Alec Rush turned his head and sank his gold teeth deep into his cigar.

Scarcely twenty feet behind the coupé, in the doorway of a garage, a dark young man with high cheek-bones, high, straight shoulders, loitered. His nose was large. His suit was brown, as were the eyes with which he seemed to pay no especial attention to anything through the thin blue drift of smoke from the tip of a drooping cigarette.

Alec Rush took his cigar from his mouth to examine it, took a knife from his pocket to trim the bitten end, restored cigar to mouth and knife to pocket, and thereafter was as indifferent to all Mount Royal Avenue as the dark youth behind him. The one drowsed in his doorway. The other dozed in his car. And the afternoon crawled past one o'clock, past one-thirty.

Hubert Landow came out of the apartment building, vanished swiftly in his blue roadster. His going stirred neither of the motionless men, scarcely their eyes. Not until another fifteen minutes had gone did either of them move.

Then the dark youth left his doorway. He moved without haste, up the street, with short, almost mincing, steps. The back of Alec Rush's black-derbied head was to the youth when he passed the coupé, which may have been chance, for none could have said that the ugly man had so much as glanced at the other since his first sight of him. The dark young man let his eyes rest on the detective's back without interest as he passed. He went on up the street toward the apartment building Landow had visited, up its steps, and out of sight into it.

When the dark young man had disappeared, Alec Rush threw away his cigar, stretched, yawned, and awakened the coupé's engine. Four blocks and two turnings from Mount Royal Avenue, he got out of the automobile, leaving it locked and empty in front of a graystone church. He walked back to Mount Royal Avenue, to halt on a corner two blocks above his earlier position.

He had another half-hour of waiting before the dark young man appeared. Alec Rush was buying a cigar in a glass-fronted cigar store when the other passed. The young man boarded a street car at North Avenue and found a seat. The detective boarded the same car at the next corner and stood on the rear platform. Warned by an indicative forward hitching of the young man's shoulders and head, Alec Rush was the first passenger off the car at Madison Avenue, and the first aboard a southbound car there. And again, he was off first at Franklin Street.

The dark youth went straight to a rooming-house in this street, while the detective came to rest beside the window of a corner drug store specializing in theatrical make-up. There he loafed until half-past three. When the dark young man came into the street again it was to walk—Alec Rush behind him—to Eutaw Street, board a car, and ride to Camden Station.

There, in the waiting-room, the dark young man met a young woman who frowned and asked:

"Where in the hell have you been at?"

Passing them, the detective heard the petulant greeting, but the young man's reply was pitched too low for him to catch, nor did he hear anything else the young woman said. They talked for perhaps ten minutes, standing together in a deserted end of the waiting-room, so that Alec Rush could not have approached them without making himself conspicuous.

The young woman seemed to be impatient, urgent. The young man seemed to explain, to reassure. Now and then he gestured with the ugly, deft hands of a skilled mechanic. His companion became more agreeable. She was short, square, as if carved economically from a cube. Consistently, her nose also was short and her chin square. She had, on the whole, now that her earlier displeasure was passing, a merry face, a pert, pugnacious, rich-blooded face that advertised inexhaustible vitality. That advertisement was in every feature, from the live ends of her cut brown hair to the earth-gripping pose of her feet on the cement flooring. Her clothes were dark, quiet, expensive, but none too gracefully worn, hanging just the least bit bunchily here and there on her sturdy body.

Nodding vigorously several times, the young man at length tapped his cap-visor with two careless fingers and went out into the street. Alec Rush let him depart unshadowed. But when, walking slowly out to the iron train-shed gates, along them to the baggage window, thence to the street door, the young woman passed out of the station, the ugly man was behind her. He was still behind her when she joined the four o'clock shopping crowd at Lexington Street.

The young woman shopped with the whole-hearted air of one with nothing else on her mind. In the second department store she visited, Alec Rush left her looking at a display of laces while he moved as swiftly and directly as intervening shoppers would permit toward a tall, thick-shouldered, gray-haired woman in black, who seemed to be waiting for someone near the foot of a flight of stairs.

"Hello, Alec!" she said when he touched her arm, and her humorous eyes actually looked with pleasure at his uncouth face. "What are you doing in my territory?"

"Got a booster for you," he mumbled. "The chunky girl in blue at the lace counter. Make her?"

The store detective looked and nodded.

"Yes. Thanks, Alec. You're sure she's boosting, of course?"

"Now, Minnie!" he complained, his rasping voice throttled down to a metallic growl. "Would I be giving you a bum rumble? She went south with a couple of silk pieces, and it's more than likely she's got herself some lace by now."

"Um-hmm," said Minnie. "Well, when she sticks her foot on the sidewalk, I'll be with her."

Alec Rush put his hand on the store detective's arm again.

"I want a line on her," he said. "What do you say we tail her around and see what she's up to before we knock her over?"

"If it doesn't take all day," the woman agreed. And when the chunky girl in blue presently left the lace counter and the store, the detectives followed, into another store, ranging too far behind her to see any thieving she might have done, content to keep her under surveillance. From this last store their prey went down to where Pratt Street was dingiest, into a dingy three-story house of furnished flats.

Two blocks away a policeman was turning a corner.

"Take a plant on the joint while I get a copper," Alex Rush ordered.

When he returned with the policeman the store detective was waiting in the vestibule.

"Second floor," she said.

Behind her the house's street door stood open to show a dark hallway and the foot of a tattered-carpeted flight of steps. Into this dismal hallway appeared a slovenly thin woman in rumpled gray cotton, saying whiningly as she came forward, "What do you want? I keep a respectable house, I'll have you understand, and I—"

"Chunky, dark-eyed girl living here," Alec Rush croaked. "Second floor. Take us up."

The woman's scrawny face sprang into startled lines, faded eyes wide, as if mistaking the harshness of the detective's voice for the harshness of great emotion.

"Why—why—" she stammered, and then remembered the first principle of shady rooming-house management—never to stand in the way of the police. "I'll take you up," she agreed, and, hitching her wrinkled skirt in one hand, led the way up the stairs.

Her sharp fingers tapped on a door near the head of the stairs.

"Who's that?" a casually curt feminine voice asked.

"Landlady."

The chunky girl in blue, without her hat now, opened the door. Alec Rush moved a big foot forward to hold it open, while the landlady said, "This is her," the policeman said, "You'll have to come along," and Minnie said, "Dearie, we want to come in and talk to you."

"My God!" exclaimed the girl. "There'd be just as much sense to it if you'd all jumped out at me and yelled 'Boo!'"

"This ain't any way," Alec Rush rasped, moving forward, grinning his hideous friendly grin. "Let's go in where we can talk it over."

Merely by moving his loose-jointed bulk a step this way, a half-step that, turning his ugly face on this one and that one, he herded the little group as he wished, sending the landlady discontentedly away, marshaling the others into the girl's rooms.

"Remember, I got no idea what this is all about," said the girl when they were in her living-room, a narrow room where blue fought with red without ever compromising on purple. "I'm easy to get along with, and if you think this is a nice place to talk about whatever you want to talk about, go ahead! But if you're counting on me talking, too, you'd better smart me up."

"Boosting, dearie," Minnie said, leaning forward to pat the girl's arm. "I'm at Goodbody's."

"You think I've been shoplifting? Is that the idea?"

"Yeah. Exactly. Uh-huh. That's what." Alec Rush left her no doubt on the point.

The girl narrowed her eyes, puckered her red mouth, squinted sidewise at the ugly man.

"It's all right with me," she announced, "so long as Goodbody's is hanging the rap on me—somebody I can sue for a million when it flops. I've got nothing to say. Take me for my ride."

"You'll get your ride, sister," the ugly man rasped good-naturedly. "Nobody's going to beat you out of it. But do you mind if I look around your place a little first?"

"Got anything with a judge's name on it that says you can?"

"No."

"Then you don't get a peep!"

Alec Rush chuckled, thrust his hands into his trouser-pockets, and began to wander through the rooms, of which there were three. Presently he came out of the bedroom carrying a photograph in a silver frame.

"Who's this?" he asked the girl.

"Try and find out!"

"I am trying," he lied.

"You big bum!" said she. "You couldn't find water in the ocean!"

Alec Rush laughed with coarse heartiness. He could afford to. The photograph in his hand was of Hubert Landow.

TWILIGHT WAS around the graystone church when the owner of the deserted coupé returned to it. The chunky girl—Polly Vanness was the name she had given—had been booked and lodged in a cell in the Southwestern Police Station. Quantities of stolen goods had been found in her flat. Her harvest of that afternoon was still on her person when Minnie and a police matron searched her. She had refused to talk. The detective had said nothing to her about his knowledge of the photograph's subject, or of her meeting in the railroad station with the dark young man. Nothing found in her rooms threw any light on either of these things.

Having eaten his evening meal before coming back to his car, Alec Rush now drove out to Charles-Street Avenue. Lights glowed normally in the Landow house when he passed it. A little beyond it he turned his coupé so that it pointed toward the city, and brought it to rest in a tree-darkened curb-side spot within sight of the house.

The night went along and no one left or entered the Landow house.

Fingernails clicked on the coupé's glass door.

A man stood there. Nothing could be said of him in the darkness except that he was not large, and that to have escaped the detective's notice until now he must have stealthily stalked the car from the rear.

Alec Rush put out a hand and the door swung open.

"Got a match?" the man asked.

The detective hesitated, said, "Yeah," and held out a box.

A match scraped and flared into a dark young face: large nose, high cheek-bones: the young man Alec Rush had shadowed that afternoon.

But recognition, when it was voiced, was voiced by the dark young man.

"I thought it was you," he said simply as he applied the flaming match to his cigarette. "Maybe you don't know me, but I knew you when you were on the force."

The ex-detective-sergeant gave no meaning at all to a husky "Yeah."

"I thought it was you in the heap on Mount Royal this afternoon, but I couldn't make sure," the young man continued, entering the coupé, sitting beside the detective, closing the door. "Scuttle Zeipp's me. I ain't as well-known as Napoleon, so if you've never heard of me there's no hard feelings."

"Yeah."

"That's the stuff! When you once think up a good answer, stick to it." Scuttle Zeipp's face was a sudden bronze mask in the glow of his cigarette. "The same answer'll do for my next question. You're interested in these here Landows? Yeah," he added in hoarse mimicry of the detective's voice.

Another inhalation lighted his face, and his words came smokily out as the glow faded.

"You ought to want to know what I'm doing hanging around 'em. I ain't tight. I'll tell you. I've been slipped half a grand to bump off the girl—twice. How do you like that?"

"I hear you," said Alec Rush. "But anybody can talk that knows the words."

"Talk? Sure it's talk," Zeipp admitted cheerfully. "But so's it talk when the judge says 'hanged by the neck until dead and may God have mercy on your soul!' Lots of things are talk, but that don't always keep 'em from being real."

"Yeah?"

"Yeah, brother, yeah! Now listen to this: it's one for the cuff. A certain party comes to me a couple of days ago with a knock-down from a party that knows me. See? This certain party asks me what I want to bump off a broad. I thought a grand would be right, and said so. Too stiff. We come together on five hundred. I got two-fifty down and get the rest when the Landow twist is cold. Not so bad for a soft trick—a slug through the side of a car—huh?"

"Well, what are you waiting for?" the detective asked. "You want to make it a fancy caper—kill her on her birthday or a legal holiday?"

Scuttle Zeipp smacked his lips and poked the detective's chest with a finger in the dark.

"Not any, brother! I'm thinking way ahead of you! Listen to this: I pocket my two-fifty advance and come up here to give the ground a good casing, not wanting to lam into anything I didn't know was here. While I'm poking around, I run into another party that's poking around. This second party gives me a tumble, I talk smart, and bingo! First thing you know she's propositioning me. What do you guess? She wants to know what I want to bump off a broad! Is it the same one *she* wants stopped? I hope to tell you it is!

"It ain't so silly! I get my hands on another two hundred and fifty berries, with that much more coming when I put over the fast one. Now do you think I'm going to do anything to that Landow baby? You're dumb if you do. She's my meal ticket. If she lives till I pop her, she'll be older than either you or the bay. I've got five hundred out of her so far. What's the matter with sticking around and waiting for more customers that don't like her? If two of 'em want to buy her out of the world, why not more? The answer is 'Yeah!' And on top of that, here you are snooping around her. Now there it is, brother, for you to look at and taste and smell."

Silence held for several minutes, in the darkness of the coupé's interior, and then the detective's harsh voice put a skeptical question:

"And who are these certain parties that want her out of the way?"

"Be yourself!" Scuttle Zeipp admonished him. "I'm laying down on 'em, right enough, but I ain't feeding 'em to you."

"What are you giving me all this for then?"

"What for? Because you're in on the lay somewhere. Crossing each other, neither of us can make a thin dimmer. If we don't hook up we'll just ruin the racket for each other. I've already made half a grand off this Landow. That's mine, but there's more to be picked up by a couple of men that know what they're doing. All right. I'm offering to throw in with you on a two-way cut of whatever else we can get. But my parties are out! I don't mind throwing them down, but I ain't rat enough to put the finger on them for you."

Alec Rush grunted and croaked another dubious inquiry.

"How come you trust me so much, Scuttle?"

The hired killer laughed knowingly.

"Why not? You're a right guy. You can see a profit when it's showed to you. They didn't chuck you off the force for forgetting to hang up your stocking. Besides, suppose you want to double-cross me, what can you do? You can't prove anything. I told you I didn't mean the woman any harm. I ain't even packing a gun. But all that's the bunk. You're a wise head. You know what's what. Me and you, Alec, we can get plenty!"

Silence again, until the detectives spoke slowly, thoughtfully.

"The first thing would be to get a line on the reasons your parties want the girl put out. Got anything on that?"

"Not a whisper."

"Both of 'em women, I take it."

Scuttle Zeipp hesitated.

"Yes," he admitted. "But don't be asking me anything about 'em. In the first place, I don't know anything, and in the second, I wouldn't tip their mitts if I did."

"Yeah," the detective croaked, as if he quite understood his companion's perverted idea of loyalty. "Now if they're women, the chances are the racket hangs on a man. What do you think of Landow? He's a pretty lad."

Scuttle Zeipp leaned over to put his finger against the detective's chest again.

"You've got it, Alec! That could be it, damned if it couldn't!"

"Yeah," Alec Rush agreed, fumbling with the levers of his car. "We'll get away from here and stay away until I look into him."

At Franklin Street, half a block from the rooming-house into which he had shadowed the young man that afternoon, the detective stopped his coupé.

"You want to drop out here?" he asked.

Scuttle Zeipp looked sidewise, speculatively, into the elder man's ugly face.

"It'll do," the young man said, "but you're a damned good guesser, just the same." He stopped with a hand on the door. "It's a go, is it, Alec? Fifty-fifty?"

"I wouldn't say so." Alec Rush grinned at him with hideous good nature. "You're not a bad lad, Scuttle, and if there's any gravy you'll get yours, but don't count on me mobbing up with you."

Zeipp's eyes jerked to slits, his lips snarled back from yellow teeth that were set edge to edge.

"You sell me out, you damned gorilla, and I'll—" He laughed the threat out of being, his dark face young and careless again. "Have it your own way, Alec. I didn't make no mistake when I throwed in with you. What you say goes."

"Yeah," the ugly man agreed. "Lay off that joint out there until I tell you. Maybe you'd better drop in to see me to-morrow. The phone book'll tell you where my office is. So long, kid."

"So long, Alec."

In the morning Alec Rush set about investigating Hubert Landow. First he went to the City Hall, where he examined the gray books in which marriage licenses are indexed. Hubert Britman Landow and Sara Falsoner had been married six months before, he learned.

The bride's maiden name thickened the red in the detective's bloodshot eyes. Air hissed sharply from his flattened nostrils. "Yeah! Yeah!" he said to himself, so raspingly that a lawyer's skinny clerk, fiddling with other records at his elbow, looked frightenedly at him and edged a little away.

From the City Hall, Alec Rush carried the bride's name to two newspaper offices, where, after studying the files, he bought an armful of six-month-old papers. He took the papers to his office, spread them on his desk, and attacked them with a pair of shears. When the last one had been cut and thrown aside, there remained on his desk a thick sheaf of clippings.

Arranging his clippings in chronological order, Alec Rush lighted a black cigar, put his elbows on the desk, his ugly head between his palms, and began to read a story with which newspaper-reading Baltimore had been familiar half a year before.

Purged of irrelevancies and earlier digressions, the story was essentially this:

Jerome Falsoner, aged forty-five, was a bachelor who lived alone in a flat in Cathedral Street, on an income more than sufficient for his comfort. He was a tall man, but of delicate physique, the result, it may have been, of excessive indulgence in pleasure on a constitution none too strong in the beginning. He was well-known, at least by sight, to all night-living Baltimoreans, and to those who frequented race-track, gambling-house, and the furtive cockpits that now and then materialize for a few brief hours in the forty miles of country that lie between Baltimore and Washington.

One Fanny Kidd, coming as was her custom at ten o'clock one morning to "do" Jerome Falsoner's rooms, found him lying on his back in his living-room, staring with dead eyes at a spot on the ceiling, a bright spot that was reflected sunlight—reflected from the metal hilt of his paper-knife, which protruded from his chest.

Police investigation established four facts:

First, Jerome Falsoner had been dead for fourteen hours when Fanny Kidd found him, which placed his murder at about eight o'clock the previous evening.

Second, the last persons known to have seen him alive were a woman named Madeline Boudin, with whom he had been intimate, and three of her friends. They had seen him, alive, at some time between seven-thirty and eight o'clock, or less than half an hour before his death. They had been driving down to a cottage on the Severn River, and Madeline Boudin had told the others she wanted to see Falsoner before she went. The others had remained in their car while she rang the bell. Jerome Falsoner opened the street door and she went in. Ten minutes later she came out and rejoined her friends. Jerome Falsoner came to the door with her, waving a hand at one of the men in the car—a Frederick Stoner, who knew Falsoner slightly, and who was connected with the district attorney's office. Two women, talking on the steps of a house across the street, had also seen Falsoner, and had seen Madeline Boudin and her friends drive away.

Third, Jerome Falsoner's heir and only near relative was his niece, Sara Falsoner, who, by some vagary of chance, was marrying Hubert Landow at the very hour that Fanny Kidd was finding her employer's dead body. Niece and uncle had seldom seen one another. The niece—for police suspicion settled on her for a short space—was definitely proved to have been at home, in her apartment in Carey Street, from six o'clock the evening of the murder until eight-thirty the next morning. Her husband, her fiancé then, had been there with her from six until eleven that evening. Prior to her marriage, the girl had been employed as stenographer by the same trust company that employed Ralph Millar.

Fourth, Jerome Falsoner, who had not the most even of dispositions, had quarreled with an Icelander named Einar Jokumsson in a gambling-house two days before he was murdered. Jokumsson had threatened him. Jokumsson—a short, heavily built man, dark-haired, dark-eyed—had vanished from his hotel, leaving his bags there, the day the body was found, and had not been seen since.

The last of these clippings carefully read, Alec Rush rocked back in his chair and made a thoughtful monster's face at the ceiling. Presently he leaned forward again to look into the telephone directory, and to call the number of Ralph Millar's trust company. But when he got his number he changed his mind.

"Never mind," he said into the instrument, and called a number that was Goodbody's. Minnie, when she came to the telephone, told him that Polly Vanness had been identified as one Polly Bangs, arrested in Milwaukee two years ago for shoplifting, and given a two-year sentence. Minnie also said that Polly Bangs had been released on bail early that morning.

Alec Rush pushed back the telephone and looked through his clippings again until he found the address of Madeline Boudin, the woman who had visited Falsoner so soon before his death. It was a Madison Avenue number. Thither his coupé carried the detective.

No, Miss Boudin did not live there. Yes, she had lived there, but had moved four months ago. Perhaps Mrs. Blender, on the third floor, would know where she lived now. Mrs. Blender did not know. She knew Miss Boudin had moved to an apartment house in Garrison Avenue, but did not think she was living there now. At the Garrison Avenue house: Miss Boudin had moved away a month and a half ago—somewhere in Mount Royal Avenue, perhaps. The number was not known.

The coupé carried its ugly owner to Mount Royal Avenue, to the apartment building he had seen first Hubert Landow and then Scuttle Zeipp visit the previous day. At the manager's office he made inquiries about a Walter Boyden, who was thought to live there. Walter Boyden was not known to the manager. There was a Miss Boudin in 604, but her name was B-o-u-d-i-n, and she lived alone.

Alec Rush left the building and got in his car again. He screwed up his savage red eyes, nodded his head in a satisfied way, and with one finger described a small circle in the air. Then he returned to his office.

Calling the trust company's number again, he gave Ralph Millar's name, and presently was speaking to the assistant cashier.

"This is Rush. Can you come up to the office right away?"

"What's that? Certainly. But how—how—? Yes, I'll be up in a minute."

None of the surprise that had been in Millar's telephone voice was apparent when he reached the detective's office. He asked no questions concerning the detective's knowledge of his identity. In brown to-day, he was as neatly inconspicuous as he had been yesterday in gray.

"Come in," the ugly man welcomed him. "Sit down. I've got to have some more facts, Mr. Millar."

Millar's thin mouth tightened and his brows drew together with obstinate reticence.

"I thought we settled that point, Rush. I told you—"

Alec Rush frowned at his client with jovial, though frightful exasperation.

"I know what you told me," he interrupted. "But that was then and this is now. The thing's coming unwound on me, and I can see just enough to get myself tangled up if I don't watch Harvey. I found your mysterious man, talked to him. He was following Mrs. Landow, right enough. According to the way he tells it, he's been hired to kill her."

Millar leaped from his chair to lean over the yellow desk, his face close to the detective's.

"My God, Rush, what are you saying? To kill her?"

"Now, now! Take it easy. He's not going to kill her. I don't think he ever meant to. But he claims he was hired to do it."

"You've arrested him? You've found the man who hired him?"

The detective squinted up his bloodshot eyes and studied the younger man's passionate face.

"As a matter of fact," he croaked calmly when he had finished his examination, "I haven't done either of those things. She's in no danger just now. Maybe the lad was stringing me, maybe he wasn't, but either way he wouldn't have spilled it to me if he meant to do anything. And when it comes right down to it, Mr. Millar, do you want him arrested?"

"Yes! That is—" Millar stepped back from the desk, sagged limply down on the chair again, and put shaking hands over his face. "My God, Rush, I don't know!" he gasped.

"Exactly," said Alec Rush. "Now here it is. Mrs. Landow was Jerome Falsoner's niece and heir. She worked for your trust company. She married Landow the morning her uncle was found dead. Yesterday Landow visited the building where Madeline Boudin lives. She was the last person known to have been in Falsoner's rooms before he was killed. But her alibi seems to be as air-tight as the Landows'. The man who claims he was hired to kill Mrs. Landow also visited Madeline Boudin's building yesterday. I saw him go in. I saw him meet another woman. A shoplifter, the second one. In her rooms I found a photograph of Hubert Landow. Your dark man claims he was hired twice to kill Mrs. Landow—by two women neither knowing the other had hired him. He won't tell me who they are, but he doesn't have to."

The hoarse voice stopped and Alec Rush waited for Millar to speak. But Millar was for the time without a voice. His eyes were wide and despairingly empty. Alec Rush raised one big hand, folded it into a fist that was almost perfectly spherical, and thumped his desk softly.

"There it is, Mr. Millar," he rasped. "A pretty tangle. If you'll tell me what you know, we'll get it straightened out, never fear. If you don't—I'm out!"

Now Millar found words, however jumbled.

"You couldn't, Rush! You can't desert me—us—her! It's not— You're not—"

But Alec Rush shook his ugly pear-shaped head with slow emphasis.

"There's murder in this and the Lord knows what all. I've got no liking for a blindfolded game. How do I know what you're up to? You can tell me what you know—everything—or you can find yourself another detective. That's flat."

Ralph Millar's fingers picked at each other, his teeth pulled at his lips, his harassed eyes pleaded with the detective.

"You can't, Rush," he begged. "She's still in danger. Even if you are right about that man not attacking her, she's not safe. The women who hired him can hire another. You've got to protect her, Rush."

"Yeah? Then you've got to talk."

"I've got to—? Yes, I'll talk, Rush. I'll tell you anything you ask. But there's really nothing—or almost nothing—I know beyond what you've already learned."

"She worked for your trust company?"

"Yes, in my department."

"Left there to be married?"

"Yes. That is— No, Rush, the truth is she was discharged. It was an outrage, but—"

"When was this?"

"It was the day before the—before she was married."

"Tell me about it."

"She had— I'll have to explain her situation to you first, Rush. She is an orphan. Her father, Ben Falsoner, had been wild in his youth—and perhaps not only in his youth—as I believe all the Falsoners have been. However, he had quarreled with his father—old Howard Falsoner—and the old man had cut him out of the will. But not altogether out. The old man hoped Ben would mend his ways, and he didn't mean to leave him with nothing in that event. Unfortunately he trusted it to his other son, Jerome.

"Old Howard Falsoner left a will whereby the income from his estate was to go to Jerome during Jerome's life. Jerome was to provide for his brother, Ben, as he saw fit. That is, he had an absolutely free hand. He could divide the income equally with his brother, or he could give him a pittance, or he could give him nothing, as Ben's conduct deserved. On Jerome's death the estate was to be divided equally among the old man's grandchildren.

"In theory, that was a fairly sensible arrangement, but not in practice— not in Jerome Falsoner's hands. You didn't know him? Well, he was the last man you'd ever trust with a thing of that sort. He exercised his power to the utmost. Ben Falsoner never got a cent from him. Three years ago Ben died, and so the girl, his only daughter, stepped into his position in relation to her grandfather's money. Her mother was already dead. Jerome Falsoner never paid her a cent.

"That was her situation when she came to the trust company two years ago. It wasn't a happy one. She had at least a touch of the Falsoner recklessness and extravagance. There she was: heiress to some two million dollars—for Jerome had never married and she was the only grandchild—but without any present income at all, except her salary, which was by no means a large one.

"She got in debt. I suppose she tried to economize at times, but there was always that two million dollars ahead to make scrimping doubly distasteful. Finally, the trust company officials heard of her indebtedness. A collector or two came to the office, in fact. Since she was employed in my department, I had the disagreeable duty of warning her. She promised to pay her debts and contract no more, and I suppose she did try, but she wasn't very successful. Our officials are old-fashioned, ultra-conservative. I did everything I could to save her, but it was no good. They simply would not have an employee who was heels over head in debt."

Millar paused a moment, looked miserably at the floor, and went on:

"I had the disagreeable task of telling her her services were no longer needed. I tried to— It was awfully unpleasant. That was the day before she married Landow. It—" He paused and, as if he could think of nothing else to say, repeated, "Yes, it was the day before she married Landow," and fell to staring miserably at the floor again.

Alec Rush, who had sat as still through the recital of this history as a carven monster on an old church, now leaned over his desk and put a husky question:

"And who is this Hubert Landow? What is he?"

Ralph Millar shook his downcast head.

"I don't know him. I've seen him. I know nothing of him."

"Mrs. Landow ever speak of him? I mean when she was in the trust company?"

"It's likely, but I don't remember."

"So you didn't know what to make of it when you heard she'd married him?"

The younger man looked up with frightened brown eyes.

"What are you getting at, Rush? You don't think— Yes, as you say, I was surprised. What are you getting at?"

"The marriage license," the detective said, ignoring his client's repeated question, "was issued to Landow four days before the wedding-day, four days before Jerome Falsoner's body was found."

Millar chewed a fingernail and shook his head hopelessly.

"I don't know what you're getting at," he mumbled around the finger. "The whole thing is bewildering."

"Isn't it a fact, Mr. Millar," the detective's voice filled the office with hoarse insistence, "that you were on more friendly terms with Sara Falsoner than with anyone else in the trust company?"

The younger man raised his head and looked Alec Rush in the eye— held his gaze with brown eyes that were doggedly level.

"The fact is," he said quietly, "that I asked Sara Falsoner to marry me the day she left."

"Yeah. And she—?"

"And she—I suppose it was my fault. I was clumsy, crude, whatever you like. God knows what she thought—that I was asking her to marry me out of pity, that I was trying to force her into marriage by discharging her when I knew she was over her head in debt! She might have thought anything. Anyhow, it was—it was disagreeable."

"You mean she not only refused you, but was—well—disagreeable about it?"

"I do mean that."

Alec Rush sat back in his chair and brought fresh grotesqueries into his face by twisting his thick mouth crookedly up at one corner. His red eyes were evilly reflective on the ceiling.

"The only thing for it," he decided, "is to go to Landow and give him what we've got."

"But are you sure he—?" Millar objected indefinitely.

"Unless he's one whale of an actor, he's a lot in love with his wife," the detective said with certainty. "That's enough to justify taking the story to him."

Millar was not convinced.

"You're sure it would be wisest?"

"Yeah. We've got to go to one of three people with the tale—him, her, or the police. I think he's the best bet, but take your choice."

The younger man nodded reluctantly.

"All right. But you don't have to bring me into it, do you?" he said with quick alarm. "You can handle it so I won't be involved. You understand what I mean? She's his wife, and it would be—"

"Sure," Alec Rush promised; "I'll keep you covered up."

HUBERT LANDOW, twisting the detective's card in his fingers, received Alec Rush in a somewhat luxuriously furnished room in the second story of the Charles-Street Avenue house. He was standing—tall, blond, boyishly handsome—in the middle of the floor, facing the door, when the detective—fat, grizzled, battered, and ugly—was shown in.

"You wish to see me? Here, sit down."

Hubert Landow's manner was neither restrained nor hearty. It was precisely the manner that might be expected of a young man receiving an unexpected call from so savage-visaged a detective.

"Yeah," said Alec Rush as they sat in facing chairs. "I've got something to tell you. It won't take much time, but it's kind of wild. It might be a surprise to you, and it might not. But it's on the level. I don't want you to think I'm kidding you."

Hubert Landow bent forward, his face all interest.

"I won't," he promised. "Go on."

"A couple of days ago I got a line on a man who might be tied up in a job I'm interested in. He's a crook. Trailing him around, I discovered he was interested in your affairs, and your wife's. He's shadowed you and he's shadowed her. He was loafing down the street from a Mount Royal Avenue apartment that you went in yesterday, and he went in there later himself."

"But what the devil is he up to?" Landow exclaimed. "You think he's—"

"Wait," the ugly man advised. "Wait until you've heard it all, and then you can tell me what you make of it. He came out of there and went to Camden Station, where he met a young woman. They talked a bit, and later in the afternoon she was picked up in a department store—shoplifting. Her name is Polly Bangs, and she's done a hitch in Wisconsin for the same racket. Your photograph was on her dresser."

"My photograph?"

Alec Rush nodded placidly up into the face of the young man, who was now standing.

"Yours. You know this Polly Bangs? A chunky, square-built girl of twenty-six or so, with brown hair and eyes—saucy looking?"

Hubert Landow's face was a puzzled blank.

"No! What the devil could she be doing with my picture?" he demanded. "Are you sure it was mine?"

"Not dead sure, maybe, but sure enough to need proof that it wasn't. Maybe she's somebody you've forgotten, or maybe she ran across the picture somewhere and kept it because she liked it."

"Nonsense!" The blond man squirmed at this tribute to his face, and blushed a vivid red beside which Alec Rush's complexion was almost colorless. "There must be some sensible reason. She has been arrested, you say?"

"Yeah, but she's out on bail now. But let me get along with my story. Last night this thug I've told you about and I had a talk. He claims he has been hired to kill your wife."

Hubert Landow, who had returned to his chair, now jerked in it so that its joints creaked strainingly. His face, crimson a second ago, drained paper-white. Another sound than the chair's creaking was faint in the room: the least of muffled gasps. The blond young man did not seem to hear it, but Alec Rush's bloodshot eyes flicked sidewise for an instant to focus fleetingly on a closed door across the room.

Landow was out of his chair again, leaning down to the detective, his fingers digging into the ugly man's loose muscular shoulders.

"This is horrible!" he was crying. "We've got to—"

The door at which the detective had looked a moment ago opened. A beautiful tall girl came through—Sara Landow. Her rumpled hair was an auburn cloud around her white face. Her eyes were dead things. She walked slowly toward the men, her body inclined a little forward, as if against a strong wind.

"It's no use, Hubert." Her voice was as dead as her eyes. "We may as well face it. It's Madeline Boudin. She has found out that I killed my uncle."

"Hush, darling, hush!" Landow caught his wife in his arms and tried to soothe her with a caressing hand on her shoulder. "You don't know what you're saying."

"Oh, but I do." She shrugged herself listlessly out of his arms and sat in the chair Alec Rush had just vacated. "It's Madeline Boudin, you know it is. She knows I killed Uncle Jerome."

Landow whirled to the detective, both hands going out to grip the ugly man's arm.

"You won't listen to what she's saying, Rush?" he pleaded. "She hasn't been well. She doesn't know what she's saying."

Sara Landow laughed with weary bitterness.

"Haven't been well?" she said. "No, I haven't been well, not since I killed him. How could I be well after that? You are a detective." Her eyes lifted their emptiness to Alec Rush. "Arrest me. I killed Jerome Falsoner."

Alec Rush, standing arms akimbo, legs apart, scowled at her, saying nothing.

"You can't, Rush!" Landow was tugging at the detective's arm again. "You can't, man. It's ridiculous! You—"

"Where does this Madeline Boudin fit in?" Alec Rush's harsh voice demanded. "I know she was chummy with Jerome, but why should she want your wife killed?"

Landow hesitated, shifting his feet, and when he replied it was reluctantly.

"She was Jerome's mistress, had a child by him. My wife, when she learned of it, insisted on making her a settlement out of the estate. It was in connection with that that I went to see her yesterday."

"Yeah. Now to get back to Jerome: you and your wife were supposed to be in her apartment at the time he was killed, if I remember right?"

Sara Landow sighed with spiritless impatience.

"Must there be all this discussion?" she asked in a small, tired voice. "I killed him. No one else killed him. No one else was there when I killed him. I stabbed him with the paper-knife when he attacked me, and he said, 'Don't! Don't!' and began to cry, down on his knees, and I ran out."

Alec Rush looked from the girl to the man. Landow's face was wet with perspiration, his hands were white fists, and something quivered in his chest. When he spoke his voice was as hoarse as the detective's, if not so loud.

"Sara, will you wait here until I come back? I'm going out for a little while, possibly an hour. You'll wait here and not do anything until I return?"

"Yes," the girl said, neither curiosity nor interest in her voice. "But it's no use, Hubert. I should have told you in the beginning. It's no use."

"Just wait for me, Sara," he pleaded, and then bent his head to the detective's deformed ear. "Stay with her, Rush, for God's sake!" he whispered, and went swiftly out of the room.

The front door banged shut. An automobile purred away from the house. Alec Rush spoke to the girl.

"Where's the phone?"

"In the next room," she said, without looking up from the handkerchief her fingers were measuring.

The detective crossed to the door through which she had entered the room, found that it opened into a library, where a telephone stood in a corner. On the other side of the room a clock indicated 3:35. The detective went to the telephone and called Ralph Millar's office, asked for Millar, and told him:

"This is Rush. I'm at the Landows'. Come up right away."

"But I can't, Rush. Can't you understand my—"

"Can't hell!" croaked Alec Rush. "Get here quick!"

The young woman with dead eyes, still playing with the hem of her handkerchief, did not look up when the ugly man returned to the room. Neither of them spoke. Alec Rush, standing with his back to a window, twice took out his watch to glare savagely at it.

The faint tingling of the doorbell came from below. The detective went across to the hall door and down the front stairs, moving with heavy swiftness. Ralph Millar, his face a field in which fear and embarrassment fought, stood in the vestibule, stammering something unintelligible to the maid who had opened the door. Alec Rush put the girl brusquely aside, brought Millar in, guided him upstairs.

"She says she killed Jerome," he muttered into his client's ear as they mounted.

Ralph Millar's face went dreadfully white, but there was no surprise in it.

"You knew she killed him?" Alec Rush growled.

Millar tried twice to speak and made no sound. They were on the second-floor landing before the words came.

"I saw her on the street that night, going toward his flat!"

Alec Rush snorted viciously and turned the younger man toward the room where Sara Landow sat.

"Landow's out," he whispered hurriedly. "I'm going out. Stay with her. She's shot to hell—likely to do anything if she's left alone. If Landow gets back before I do, tell him to wait for me."

Before Millar could voice the confusion in his face they were across the sill and into the room. Sara Landow raised her head. Her body was lifted from the chair as if by an invisible power. She came up tall and erect on her feet. Millar stood just inside the door. They looked eye into eye, posed each as if in the grip of a force pushing them together, another holding them apart.

Alec Rush hurried clumsily and silently down to the street.

In Mount Royal Avenue, Alec Rush saw the blue roadster at once. It was standing empty before the apartment building in which Madeline Boudin lived. The detective drove past it and turned his coupé in to the curb three blocks below. He had barely come to rest there when Landow ran out of the apartment building, jumped into his car, and drove off. He drove to a Charles Street hotel. Behind him went the detective.

In the hotel, Landow walked straight to the writing-room. For half an hour he sat there, bending over a desk, covering sheet after sheet of paper with rapidly written words, while the detective sat behind a newspaper in a secluded angle of the lobby, watching the writing-room exit. Landow came out of the room stuffing a thick envelope in his pocket, left the hotel, got into his machine, and drove to the office of a messenger service company in St. Paul Street.

He remained in this office for five minutes. When he came out he ignored his roadster at the curb, walking instead to Calvert Street, where he boarded a northbound street car. Alec Rush's coupé rolled along behind the car. At Union Station, Landow left the street car and went to the ticket-window. He had just asked for a one-way ticket to Philadelphia when Alec Rush tapped him on the shoulder.

Hubert Landow turned slowly, the money for his ticket still in his hand. Recognition brought no expression to his handsome face.

"Yes," he said coolly, "what is it?"

Alec Rush nodded his ugly head at the ticket-window, at the money in Landow's hand.

"This is nothing for you to be doing," he growled.

"Here you are," the ticket-seller said through his grille. Neither of the men in front paid any attention to him. A large woman in pink, red, and violet, jostling Landow, stepped on his foot and pushed past him to the window. Landow stepped back, the detective following.

"You shouldn't have left Sara alone," said Landow. "She's—"

"She's not alone. I got somebody to stay with her."

"Not—?"

"Not the police, if that's what you're thinking."

Landow began to pace slowly down the long concourse, the detective keeping step with him. The blond man stopped and looked sharply into the other's face.

"Is it that fellow Millar who's with her?" he demanded.

"Yeah."

"Is he the man you're working for, Rush?"

"Yeah."

Landow resumed his walking. When they had reached the northern extremity of the concourse, he spoke again.

"What does he want, this Millar?"

Alec Rush shrugged his thick, limber shoulders and said nothing.

"Well, what do you want?" the young man asked with some heat, facing the detective squarely now.

"I don't want you going out of town."

Landow pondered that, scowling.

"Suppose I insist on going," he asked, "how will you stop me?"

"Accomplice after the fact in Jerome's murder would be a charge I could hold you on."

Silence again, until broken by Landow.

"Look here, Rush. You're working for Millar. He's out at my house. I've just sent a letter out to Sara by messenger. Give them time to read it, and then phone Millar there. Ask him if he wants me held or not."

Alec Rush shook his head decidedly.

"No good," he rasped. "Millar's too rattle-brained for me to take his word for anything like that over the phone. We'll go back there and have a talk all around."

Now it was Landow who balked.

"No," he snapped. "I won't!" He looked with cool calculation at the detective's ugly face. "Can I buy you, Rush?"

"No, Landow. Don't let my looks and my record kid you."

"I thought not." Landow looked at the roof and at his feet, and he blew his breath out sharply. "We can't talk here. Let's find a quiet place."

"The heap's outside," Alec Rush said, "and we can sit in that."

Seated in Alec Rush's coupé, Hubert Landow lighted a cigarette, the detective one of his black cigars.

"That Polly Bangs you were talking about, Rush," the blond man said without preamble, "is my wife. My name is Henry Bangs. You won't find my fingerprints anywhere. When Polly was picked up in Milwaukee a couple of years ago and sent over, I came east and fell in with Madeline Boudin. We made a good team. She had brains in chunks, and if I've got somebody to do my thinking for me, I'm a pretty good worker myself."

He smiled at the detective, pointing at his own face with his cigarette. While Alec Rush watched, a tide of crimson surged into the blond man's face until it was as rosy as a blushing school-girl's. He laughed again and the blush began to fade.

"That's my best trick," he went on. "Easy if you have the gift and keep in practice: fill your lungs, try to force the air out while keeping it shut off at the larynx. It's a gold mine for a grifter! You'd be surprised how people will trust me after I've turned on a blush or two for 'em. So Madeline and I were in the money. She had brains, nerve, and a good front. I have everything but brains. We turned a couple of tricks—one con and one blackmail—and then she ran into Jerome Falsoner. We were going to give him the squeeze at first. But when Madeline found out that Sara was his heiress, that she was in debt, and that she and her uncle were on the outs, we ditched that racket and cooked a juicier one. Madeline found somebody to introduce me to Sara. I made myself agreeable, playing the boob—the shy but worshipful young man.

"Madeline had brains, as I've said. She used 'em all this time. I hung around Sara, sending her candy, books, flowers, taking her to shows and dinner. The books and shows were part of Madeline's work. Two of the books mentioned the fact that a husband can't be made to testify against his wife in court, nor wife against husband. One of the plays touched the same thing. That was planting the seeds. We planted another with my blushing and mumbling—persuaded Sara, or rather let her discover for herself, that I was the clumsiest liar in the world.

"The planting done, we began to push the game along. Madeline kept on good terms with Jerome. Sara was getting deeper in debt. We helped her in still deeper. We had a burglar clean out her apartment one night—Ruby Sweeger, maybe you know him. He's in stir now for another caper. He got what money she had and most of the things she could have hocked in a pinch. Then we stirred up some of the people she owed, sent them anonymous letters warning them not to count too much on her being Jerome's heir. Foolish letters, but they did the trick. A couple of her creditors sent collectors to the trust company.

"Jerome got his income from the estate quarterly. Madeline knew the dates, and Sara knew them. The day before the next one, Madeline got busy on Sara's creditors again. I don't know what she told them this time, but it was enough. They descended on the trust company in a flock, with the result that the next day Sara was given two weeks' pay and discharged. When she came out I met her—by chance—yes, I'd been watching for her since morning. I took her for a drive and got her back to her apartment at six o'clock. There we found more frantic creditors waiting to pounce on her. I chased them out, played the big-hearted boy, making embarrassed offers of all sorts of help. She refused them, of course, and I could see decision coming into her face. She knew this was the day on which Jerome got his quarterly check. She determined to go see him, to demand that he pay her debts at least. She didn't tell me where she was going, but I could see it plain enough, since I was looking for it.

"I left her and waited across the street from her apartment, in Franklin Square, until I saw her come out. Then I found a telephone, called up Madeline, and told her Sara was on her way to her uncle's flat."

Landow's cigarette scorched his fingers. He dropped it, crushed it under his foot, lighted another.

"This is a long-winded story, Rush," he apologized, "but it'll soon be over now."

"Keep talking, son," said Alec Rush.

"There were some people in Madeline's place when I phoned her—people trying to persuade her to go down the country on a party. She agreed now. They would give her an even better alibi than the one she had cooked up. She told them she had to see Jerome before she left, and they drove her over to his place and waited in their car while she went in with him.

"She had a pint bottle of cognac with her, all doped and ready. She poured out a drink of it for Jerome, telling him of the new bootlegger she had found who had a dozen or more cases of this cognac to sell at a reasonable price. The cognac was good enough and the price low enough to make Jerome think she had dropped in to let him in on something good. He gave her an order to pass on to the bootlegger. Making sure his steel paper-knife was in full view on the table, Madeline rejoined her friends, taking Jerome as far as the door so they would see he was still alive, and drove off.

"Now I don't know what Madeline had put in that cognac. If she told me, I've forgotten. It was a powerful drug—not a poison, you understand, but an excitant. You'll see what I mean when you hear the rest. Sara must have reached her uncle's flat ten or fifteen minutes after Madeline's departure. Her uncle's face, she says, was red, inflamed, when he opened the door for her. But he was a frail man, while she was strong, and she wasn't afraid of the devil himself, for that matter. She went in and demanded that he settle her debts, even if he didn't choose to make her an allowance out of his income.

"They were both Falsoners, and the argument must have grown hot. Also the drug was working on Jerome, and he had no will with which to fight it. He attacked her. The paper-knife was on the table, as Madeline had seen. He was a maniac. Sara was not one of your corner-huddling, screaming girls. She grabbed the paper-knife and let him have it. When he fell, she turned and ran.

"Having followed her as soon as I'd finished telephoning to Madeline, I was standing on Jerome's front steps when she dashed out. I stopped her and she told me she'd killed her uncle. I made her wait there while I went in, to see if he was really dead. Then I took her home, explaining my presence at Jerome's door by saying, in my boobish, awkward way, that I had been afraid she might do something reckless and had thought it best to keep an eye on her.

"Back in her apartment, she was all for giving herself up to the police. I pointed out the danger in that, arguing that, in debt, admittedly going to her uncle for money, being his heiress, she would most certainly be convicted of having murdered him so she would get the money. Her story of his attack, I persuaded her, would be laughed at as a flimsy yarn. Dazed, she wasn't hard to convince. The next step was easy. The police would investigate her, even if they didn't especially suspect her. I was, so far as we knew, the only person whose testimony could convict her. I was loyal enough, but wasn't I the clumsiest liar in the world? Didn't the mildest lie make me blush like an auctioneer's flag? The way around that difficulty lay in what two of the books I had given her, and one of the plays we had seen, had shown: if I was her husband I couldn't be made to testify against her. We were married the next morning, on a license I had been carrying for nearly a week.

"Well, there we were. I was married to her. She had a couple of million coming when her uncle's affairs were straightened out. She couldn't possibly, it seemed, escape arrest and conviction. Even if no one had seen her entering or leaving her uncle's flat, everything still pointed to her guilt, and the foolish course I had persuaded her to follow would simply ruin her chance of pleading self-defense. If they hanged her, the two million would come to me. If she got a long term in prison, I'd have the handling of the money at least."

Landow dropped and crushed his second cigarette and stared for a moment straight ahead into distance.

"Do you believe in God, or Providence, or Fate, or any of that, Rush?" he asked. "Well, some believe in one thing and some in another, but listen. Sara was never arrested, never even really suspected. It seems there was some sort of Finn or Swede who had had a run-in with Jerome and threatened him. I suppose he couldn't account for his whereabouts the night of the killing, so he went into hiding when he heard of Jerome's murder. The police suspicion settled on him. They looked Sara up, of course, but not very thoroughly. No one seems to have seen her in the street, and the people in her apartment house, having seen her come in at six o'clock with me, and not having seen her—or not remembering if they did—go out or in again, told the police she had been in all evening. The police were too much interested in the missing Finn, or whatever he was, to look any further into Sara's affairs.

"So there we were again. I was married into the money, but I wasn't fixed so I could hand Madeline her cut. Madeline said we'd let things run along as they were until the estate was settled up, and then we could tip Sara off to the police. But by the time the money was settled up there was another hitch. This one was my doing. I—I—well, I wanted to go on just as we were. Conscience had nothing to do with it, you understand? It was simply that—well—that living on with Sara was the only thing I wanted. I wasn't even sorry for what I'd done, because if it hadn't been for that I would never have had her.

"I don't know whether I can make this clear to you, Rush, but even now I don't regret any of it. If it could have been different—but it couldn't. It had to be this way or none. And I've had those six months. I can see that I've been a chump. Sara was never for me. I got her by a crime and a trick, and while I held on to a silly hope that some day she'd—she'd look at me as I did at her, I knew in my heart all the time it was no use. There had been a man—your Millar. She's free now that it's out about my being married to Polly, and I hope she—I hope— Well, Madeline began to howl for action. I told Sara that Madeline had had a child by Jerome, and Sara agreed to settle some money on her. But that didn't satisfy Madeline. It wasn't sentiment with her. I mean, it wasn't any feeling for me, it was just the money. She wanted every cent she could get, and she couldn't get enough to satisfy her in a settlement of the kind Sara wanted to make.

"With Polly, it was that too, but maybe a little more. She's fond of me, I think. I don't know how she traced me here after she got out of the Wisconsin big house, but I can see how she figured things. I was married to a wealthy woman. If the woman died—shot by a bandit in a hold-up attempt—then I'd have money, and Polly would have both me and money. I haven't seen her, wouldn't know she was in Baltimore if you hadn't told me, but that's the way it would work out in her mind. The killing idea would have occurred just as easily to Madeline. I had told her I wouldn't stand for pushing the game through on Sara. Madeline knew that if she went ahead on her own hook and hung the Falsoner murder on Sara I'd blow up the whole racket. But if Sara died, then I'd have the money and Madeline would draw her cut. So that was it.

"I didn't know that until you told me, Rush. I don't give a damn for your opinion of me, but it's God's truth that I didn't know that either Polly or Madeline was trying to have Sara killed. Well, that's about all. Were you shadowing me when I went to the hotel?"

"Yeah."

"I thought so. That letter I wrote and sent home told just about what I've told you, spilled the whole story. I was going to run for it, leaving Sara in the clear. She's clear, all right, but now I'll have to face it. But I don't want to see her again, Rush."

"I wouldn't think you would," the detective agreed. "Not after making a killer of her."

"But I didn't," Landow protested. "She isn't. I forgot to tell you that, but I put it in the letter. Jerome Falsoner was not dead, not even dying, when I went past her into the flat. The knife was too high in his chest. I killed him, driving the knife into the same wound again, but downward. That's what I went in for, to make sure he was finished!"

Alec Rush screwed up his savage bloodshot eyes, looked long into the confessed murderer's face.

"That's a lie," he croaked at last, "but a decent one. Are you sure you want to stick to it? The truth will be enough to clear the girl, and maybe won't swing you."

"What difference does it make?" the younger man asked. "I'm a gone baby anyhow. And I might as well put Sara in the clear with herself as well as with the law. I'm caught to rights and another rap won't hurt. I told you Madeline had brains. I was afraid of them. She'd have had something up her sleeve to spring on us—to ruin Sara with. She could out-smart me without trying. I couldn't take any chances."

He laughed into Alec Rush's ugly face and, with a somewhat theatrical gesture, jerked one cuff an inch or two out of his coat-sleeve. The cuff was still damp with a maroon stain.

"I killed Madeline an hour ago," said Henry Bangs, alias Hubert Landow.

HIS BROTHER'S
KEEPER

I knew what a lot of people said about Loney but he was always swell to me. Ever since I remember he was swell to me and I guess I would have liked him just as much even if he had been just somebody else instead of my brother; but I was glad he was not just somebody else.

He was not like me. He was slim and would have looked swell in any kind of clothes you put on him, only he always dressed classy and looked like he had stepped right out of the bandbox even when he was just loafing around the house, and he had slick hair and the whitest teeth you ever saw and long, thin, clean-looking fingers. He looked like the way I remembered my father, only better-looking. I took more after Ma's folks, the Malones, which was funny because Loney was the one that was named after them. Malone Bolan. He was smart as they make them, too. It was no use trying to put anything over on him and maybe that was what some people had against him, only that was kind of hard to fit in with Pete Gonzalez.

Pete Gonzalez not liking Loney used to bother me sometimes because he was a swell guy too, and he was never trying to put anything over on anybody. He had two fighters and a wrestler named Kilchak and he always sent them in to do the best they could, just like Loney sent me in. He was the topnotch manager in our part of the country and a lot of people said there was no better anywhere, so I felt pretty good about him wanting to handle me, even if I did say no.

It was in the hall leaving Tubby White's gym that I ran into him that afternoon and he said, "Hello, Kid, how's it?" moving his cigar farther over in a corner of his mouth so he could talk.

"Hello. All right."

He looked me up and down, squinting on account of the smoke from his cigar. "Going to take this guy Saturday?"

"I guess so."

He looked me up and down again like he was weighing me in. His eyes were little enough anyhow and when he squinted like that you could hardly see them at all. "How old are you, Kid?"

"Going on nineteen."

"And you'll weigh about a hundred and sixty," he said.

"Sixty-seven and a half. I'm growing pretty fast."

"Ever see this guy you're fighting Saturday?"

"No."

"He's plenty tough."

I grinned and said, "I guess he is."

"And plenty smart."

I said, "I guess he is," again.

He took his cigar out of his mouth and scowled at me and said like he was sore at me, "You know you got no business in the ring with him, don't you?" Before I could think up anything to say he stuck the cigar back in his mouth and his face and his voice changed. "Why don't you let me handle you, Kid? You got the stuff. I'll handle you right, build you up, not use you up, and you'll be good for a long trip."

"I couldn't do that," I said. "Loney taught me all I know and—"

"Taught you what?" Pete snarled. He looked mad again. "If you think you been taught anything at all you just take a look at your mug in the next looking-glass you come across." He took the cigar out of his mouth and spat out a piece of tobacco that had come loose. "Only eighteen years old and ain't been fighting a year and look at the mug on him!"

I felt myself blushing. I guess I was never any beauty but, like Pete said, I had been hit in the face a lot and I guess my face showed it. I said, "Well, of course, I'm not a boxer."

"And that's the God's truth," Pete said. "And why ain't you?"

"I don't know. I guess it's just not my way of fighting."

"You could learn. You're fast and you ain't dumb. What's this stuff getting you? Every week Loney sends you in against some guy you're not ready for yet and you soak up a lot of fists and—"

"I win, don't I?" I said.

"Sure you win—so far—because you're young and tough and got the moxie and can hit, but I wouldn't want to pay for winning what you're paying, and I wouldn't want any of my boys to. I seen kids—maybe some of them as promising as you—go along the way you're going, and I seen what was left of them a couple years later. Take my word for it, Kid, you'll do better than that with me."

"Maybe you're right," I said, "and I'm grateful to you and all that, but I couldn't leave Loney. He—"

"I'll give Loney a piece of change for your contract, even if you ain't got one with him."

"No, I'm sorry, I—I couldn't."

Pete started to say something and stopped and his face began to get red. The door of Tubby's office had opened and Loney was coming out. Loney's face was white and you could hardly see his lips because they were so tight together, so I knew he had heard us talking.

He walked up close to Pete, not even looking at me once, and said, "You chiseling dago rat."

Pete said, "I only told him what I told you when I made you the offer last week."

Loney said, "Swell. So now you've told everybody. So now you can tell 'em about this." He smacked Pete across the mouth with the back of his hand.

I moved over a little because Pete was a lot bigger than Loney, but Pete just said, "O.K., pal, maybe you won't live forever. Maybe you won't live forever even if Big Jake don't never get hep to the missus."

Loney swung at him with a fist this time but Pete was backing away down the hall and Loney missed him by about a foot and a half, and when Loney started after him Pete turned and ran toward the gym.

Loney came back to me grinning and not looking mad any more. He could change that way quicker than anybody you ever saw. He put an arm around my shoulders and said, "The chiseling dago rat. Let's blow." Outside he turned me around to look at the sign advertising the fights. "There you are, Kid. I don't blame him for wanting you. There'll be a lot of 'em wanting you before you're through."

It did look swell, KID BOLAN VS. SAILOR PERELMAN, in red letters that were bigger than any of the other names and up at the top of the card. That was the first time I ever had had my name at the top. I thought, *I'm going to have it there like that all the time now and maybe in New York some time*, but I just grinned at Loney without saying anything and we went on home.

Ma was away visiting my married sister in Pittsburgh and we had a nigger woman named Susan taking care of the house for us and after she washed up the supper dishes and went home Loney went to the telephone and I could hear him talking low. I wanted to say something to him when he came back but I was afraid I would say the wrong thing because Loney might think I was trying to butt into his business, and before I could find a safe way to start, the doorbell rang.

Loney went to the door. It was Mrs. Schiff, like I had a hunch it would be, because she had come over the first night Ma was away.

She came in laughing, with Loney's arm around her waist, and said, "Hello, Champ," to me.

I said "Hello," and shook hands with her.

I liked her, I guess, but I guess I was kind of afraid of her. I mean not only afraid of her on Loney's account but in a different way. You know, like sometimes when you were a kid and you found yourself all alone in a strange neighborhood on the other side of town. There was nothing you could see to be downright afraid of but you kept halfway expecting something. It was something like that. She was awful pretty but there was something kind of wild-looking about her. I don't mean wild-looking like some floozies you see; I mean almost like an animal, like she was always on the watch for something. It was like she was hungry. I mean just her eyes and maybe her mouth because you could not call her skinny or anything or fat either.

Loney got out a bottle of whisky and glasses and they had a drink. I stalled around for a few minutes just being polite and then said I guessed I was tired and I said good night to them and took my magazine upstairs to my room. Loney was beginning to tell her about his run-in with Pete Gonzalez when I went upstairs.

After I got undressed I tried to read but I kept worrying about Loney. It was this Mrs. Schiff that Pete made the crack about in the afternoon. She was the wife of Big Jake Schiff, the boss of our ward, and a lot of people must have known about her running around with Loney on the side. Anyhow Pete knew about it and he and Big Jake were pretty good friends besides him now having something to pay Loney back for. I wished Loney would cut it out. He could have had a lot of other girls and Big Jake was nobody to have trouble with, even leaving aside the pull he had down at the City Hall. Every time I tried to read I would get to thinking things like that so finally I gave it up and went to sleep pretty early, even for me.

That was a Monday. Tuesday night when I got home from the movies she was waiting in the vestibule. She had on a long coat but no hat, and she looked pretty excited.

"Where's Loney?" she asked, not saying hello or anything.

"I don't know. He didn't say where he was going."

"I've got to see him," she said. "Haven't you any idea where he'd be?"

"No, I don't know where he is."

"Do you think he'll be late?"

I said, "I guess he usually is."

She frowned at me and then she said, "I've got to see him. I'll wait a little while anyhow." So we went back to the dining-room.

She kept her coat on and began to walk around the room looking at things but without paying much attention to them. I asked her if she wanted a drink and she said, "Yes," sort of absent-minded, but when I started to get it for her she took hold of the lapel of my coat and said, "Listen, Eddie, will you tell me something? Honest to God?"

I said, "Sure," feeling kind of embarrassed looking in her face like that, "if I can."

"Is Loney really in love with me?"

That was a tough one. I could feel my face getting redder and redder. I wished the door would open and Loney would come in. I wished a fire would break out or something.

She jerked my lapel. "Is he?"

I said, "I guess so. I guess he is, all right."

"Don't you know?"

I said, "Sure, I know, but Loney don't ever talk to me about things like that. Honest, he don't."

She bit her lip and turned her back on me. I was sweating. I spent as long a time as I could in the kitchen getting the whisky and things. When I went back in the dining-room she had sat down and was putting lip-stick on her mouth. I set the whisky down on the table beside her.

She smiled at me and said, "You're a nice boy, Eddie. I hope you win a million fights. When do you fight again?"

I had to laugh at that. I guess I had been going around thinking that everybody in the world knew I was going to fight Sailor Perelman that Saturday just because it was my first main event. I guess that is the way you get a swelled head. I said, "This Saturday."

"That's fine," she said, and looked at her wrist-watch. "Oh, why doesn't he come? I've got to be home before Jake gets there." She jumped up. "Well, I can't wait any longer. I shouldn't have stayed this long. Will you tell Loney something for me?"

"Sure."

"And not another soul?"

"Sure."

She came around the table and took hold of my lapel again. "Well, listen. You tell him that somebody's been talking to Jake about—about us. You tell him we've got to be careful, Jake'd kill both of us. You tell him I don't think Jake knows for sure yet, but we've got to be careful. Tell Loney not to phone me and to wait here till I phone him to-morrow afternoon. Will you tell him that?"

"Sure."

"And don't let him do anything crazy."

I said, "I won't." I would have said anything to get it over with.

She said, "You're a nice boy, Eddie," and kissed me on the mouth and went out of the house.

I did not go to the door with her. I looked at the whisky on the table and thought maybe I ought to take the first drink of my life, but instead I sat down and thought about Loney. Maybe I dozed off a little but I was awake when he came home and that was nearly two o'clock.

He was pretty tight. "What the hell are you doing up?" he said.

I told him about Mrs. Schiff and what she told me to tell him.

He stood there in his hat and overcoat until I had told it all, then he said, "That chiseling dago rat," kind of half under his breath and his face began to get like it got when he was mad.

"And she said you mustn't do anything crazy."

"Crazy?" He looked at me and kind of laughed. "No, I won't do anything crazy. How about you scramming off to bed?"

I said, "All right," and went upstairs.

The next morning he was still in bed when I left for the gym and he had gone out before I got home. I waited supper for him until nearly seven o'clock and then ate it by myself. Susan was getting sore because it was going to be late before she got through. Maybe he stayed out all night but he looked all right when he came in Tubby's the next afternoon to watch me work out, and he was making jokes and kidding along with the fellows hanging around there just like he had nothing at all on his mind.

He waited for me to dress and we walked over home together. The only thing that was kind of funny, he asked me, "How do you feel, Kid?" That was kind of funny because he knew I always felt all right. I guess I never even had a cold all my life.

I said, "All right."

"You're working good," he said. "Take it easy to-morrow. You want to be rested up for this baby from Providence. Like that chiseling dago rat said, he's plenty tough and plenty smart."

I said, "I guess he is. Loney, do you think Pete really tipped Big Jake off about—"

"Forget it," he said. "Hell with 'em." He poked my arm. "You got nothing to worry about but how you're going to be in there Saturday night."

"I'll be all right."

"Don't be too sure," he said. "Maybe you'll be lucky to get a draw."

I stopped still in the street, I was so surprised. Loney never talked like that about any of my fights before. He was always saying, "Don't worry about how tough this mug looks, just go in and knock him apart," or something like that.

I said, "You mean—?"

He took hold of my arm to start me walking again. "Maybe I overmatched you this time, Kid. This sailor's pretty good. He can box and he hits a lot harder than anybody you been up against so far."

"Oh, I'll be all right," I said.

"Maybe," he said, scowling straight ahead. "Listen, what do you think about what Pete said about you needing more boxing?"

"I don't know. I don't ever pay attention much to what anybody says but you."

"Well, what do you think about it now?" he asked.

"Sure, I'd like to learn to box better, I guess."

He grinned at me without moving his lips much. "You're liable to get some fine lessons from this Sailor whether you want 'em or not. But no kidding, suppose I told you to box him instead of tearing in, would you do it? I mean for the experience, even if you didn't make much of a showing that way."

I said, "Don't I always fight the way you tell me?"

"Sure you do. But suppose it meant maybe losing this once but learning something?"

"I want to win, of course," I said, "but I'll do anything you tell me. Do you want me to fight him that way?"

"I don't know," he said. "We'll see."

Friday and Saturday I just loafed around. Friday I tried to find somebody to go out and shoot pheasants with but all I could find was Bob Kirby and I was tired of listening to him make the same jokes over and over, so I changed my mind and stayed home.

Loney came home for supper and I asked him what the odds were on our fight.

He said, "Even money. You got a lot of friends."

"Are we betting?" I asked.

"Not yet. Maybe if the price gets better. I don't know."

I wished he had not been so afraid I was going to lose but I thought it might sound kind of conceited if I said anything about it, so I just went on eating.

We had a swell house that Saturday night. The armory was packed and we got a pretty good hand when we went in the ring. I felt fine and I guess Dick Cohen, who was going to be in my corner with Loney, felt fine too, because he looked like he was trying to keep from grinning. Only Loney looked kind of worried, not enough that you would notice it unless you knew him as well as I did, but I could notice it.

"I'm all right," I told him. A lot of fighters say they feel uncomfortable waiting for their fight to start but I always feel fine.

Loney said, "Sure you are," and slapped me on my back.

"Listen, Kid," he said, and cleared his throat. He put his mouth over close to my ear so nobody else would hear him. "Listen, Kid, maybe—maybe you better box him like we said. O.K.?"

I said, "O.K."

"And don't let those mugs out front yell you into anything. You're doing the fighting up there."

I said, "O.K."

The first couple of rounds were kind of fun in a way because this was new stuff to me, this moving around him on my toes and going in and out with my hands high. Of course I had done some of that with fellows in the gym but not in the ring before and not with anybody that was as good at it as he was. He was pretty good and had it all over me both of those rounds but nobody hurt anybody else.

But in the first minute of the third he got to my jaw with a honey of a right cross and then whammed me in the body twice fast with his left. Pete and Loney had not been kidding when they said he could hit. I forgot about boxing and went in pumping with both hands, driving him all the way across the ring before he tied me up in a clinch. Everybody yelled so I guess it looked pretty good but I only really hit him once; he took the rest of them on his arms. He was the smartest fighter I had ever been up against.

By the time Pop Agnew broke us I remembered I was supposed to be boxing so I went back to that, but Perelman was going faster and I spent most of the rest of the round trying to keep his left out of my face.

"Hurt you?" Loney asked when I was back in my corner.

"Not yet," I said, "but he can hit."

In the fourth I stopped another right cross with my eye and a lot of lefts with other parts of my face and the fifth round was still tougher. For one thing, the eye he had hit me in was almost shut by that time and for another thing I guess he had me pretty well figured out. He went around and around me, not letting me get set.

"How do you feel?" Loney asked when he and Dick were working on me after that round. His voice was funny, like he had a cold.

I said, "All right." It was hard to talk much because my lips were puffed out.

"Cover up more," Loney said.

I shook my head up and down to say I would.

"And don't pay any attention to those mugs out front."

I had been too busy with Sailor Perelman to pay much attention to anybody else but when we came out for the sixth round I could hear people hollering things like, "Go in and fight him, Kid," and "Come on, Kid, go to work on this guy," and "What are you waiting for, Kid?" so I guessed they had been hollering like that all along. Maybe that had something to do with it or maybe I just wanted to show Loney that I was still all right so he would not worry about me. Anyway, along toward the last part of the round, when Perelman jarred me with another one of those right crosses that I was having so much trouble with, I got down low and went in after him. He hit me some but not enough to keep me away and, even if he did take care of most of my punches, I got in a couple of good ones and I could tell that he felt them. And when he tied me up in a clinch I knew he could do it because he was smarter than me and not because he was stronger.

"What's the matter with you?" he growled in my ear. "Are you gone nuts?" I never liked to talk in the ring so I just grinned to myself without saying anything and kept trying to get a hand loose.

Loney scowled at me when I sat down after that round. "What's the matter with you?" he said. "Didn't I tell you to box him?" He was awful pale and his voice was hoarse.

I said, "All right, I will."

Dick Cohen began to curse over on the side I could not see out of. He did not seem to be cursing anybody or anything, just cursing in a low voice until Loney told him to shut up.

I wanted to ask Loney what I ought to do about that right cross but, with my mouth the way it was, talking was a lot of work and, besides, my nose was stopped up and I had to use my mouth for breathing, so I kept quiet. Loney and Dick worked harder on me than they had between any of the other rounds. When Loney crawled out of the ring just before the gong he slapped me on the shoulder and said in a sharp voice, "Now box."

I went out and boxed. Perelman must have got to my face thirty times that round; anyway it felt like he did, but I kept on trying to box him. It seemed like a long round.

I went back to my corner not feeling exactly sick but like I might be going to get sick, and that was funny because I could not remember being hit in the stomach to amount to anything. Mostly Perelman had been working on my head. Loney looked a lot sicker than I felt. He looked so sick I tried not to look at him and I felt kind of ashamed of making a bum out of him by letting this Perelman make a monkey out of me like he was doing.

"Can you last it out?" Loney asked.

When I tried to answer him I found that I could not move my lower lip because the inside of it was stuck on a broken tooth. I put a thumb up to it and Loney pushed my glove away and pulled my lip loose from the tooth.

Then I said, "Sure. I'll get the hang of it pretty soon."

Loney made a queer gurgling kind of noise down in his throat and all of a sudden put his face up close in front of mine so that I had to stop looking at the floor and look at him. His eyes were like you think a hophead's are. "Listen, Kid," he says, his voice sounding cruel and hard, almost like he hated me. "To hell with this stuff. Go in and get that mug. What the hell are you boxing for? You're a fighter. Get in there and fight."

I started to say something and then stopped, and I had a goofy idea that I would like to kiss him or something and then he was climbing through the ropes and the gong rang.

I did like Loney said and I guess I took that round by a pretty good edge. It was swell, fighting my own way again, going in banging away with both hands, not swinging or anything silly like that, just shooting them in short and hard, leaning from side to side to get everything from the ankles up into them. He hit me of course but I figured he was not likely to be able to hit me any harder than he had in the other rounds and I had stood up under that, so I was not worrying about it now. Just before the gong rang I threw him out of a clinch and when it rang I had him covering up in a corner.

It was swell back in my corner. Everybody was yelling all around except Loney and Dick and neither of them said a single word to me. They hardly looked at me, just at the parts they were working on and they were rougher with me than they ever were before. You would have thought I was a machine they were fixing up. Loney was not looking sick any more. I could tell he was excited because his face was set hard and still. I like to remember him that way, he was awful good-looking. Dick was whistling between his teeth very low while he doused my head with a sponge.

I got Perelman sooner than I expected, in the ninth. The first part of the round was his because he came out moving fast and left-handing me and making me look pretty silly, I guess, but he could not keep it up and I got in under one of his lefts and cracked him on the chin with a left hook, the first time I had been able to lay one on his head the way I wanted to. I knew it was a good one even before his head went back and I threw six punches at him as fast as I could get them out—left, right, left, right, left, right. He took care of four of them but I got him on the chin again with a right and just above his trunks with another, and when his knees bent a little and he tried to clinch I pushed him away and smacked him on the cheek-bone with everything I had.

Then Dick Cohen was putting my bathrobe over my shoulders and hugging me and sniffling and cursing and laughing all at the same time, and across the ring they were propping Perelman up on his stool.

"Where's Loney?" I asked.

Dick looked around. "I don't know. He was here. Boy, was that a mill!"

Loney caught up to us just as we were going in the dressing-room. "I had to see a fellow," he said. His eyes were bright like he was laughing at something, but he was white as a ghost and he held his lips tight against his teeth even when he grinned kind of lopsided at me and said, "It's going to be a long time before anybody beats you, Kid."

I said I hoped it was. I was awful tired now that it was all over. Usually I get awful hungry after a fight but this time I was just awful tired.

Loney went across to where he had hung his coat and put it on over his sweater, and when he put it on the tail of it caught and I saw he had a gun in his hip pocket. That was funny because I never knew him to carry a gun before and if he had had it in the ring everybody would have been sure to see it when he bent over working on me. I could not ask him about it because there were a lot of people in there talking and arguing.

Pretty soon Perelman came in with his manager and two other men who were strangers to me, so I guessed they had come down from Providence with him too. He was looking straight ahead but the others looked kind of hard at Loney and me and went up to the other end of the room without saying anything. We all dressed in one long room there.

Loney said to Dick, who was helping me, "Take your time. I don't want the Kid to go out till he's cooled off."

Perelman got dressed pretty quick and went out still looking straight ahead. His manager and the two men with him stopped in front of us. The manager was a big man with green eyes like a fish and a dark kind of flat face. He had an accent, too, maybe he was a Polack. He said, "Smart boys, huh?"

Loney was standing up with one hand behind him. Dick Cohen put his hands on the back of a chair and kind of leaned over it. Loney said, "I'm smart. The Kid fights the way I tell him to fight."

The manager looked at me and looked at Dick and looked at Loney again and said, "M-m-m, so that's the way it is." He thought a minute and said, "That's something to know." Then he pulled his hat down tighter on his head and turned around and went out with the other two men following.

I asked Loney, "What's the matter?"

He laughed, but not like it was anything funny. "Bad losers."

"But you've got a gun in—"

He cut me off. "Uh-huh, a fellow asked me to hold it for him. I got to go give it back to him now. You and Dick go on home and I'll see you there in a little while. But don't hurry, because I want you to cool off before you go out. You two take the car, you know where we parked it. Come here, Dick."

He took Dick over in a corner and whispered to him. Dick kept nodding his head up and down and looking more and more scared, even if he did try to hide it when he turned around to me. Loney said, "Be seeing you," and went out.

"What's the matter?" I asked Dick.

He shook his head and said, "It's nothing to worry about," and that was every word I could get out of him.

Five minutes later Bob Kirby's brother Pudge ran in and yelled, "Jees, they shot Loney!"

I shot Loney. If I was not so dumb he would still be alive any way you figure it. For a long time I blamed it on Mrs. Schiff, but I guess that was just to keep from admitting that it was my own fault. I mean I never thought she actually did the shooting, like the people who said that when he missed the train that they were supposed to go away on together she came back and waited outside the armory and when he came out he told her he had changed his mind and she shot him. I mean I blamed her for lying to him, because it came out that nobody had tipped Big Jake off about her and Loney. Loney had put the idea in her head, telling her about what Pete had said, and she had made up the lie so Loney would go away with her. But if I was not so dumb Loney would have caught that train.

Then a lot of people said Big Jake killed Loney. They said that was why the police never got very far, on account of Big Jake's pull down at the City Hall. It was a fact that he had come home earlier than Mrs. Schiff had expected and she had left a note for him saying that she was running away with Loney, and he could have made it down to the street near the armory where Loney was shot in time to do it, but he could not have got to the railroad station in time to catch their train, and if I was not so dumb Loney would have caught that train.

And the same way if that Sailor Perelman crowd did it, which is what most people including the police thought even if they did have to let him go because they could not find enough evidence against him. If I was not so dumb Loney could have said to me right out, "Listen, Kid, I've got to go away and I've got to have all the money I can scrape up and the best way to do it is to make a deal with Perelman for you to go in the tank and then bet all we got against you." Why, I would have thrown a million fights for Loney, but how could he know he could trust me, with me this dumb?

Or I could have guessed what he wanted and I could have gone down when Perelman copped me with that uppercut in the fifth. That would have been easy. Or if I was not so dumb I would have learned to box better and, even losing to Perelman like I would have anyway, I could have kept him from chopping me to pieces so bad that Loney could not stand it any more and had to throw away everything by telling me to stop boxing and go in and fight.

Or even if everything had happened like it did up to then he could still have ducked out at the last minute if I was not so dumb that he had to stick around to look out for me by telling those Providence guys that I had nothing to do with double-crossing them.

I wish I was dead instead of Loney.

TWO SHARP
KNIVES

design, art

On my way home from the regular Wednesday night poker game at
Ben Kamsley's I stopped at the railroad station to see the 2:11 come
in—what we called putting the town to bed—and as soon as this
fellow stepped down from the smoking-car I recognized him.
There was no mistaking his face, the pale eyes with lower lids that were as
straight as if they had been drawn with a ruler, the noticeably flat-tipped
bony nose, the deep cleft in his chin, the slightly hollow grayish cheeks. He
was tall and thin and very neatly dressed in a dark suit, long dark overcoat,
and derby hat, and carried a black Gladstone bag. He looked a few years
older than the forty he was supposed to be. He went past me toward the
street steps.

When I turned around to follow him I saw Wally Shane coming out of
the waiting-room. I caught Wally's eye and nodded at the man carrying the
black bag. Wally examined him carefully as he went by. I could not see
whether the man noticed the examination. By the time I came up to Wally
the man was going down the steps to the street.

Wally rubbed his lips together and his blue eyes were bright and hard.
"Look," he said out of the side of his mouth, "that's a ringer for the guy we
got—"

"That's the guy," I said, and we went down the steps behind him.

Our man started toward one of the taxicabs at the curb, then saw the
lights of the Deerwood Hotel two blocks away, shook his head at the taxi
driver, and went up the street afoot.

"What do we do?" Wally asked. "See what he's—?"

"It's nothing to us. We take him. Get my car. It's at the corner of the alley."

I gave Wally the few minutes he needed to get the car and then closed in. "Hello, Furman," I said when I was just behind the tall man.

His face jerked around to me. "How do you—" He halted. "I don't believe I—" He looked up and down the street. We had the block to ourselves.

"You're Lester Furman, aren't you?" I asked.

He said, "Yes," quickly.

"Philadelphia?"

He peered at me in the light that was none too strong where we stood. "Yes."

"I'm Scott Anderson," I said. "Chief of police here. I—"

His bag thudded down on the pavement. "What's happened to her?" he asked hoarsely.

"Happened to whom?"

Wally arrived in my car then, abruptly, skidding into the curb. Furman, his face stretched by fright, leaped back away from me. I went after him, grabbing him with my good hand, jamming him back against the front wall of Henderson's warehouse. He fought with me there until Wally got out of the car. Then he saw Wally's uniform and immediately stopped fighting.

"I'm sorry," he said weakly. "I thought—for a second I thought maybe you weren't the police. You're not in uniform and— It was silly of me. I'm sorry."

"It's all right," I told him. "Let's get going before we have a mob around us." Two cars had stopped just a little beyond mine and I could see a bell-boy and a hatless man coming toward us from the direction of the hotel. Furman picked up his bag and went willingly into my car ahead of me. We sat in the rear. Wally drove. We rode a block in silence, then Furman asked, "You're taking me to police headquarters?"

"Yes."

"What for?"

"Philadelphia."

"I"—he cleared his throat—"I don't think I understand you."

"You understand that you're wanted in Philadelphia, don't you, for murder?"

He said indignantly, "That's ridiculous. Murder! That's—" He put a hand on my arm, his face close to mine, and instead of indignation in his voice there was now a desperate sort of earnestness. "Who told you that?"

"I didn't make it up. Well, here we are. Come on, I'll show you."

We took him into my office. George Propper, who had been dozing in a chair in the front office, followed us in. I found the Trans-American Detective Agency circular and handed it to Furman. In the usual form it offered fifteen hundred dollars for the arrest and conviction of Lester Furman, alias Lloyd Fields, alias J. D. Carpenter, for the murder of Paul Frank Dunlap in Philadelphia on the twenty-sixth of the previous month.

Furman's hands holding the circular were steady and he read it carefully. His face was pale, but no muscles moved in it until he opened his mouth to speak. He tried to speak calmly. "It's a lie." He did not look up from the circular.

"You're Lester Furman, aren't you?" I asked.

He nodded, still not looking up.

"That's your description, isn't it?"

He nodded.

"That's your photograph, isn't it?"

He nodded, and then, staring at his photograph on the circular, he began to tremble—his lips, his hands, his legs.

I pushed a chair up behind him and said, "Sit down," and he dropped down on it and shut his eyes, pressing the lids together. I took the circular from his limp hands.

George Propper, leaning against a side of the doorway, turned his loose grin from me to Wally and said, "So that's that and so you lucky stiffs split a grand and a half reward money. Lucky Wally! If it ain't vacations in New York at the city's expense it's reward money."

Furman jumped up from the chair and screamed, "It's a lie. It's a frame-up. You can't prove anything. There's nothing to prove. I never killed anybody. I won't be framed. I won't be—"

I pushed him down on the chair again. "Take it easy," I told him. "You're wasting your breath on us. Save it for the Philadelphia police. We're just holding you for them. If anything's wrong it's there, not here."

"But it's not the police. It's the Trans-American De—"

"We turn you over to the police."

He started to say something, broke off, sighed, made a little hopeless gesture with his hands, and tried to smile. "Then there's nothing I can do now?"

"There's nothing any of us can do till morning," I said. "We'll have to search you, then we won't bother you any more till they come for you."

In the black Gladstone bag we found a couple of changes of clothes, some toilet articles, and a loaded .38 automatic. In his pockets we found a hundred and sixty-some dollars, a book of checks on a Philadelphia bank, business cards and a few letters that seemed to show he was in the real-estate business, and the sort of odds and ends that you usually find in men's pockets. While Wally was putting these things in the vault I told George Propper to lock Furman up.

George rattled keys in his pocket and said, "Come along, darling. We ain't had anybody in our little hoosegow for three days. You'll have it all to yourself, just like a suite in the Ritz."

Furman said, "Good night and thank you," to me, and followed George out.

When George came back he leaned against the doorframe again and asked, "How about you big-hearted boys cutting me in on a little of that blood money?"

Wally said, "Sure. I'll forget that two and a half you been owing me three months."

I said, "Make him as comfortable as you can, George. If he wants anything sent in, O.K."

"He's valuable, huh? If it was some bum that didn't mean a nickel to you— Maybe I ought to take a pillow off my bed for him." He spat at the cuspidor and missed. "He's just like the rest of 'em to me."

I thought, *Any day now I'm going to forget that your uncle is county chairman and throw you back in the gutter.* I said, "Do all the talking you want, but do what I tell you."

It was about four o'clock when I got home—my farm was a little outside the town—and maybe half an hour after that before I went to sleep. The telephone woke me up at five minutes past six.

Wally's voice: "You better come down, Scott. The fellow Furman's hung himself."

"What?"

"By his belt—from a window bar—deader'n hell."

"All right. I'm on my way. Phone Ben Kamsley I'll pick him up on my way in."

"No doctor's going to do this man any good, Scott."

"It won't hurt to have him looked at," I insisted. "You'd better phone Douglassville, too." Douglassville was the county seat.

"O.K."

Wally phoned me back while I was dressing to tell me that Ben Kamsley had been called out on an emergency case and was somewhere on the other side of town, but that his wife would get in touch with him and tell him to stop at headquarters on his way home.

When, riding into town, I was within fifty or sixty feet of the Red Top Diner, Heck Jones ran out with a revolver in his hand and began to shoot at two men in a black roadster that had just passed me.

I leaned out and yelled, "What's it?" at him while I was turning my car.

"Hold-up," he bawled angrily. "Wait for me." He let loose another shot that couldn't have missed my front tire by more than an inch, and galloped up to me, his apron flapping around his fat legs. I opened the door for him, he squeezed his bulk in beside me, and we set off after the roadster.

"What gets me," he said when he had stopped panting, "is they done it like a joke. They come in, they don't want nothing but ham and eggs and coffee and then they get kind of kidding together under their breath and then they put the guns on me like a joke."

"How much did they take?"

"Sixty or thereabouts, but that ain't what gripes me so much. It's them doing it like a joke."

"Never mind," I said. "We'll get 'em."

We very nearly didn't, though. They led us a merry chase. We lost them a couple of times and finally picked them up more by luck than anything else, a couple of miles over the state line.

We didn't have any trouble taking them, once we had caught up to them, but they knew they had crossed the state line and they insisted on a regular extradition or nothing, so we had to carry them on to Badington and stick them in the jail there until the necessary papers could be sent through. It was ten o'clock before I got a chance to phone my office.

Hammill answered the phone and told me Ted Carroll, our district attorney, was there, so I talked to Ted—though not as much as he talked to me.

"Listen, Scott," he asked excitedly, "what is all this?"

"All what?"

"This fiddlededee, this hanky-panky."

"I don't know what you mean," I said. "Wasn't it suicide?"

"Sure it was suicide, but I wired the Trans-American and they phoned me just a few minutes ago and said they'd never sent out any circulars on Furman, didn't know about any murder he was wanted for. All they knew about him was he used to be a client of theirs."

I couldn't think of anything to say except that I would be back in Deerwood by noon. And I was.

Ted was at my desk with the telephone receiver clamped to his ear, saying, "Yes. . . . Yes. . . . Yes," when I went into the office. He put down the receiver and asked, "What happened to you?"

"A couple of boys knocked over the Red Top Diner and I had to chase 'em almost to Badington."

He smiled with one side of his mouth. "The town getting out of your hands?" He and I were on opposite sides of the fence politically and we took our politics seriously in Candle County.

I smiled back at him. "Looks like it—with one felony in six months."

"And this." He jerked a thumb toward the rear of the building, where the cells were.

"What about this? Let's talk about this."

"It's plenty wrong," he said. "I just finished talking to the Philly police. There wasn't any Paul Frank Dunlap murdered there that they know about; they've got no unexplained murder on the twenty-sixth of last month." He looked at me as if it were my fault. "What'd you get out of Furman before you let him hang himself?"

"That he was innocent."

"Didn't you grill him? Didn't you find out what he was doing in town? Didn't you—"

"What for?" I asked. "He admitted his name was Furman, the description fitted him, the photograph was him, the Trans-American's supposed to be on the level. Philadelphia wanted him, I didn't. Sure, if I'd known he was going to hang himself— You said he'd been a client of the Trans-American. They tell you what the job was?"

"His wife left him a couple of years ago and he had them hunting for her for five or six months, but they never found her. They're sending a man up to-night to look it over." He stood up. "I'm going to get some lunch." At the door he turned his head over his shoulder to say, "There'll probably be trouble over this."

I knew that; there usually is when somebody dies in a cell.

George Propper came in grinning happily. "So what's become of that fifteen hundred fish?"

"What happened last night?" I asked.

"Nothing. He hung hisself."

"Did you find him?"

He shook his head. "Wally took a look in there to see how things was before he went off duty, and found him."

"You were asleep, I suppose."

"Well, I was catching a nap, I guess," he mumbled, "but everybody does that sometimes—even Wally sometimes when he comes in off his beat between rounds—and I always wake up when the phone rings or anything. And suppose I had been awake. You can't hear a guy hanging hisself."

"Did Kamsley say how long he'd been dead?"

"He done it about five o'clock, he said he guessed. You want to look at the remains? They're over at Fritz's undertaking parlor."

I said, "Not now. You'd better go home and get some more sleep, so your insomnia won't keep you awake to-night."

He said, "I feel almost as bad about you and Wally losing all that dough as you do," and went out chuckling.

Ted Carroll came back from lunch with the notion that perhaps there was some connection between Furman and the two men who had robbed Heck Jones. That didn't seem to make much sense, but I promised to look into it. Naturally, we never did find any such connection.

That evening a fellow named Rising, assistant manager of the Trans-American Detective Agency's Philadelphia branch, arrived. He brought the dead man's lawyer, a scrawny, asthmatic man named Wheelock, with him. After they had identified the body we went back to my office for a conference.

It didn't take me long to tell them all I knew, with the one additional fact I had picked up during the afternoon, which was that the police in most towns in our corner of the state had received copies of the reward circular. Rising examined the circular and called it an excellent forgery: paper, style, type were all almost exactly those used by his agency.

They told me the dead man was a well-known, respectable, and prosperous citizen of Philadelphia. In 1938 he had married a twenty-two-year-old girl named Ethel Brian, the daughter of a respectable, if not prosperous, Philadelphia family. They had a child born in 1940, but it lived only a few months. In 1941 Furman's wife had disappeared and neither he nor her family had heard of her since, though he had spent a good deal of money trying to find her. Rising showed me a photograph of her, a small-featured, pretty blonde with a weak mouth and large, staring eyes.

"I'd like to have a copy made," I said.

"You can keep that. It's one of them that we had made. Her description's on the back."

"Thanks. And he didn't divorce her?"

Rising shook his head with emphasis. "No, sir. He was a lot in love with her and he seemed to think the kid's dying had made her a little screwy and she didn't know what she was doing." He looked at the lawyer. "That right?"

Wheelock made a couple of asthmatic sounds and said, "That is my belief."

"You said he had money. About how much, and who gets it?"

The scrawny layer wheezed some more, said, "I should say his estate will amount to perhaps half a million dollars, left in its entirety to his wife." That gave me something to think about, but the thinking didn't help me out then.

They couldn't tell me why he had come to Deerwood. He seemed to have told nobody where he was going, had simply told his servants and his employees that he was leaving town for a day or two. Neither Rising nor Wheelock knew of any enemies he had. That was the crop.

And that was still the crop at the inquest the next day. Everything showed that somebody had framed Furman into our jail and that the frame-up had driven him to suicide. Nothing showed anything else. And there had to be something else, a lot else.

Some of the else began to show up immediately after the inquest. Ben Kamsley was waiting for me when I left the undertaking parlor, where the inquest had been held. "Let's get out of the crowd," he said. "I want to tell you something."

"Come on over to the office."

We went over there. He shut the door, which usually stayed open, and sat on a corner of my desk. His voice was low. "Two of those bruises showed."

"What bruises?"

He looked curiously at me for a second, then put a hand on the top of his head. "Furman—up under the hair—there were two bruises."

I tried to keep from shouting. "Why didn't you tell me?"

"I am telling you. You weren't here that morning. This is the first time I've seen you since."

I cursed the two hoodlums who had kept me away by sticking up the Red Top Diner and demanded, "Then why didn't you spill it when you were testifying at the inquest?"

He frowned. "I'm a friend of yours. Do I want to put you in a spot where people can say you drove this chap to suicide by third-degreeing him too rough?"

"You're nuts," I said. "How bad was his head?"

"That didn't kill him, if that's what you mean. There's nothing the matter with his skull. Just a couple of bruises nobody would notice unless they parted the hair."

"It killed him just the same," I growled. "You and your *friendship—*"

The telephone rang. It was Fritz. "Listen, Scott," he said, "there's a couple ladies here that want a look at that fellow. Is it all right?"

"Who are they?"

"I don't know 'em—strangers."

"Why do they want to see him?"

"I don't know. Wait a minute."

A woman's voice came over the wire: "Can't I please see him?" It was a very pleasant, earnest voice.

"Why do you want to see him?" I asked.

"Well, I"—there was a long pause—"I am"—a shorter pause, and when she finished the sentence her voice was not much more than a whisper—"his wife."

"Oh, certainly," I said. "I'll be right over."

I hurried out.

Leaving the building, I ran into Wally Shane. He was in civilian clothes, since he was off duty. "Hey, Scott?" He took my arm and dragged me back into the vestibule, out of sight of the street. "A couple of dames came into Fritz's just as I was leaving. One of 'em's Hotcha Randall, a baby with a record as long as your arm. You know she's one of that mob you had me working on in New York last summer."

"She know you?"

He grinned. "Sure. But not by my right name, and she thinks I'm a Detroit hoodlum."

"I mean did she know you just now?"

"I don't think she saw me. Anyway, she didn't give me a tumble."

"You don't know the other one?"

"No. She's a blonde, kind of pretty."

"O.K.," I said. "Stick around a while, but out of sight. Maybe I'll be bringing them back with me." I crossed the street to the undertaking parlor.

Ethel Furman was prettier than her photograph had indicated. The woman with her was five or six years older, quite a bit larger, handsome in a big, somewhat coarse way. Both of them were attractively dressed in styles that hadn't reached Deerwood yet.

The big woman was introduced to me as Mrs. Crowder. I said, "I thought your name was Randall."

She laughed. "What do you care, Chief? I'm not hurting your town."

I said, "Don't call me Chief. To you big-city slickers I'm the town whittler. We go back through here."

Ethel Furman didn't make any fuss over her husband when she saw him. She simply looked gravely at his face for about three minutes, then turned away and said, "Thank you," to me.

"I'll have to ask you some questions," I said, "so if you'll come across the street . . ."

She nodded. "And I'd like to ask you some." She looked at her companion. "If Mrs. Crowder will—"

"Call her Hotcha," I said. "We're all among friends. Sure, she'll come along, too."

The Randall woman said, "Aren't you the cut-up?" and took my arm.

IN MY OFFICE   I gave them chairs and said, "Before I ask you anything I want to tell you something. Furman didn't commit suicide. He was murdered."

Ethel Furman opened her eyes wide. "Murdered?"

Hotcha Randall said, as if she had had the words on the tip of her tongue right along, "We've got alibis. We were in New York. We can prove it."

"You're likely to get a chance to, too," I told her. "How'd you people happen to come down here?"

Ethel Furman repeated, "Murdered?" in a dazed tone.

The Randall woman said, "Who's got a better right to come down here? She was still his wife, wasn't she? She's entitled to some of his estate, isn't she? She's got a right to look out for her own interests, hasn't she?"

That reminded me of something. I picked up the telephone and told Hammill to have somebody get hold of the lawyer Wheelock—he had stayed over for the inquest, of course—before he left town, and tell him I wanted to see him. "And is Wally around?"

"He's not here. He said you told him to keep out of sight. I'll find him, though."

"Right. Tell him I want him to go to New York to-night. Send Mason home to get some sleep. He'll have to take over Wally's night trick."

Hammill said, "Oke," and I turned back to my guests.

Ethel Furman had come out of her daze. She leaned forward and asked, "Mr. Anderson, do you think I had—had anything to do with Lester's—with his death?"

"I don't know. I know he was killed. I know he left you something like half a million."

The Randall woman whistled softly. She came over and put a diamond-ringed hand on my shoulder. "Dollars?"

When I nodded, the delight went out of her face, leaving it serious. "All right, Chief," she said, "now don't be a clown. The kid didn't have a thing to do with whatever you think happened. We read about him committing suicide in yesterday morning's paper, and about there being something funny about it, and I persuaded her to come down and—"

Ethel Furman interrupted her friend. "Mr. Anderson, I wouldn't have done anything to hurt Lester. I left him because I wanted to leave him, but I wouldn't have done anything to him for money or anything else. Why, if I'd wanted money from him all I'd've had to do would've been to ask him. Why, he used to put ads in papers telling me if I wanted anything to let him know, but I never did. You can—his lawyer—anybody who knew anything about it can tell you that."

The Randall woman took up the story. "That's the truth, Chief. I've been telling her she was a chump not to tap him, but she never would. I had a hard enough time getting her to come for her share now he's dead and got nobody else to leave it to."

Ethel Furman said, "I wouldn't've hurt him."

"Why'd you leave him?"

She moved her shoulders. "I don't know how to say it. The way we lived wasn't the way I wanted to live. I wanted—I don't know what. Anyway, after the baby died I couldn't stand it any more and cleared out, but I didn't want anything from him and I wouldn't've hurt him. He was always good to me. I was—I was the one that was wrong."

The telephone rang. Hammill's voice. "I found both of 'em. Wally's home. I told him. The old guy Wheelock is on his way over."

I dug out the phony reward circular and showed it to Ethel Furman. "This is what got him into the can. Did you ever see that picture before?"

She started to say "No," then a frightened look came into her face. "Why, that's—it can't be. It's—it's a snapshot I had—have. It's an enlargement of it."

"Who else has one?"

Her face became more frightened, but she said, "Nobody that I know of. I don't think anybody else could have one."

"You've still got yours?"

"Yes. I don't remember whether I've seen it recently—it's with some old papers and things—but I must have it."

I said, "Well, Mrs. Furman, it's stuff like that that's got to be checked up, and neither of us can dodge it. Now there are two ways we can play it. I can hold you here on suspicion till I've had time to check things up, or I can send one of my men back to New York with you for the check-up. I'm willing to do that if you'll speed things up by helping him all you can and if you'll promise me you won't try any tricks."

"I promise," she said. "I'm as anxious as you are to—"

"All right. How'd you come down?"

"I drove," the Randall woman said. "That's my car, the big green one across the street."

"Fine. Then he can ride back with you, but no funny business."

The telephone rang again while they were assuring me there would be no funny business. Hammill said, "Wheelock's here."

"Send him in."

The lawyer's asthma nearly strangled him when he saw Ethel Furman. Before he could get himself straightened out I asked, "This is really Mrs. Furman?"

He wagged his head up and down, still wheezing.

"Fine," I said. "Wait for me. I'll be back in a little while." I herded the two women out and across the street to the green car. "Straight up to the end of the street and then two blocks left," I told the Randall woman, who was at the wheel.

"Where are we going?" she asked.

"To see Shane, the man who's going to New York with you."

Mrs. Dober, Wally's landlady, opened the door for us.

"Wally in?" I asked.

"Yes, indeedy, Mr. Anderson. Go right on up." She was staring with wide-eyed curiosity at my companions while talking to me.

We went up a flight of stairs and I knocked on his door.

"Who is it?" he called.

"Scott."

"Come on in."

I pushed the door open and stepped aside to let the women in.

Ethel Furman gasped, "Harry," and stepped back.

Wally had a hand behind him, but my gun was already out in my hand. "I guess you win," he said.

I said I guessed I did and we all went back to headquarters.

"I'm a sap," he complained when he and I were alone in my office. "I knew it was all up as soon as I saw those two dames going into Fritz's. Then, when I was ducking out of sight and ran into you, I was afraid you'd take me over with you, so I had to tell you one of 'em knew me, figuring you'd want to keep me under cover for a little while anyhow—long enough for me to get out of town. And then I didn't have sense enough to go.

"I drop in home to pick up a couple of things before I scram and that call of Hammill's catches me and I fall for it plenty. I figure I'm getting a break. I figure you're not on yet and are going to send me back to New York as the Detroit hood again to see what dope I can get out of these folks, and I'll be sitting pretty. Well, you fooled me, brother, or didn't— Listen, Scott, you didn't just stumble into that accidentally, did you?"

"No. Furman had to be murdered by a copper. A copper was most likely to know reward circulars well enough to make a good job of forging one. Who printed that for you?"

"Go on with your story," he said. "I'm not dragging anybody in with me. It was only a poor mug of a printer that needed dough."

"Okay. Only a copper would be sure enough of the routine to know how things would be handled. Only a copper—one of my coppers—would be able to walk into his cell, bang him across the head, and string him up on the— Those bruises showed."

"They did? I wrapped the blackjack in a towel, figuring it would knock him out without leaving a mark anybody'd find under the hair. I seem to've slipped up a lot."

"So that narrows it down to my coppers," I went on, "and—well—you told me you knew the Randall woman, and there it was, only I figured you were working with them. What got you into this?"

He made a sour mouth. "What gets most saps in jams? A yen for easy dough. I'm in New York, see, working on that Dutton job for you, palling around with gamblers, and racketeers, passing for one of them; and I get to figuring that here my work takes as much brains as theirs, and is as tough and dangerous as theirs, but they're taking in big money and I'm working for coffee and doughnuts. That kind of stuff gets you.

"Then I run into this Ethel and she goes for me like a house afire. I like her, too, so that's dandy; but one night she tells me about this husband of hers and how much dough he's got and how nuts he is about her and how he's still trying to find her, and I get to thinking. I think she's nuts enough about me to marry me. I still think she'd marry me if she didn't know I killed him. Divorcing him's no good, because the chances are she wouldn't take any money from him and, anyway, it would only be part. So I got to thinking about suppose he died and left her the roll.

"That was more like it. I ran down to Philly a couple of afternoons and looked him up and everything looked fine. He didn't even have anybody else close enough to leave more than a little of his dough to. So I did it. Not right away; I took my time working out the details, meanwhile writing to her through a fellow in Detroit.

"And then I did it. I sent those circulars out—to a lot of places—not wanting to point too much at this one. And when I was ready I phoned him, telling him if he'd come to the Deerwood Hotel that night, some time between then and the next night, he'd hear from Ethel. And, like I thought, he'd've fallen for any trap that was baited with her. You picking him up at the station was a break. If you hadn't, I'd've had to discover he was registered at the hotel that night. Anyway, I'd've killed him and pretty soon I'd've started drinking or something, and you'd've fired me and I'd've gone off and married Ethel and her half-million under my Detroit name." He made the sour mouth again. "Only I guess I'm not as sharp as I thought."

"Maybe you are," I said, "but that doesn't always help. Old man Kamsley, Ben's father, used to have a saying, 'To a sharp knife comes a tough steak.' I'm sorry you did it, Wally. I always liked you."

He smiled wearily. "I know you did," he said. "I was counting on that."

DEATH ON
PINE STREET

A plump maid with bold green eyes and a loose, full-lipped mouth led me up two flights of steps and into an elaborately furnished boudoir, where a woman in black sat at a window. She was a thin woman of a little more than thirty, this murdered man's widow, and her face was white and haggard.

"You are from the Continental Detective Agency?" she asked before I was two steps inside the room.

"Yes."

"I want you to find my husband's murderer." Her voice was shrill, and her dark eyes had wild lights in them. "The police have done nothing. Four days, and they have done nothing. They say it was a robber, but they haven't found him. They haven't found anything!"

"But, Mrs. Gilmore," I began, not exactly tickled to death with this explosion, "you must—"

"I know! I know!" she broke in. "But they have done nothing, I tell you—nothing. I don't believe they've made the slightest effort. I don't believe they want to find h-him!"

"Him?" I asked, because she had started to say *her*. "You think it was a man?"

She bit her lip and looked away from me, out of the window to where San Francisco Bay, the distance making toys of its boats, was blue under the early afternoon sun.

"I don't know," she said hesitantly; "it might have—"

Her face spun toward me—a twitching face—and it seemed impossible that anyone could talk so fast, hurl words out so rapidly one after the other.

"I'll tell you. You can judge for yourself. Bernard wasn't faithful to me. There was a woman who calls herself Cara Kenbrook. She wasn't the first. But I learned about her last month. We quarreled. Bernard promised to give her up. Maybe he didn't. But if he did, I wouldn't put it past her— A woman like that would do anything—anything. And down in my heart I really believe she did it!"

"And you think the police don't want to arrest her?"

"I didn't mean exactly that. I'm all unstrung, and likely to say anything. Bernard was mixed up in politics, you know; and if the police found, or thought, that politics had anything to do with his death, they might—I don't know just what I mean. I'm a nervous, broken woman, and full of crazy notions." She stretched a thin hand out to me. "Straighten this tangle out for me! Find the person who killed Bernard!"

I nodded with empty assurance, still not any too pleased with my client.

"Do you know this Kenbrook woman?" I asked.

"I've seen her on the street, and that's enough to know what sort of person she is!"

"Did you tell the police about her?"

"No-o." She looked out of the window again, and then, as I waited, she added, defensively:

"The police detectives who came to see me acted as if they thought I might have killed Bernard. I was afraid to tell them that I had cause for jealousy. Maybe I shouldn't have kept quiet about that woman, but I didn't think she had done it until afterward, when the police failed to find the murderer. Then I began to think she had done it; but I couldn't make myself go to the police and tell them that I had withheld information. I knew what they'd think. So I— You can twist it around so it'll look as if I hadn't known about the woman, can't you?"

"Possibly. Now as I understand it, your husband was shot on Pine Street, between Leavenworth and Jones, at about three o'clock Tuesday morning. That right?"

"Yes."

"Where was he going?"

"Coming home, I suppose; but I don't know where he had been. Nobody knows. The police haven't found out, if they have tried. He told me Monday evening that he had a business engagement. He was a building contractor, you know. He went out at about half-past eleven, saying he would probably be gone four or five hours."

"Wasn't that an unusual hour to be keeping a business engagement?"

"Not for Bernard. He often had men come to the house at midnight."

"Can you make any guess at all where he was going that night?"

She shook her head with emphasis.

"No. I knew nothing at all about his business affairs, and even the men in his office don't seem to know where he went that night."

That wasn't unlikely. Most of the B. F. Gilmore Construction Company's work had been on city and state contracts, and it isn't altogether unheard-of for secret conferences to go with that kind of work. Your politician-contractor doesn't always move in the open.

"How about enemies?" I asked.

"I don't know anybody that hated him enough to kill him."

"Where does this Kenbrook woman live, do you know?"

"Yes—in the Garford Apartments on Bush Street."

"Nothing you've forgotten to tell me, is there?" I asked, stressing the *me* a little.

"No, I've told you everything I know—every single thing."

Walking over to California Street, I shook down my memory for what I had heard here and there of Bernard Gilmore. I could remember a few things—the opposition papers had been in the habit of exposing him every election year—but none of them got me anywhere. I had known him by sight: a boisterous, red-faced man who had hammered his way up from hod-carrier to the ownership of a half-million-dollar business and a pretty place in politics. "A roughneck with a manicure," somebody had called him; a man with a lot of enemies and more friends; a big, good-natured, hard-hitting rowdy.

Odds and ends of a dozen graft scandals in which he had been mixed up, without anybody ever really getting anything on him, flitted through my head as I rode downtown on the too-small outside seat of a cable car. Then there had been some talk of a bootlegging syndicate of which he was sup-posed to be the head. . . .

I left the car at Kearny Street and walked over to the Hall of Justice. In the detectives' assembly-room I found O'Gar, the detective-sergeant in charge of the Homicide Detail: a squat man of fifty who went in for wide-brimmed hats of the movie-sheriff sort, but whose little blue eyes and bullet-head weren't handicapped by the trick headgear.

"I want some dope on the Gilmore killing," I told him.

"So do I," he came back. "But if you'll come along I'll tell you what little I know while I'm eating. I ain't had lunch yet."

Safe from eavesdroppers in the clatter of a Sutter Street lunchroom, the detective-sergeant leaned over his clam chowder and told me what he knew about the murder, which wasn't much.

"One of the boys, Kelly, was walking his beat early Tuesday morning, coming down the Jones Street hill from California Street to Pine. It was about three o'clock—no fog or nothing—a clear night. Kelly's within maybe twenty feet of Pine Street when he hears a shot. He whisks around the corner, and there's a man dying on the north sidewalk of Pine Street, halfway between Jones and Leavenworth. Nobody else is in sight. Kelly runs up to the man and finds it's Gilmore. Gilmore dies before he can say a word. The doctors say he was knocked down and then shot; because there's a bruise on his forehead, and the bullet slanted upward in his chest. See what I mean? He was lying on his back when the bullet hit him, with his feet pointing toward the gun it came from. It was a thirty-eight."

"Any money on him?"

O'Gar fed himself two spoons of chowder and nodded.

"Six hundred smacks, a coupla diamonds, and a watch. Nothing touched."

"What was he doing on Pine Street at that time in the morning?"

"Damned if I know, brother. Chances are he was going home, but we can't find out where he'd been. Don't even know what direction he was walking in when he was knocked over. He was lying across the sidewalk with his feet to the curb; but that don't mean nothing—he could of turned around three or four times after he was hit."

"All apartment buildings in that block, aren't there?"

"Uh-huh. There's an alley or two running off from the south side; but Kelly says he could see the mouths of both alleys when the shot was fired—before he turned the corner—and nobody got away through them."

"Reckon somebody who lives in that block did the shooting?" I asked.

O'Gar tilted his bowl, scooped up the last drops of the chowder, put them in his mouth, and grunted.

"Maybe. But we got nothing to show that Gilmore knew anybody in that block."

"Many people gather around afterward?"

"A few. There's always people on the street to come running if anything happens. But Kelly says there wasn't anybody that looked wrong—just the ordinary night crowd. The boys gave the neighborhood a combing, but didn't turn up anything."

"Any cars around?"

"Kelly says there wasn't, that he didn't see any, and couldn't of missed seeing it if there'd been one."

"What do you think?" I asked.

He got to his feet, glaring at me.

"I don't think," he said disagreeably; "I'm a police detective."

I knew by that that somebody had been panning him for not finding the murderer.

"I have a line on a woman," I told him. "Want to come along and talk to her with me?"

"I want to," he growled, "but I can't. I got to be in court this afternoon."

In the vestibule of the Garford Apartments, I pressed the button tagged Miss Cara Kenbrook several times before the door clicked open. Then I mounted a flight of stairs and walked down a hall to her door. It was opened presently by a tall girl of twenty-three or -four in a black and white crêpe dress.

"Miss Cara Kenbrook?"

"Yes."

I gave her a card—one of those that tell the truth about me.

"I'd like to ask you a few questions; may I come in?"

"Do."

Languidly she stepped aside for me to enter, closed the door behind me, and led me back into a living room that was littered with newspapers, cigarettes in all stages of consumption from unlighted freshness to cold ash, and miscellaneous articles of feminine clothing. She made room for me on a chair by dumping off a pair of pink silk stockings and a hat, and herself sat on some magazines that occupied another chair.

"I'm interested in Bernard Gilmore's death," I said, watching her face.

It wasn't a beautiful face, although it should have been. Everything was there—perfect features; smooth, white skin; big, almost enormous, brown eyes—but the eyes were dead-dull, and the face was as empty of expression as a china doorknob, and what I said didn't change it.

"Bernard Gilmore," she said without interest. "Oh, yes."

"You and he were pretty close friends, weren't you?" I asked, puzzled by her blankness.

"We had been—yes."

"What do you mean by *had been*?"

She pushed back a lock of her short-cut brown hair with a lazy hand.

"I gave him the air last week," she said casually, as if speaking of something that had happened years ago.

"When was the last time you saw him?"

"Last week—Monday, I think—a week before he was killed."

"Was that the time when you broke off with him?"

"Yes."

"Have a row, or part friends?"

"Not exactly either. I just told him that I was through with him."

"How did he take it?"

"It didn't break his heart. I guess he'd heard the same thing before."

"Where were you the night he was killed?"

"At the Coffee Cup, eating and dancing with friends until about one o'clock. Then I came home and went to bed."

"Why did you split with Gilmore?"

"Couldn't stand his wife."

"Huh?"

"She was a nuisance." This without the faintest glint of either annoyance or humor. "She came here one night and raised a racket; so I told Bernie that if he couldn't keep her away from me he'd have to find another playmate."

"Have you any idea who might have killed him?" I asked.

"Not unless it was his wife—these excitable women always do silly things."

"If you had given her husband up, what reason would she have for killing him, do you think?"

"I'm sure I don't know," she replied with complete indifference. "But I'm not the only girl that Bernie ever looked at."

"Think there were others, do you? Know anything, or are you just guessing?"

"I don't know any names," she said, "but I'm not just guessing."

I let that go at that and switched back to Mrs. Gilmore, wondering if this girl could be full of dope.

"What happened the night his wife came here?"

"Nothing but that. She followed Bernie here, rang the bell, rushed past me when I opened the door, and began to cry and call Bernie names. Then she started on me, and I told him that if he didn't take her away I'd hurt her, so he took her home."

Admitting I was licked for the time, I got up and moved to the door. I couldn't do anything with this baby just now. I didn't think she was telling the whole truth, but on the other hand it wasn't reasonable to believe that anybody would lie so woodenly—with so little effort to be plausible.

"I may be back later," I said as she let me out.

"All right."

Her manner didn't even suggest that she hoped I wouldn't.

From this unsatisfactory interview I went to the scene of the killing, only a few blocks away, to get a look at the neighborhood. I found the block just as I had remembered it and as O'Gar had described it: lined on both sides by apartment buildings, with two blind alleys—one of which was dignified with a name, Touchard Street—running from the south side.

The murder was four days old; I didn't waste any time snooping around the vicinity; but, after strolling the length of the block, boarded a Hyde Street car, transferred at California Street, and went up to see Mrs. Gilmore again. I was curious to know why she hadn't told me about her call on Cara Kenbrook.

The same plump maid who had admitted me earlier in the afternoon opened the door.

"Mrs. Gilmore is not at home," she said. "But I think she'll be back in half an hour or so."

"I'll wait," I decided.

The maid took me into the library, an immense room on the second floor, with barely enough books in it to give it that name. She switched on a light—the windows were too heavily curtained to let in much daylight—crossed to the door, stopped, moved over to straighten some books on a shelf, and looked at me with a half-questioning, half-inviting look in her green eyes, started for the door again, and halted.

By that time I knew she wanted to say something, and needed encouragement. I leaned back in my chair and grinned at her, and decided I had made a mistake—the smile into which her slack lips curved held more coquetry than anything else. She came over to me, walking with an exaggerated swing of the hips, and stood close in front of me.

"What's your mind?" I asked.

"Suppose—suppose a person knew something that nobody else knew; what would it be worth to them?"

"That," I stalled, "would depend on how valuable it was."

"Suppose I knew who killed the boss?" She bent her face close down to mine, and spoke in a husky whisper. "What would that be worth?"

"The newspapers say that one of Gilmore's clubs has offered a thousand-dollar reward. You'd get that."

Her green eyes went greedy, and then suspicious.

"If *you* didn't."

I shrugged. I knew she'd go through with it—whatever it was—now; so I didn't even explain to her that the Continental doesn't touch rewards, and doesn't let its hired men touch them.

"I'll give you my word," I said; "but you'll have to use your own judgment about trusting me."

She licked her lips.

"You're a good fellow, I guess. I wouldn't tell the police, because I know they'd beat me out of the money. But you look like I can trust you." She leered into my face. "I used to have a gentleman friend who was the very image of you, and he was the grandest—"

"Better speak your piece before somebody comes in," I suggested.

She shot a look at the door, cleared her throat, licked her loose mouth again, and dropped on one knee beside my chair.

"I was coming home late Monday night—the night the boss was killed—and was standing in the shadows saying good night to my friend, when the boss came out of the house and walked down the street. And he had hardly got to the corner, when she—Mrs. Gilmore—came out, and went down the street after him. Not trying to catch up with him, you understand; but following him. What do you think of that?"

"What do *you* think of it?"

"*I* think that she finally woke up to the fact that all of her Bernie's dates didn't have anything to do with the building business."

"Do you know that they didn't?"

"Do I know it? I knew that man! He liked 'em—liked 'em all." She smiled into my face, a smile that suggested all evil. "I found *that* out soon after I first came here."

"Do you know when Mrs. Gilmore came back that night—what time?"

"Yes," she said, "at half-past three."

"Sure?"

"Absolutely! After I got undressed I got a blanket and sat at the head of the front stairs. My room's in the rear of the top floor. I wanted to see if they came home together, and if there was a fight. After she came in alone I went back to my room, and it was just twenty-five minutes to four then. I looked at my alarm clock."

"Did you see her when she came in?"

"Just the top of her head and shoulders when she turned toward her room at the landing."

"What's your name?" I asked.

"Lina Best."

"All right, Lina," I told her. "If this is the goods I'll see that you collect on it. Keep your eyes open, and if anything else turns up you can get in touch with me at the Continental office. Now you'd better beat it, so nobody will know we've had our heads together."

Alone in the library, I cocked an eye at the ceiling and considered the information Lina Best had given me. But I soon gave that up—no use trying to guess at things that will work out for themselves in a while. I found a book, and spent the next half-hour reading about a sweet young she-chump and a big strong he-chump and all their troubles.

Then Mrs. Gilmore came in, apparently straight from the street.

I got up and closed the door behind her, while she watched me with wide eyes.

"Mrs. Gilmore," I said, when I faced her again, "why didn't you tell me that you followed your husband the night he was killed?"

"That's a lie!" she cried; but there was no truth in her voice. "That's a lie!"

"Don't you think you're making a mistake?" I urged. "Don't you think you'd better tell me the whole thing?"

She opened her mouth, but only a dry sobbing sound came out; and she began to sway with a hysterical rocking motion, the fingers of one black-gloved hand plucking at her lower lip, twisting and pulling it.

I stepped to her side and set her down in the chair I had been sitting in, making foolish clucking sounds—meant to soothe her—with my tongue. A disagreeable ten minutes—and gradually she pulled herself together; her eyes lost their glassiness, and she stopped clawing at her mouth.

"I did follow him." It was a hoarse whisper, barely audible.

Then she was out of the chair, kneeling, with arms held up to me, and her voice was a thin scream.

"But I didn't kill him! I didn't! Please believe that I didn't!"

I picked her up and put her back in the chair.

"I didn't say you did. Just tell me what did happen."

"I didn't believe him when he said he had a business engagement," she moaned. "I didn't trust him. He had lied to me before. I followed him to see if he went to that woman's rooms."

"Did he?"

"No. He went into an apartment house on Pine Street, in the block where he was killed. I don't know exactly which house it was—I was too far behind him to make sure. But I saw him go up the steps and into one—near the middle of the block."

"And then what did you do?"

"I waited, hiding in a dark doorway across the street. I knew the woman's apartment was on Bush Street, but I thought she might have moved, or be meeting him here. I waited a long time, shivering and trembling. It was chilly and I was frightened—afraid somebody would come into the vestibule where I was. But I made myself stay. I wanted to see if he came out alone, or if that woman came out. I had a right to do it—he had deceived me before.

"It was terrible, horrible—crouching there in the dark—cold and scared. Then—it must have been about half-past two—I couldn't stand it any longer. I decided to telephone the woman's apartment and find out if she was home. I went down to an all-night lunchroom on Ellis Street and called her up."

"Was she home?"

"No! I tried for fifteen minutes, or maybe longer, but nobody answered the phone. So I *knew* she was in that Pine Street building."

"And what did you do then?"

"I went back there, determined to wait until he came out. I walked up Jones Street. When I was between Bush and Pine I heard a shot. I thought it was a noise made by an automobile then, but now I know that it was the shot that killed Bernie.

"When I reached the corner of Pine and Jones, I could see a policeman bending over Bernie on the sidewalk, and I saw people gathering around. I didn't know then that it was Bernie lying on the sidewalk. In the dark and at that distance I couldn't even see whether it was a man or a woman.

"I was afraid that Bernard would come out to see what was going on, or look out of a window, and discover me; so I didn't go down that way. I was afraid to stay in the neighborhood now, for fear the police would ask me what I was doing loitering in the street at three in the morning—and have it come out that I had been following my husband. So I kept on walking up Jones Street, to California, and then straight home."

"And then what?" I led her on.

"Then I went to bed. I didn't go to sleep—lay there worrying over Bernie; but still not thinking it was he I had seen lying in the street. At nine o'clock that morning two police detectives came and told me Bernie had been killed. They questioned me so sharply that I was afraid to tell them the whole truth. If they had known I had reason for being jealous, and had followed my husband that night, they would have accused me of shooting him. And what could I have done? Everybody would have thought me guilty.

"So I didn't say anything about the woman. I thought they'd find the murderer, and then everything would be all right. I didn't think *she* had done it then, or I would have told you the whole thing the first time you were here. But four days went by without the police finding the murderer, and I began to think they suspected *me!* It was terrible! I couldn't go to them and confess that I had lied to them, and I was sure that the woman had killed him and that the police had failed to suspect her because I hadn't told them about her.

"So I employed you. But I was afraid to tell even you the whole truth. I thought that if I just told you there had been another woman and who she was, you could do the rest without having to know that I had followed Bernie that night. I was afraid *you* would think I had killed him, and would turn me over to the police if I told you everything. And now you *do* believe it! And you'll have me arrested! And they'll hang me! I know it! I know it!"

She began to rock crazily from side to side in her chair.

"Sh-h-h," I soothed her. "You're not arrested yet. Sh-h-h."

I didn't know what to make of her story. The trouble with these nervous, hysterical women is that you can't possibly tell when they're lying and when telling the truth unless you have outside evidence—half of the time they themselves don't know.

"When you heard the shot," I went on when she had quieted down a bit, "you were walking north on Jones, between Bush and Pine? You could see the corner of Pine and Jones?"

"Yes—clearly."

"See anybody?"

"No—not until I reached the corner and looked down Pine Street. Then I saw a policeman bending over Bernie, and two men walking toward them."

"Where were the two men?"

"On Pine Street east of Jones. They didn't have hats on—as if they had come out of a house when they heard the shot."

"Any automobiles in sight either before or after you heard the shot?"

"I didn't see or hear any."

"I have some more questions, Mrs. Gilmore," I said, "but I'm in a hurry now. Please don't go out until you hear from me again."

"I won't," she promised, "but—"

I didn't have any answers for anybody's questions, so I ducked my head and left the library.

Near the street door Lina Best appeared out of a shadow, her eyes bright and inquisitive.

"Stick around," I said without any meaning at all, stepped around her, and went on out into the street.

I returned then to the Garford Apartments, walking, because I had a lot of things to arrange in my mind before I faced Cara Kenbrook again. And, even though I walked slowly, they weren't all exactly filed in alphabetical order when I got there. She had changed the black and white dress for a plushlike gown of bright green, but her empty doll's face hadn't changed.

"Some more questions," I explained when she opened the door.

She admitted me without word or gesture, and led me back into the room where we had talked before.

"Miss Kenbrook," I asked, standing beside the chair she had offered me, "why did you tell me you were home in bed when Gilmore was killed?"

"Because it's so." Without the flicker of a lash.

"And you wouldn't answer the doorbell?"

I had to twist the facts to make my point. Mrs. Gilmore had phoned, but I couldn't afford to give this girl a chance to shunt the blame for her failure to answer off on central.

She hesitated for a split second.

"No—because I didn't hear it."

One cool article, this baby! I couldn't figure her. I didn't know then, and I don't know now, whether she was the owner of the world's best poker face or was just naturally stupid. But whichever she was, she was thoroughly and completely it!

I stopped trying to guess and got on with my probing.

"And you wouldn't answer the phone either?"

"It didn't ring—or not enough to awaken me."

I chuckled—an artificial chuckle—because central could have been ringing the wrong number. However . . .

"Miss Kenbrook," I lied, "your phone rang at two-thirty and at two-forty that morning. And your doorbell rang almost continually from about two-fifty until after three."

"Perhaps," she said, "but I wonder who'd be trying to get me at that hour."

"You didn't hear either?"

"No."

"But you were here?"

"Yes—who was it?" carelessly.

"Get your hat," I bluffed, "and I'll show them to you down at headquarters."

She glanced down at the green gown and walked toward an open bed-room door.

"I suppose I'd better get a cloak, too," she said.

"Yes," I advised her, "and bring your toothbrush."

She turned around then and looked at me, and for a moment it seemed that some sort of expression—surprise, maybe—was about to come into her big brown eyes; but none actually came. The eyes stayed dull and empty.

"You mean you're arresting me?"

"Not exactly. But if you stick to your story about being home in bed at three o'clock last Tuesday morning, I can promise you you *will* be arrested. If I were you I'd think up another story."

She left the doorway slowly and came back into the room, as far as a chair that stood between us, put her hands on its back, and leaned over it to look at me. For perhaps a minute neither of us spoke—just stood there staring at each other, while I tried to keep my face as expressionless as hers.

"Do you really think," she asked at last, "that I wasn't here when Bernie was killed?"

"I'm a busy man, Miss Kenbrook." I put all the certainty I could fake into my voice. "If you want to stick to your funny story, it's all right with me. But please don't expect me to stand here and argue about it. Get your hat and cloak."

She shrugged, and came around the chair on which she had been leaning.

"I suppose you *do* know something," she said, sitting down. "Well, it's tough on Stan, but women and children first."

My ears twitched at the name *Stan*, but I didn't interrupt her.

"I *was* in the Coffee Cup until one o'clock," she was saying, her voice still flat and emotionless. "And I *did* come home afterward. I'd been drinking *vino* all evening, and it always makes me blue. So after I came home I got to worrying over things. Since Bernie and I split, finances haven't been so good. I took stock that night—or morning—and found only four dollars in my purse. The rent was due, and the world looked damned blue.

"Half-lit on dago wine as I was, I decided to run over and see Stan, tell him all my troubles, and make a touch. Stan is a good egg and he's always willing to go the limit for me. Sober, I wouldn't have gone to see him at three in the morning; but it seemed a perfectly sensible thing to do at the time.

"It's only a few minutes' walk from here to Stan's. I went down Bush Street to Leavenworth, and up Leavenworth to Pine. I was in the middle of that last block when Bernie was shot—I heard it. And when I turned the corner into Pine Street I saw a copper bending over a man on the pavement right in front of Stan's. I hesitated for a couple of minutes, standing in the shadow of a pole, until three or four men had gathered around the man on the sidewalk. Then I went over.

"It was Bernie. And just as I got there I heard the copper tell one of the men that he had been shot. It was an awful shock to me. You know how things like that will hit you!"

I nodded, though God knows there was nothing in this girl's face, manner, or voice to suggest shock. She might have been talking about the weather.

"Dumbfounded, not knowing what to do," she went on, "I didn't even stop. I went on, passing as close to Bernie as I am to you now, and rang Stan's bell. He let me in. He had been half-undressed when I rang. His rooms are in the rear of the building, and he hadn't heard the shot, he said. He didn't know Bernie had been killed until I told him. It sort of knocked the wind out of him. He said Bernie had been there—in Stan's rooms— since midnight, and had just left.

"Stan asked me what I was doing there, and I told him my tale of woe. That was the first time Stan knew that Bernie and I were so thick. I met Bernie through Stan, but Stan didn't know we had got so chummy.

"Stan was worried for fear it would come out that Bernie had been to see him that night, because it would make a lot of trouble for him—some sort of shady deal they had on, I guess. So he didn't go out to see Bernie. That's about all there is to it. I got some money from Stan, and stayed in his rooms until the police had cleared out of the neighborhood; because neither of us wanted to get mixed up in anything. Then I came home. That's straight— on the level."

"Why didn't you get this off your chest before?" I demanded, knowing the answer.

It came.

"I was afraid. Suppose I told about Bernie throwing me down, and said I was close to him—a block or so away—when he was killed, and was half-full of *vino*? The first thing everybody would have said was that I had shot him! I'd lie about it still if I thought you'd believe me."

"So Bernie was the one who broke off, and not you?"

"Oh, yes," she said lightly.

I lit a Fatima and breathed smoke in silence for a while, and the girl sat placidly watching me.

Here I had two women—neither normal. Mrs. Gilmore was hysterical, abnormally nervous. This girl was dull, subnormal. One was the dead man's wife; the other his mistress; and each with reason for believing she had been thrown down for the other. Liars, both; and both finally confessing that they had been near the scene of the crime at the time of the crime, though neither admitted seeing the other. Both, by their own accounts, had been at that time even further from normal than usual—Mrs. Gilmore filled with jealousy; Cara Kenbrook, half-drunk.

What was the answer? Either could have killed Gilmore; but hardly both—unless they had formed some sort of crazy partnership, and in that event—

Suddenly all the facts I had gathered—true and false—clicked together in my head. I had the answer—the one simple, satisfying answer!

I grinned at the girl, and set about filling in the gaps in my solution.

"Who is Stan?" I asked.

"Stanley Tennant—he has something to do with the city."

Stanley Tennant. I knew him by reputation, a—

A key rattled in the hall door.

The hall door opened and closed, and a man's footsteps came toward the open doorway of the room in which we were. A tall, broad-shouldered man in tweeds filled the doorway—a ruddy-faced man of thirty-five or so, whose appearance of athletic blond wholesomeness was marred by close-set eyes of an indistinct blue.

Seeing me, he stopped—a step inside the room.

"Hello, Stan!" the girl said lightly. "This gentleman is from the Continental Detective Agency. I've just emptied myself to him about Bernie. Tried to stall him at first, but it was no good."

The man's vague eyes switched back and forth between the girl and me. Around the pale irises his eyeballs were pink.

He straightened his shoulders and smiled too jovially.

"And what conclusion have you come to?" he inquired.

The girl answered for me.

"I've already had *my* invitation to take a ride."

Tennant bent forward. With an unbroken swing of his arms, he swept a chair up from the floor into my face. Not much force behind it, but quick.

I went back against the wall, fending off the chair with both arms—threw it aside—and looked into the muzzle of a nickeled revolver.

A table drawer stood open—the drawer from which he had grabbed the gun while I was busy with the chair. The revolver, I noticed, was of .38 caliber.

"Now"—his voice was thick, like a drunk's—"turn around."

I turned my back to him, felt a hand moving over my body, and my gun was taken away.

"All right," he said, and I faced him again.

He stepped back to the girl's side, still holding the nickel-plated revolver on me. My own gun wasn't in sight—in his pocket perhaps. He was breathing noisily, and his eyeballs had gone from pink to red. His face, too, was red, with veins bulging in the forehead.

"You know me?" he snapped.

"Yes, I know you. You're Stanley Tennant, assistant city engineer, and your record is none too lovely." I chattered away on the theory that conversation is always somehow to the advantage of the man who is looking into the gun. "You're supposed to be the lad who supplied the regiment of well-trained witnesses who turned last year's investigation of graft charges against the engineer's office into a comedy. Yes, Mr. Tennant, I know you. You're the answer to why Gilmore was so lucky in landing city contracts with bids only a few dollars beneath his competitors. Yes, Mr. Tennant, I know you. You're the bright boy who—"

I had a lot more to tell him, but he cut me off.

"That will do out of you!" he yelled. "Unless you want me to knock a corner off your head with this gun."

Then he addressed the girl, not taking his eyes from me.

"Get up, Cara."

She got out of her chair and stood beside him. His gun was in his right hand, and that side was toward her. He moved around to the other side.

The fingers of his left hand hooked themselves inside the girl's green gown where it was cut low over the swell of her breasts. His gun never wavered from me. He jerked his left hand, ripping her gown down to the waistline.

"*He* did that, Cara," Tennant said.

She nodded.

His fingers slid inside the flesh-colored undergarment that was now exposed, and he tore that as he had torn the gown.

"*He* did that."

She nodded again.

His bloodshot eyes darted little measuring glances at her face—swift glances that never kept his eyes from me for the flash of time I would have needed to tie into him.

Then—eyes and gun on me—he smashed his left fist into the girl's blank white face.

One whimper—low and not drawn out—came from her as she went down in a huddle against the wall. Her face—well, there wasn't *much* change in it. She looked dumbly up at Tennant from where she had fallen.

"*He* did that," Tennant was saying.

She nodded, got up from the floor, and returned to her chair.

"Here's our story." The man talked rapidly, his eyes alert on me. "Gilmore was never in my rooms in his life, Cara, and neither were you. The night he was killed you were home shortly after one o'clock, and stayed here. You were sick—probably from the wine you had been drinking—and called a doctor. His name is Howard. I'll see that he's fixed. He got here at two-thirty and stayed until three-thirty.

"To-day, this gumshoe, learning that you had been intimate with Gilmore, came here to question you. He knew you hadn't killed Gilmore, but he made certain suggestions to you—you can play them up as strong as you like; maybe say that he's been annoying you for months—and when you turned him down he threatened to frame you.

"You refused to have anything to do with him, and he grabbed you, tearing your clothes, and bruising your face when you resisted. I happened to come along then, having an engagement with you, and heard you scream. Your front door was unlocked, so I rushed in, pulled this fellow away, and disarmed him. Then we held him until the police—whom we will phone for—came. Got that?"

"Yes, Stan."

"Good! Now listen: When the police get here this fellow will spill all he knows of course, and the chances are that all three of us will be taken in. That's why I want you to know what's what right now. I ought to have enough pull to get you and me out on bail to-night, or, if worse comes to worst, to see that my lawyer gets to me to-night—so I can arrange for the witnesses we'll need. Also I ought to be able to fix it so our little fat friend will be held for a day or two, and not allowed to see anybody until late to-morrow—which will give us a good start on him. I don't know how much he knows, but between your story and the stories of a couple of other smart little ladies I have in mind, I'll fix him up with a rep that will keep any jury in the world from ever believing him about anything."

"How do you like that?" he asked me, triumphantly.

"You big clown," I laughed at him, "I think it's funny!"

But I didn't really think so. In spite of what I thought I knew about Gilmore's murder—in spite of my simple, satisfactory solution—something was crawling up my back, my knees felt jerky, and my hands were wet with sweat. I had had people try to frame me before—no detective stays in the business long without having it happen—but I had never got used to it. There's a peculiar deadliness about the thing—especially if you know how erratic juries can be—that makes your flesh crawl, no matter how safe your judgment tells you you are.

"Phone the police," Tennant told the girl, "and for God's sake keep your story straight!"

As he tried to impress that necessity on the girl his eyes left me.

I was perhaps five feet from him and his level gun.

A jump—not straight at him—off to one side—put me close.

The gun roared under my arm. I was surprised not to feel the bullet. It seemed that he *must* have hit me.

There wasn't a second shot.

I looped my right fist over as I jumped. It landed when I landed. It took him too high—up on the cheek-bone—but it rocked him back a couple of steps.

I didn't know what had happened to his gun. It wasn't in his hand any more. I didn't stop to look for it. I was busy, crowding him back—not letting him set himself—staying close to him—driving at him with both hands.

He was a head taller than I, and had longer arms, but he wasn't any heavier or stronger. I suppose he hit me now and then as I hammered him across the room. He must have. But I didn't feel anything.

I worked him into a corner. Jammed him back in a corner with his legs cramped under him—which didn't give him much leverage to hit from. I got my left arm around his body, holding him where I wanted him. And I began to throw my right fist into him.

I liked that. His belly was flabby, and it got softer every time I hit it. I hit it often.

He was chopping at my face, but by digging my nose into his chest and holding it there I kept my beauty from being altogether ruined. Meanwhile I threw my right fist into him.

Then I became aware that Cara Kenbrook was moving around behind me; and I remembered the revolver that had fallen somewhere when I had charged Tennant. I didn't like that; but there was nothing I could do about it—except put more weight in my punches. My own gun, I thought, was in one of his pockets. But neither of us had time to hunt for it now.

Tennant's knees sagged the next time I hit him.

Once more, I said to myself, and then I'll step back, let him have one on the button, and watch him fall.

But I didn't get that far.

Something that I knew was the missing revolver struck me on the top of the head. An ineffectual blow—not clean enough to stun me—but it took the steam out of my punches.

Another.

They weren't hard, these taps, but to hurt a skull with a hunk of metal you don't have to hit it hard.

I tried to twist away from the next bump, and failed. Not only failed, but let Tennant wiggle away from me.

That was the end.

I wheeled on the girl just in time to take another rap on the head, and then one of Tennant's fists took me over the ear.

I went down in one of those falls that get pugs called quitters—my eyes were open, my mind was alive, but my legs and arms wouldn't lift me up from the floor.

Tennant took my own gun out of a pocket, and with it held on me, sat down in a Morris chair, to gasp for the air I had pounded out of him. The girl sat in another chair; and I, finding I could manage it, sat up in the middle of the floor and looked at them.

Tennant spoke, still panting.

"This is fine—all the signs of a struggle we need to make our story good!"

"If they don't believe you were in a fight," I suggested sourly, pressing my aching head with both hands, "you can strip and show them your little tummy."

"And you can show them this!"

He leaned down and split my lip with a punch that spread me on my back.

Anger brought my legs to life. I got up on them. Tennant moved around behind the Morris chair. My black gun was steady in his hand.

"Go easy," he warned me. "My story will work if I have to kill you— maybe work better."

That was sense. I stood still.

"Phone the police, Cara," he ordered.

She went out of the room, closing the door behind her; and all I could hear of her talk was a broken murmur.

Ten minutes later three uniformed policemen arrived. All three knew

Tennant, and they treated him with respect. Tennant reeled off the story he and the girl had cooked up, with a few changes to take care of the shot that had been fired from the nickeled gun and our rough-house. She nodded her head vigorously whenever a policeman looked at her. Tennant turned both guns over to the white-haired sergeant in charge.

I didn't argue, didn't deny anything, but told the sergeant:

"I'm working with Detective Sergeant O'Gar on a job. I want to talk to him over the phone and then I want you to take all three of us down to the detective bureau."

Tennant objected to that, of course; not because he expected to gain anything, but on the off-chance that he might. The white-haired sergeant looked from one of us to the other in puzzlement. Me, with my skinned face and split lip; Tennant, with a red lump under one eye where my first wallop had landed; and the girl, with most of the clothes above the waistline ripped off and a bruised cheek.

"It has a queer look, this thing," the sergeant decided aloud, "and I shouldn't wonder but what the detective bureau was the place for the lot of you."

One of the policemen went into the hall with me, and I got O'Gar on the phone at his home. It was nearly ten o'clock by now, and he was preparing for bed.

"Cleaning up the Gilmore murder," I told him. "Meet me at the Hall. Will you get hold of Kelly, the patrolman who found Gilmore, and bring him down there? I want him to look at some people."

"I will that," O'Gar promised, and I hung up.

The "wagon" in which the three policemen had answered Cara Kenbrook's call carried us down to the Hall of Justice, where we all went into the captain of detectives' office. McTighe, a lieutenant, was on duty.

I knew McTighe, and we were on pretty good terms, but I wasn't an influence in local politics, and Tennant was. I don't mean that McTighe would have knowingly helped Tennant frame me; but with me stacked up against the assistant city engineer, I knew who would get the benefit of any doubt there might be.

My head was thumping and roaring just now, with knots all over it where the girl had beaned me. I sat down, kept quiet, and nursed my head while Tennant and Cara Kenbrook, with a lot of details that they had not wasted on the uniformed men, told their tale and showed their injuries.

Tennant was talking—describing the terrible scene that had met his eyes when, drawn by the girl's screams, he had rushed into her apartment—

when O'Gar came into the office. He recognized Tennant with a lifted eyebrow, and came over to sit beside me.

"What the hell is all this?" he muttered.

"A lovely mess," I whispered back. "Listen—in that nickel gun on the desk there's an empty shell. Get it for me."

He scratched his head doubtfully, listened to the next few words of Tennant's yarn, glanced at me out of the corner of his eye, and then went over to the desk and picked up the revolver.

McTighe looked at him—a sharp, questioning look.

"Something on the Gilmore killing," the detective-sergeant said, breaking the gun.

The lieutenant started to speak, changed his mind, and O'Gar brought the shell over and handed it to me.

"Thanks," I said, putting it in my pocket. "Now listen to my friend there. It's a good act, if you like it."

Tennant was winding up his history.

". . . Naturally a man who tried a thing like that on an unprotected woman would be yellow, so it wasn't very hard to handle him after I got his gun away from him. I hit him a couple of times, and he quit—begging me to stop, getting down on his knees. Then we called the police."

McTighe looked at me with eyes that were cold and hard. Tennant had made a believer of him, and not only of him—the police-sergeant and his two men were glowering at me. I suspected that even O'Gar—with whom I had been through a dozen storms—would have been half-convinced if the engineer hadn't added the neat touches about my kneeling.

"Well, what have *you* got to say?" McTighe challenged me in a tone which suggested that it didn't make much difference what I said.

"I've got nothing to say about this dream," I said shortly. "I'm interested in the Gilmore murder—not in this stuff." I turned to O'Gar. "Is the patrolman here?"

The detective-sergeant went to the door, and called: "Oh, Kelly!"

Kelly came in—a big, straight-standing man, with iron-gray hair and an intelligent fat face.

"You found Gilmore's body?" I asked.

"I did."

I pointed at Cara Kenbrook.

"Ever see her before?"

His gray eyes studied her carefully.

"Not that I remember," he answered.

"Did she come up the street while you were looking at Gilmore, and go into the house he was lying in front of?"

"She did not."

I took out the empty shell O'Gar had got for me, and chucked it down on the desk in front of the patrolman.

"Kelly," I asked, *"why did you kill Gilmore?"*

Kelly's right hand went under his coat-tail at his hip.

I jumped for him.

Somebody grabbed me by the neck. Somebody else piled on my back. McTighe aimed a big fist at my face, but it missed. My legs had been suddenly kicked from under me, and I went down hard with men all over me.

When I was yanked to my feet again, big Kelly stood straight up by the desk, weighing his service revolver in his hand. His clear eyes met mine, and he laid the weapon on the desk. Then he unfastened his shield and put it with the gun.

"It was an accident," he said simply.

By this time the birds who had been manhandling me woke up to the fact that maybe they were missing part of the play—that maybe I wasn't a maniac. Hands dropped off me, and presently everybody was listening to Kelly.

He told his story with unhurried evenness, his eyes never wavering or clouding. A deliberate man, though unlucky.

"I was walkin' my beat that night, an' as I turned the corner of Jones into Pine I saw a man jump back from the steps of a buildin' into the vestibule. A burglar, I thought, an' cat-footed it down there. It was a dark vestibule, an' deep, an' I saw somethin' that looked like a man in it, but I wasn't sure.

"'Come out o' there!' I called, but there was no answer. I took my gun in my hand an' started up the steps. I saw him move just then, comin' out. An' then my foot slipped. It was worn smooth, the bottom step, an' my foot slipped. I fell forward, the gun went off, an' the bullet hit him. He had come out a ways by then, an' when the bullet hit him he toppled over frontwise, tumblin' down the steps onto the sidewalk.

"When I looked at him I saw it was Gilmore. I knew him to say 'howdy' to, an' he knew me—which is why he must o' ducked out of sight when he saw me comin' around the corner. He didn't want me to see him comin' out of a buildin' where I knew Mr. Tennant lived, I suppose, thinkin' I'd put two an' two together, an' maybe talk.

"I don't say that I did the right thing by lyin', but it didn't hurt anybody. It was an accident, but he was a man with a lot of friends up in high places, an'—accident or no—I stood a good chance of bein' broke, an' maybe sent over for a while. So I told my story the way you people know it. I couldn't say I'd seen anything suspicious without maybe puttin' the blame on some innocent party, an' I didn't want that. I'd made up my mind that if anybody was arrested for the murder, an' things looked bad for them, I'd come out an' say I'd done it. Home, you'll find a confession all written out—written out in case somethin' happened to me—so nobody else'd ever be blamed.

"That's why I had to say I'd never seen the lady here. I did see her—saw her go into the buildin' that night—the buildin' Gilmore had come out of. But I couldn't say so without makin' it look bad for her; so I lied. I could have thought up a better story if I'd had more time, I don't doubt, but I had to think quick. Anyways, I'm glad it's all over."

KELLY AND the other uniformed policeman had left the office, which now held McTighe, O'Gar, Cara Kenbrook, Tennant, and me. Tennant had crossed to my side, and was apologizing.

"I hope you'll let me square myself for this evening's work. But you know how it is when somebody you care for is in a jam. I'd have killed you if I had thought it would help Cara—on the level. Why didn't you tell us that you didn't suspect her?"

"But I did suspect the pair of you," I said. "It looked as if Kelly had to be the guilty one; but you people carried on so much that I began to feel doubtful. For a while it was funny—you thinking she had done it, and she thinking you had, though I suppose each had sworn to his or her innocence. But after a time it stopped being funny. You carried it too far."

"How did you rap to Kelly?" O'Gar, at my shoulder, asked.

"Miss Kenbrook was walking north on Leavenworth—and was halfway between Bush and Pine—when the shot was fired. She saw nobody, no cars, until she rounded the corner. Mrs. Gilmore, walking north on Jones, was about the same distance away when *she* heard the shot, and she saw nobody until she reached Pine Street. If Kelly had been telling the truth, she would have seen him on Jones Street. He said he didn't turn the corner until after the shot was fired.

"Either of the women could have killed Gilmore, but hardly both; and I doubted that either could have shot him and got away without running into Kelly or the other. Suppose both of them were telling the truth—what then? Kelly must have been lying! He was the logical suspect anyway—the nearest known person to the murdered man when the shot was fired.

"To back all this up, he had let Miss Kenbrook go into the apartment building at three in the morning, in front of which a man had just been killed, without questioning her or mentioning her in his report. That looked as if he *knew* who had done the killing. So I took a chance with the empty-shell trick, it being a good bet that he would have thrown his away, and would think that—"

McTighe's heavy voice interrupted my explanation.

"How about this assault charge?" he asked, and had the decency to avoid my eye when I turned toward him with the others.

Tennant cleared his throat.

"Er—ah—in view of the way things have turned out, and knowing that Miss Kenbrook doesn't want the disagreeable publicity that would accompany an affair of this sort, why, I'd suggest that we drop the whole thing." He smiled brightly from McTighe to me. "You know nothing has gone on the records yet."

"Make the big heap play his hand out," O'Gar growled in my ear. "Don't let him drop it."

"Of course if Miss Kenbrook doesn't want to press the charge," McTighe was saying, watching me out of the tail of his eye, "I suppose—"

"If everybody understands that the whole thing was a plant," I said, "and if the policemen who heard the story are brought in here now and told by Tennant and Miss Kenbrook that it was all a lie—then I'm willing to let it go at that. Otherwise, I won't stand for a hush-up."

"You're a damned fool!" O'Gar whispered. "Put the screws on them!"

But I shook my head. I didn't see any sense in making a lot of trouble for myself just to make some for somebody else—and suppose Tennant *proved* his story . . .

So the policemen were found, and brought into the office again, and told the truth.

And presently Tennant, the girl, and I were walking together like three old friends through the corridors toward the door, Tennant still asking me to let him make amends for the evening's work.

"You've *got* to let me do something!" he insisted. "It's only right!"

His hand dipped into his coat, and came out with a thick billfold.

"Here," he said, "let me—"

We were going, at that happy moment, down the stone vestibule steps that lead to Kearny Street—six or seven steps there are.

"No," I said, "let me—"

He was on the next to the top step, when I reached up and let go.

He settled in a rather limp pile at the bottom.

Leaving his empty-faced lady love to watch over him, I strolled up through Portsmouth Square toward a restaurant where the steaks come thick.

THE SECOND-STORY
ANGEL

Carter Brigham — Carter Webright Brigham in the tables of contents of various popular magazines — woke with a start, passing from unconsciousness into full awareness too suddenly to doubt that his sleep had been disturbed by something external.

The moon was not up and his apartment was on the opposite side of the building from the street-lights; the blackness about him was complete — he could not see so far as the foot of his bed.

Holding his breath, not moving after that first awakening start, he lay with straining eyes and ears. Almost at once a sound — perhaps a repetition of the one that had aroused him — came from the adjoining room: the furtive shuffling of feet across the wooden floor. A moment of silence, and a chair grated on the floor, as if dislodged by a careless shin. Then silence again, and a faint rustling as of a body scraping against the rough paper of the wall.

Now Carter Brigham was neither a hero nor a coward, and he was not armed. There was nothing in his rooms more deadly than a pair of candlesticks, and they — not despicable weapons in an emergency — were on the far side of the room from which the sounds came.

If he had been awakened to hear very faint and not often repeated noises in the other room — such rustlings as even the most adept burglar might not avoid — the probabilities are that Carter would have been content to remain in his bed and try to frighten the burglar away by yelling at him. He would not have disregarded the fact that in an encounter at close quarters under these conditions every advantage would lie on the side of the prowler.

But this particular prowler had made quite a lot of noise, had even stumbled against a chair, had shown himself a poor hand at stealthiness. That an inexpert burglar might easily be as dangerous as an adept did not occur to the man in the bed.

Perhaps it was that in the many crook stories he had written, deadliness had always been wedded to skill and the bunglers had always been comparatively harmless and easily overcome, and that he had come to accept this theory as a truth. After all, if a man says a thing often enough, he is very likely to acquire some sort of faith in it sooner or later.

Anyhow, Carter Brigham slid his not unmuscular body gently out from between the sheets and crept on silent bare feet toward the open doorway of the room from which the sounds had come. He passed from his bed to a position inside the next room, his back against the wall beside the door during an interlude of silence on the intruder's part.

The room in which Carter now stood was every bit as black as the one he had left; so he stood motionless, waiting for the prowler to betray his position.

His patience was not taxed. Very soon the burglar moved again, audibly; and then against the rectangle of a window—scarcely lighter than the rest of the room—Carter discerned a man-shaped shadow just a shade darker coming toward him. The shadow passed the window and was lost in the enveloping darkness.

Carter, his body tensed, did not move until he thought the burglar had had time to reach a spot where no furniture intervened. Then, with clutching hands thrown out on wide-spread arms, Carter hurled himself forward.

His shoulder struck the intruder and they both crashed to the floor. A forearm came up across Carter's throat, pressing into it. He tore it away and felt a blow on his cheek. He wound one arm around the burglar's body, and with the other fist struck back. They rolled over and over across the floor until they were stopped by the legs of a massive table, the burglar uppermost.

With savage exultance in his own strength, which the struggle thus far had shown to be easily superior to the other's, Carter twisted his body, smashing his adversary into the heavy table. Then he drove a fist into the body he had just shaken off and scrambled to his knees, feeling for a grip on the burglar's throat. When he had secured it he found that the prowler was lying motionless, unresisting. Laughing triumphantly, Carter got to his feet and switched on the lights.

The girl on the floor did not move.

Half lying, half hunched against the table where he had hurled her, she was inanimate. A still, twisted figure in an austerely tailored black suit—one sleeve of which had been torn from the shoulder—with an unended con-fusion of short chestnut hair above a face that was linen-white except where blows had reddened it. Her eyes were closed. One arm was outflung across the floor, the other lay limply at her side; one silken leg was extended, the other folded under her.

Into a corner of the room her hat, a small black toque, had rolled; not far from the hat lay a very small pinch-bar, the jimmy with which she had forced an entrance.

The window over the fire escape—always locked at night—was wide-open. Its catch hung crookedly.

Mechanically, methodically—because he had been until recently a reporter on a morning paper, and the lessons of years are not unlearned in a few weeks—Carter's eyes picked up these details and communicated them to his brain while he strove to conquer his bewilderment.

After a while his wits resumed their functions and he went over to kneel beside the girl. Her pulse was regular, but she gave no other indications of life. He lifted her from the floor and carried her to the leather couch on the other side of the room. Then he brought cold water from the bathroom and brandy from the bookcase. Generous applications of the former to her tem-ples and face and of the latter between her lips finally brought a tremor to her mouth and a quiver to her eyelids.

Presently she opened her eyes, looked confusedly around the room, and endeavored to sit up. He pressed her head gently down on the couch.

"Lie still a moment longer—until you feel all right."

She seemed to see him then for the first time, and to remember where she was. She shook her head clear of his restraining hand and sat up, swing-ing her feet down to the floor.

"So I lose again," she said, with an attempt at nonchalance that was only faintly tinged with bitterness, her eyes meeting his.

They were green eyes and very long, and they illuminated her face which, without their soft light, had seemed of too sullen a cast for beauty, despite the smooth regularity of the features.

Carter's glance dropped to her discolored cheek, where his knuckles had left livid marks.

"I'm sorry I struck you," he apologized. "In the dark I naturally thought you were a man. I wouldn't have—"

"Forget it," she commanded coolly. "It's all in the game."

"But I—"

"Aw, stop it!" Impatiently. "It doesn't amount to anything. I'm all right."

"I'm glad of that."

His bare toes came into the range of his vision, and he went into his bedroom for slippers and a robe. The girl watched him silently when he returned to her, her face calmly defiant.

"Now," he suggested, drawing up a chair, "suppose you tell me all about it."

She laughed briefly. "It's a long story, and the bulls ought to be here any minute now. There wouldn't be time to tell it."

"The police?"

"Uh-huh."

"But I didn't send for them! Why should I?"

"God knows!" She looked around the room and then abruptly straight into his eyes. "If you think I'm going to buy my liberty, brother"—her voice was icy insolent—"you're way off!"

He denied the thought. Then: "Suppose you tell me about it."

"All primed to listen to a sob story?" she mocked. "Well, here goes: I got some bad breaks on the last couple of jobs I pulled and had to lay low—so low that I didn't even get anything to eat for a day or two. I figured I'd have to pull another job for getaway money—so I could blow town for a while. And this was it! I was sort of giddy from not eating and I made too much noise; but even at that"—with a scornful laugh—"you'd never have nailed me if I'd had a gun on me!"

Carter was on his feet.

"There's food of some sort in the icebox. We'll eat before we do any more talking."

A grunt came from the open window by which the girl had entered. Both of them wheeled toward it. Framed in it was a burly, red-faced man who wore a shiny blue serge suit and a black derby hat. He threw one thick leg over the sill and came into the room with heavy, bearlike agility.

"Well, well"—the words came complacently from his thick-lipped mouth, under a close-clipped gray mustache—"if it ain't my old friend Angel Grace!"

"Cassidy!" the girl exclaimed weakly, and then relapsed into sullen stoicism.

Carter took a step forward.

"What—"

"'S all right!" the newcomer assured him, displaying a bright badge. "Detective-Sergeant Cassidy. I was passin' and spotted somebody makin' your fire escape. Decided to wait until they left and nab 'em with the goods. Got tired of waitin' and came up for a look-see."

He turned jovially to the girl.

"And here it turns out to be the Angel herself! Come on, kid, let's take a ride."

Carter put out a detaining hand as she started submissively toward the detective.

"Wait a minute! Can't we fix this thing up? I don't want to prosecute the lady."

Cassidy leered from the girl to Carter and back, and then shook his head.

"Can't be done! The Angel is wanted for half a dozen jobs. Don't make no diff' whether you make charges against her or not—she'll go over for plenty anyways."

The girl nodded concurrence.

"Thanks, old dear," she told Carter, with an only partially successful attempt at nonchalance, "but they want me pretty bad."

But Carter would not submit without a struggle. The gods do not send a real flesh-and-blood feminine crook into a writer's rooms every evening in the week. The retention of such a gift was worth contending for. The girl must have within her, he thought, material for thousands, tens of thousands, of words of fiction. Was that a boon to be lightly surrendered? And then her attractiveness was in itself something; and a still more potent claim on his assistance—though not perhaps so clearly explainable—was the mottled area his fists had left on the smooth flesh of her cheek.

"Can't we arrange it somehow?" he asked. "Couldn't we fix it so that the charges might be—er—unofficially disregarded for the present?"

Cassidy's heavy brows came down and the red of his face darkened.

"Are you tryin' to—"

He stopped, and his small blue eyes narrowed almost to the point of vanishing completely.

"Go ahead! You're doin' the talkin'."

Bribery, Carter knew, was a serious matter, and especially so when directed toward an officer of the law. The law is not to be lightly set aside, perverted, by an individual. To fling to this gigantic utensil a few bits of green-engraved paper, expecting thus to turn it from its course, was, to say the least, a foolhardy proceeding.

Yet the law as represented by this fat Cassidy in baggy, not too immaculate garments, while indubitably the very same law, seemed certainly less awe-inspiring, less unapproachable. Almost it took on a human aspect—the aspect of a man who was not entirely without his faults. The law just now, in fact, looked out through little blue eyes that were manifestly greedy, for all their setting in a poker face.

Carter hesitated, trying to find the words in which his offer would be most attractively dressed; but the detective relieved him of the necessity of broaching the subject.

"Listen, mister," he said candidly. "I get you all right! But on the level, I don't think it'd be worth what it'd cost you."

"What would it cost?"

"Well, there's four hundred in rewards offered for her that I know of—maybe more."

Four hundred dollars! That was considerably more than Carter had expected to pay. Still, he could get several times four hundred dollars' worth of material from her.

"Done!" he said. "Four hundred it is!"

"Woah!" Cassidy rumbled. "That don't get me nothin'! What kind of chump do you think I am? If I turn her in I get that much, besides credits for promotion. Then what the hell's the sense of me turnin' her loose for that same figure and runnin' the risk of bein' sent over myself if it leaks out?"

Carter recognized the justice of the detective's stand.

"Five hundred," he bid.

Cassidy shook his head emphatically.

"On the level, I wouldn't touch it for less'n a thousan'—and you'd be a sucker to pay that much! She's a keen kid all right, but the world's full of just as keen ones that'll come a lot cheaper."

"I can't pay a thousand," Carter said slowly; he had only a few dollars more than that in his bank.

His common sense warned him not to impoverish himself for the girl's sake, warned him that the payment of even five hundred dollars for her liberty would be a step beyond the limits of rational conduct.

He raised his head to acknowledge his defeat, and to tell Cassidy that he might take the girl away; then his eyes focused on the girl. Though she still struggled to maintain her attitude of ironic indifference to her fate, and did attain a reckless smile, her chin quivered and her shoulders were no longer jauntily squared.

The dictates of reason went for nothing in the face of these signs of distress.

Without conscious volition, Carter found himself saying, "The best I can do is seven hundred and fifty."

Cassidy shook his head briskly, but he caught one corner of his lower lip between his teeth, robbing the rejecting gesture of its finality.

The girl, stirred into action by the detective-sergeant's indecision, put an impulsive hand on his arm and added the weight of her personality to the temptation of the money.

"Come on, Cassidy," she pleaded. "Be a good guy—give me a break! Take the seven fifty! You got rep enough without turning me in!"

Cassidy turned abruptly to Carter. "I'm makin' a sap o' myself, but give me the dough!"

At the sight of the check book that Carter took from a desk drawer, Cassidy balked again, demanding cash. Finally they persuaded him to accept a check made payable to "Cash."

At the door he turned and wagged a fat finger at Carter.

"Now remember," he threatened, "if you try any funny business on this check I'm going to nail you if I have to frame you to do it!"

"There'll be no funny business," Carter assured him.

There was no doubt of the girl's hunger; she ate ravenously of the cold beef, salad, rolls, pastry, and coffee that Carter put before her. Neither of them talked much while she ate. The food held her undivided attention, while Carter's mind was busy planning how his opportunity might be utilized to the utmost.

Over their cigarettes the girl mellowed somewhat, and he persuaded her to talk of herself. But clearly she had not accepted him without many reservations, and she made no pretense of lowering her guard.

She told him her story briefly, without going into any details.

"My old man was named John Cardigan, but he was a lot better known as 'Paper-Box John,' from his trick of carrying his tools around in an unsuspicious-looking shoebox. If I do say it myself, he was as slick a burglar as there was in the grift! I don't remember Ma very well. She died or left or something when I was a little kid and the old man didn't like to talk about her.

"But I had as good a bringing up, criminally speaking, as you ever heard of. There was the old man, a wizard in his line; and my older brother Frank—he's doing a one-to-fourteen-year stretch in Deer Lodge now—who wasn't a dub by any means with a can opener—safe-ripping, you know. Between them and the mobs they ran with, I got a pretty good education along certain lines.

"Everything went along fine, with me keeping house for the old man and Frank, and them giving me everything I wanted, until the old man got wiped out by a night watchman in Philly one night. Then, a couple weeks later, Frank got picked up in some burg out in Montana—Great Falls. That put me up against it. We hadn't saved much money—easy come, easy go— and what we had I sent out to Frank's mouthpiece—a lawyer—to try to spring him. But it was no go—they had him cold, and they sent him over.

"After that I had to shift for myself. It was a case of either cashing in on what the old man and Frank had taught me or going on the streets. Of course, I wouldn't have had to go on the streets actually—there were plenty of guys who were willing to take me in—it's just that it's a rotten way of making a living. I don't want to be owned!

"Maybe you think I could have got a job somewhere in a store or factory or something. But in the first place, a girl with no experience has a hard time knocking down enough jack to live on; and then again, half the dicks in town know me as the old man's daughter, and they wouldn't keep it a secret if they found me working any place—they'd think I was getting a job lined up for some mob.

"So, after thinking it all over, I decided to try the old man's racket. It went easy from the first. I knew all the tricks and it wasn't hard to put them into practice. Being a girl helped, too. A couple times, when I was caught cold, people took my word for it that I had got into the wrong place by mistake.

"But being a girl had its drawbacks, too. As the only she-burglar in action, my work was sort of conspicuous, and it wasn't long before the bulls had a line on me. I was picked up a couple times, but I had a good lawyer, and they couldn't make anything stick, so they turned me loose; but they didn't forget me.

"Then I got some bad breaks, and pulled some jobs that they knew they could tie on me; and they started looking for me proper. To make things worse, I had hurt the feelings of quite a few guys who had tried to get mushy with me at one time or another, and they had been knocking me—saying I was up-stage and so on—to everybody, and that hadn't helped me any with the people who might have helped me when I was up against it.

"So besides hiding from the dicks I had to dodge half the guns in the burg for fear they'd put the finger on me—turn me up to the bulls. This honor among thieves stuff doesn't go very big in New York!

"Finally it got so bad that I couldn't even get to my room, where my clothes and what money I had were. I was cooped up in a hang-out I had across town, peeping out at dicks who were watching the joint, and knowing that if I showed myself I was a goner.

"I couldn't keep that up, especially as I had no food there and couldn't get hold of anybody I could trust; so I took a chance to-night and went over the roof, intending to knock over the first likely-looking dump I came to for the price of some food and a ducat out of town.

"And this was the place I picked, and that brings my tale up to date."

They were silent for a moment, she watching Carter out of the corners of her eyes, as if trying to read what was going on in his mind, and he turning her story around in his head, admiring its literary potentialities.

She was speaking again, and now her voice held the slightly metallic quality that it had before she had forgotten some of her wariness in her preoccupation with her story.

"Now, old top, I don't know what your game is; but I warned you right off the reel that I wasn't buying anything."

Carter laughed. "Angel Grace, your name suits you—heaven must have sent you here," he said, and then added, a little self-consciously, "My name is Brigham—Carter Webright Brigham."

He paused, half expectantly, and not in vain.

"Not the writer?"

Her instantaneous recognition caused him to beam on her—he had not reached the stage of success when he might expect everyone to be familiar with his name.

"You've read some of my stuff?" he asked.

"Oh, yes! 'Poison for One' and 'The Settlement' in *Warner's Magazine*, 'Nemesis, Incorporated' in the *National*, and all your stories in *Cody's!*"

Her voice, even without the added testimony of the admiration that had replaced the calculation in her eyes, left no doubt in his mind that she had indeed liked his stories.

"Well, that's the answer," he told her. "That money I gave Cassidy was an investment in a gold mine. The things you can tell me will fairly write themselves and the magazines will eat 'em up!"

Oddly enough, the information that his interest had been purely professional did not seem to bring her pleasure; on the contrary, little shadows appeared in the clear green field of her eyes.

Seeing them, Carter, out of some intuitive apprehension, hastened to add: "But I suppose I'd have done the same even if you hadn't promised stories—I couldn't very well let him carry you off to jail."

She gave him a skeptical smile at that, but her eyes cleared.

"That's all very fine," she observed, "as far as it goes. But you mustn't forget that Cassidy isn't the only sleuth in the city that's hunting for me.

And don't forget that you're likely to get yourself in a fine hole by helping me."

Carter came back to earth.

"That's right! We'll have to figure out what is the best thing to do."

Then the girl spoke: "It's a cinch I'll have to get out of town! Too many of them are looking for me, and I'm too well-known. Another thing: you can trust Cassidy as long as he hasn't spent that money, but that won't be long. Most likely he's letting it go over a card table right now. As soon as he's flat he'll be back to see you again. You'll be safe enough so far as he's concerned—he can't prove anything on you without giving himself away—but if I'm where he can find me he'll pinch me unless you put up more coin; and he'll try to find me through you. There's nothing to it but for me to blow town."

"That's just what we'll do," Carter cried. "We'll pick out some safe place not far away, where you can go to-day. Then I'll meet you there to-morrow and we can make some permanent arrangements."

It was late in the morning before their plans were completed.

CARTER WENT to his bank as soon as it was open and withdrew all but sufficient money to cover the checks he had out, including the one he had given the detective-sergeant. The girl would need money for food and fare, and even clothing, for her room, she was confident, was still watched by the police.

She left Carter's apartment in a taxicab, and was to buy clothes of a different color and style from those she was wearing and whose description the police had. Then she was to dismiss the taxicab and engage another to drive her to a railroad station some distance from the city—they were afraid that the detectives on duty at the railroad stations in the city, and at the ferries, would recognize her in spite of the new clothes. At the distant station she would board a train for the upstate town they had selected for their rendezvous.

Carter was to join her there the following day.

He did not go down to the street door with her when she left, but said goodbye in his rooms. At the leave-taking she shed her coating of worldly cynicism and tried to express her gratitude.

But he cut her short with an embarrassed mockery of her own earlier admonition: "Aw, stop it!"

Carter Brigham did not work that day. The story on which he had been engaged now seemed stiff and lifeless and altogether without relation to actuality. The day and the night dragged along, but no matter how slowly, they did pass in the end, and he was stepping down from a dirty local train in the town where she was to wait for him.

Registering at the hotel they had selected, he scanned the page of the book given over to the previous day's business. "Mrs. H. H. Moore," the name she was to have used, did not appear thereon. Discreet inquiries revealed that she had not arrived.

Sending his baggage up to his room, Carter went out and called at the two other hotels in the town. She was at neither. At a newsstand he bought an armful of New York papers. Nothing about her arrest was in them. She had not been picked up before leaving the city, or the newspapers would have made much news of her.

For three days he clung obstinately to the belief that she had not run away from him. He spent the three days in his New York rooms, his ears alert for the ringing of the telephone bell, examining his mail frantically, constantly expecting the messenger, who didn't come. Occasionally he sent telegrams to the hotel in the upstate town—futile telegrams.

Then he accepted the inescapable truth: she had decided—perhaps had so intended all along—not to run the risk incidental to a meeting with him, but had picked out a hiding place of her own; she did not mean to fulfill her obligations to him, but had taken his assistance and gone.

Another day passed in idleness while he accustomed himself to the bitterness of this knowledge. Then he set to work to salvage what he could. Fortunately, it seemed to be much. The bare story that the girl had told him over the remains of her meal could with little effort be woven into a novelette that should be easily marketed. Crook stories were always in demand, especially one with an authentic girl-burglar drawn from life.

As he bent over his typewriter, concentrating on his craft, his disappointment began to fade. The girl was gone. She had treated him shabbily, but perhaps it was better that way. The money she had cost him would come back with interest from the sale of the serial rights of this story. As for the personal equation: she had been beautiful, fascinating enough—and friendly—but still she *was* a crook. . . .

For days he hardly left his desk except to eat and sleep, neither of which did he do excessively.

Finally the manuscript was completed and sent out in the mail. For the next two days he rested as fully as he had toiled, lying abed to all hours, idling through his waking hours, replacing the nervous energy his work always cost him.

On the third day a note came from the editor of the magazine to which he had sent the story, asking if it would be convenient for him to call at two-thirty the next afternoon.

Four men were with the editor when Carter was ushered into his office. Two of them he knew: Gerald Gulton and Harry Mack, writers like himself. He was introduced to the others: John Deitch and Walton Dohlman. He was familiar with their work, though he had not met them before; they contributed to some of the same magazines that bought his stories.

When the group had been comfortably seated and cigars and cigarettes were burning, the editor smiled into the frankly curious faces turned toward him.

"Now we'll get down to business," he said. "You'll think it a queer business at first, but I'll try to mystify you no longer than necessary."

He turned to Carter. "You wouldn't mind telling us, Mr. Brigham, just how you got hold of the idea for your story 'The Second-Story Angel,' would you?"

"Of course not," Carter said. "It was rather peculiar. I was roused one night by the sound of a burglar in my rooms and got up to investigate. I tackled him and we fought in the dark for a while. Then I turned on the lights and—"

"And it was a woman—a girl!" Gerald Fulton prompted hoarsely.

Carter jumped.

"How did you know?" he demanded.

Then he saw that Fulton, Mack, Deitch, and Dohlman were all sitting stiffly in their chairs and that their dissimilar faces held for the time identical expressions of bewilderment.

"And after a while a detective came in?"

It was Mack's voice, but husky and muffled.

"His name was Cassidy!"

"And for a price things could be fixed," Deitch took up the thread.

After that there was a long silence, while the editor pretended to be intrigued by the contours of a hemispherical glass paperweight on his desk, and the four professional writers, their faces beet-red and sheepish, all stared intently at nothing.

The editor opened a drawer and took out a stack of manuscripts.

"Here they are," he said. "I knew there was something wrong when within ten days I got five stories that were, in spite of the differences in treatment, unmistakably all about the same girl!"

"Chuck mine in the wastebasket," Mack instructed softly, and the others nodded their endorsement of that disposition. All but Dohlman, who seemed to be struggling with an idea. Finally he addressed the editor.

"It's a pretty good story, at that, isn't it, all five versions?"

The editor nodded.

"Yes, I'd have bought one, but five—"

"Why not buy one? We'll match coins—"

"Sure, that's fair enough," said the editor.

It was done. Mack won.

Gerald Fulton's round blue eyes were wider than ever with a look of astonishment. At last he found words.

"My God! I wonder how many other men are writing that same story right now!"

But in Carter's mind an entirely different problem was buzzing around. *Lord! I wonder if she kissed this whole bunch, too!*

AFRAID
OF A GUN

wen Sack turned from the stove as the door of his cabin opened to admit "Rip" Yust, and with the hand that did not hold the coffeepot Owen Sack motioned hospitably toward the table, where food steamed before a ready chair.

"Hullo, Rip! Set down and go to it while it's hot. 'Twon't take me but a minute to throw some more together for myself."

That was Owen Sack, a short man of compact wiriness, with round china-blue eyes and round ruddy cheeks, and only the thinness of his straw-colored hair to tell of his fifty-odd years, a quiet little man whose too-eager friendliness at times suggested timidity.

Rip Yust crossed to the table, but he paid no attention to its burden of food. Instead, he placed two big fists on the tabletop, leaned his weight on them, and scowled at Owen Sack. He was big, this Rip Yust, barrel-bodied, slope-shouldered, thick-limbed, and his usual manner was a phlegmatic sort of sullenness. But now his heavy features were twisted into a scowl.

"They got 'Lucky' this morning," he said after a moment, and his voice wasn't the voice of one who brings news. It was accusing.

"Who got him?"

But Owen Sack's eyes swerved from the other's as he put the question, and he moistened his lips nervously. He knew who had got Rip's brother.

"Who do you guess?" with heavy derision. "The Prohis! You know it!"

The little man winced.

"Aw, Rip! How would I know it? I ain't been to town for a week, and nobody never comes past here any more."

"Yeah, I wonder how you would know it."

Yust walked around the table, to where Owen Sack—with little globules of moisture glistening on his round face—stood, caught him by the slack of his blue shirt bosom and lifted him clear of the floor. Twice Yust shook the little man—shook him with a lack of vehemence that was more forcible than any violence could have been—and set him down on his feet again.

"You knowed where our cache was at," he accused, still holding the looseness of the shirt bosom in one muscular hand, "and nobody else that ain't in with us did. The Prohis showed up there this morning and grabbed Lucky. Who told 'em where it was? You did, you rat!"

"I didn't, Rip! I didn't! I swear to—"

Yust cut off the little man's whimpering by placing a broad palm across his mouth.

"Maybe you didn't. To tell the truth, I ain't exactly positive yet that you done it—or I wouldn't be talking to you." He flicked his coat aside, baring for a suggestive half-second the brown butt of a revolver that peeped out of a shoulder holster. "But it looks like it couldn't of been nobody else. But I ain't aiming to hurt nobody that don't hurt me, so I'm looking around a while to make sure. But if I find out that you done it for sure—"

He snapped his big jaws together. His right hand made as if to dart under his coat near the left armpit. He nodded with slow emphasis, and left the cabin.

For a while Owen Sack did not move. He stood stiffly still, staring with barren blue eyes at the door through which his caller had vanished; and Owen Sack looked old now. His face held lines that had not been there before; and his body, for all its rigidity, seemed frailer.

Presently he shook his shoulders briskly, and turned back to the stove with an appearance of having put the episode out of his mind; but immediately afterward his body drooped spiritlessly. He crossed to the chair, dropped down on it, and pushed the cooling meal back a way, to pillow his head upon his forearms.

He shuddered now and his knees trembled, just as he had shuddered and his knees had trembled when he had helped carry Cardwell home. Cardwell, so gossip said, had talked too much about certain traffic on the Kootenai River. Cardwell had been found one morning in a thicket below Dime, with a hole in the back of his neck where a bullet had gone in and another and larger hole in front where the bullet had come out. No one could say who had fired the bullet, but gossip in Dime had made guesses, and had taken pains to keep those guesses from the ears of the Yust brothers.

If it hadn't been for Cardwell, Owen knew that he could have convinced

Rip Yust of his own innocence. But he saw the dead man again whenever he saw one of the Yusts; and this afternoon, when Rip had come into his cabin and hurled that accusing "They got Lucky this morning" across the table, Cardwell had filled Owen Sack's mind to the exclusion of all else— filled it with a fear that had made him talk and act as if he had in fact guided the Prohibition enforcement officers to the Yusts' cache. And so Yust had gone away more than half convinced that his suspicions were correct.

Rip Yust was, Owen Sack knew, a fair man according to his lights. He would do nothing until he was certain that he had the right man. Then he would strike with neither warning nor mercy.

An eye for an eye was the code of the Rip Yusts of the world, and an enemy was one to be removed without scruple. And that Yust would not strike until he had satisfied himself that he had the right man was small comfort to Owen Sack.

Yust was not possessed of the clearest of minds; he was not fitted, for all his patience and deliberation, to unerringly sift the false from the true. Many things that properly were meaningless might, to him, seem irrefragable evidence of Owen Sack's guilt—now that Owen Sack's fears had made him act the part of a witness against himself.

And some morning Owen Sack's body would be found as Cardwell's had been found. Perhaps Cardwell had been unjustly suspected too.

Owen Sack sat up straight now, squaring his shoulders and tightening his mouth in another halfhearted attempt to pull himself together. He ground his fists into his temples, and for a moment pretended to himself that he was trying to arrive at a decision, to map out a course of action. But in his heart he knew all the time that he was lying to himself. He was going to run away again. He always did. The time for making a stand was gone.

Thirty years ago he might have done it.

That time in a Marsh Market Space dive in Baltimore, when a dispute over a reading of the dice had left him facing a bull-dog pistol in the hands of a cockney sailor. The cockney's hand had shaken; they had stood close together; the cockney was as frightened as he. A snatch, a blow—it would have been no trick at all. But he had, after a moment's hesitancy, submitted; he had let the cockney not only run him out of the game but out of the city.

His fear of bullets had been too strong for him. He wasn't a coward (not then); a knife, which most men dread, hadn't seemed especially fearful in those days. It traveled at a calculable and discernible rate of speed; you could see it coming; judge its speed; parry, elude it; or twist about so that its wound was shallow. And even if it struck, went deep, it was sharp and slid easily through the flesh, a clean, neat separation of the tissues.

But a bullet, a ball of metal, hot from the gases that propelled it, hurtling invisibly toward you—nobody could say how fast—not to make a path for itself with a fine keen edge, but to hammer out a road with a dull blunt nose, driving through whatever stood in its way. A lump of hot lead battering its irresistible tunnel through flesh and sinew, splintering bones! That he could not face.

So he had fled from the Maryland city to avoid the possibility of another meeting with the cockney sailor and his bull-dog pistol.

And that was only the first time.

No matter where he had gone, he had sooner or later found himself looking into the muzzle of a threatening gun. It was as if his very fear attracted the thing he feared. A dog, he had been told as a boy, would bite you if he thought you were afraid of him. It had been that way with guns.

Each repetition had left him in worse case than before; until now the sight of a menacing firearm paralyzed him, and even the thought of one blurred his mind with terror.

In those earlier days he hadn't been a coward, except where guns were concerned; but he had run too often; and that fear, growing, had spread like the seepage from some cancerous growth, until, little by little, he had changed from a man of reasonable courage with one morbid fear to a man of no courage at all with fears that included most forms of physical violence.

But, in the beginning, his fear hadn't been too great to have been outfaced. He could have overcome it that time in Baltimore. It would have required an enormous effort, but he could have overcome it. He could have overcome it the next time, in New South Wales, when, instead, he had gone riding madly to Bourke, across a hundred-mile paddock, away from a gun in the hands of a quarrelsome boundary rider—a desperate flight along a road whose ruts stood perversely up out of the ground like railway tracks, with frightened rabbits and paddy-mellons darting out of the infrequent patches of white-bearded spear grass along his way.

Nor would it have been too late three months after that, in north Queensland. But he had run away again. Hurrying down to Cairns and the Cooktown boat, this time, away from the menace of a rusty revolver in the giant black hand of a Negro beside whom he had toiled thigh-deep in the lime-white river of the Muldiva silver fields.

After that, however, he was beyond recovery. He could not then by any effort have conquered his fear. He was beaten and he knew it. Henceforth, he had run without even decent shame in his cowardice, and he had begun to flee from other things than guns.

He had, for instance, let a jealous half-caste *garimpeiro* drive him out of Morro Velho, drive him away from his job with the British São João del Rey Mining Company and Tita. Tita's red mouth had gone from smiling allure to derision, but neither the one nor the other was strong enough to keep Owen Sack from retreating before the flourish of a knife in the hand of a man he could have tied in knots, knife and all. Out of the Bakersfield oil fields he had been driven by the bare fists of an undersized rigger. And now from here. . . .

The other times hadn't, in a way, been so bad as this. He was younger then, and there was always some other place to attract him—one place was as good as another. But now it was different.

He was no longer young, and here in the Cabinet Mountains he had meant to stop for good. He had come to look upon his cabin as his home. He wanted but two things now: a living and tranquillity, and until now he had found them here. In the year 1923 it was still possible to wash out of the Kootenai enough dust to make wages—good wages. Not wealth, certainly, but he didn't want wealth; he wanted a quiet home, and for six months he had had it here.

And then he had stumbled upon the Yusts' cache. He had known, as all Dime knew, that the Kootenai River—winding down from British Columbia to spend most of its four hundred miles in Montana and Idaho before returning to the province of its birth to join the great Columbia—was the moving road along which came much liquor, to be relayed to Spokane, not far away. That was a matter of common knowledge, and Owen Sack of all men had no desire for more particular knowledge of the river traffic.

Why, then, had his luck sent him blundering upon the place where that liquor was concealed until ready for its overland journey? And at a time when the Yusts were there to witness his discovery? And then, as if that were not enough in itself, the Prohibition enforcement officers had swooped down on that hiding-place within a week.

Now the Yusts suspected him of having informed; it was but a matter of time before their stupid brains would be convinced of that fact; then they would strike—with a gun. A pellet of metal would drive through Owen Sack's tissues as one had driven through Cardwell's. . . .

He got up from the chair and set about packing such of his belongings as he intended taking with him—to where? It didn't matter. One place was like another—a little of peace and comfort, and then the threat of another gun, to send him elsewhere. Baltimore, New South Wales, north Queensland, Brazil, California, here—thirty years of it! He was old now and his legs were stiff for flight, but running had become an integral part of him.

He packed a little breathlessly, his fingers fumbling clumsily in their haste.

DUSK WAS THICKENING in the valley of the Kootenai when Owen Sack, bent beneath the blanketed pack across his shoulders, tramped over the bridge into Dime. He had remained in his cabin until the last minute, so that he might catch the stage which would carry him to the railroad just before it left, avoiding farewells or embarrassing meetings. He hurried now.

But, again, luck ran against him.

As he turned the corner of the New Dime Hotel toward the stage terminus—two doors beyond Henny Upshaw's soft-drink parlor and poolroom—he spied Rip Yust coming down the street toward him. Yust's face, he could see, was red and swollen, and Yust's walk was a swagger. Yust was drunk.

Owen Sack halted in the middle of the sidewalk, and realized immediately that that was precisely the wrong thing to do. Safety lay—if safety lay anywhere now—in going on as if nothing out of the ordinary were happening.

He crossed the street to the opposite sidewalk, cursing himself for this open display of his desire to avoid the other, but nevertheless unable to keep his legs from hurrying him across the dusty roadway. Perhaps, he thought, Rip Yust's whisky-clouded eyes would not see him hurrying toward the stage depot with a pack on his back. But even while the hope rose in him he knew it for a futile, childish one.

Rip Yust did see him, and came to the curb on his own side of the street, to bellow:

"Hey, you! Where you going?"

Owen Sack became motionless, a frightened statue. Fear froze his mind—fear and thoughts of Cardwell.

Yust grinned stupidly across the street, and repeated:

"Where you going?"

Owen Sack tried to answer, to say something—safety seemed to lie in words—but, though he did achieve a sound, it was inarticulate, and would have told the other nothing, even if it had traveled more than ten feet from the little man's throat.

Yust laughed boomingly. He was apparently in high good humor.

"Now, you mind what I told you this afternoon," he roared, wagging a thick forefinger at Owen Sack. "If I find that you done it—"

The thick forefinger flashed back to tap the left breast of his coat.

Owen Sack screamed at the suddenness of the gesture—a thin, shrill scream of terror, which struck amusingly upon the big man's drunken fancy.

Laughter boomed out of his throat again, and his gun came into his hand. His brother's arrest and Owen Sack's supposed part in that arrest were, for the time, forgotten in his enjoyment of the little man's ridiculous fright.

With the sight of the gun, Owen Sack's last shred of sanity departed. Terror had him fast. He tried to plead, but his mouth could not frame the words. He tried to raise both his hands high above his head in the universal posture of submission, a posture that had saved him many times before. But the strap holding his pack hampered him. He tried to loosen the strap, to fling it off.

To the alcohol-muddled eyes and brain of the man across the street Owen Sack's right hand was trying to get beneath his coat on the left side. Rip Yust could read but one meaning into that motion—the little man was going for his gun.

The weapon in Yust's hand spat flame!

Owen Sack sobbed. Something struck him heavily on one side. He fell, sat down on the sidewalk, his eyes wide and questioning and fixed upon the smoking gun across the street.

Somebody, he found, was bending over him. It was Henny Upshaw, in front of whose establishment he had fallen. Owen Sack's eyes went back to the man on the opposite curb, who, cold sober now, his face granite, stood awaiting developments, the gun still in his hand.

Owen Sack didn't know whether to get up, to remain still, or to lie down. Upshaw had struck him aside in time to save him from the first bullet; but suppose the big man fired again?

"Where'd he get you?" Upshaw was asking.

"What's that?"

"Now take it easy," Upshaw advised. "You'll be all right. I'll get one of the boys to help me with you."

Owen Sack's fingers wound into one of Upshaw's sleeves.

"Wh-what happened?" he asked.

"Rip shot you, but you'll be all right. Just lay—"

Owen Sack released Upshaw's sleeve, and his hands went feeling about his body, exploring. One of them came away red and sticky from his right side, and that side—where he had felt the blow that had taken him off his feet—was warm and numb.

"Did he *shoot* me?" he demanded in an excited screech.

"Sure, but you're all right," Upshaw soothed him, and beckoned to the men who were coming slowly into the street, drawn forward by their curiosity, but retarded in their approach by the sight of Yust, who still stood, gun in hand, waiting to see what happened next.

"My God!" Owen Sack gasped in utter bewilderment. "And it ain't no worse than that!"

He bounded to his feet—his pack sliding off—eluded the hands that grasped at him, and ran for the door of Upshaw's place. On a shelf beneath the cash register he found Upshaw's black automatic, and, holding it stiffly in front of him at arm's length, turned back to the street.

His china-blue eyes were wide with wonder, and from out of his grinning mouth issued a sort of chant:

> "All these years I been running,
> And it ain't no worse than that!
> All these years I been running,
> And it ain't no worse than that!"

Rip Yust, crossing the roadway now, was in the middle when Owen Sack popped out of Upshaw's door.

The onlookers scattered. Rip's revolver swung up, and roared. A spray of Owen Sack's straw-colored hair whisked back.

He giggled, and fired three times, rapidly. None of the bullets hit the big man. Owen Sack felt something burn his left arm. He fired again, and missed.

"I got to get closer," he told himself aloud.

He walked across the sidewalk—the automatic held stiffly before him— stepped down into the roadway, and began to stride toward where pencils of fire sprang to meet him from Yust's gun.

And as the little man strode he chanted his silly chant, and fired, fired, fired. . . . Once something tugged at one of his shoulders, and once at his arm—above where he had felt the burn—but he did not even wonder what it was.

When he was within ten feet of Rip Yust, that man turned as if to walk away, took a step, his big body curved suddenly in a grotesque arc, and he slid down into the sand of the roadway.

Owen Sack found that the weapon in his own hand was empty, had been empty for some time. He turned around. Dimly he made out the broad doorway of Upshaw's place. The ground clung to his feet, trying to pull him down, to hold him back, but he gained the doorway, gained the cash register, found the shelf, and returned the automatic to it.

Voices were speaking to him, arms were around him. He ignored the voices, shook off the arms, reached the street again. More hands to be shaken off. But the air lent him strength. He was indoors again, leaning over the firearm showcase in Jeff Hamline's store.

"I want the two biggest handguns you got, Jeff, and a mess of cartridges. Fix 'em up for me and I'll be back to get 'em in a little while."

He knew that Jeff answered him, but he could not separate Jeff's words from the roaring in his head.

The warmer air of the street once more. The ankle-deep dust of the roadway pulling at his feet. The opposite sidewalk. Doc Johnstone's door. Somebody helping him up the narrow stairs. A couch or table under him; he could see and hear better now that he was lying down.

"Fix me up in a hurry, Doc! I got a lot of things to tend to."

The doctor's smooth professional voice:

"You've nothing to attend to for a while except taking care of yourself."

"I got to travel a lot, Doc. Hurry!"

"You're all right, Sack. There's no need of your going away. I saw Yust down you first from my window, and half a dozen others saw it. Self-defense if there ever was a case of it!"

" 'Tain't that!" A nice man was Doc, but there was a lot he didn't understand. "I got a lot of places to go to, a lot of men I got to see."

"Certainly. Certainly. Just as soon as you like."

"You don't understand, Doc!" The doc was talking to him like he was a child to be humored, or a drunk. "My God, Doc! I got to back-track my whole life, and I ain't young no more. There's men I got to find in Baltimore, and Australia, and Brazil, and California, and God knows where-all. And some of 'em will take a heap of finding. I got to do a lot of shootin'. I ain't young no more, and it's a mighty big job. I got to get going! You got to hurry me up, Doc! You got to . . ."

Owen Sack's voice thickened to a mumble, to a murmur, and subsided.

TOM, DICK,
OR HARRY

don't know whether Frank Toplin was tall or short. All of him I ever got a look at was his round head—naked scalp and wrinkled face, both of them the color and texture of Manila paper—propped up on white pillows in a big four-poster bed. The rest of him was buried under a thick pile of bedding.

Also in the room that first time were his wife, a roly-poly woman with lines in a plump white face like scratches in ivory; his daughter Phyllis, a smart popular-member-of-the-younger-set type; and the maid who had opened the door for me, a big-boned blond girl in apron and cap.

I had introduced myself as a representative of the North American Casualty Company's San Francisco office, which I was in a way. There was no immediate profit in admitting I was a Continental Detective Agency sleuth, just now in the casualty company's hire, so I held back that part.

"I want a list of the stuff you lost," I told Toplin, "but first—"

"Stuff?" Toplin's yellow sphere of a skull bobbed off the pillows, and he wailed to the ceiling, "A hundred thousand dollars if a nickel, and he calls it stuff!"

Mrs. Toplin pushed her husband's head down on the pillows again with a short-fingered fat hand.

"Now, Frank, don't get excited," she soothed him.

Phyllis Toplin's dark eyes twinkled, and she winked at me.

The man in bed turned his face to me again, smiled a bit shame-facedly, and chuckled.

"Well, if you people want to call your seventy-five-thousand-dollar loss stuff, I guess I can stand it for twenty-five thousand."

"So it adds up to a hundred thousand?" I asked.

"Yes. None of them were insured to their full value, and some weren't insured at all."

That was very usual. I don't remember ever having anybody admit that anything stolen from them was insured to the hilt—always it was half, or at most, three-quarters covered by the policy.

"Suppose you tell me exactly what happened," I suggested, and added, to head off another speech that usually comes, "I know you've already told the police the whole thing, but I'll have to have it from you."

"Well, we were getting dressed to go to the Bauers' last night. I brought my wife's and daughter's jewelry—the valuable pieces—home with me from the safe-deposit box. I had just got my coat on and had called to them to hurry up when the doorbell rang."

"What time was this?"

"Just about half-past eight. I went out of this room into the sitting-room across the passageway and was putting some cigars in my case when Hilda"—nodding at the blond maid—"came walking into the room, back-ward. I started to ask her if she had gone crazy, walking around backward, when I saw the robber. He—"

"Just a moment." I turned to the maid. "What happened when you answered the bell?"

"Why, I opened the door, of course, and this man was standing there, and he had a revolver in his hand, and he stuck it against my—my stomach, and pushed me back into the room where Mr. Toplin was, and he shot Mr. Toplin, and—"

"When I saw him and the revolver in his hand"—Toplin took the story away from his servant—"it gave me a fright, sort of, and I let my cigar case slip out of my hand. Trying to catch it again—no sense in ruining good ci-gars even if you are being robbed—he must have thought I was trying to get a gun or something. Anyway, he shot me in the leg. My wife and Phyllis came running in when they heard the shot and he pointed the revolver at them, took all their jewels, and had them empty my pockets. Then he made them drag me back into Phyllis's room, into the closet, and he locked us all in there. And mind you, he didn't say a word all the time, not a word—just made motions with his gun and his left hand."

"How bad did he bang your leg?"

"Depends on whether you want to believe me or the doctor. He says it's nothing much. Just a scratch, he says, but it's my leg that's shot, not his!"

"Did he say anything when you opened the door?" I asked the maid.

"No, sir."

"Did any of you hear him say anything while he was here?"

None of them had.

"What happened after he locked you in the closet?"

"Nothing that we knew about," Toplin said, "until McBirney and a policeman came and let us out."

"Who's McBirney?"

"The janitor."

"How'd he happen along with a policeman?"

"He heard the shot and came upstairs just as the robber was starting down after leaving here. The robber turned around and ran upstairs, then into an apartment on the seventh floor, and stayed there—keeping the woman who lives there, a Miss Eveleth, quiet with his revolver—until he got a chance to sneak out and get away. He knocked her unconscious before he left, and—and that's all. McBirney called the police right after he saw the robber, but they got here too late to be any good."

"How long were you in the closet?"

"Ten minutes—maybe fifteen."

"What sort of looking man was the robber?"

"Short and thin and—"

"How short?"

"About your height, or maybe shorter."

"About five feet five or six, say? What would he weigh?"

"Oh, I don't know—maybe a hundred and fifteen or twenty. He was kind of puny."

"How old?"

"Not more than twenty-two or -three."

"Oh, Papa," Phyllis objected, "he was thirty, or near it!"

"What do you think?" I asked Mrs. Toplin.

"Twenty-five, I'd say."

"And you?" to the maid.

"I don't know exactly, sir, but he wasn't very old."

"Light or dark?"

"He was light," Toplin said. "He needed a shave and his beard was yellowish."

"More of a light brown," Phyllis amended.

"Maybe, but it was light."

"What color eyes?"

"I don't know. He had a cap pulled down over them. They looked dark, but that might have been because they were in the shadow."

"How would you describe the part of his face you could see?"

"Pale, and kind of weak-looking—small chin. But you couldn't see much of his face; he had his coat collar up and his cap pulled down."

"How was he dressed?"

"A blue cap pulled down over his eyes, a blue suit, black shoes, and black gloves—silk ones."

"Shabby or neat?"

"Kind of cheap-looking clothes, awfully wrinkled."

"What sort of gun?"

Phyllis Toplin put in her word ahead of her father.

"Papa and Hilda keep calling it a revolver, but it was an automatic—a thirty-eight."

"Would you folks know him if you saw him again?"

"Yes," they agreed.

I cleared a space on the bedside table and got out a pencil and paper.

"I want a list of what he got, with as thorough a description of each piece as possible, and the price you paid for it, where you bought it, and when." I got the list half an hour later.

"Do you know the number of Miss Eveleth's apartment?" I asked.

"702, two floors above."

I went up there and rang the bell. The door was opened by a girl of twenty-something, whose nose was hidden under adhesive tape. She had nice clear hazel eyes, dark hair, and athletics written all over her.

"Miss Eveleth?"

"Yes."

"I'm from the insurance company that insured the Toplin jewelry, and I'm looking for information about the robbery."

She touched her bandaged nose and smiled ruefully.

"This is some of my information."

"How did it happen?"

"A penalty of femininity. I forgot to mind my own business. But what you want, I suppose, is what I know about the scoundrel. The doorbell rang a few minutes before nine last night and when I opened the door he was there. As soon as I got the door opened he jabbed a pistol at me and said, 'Inside, kid!'

"I let him in with no hesitancy at all; I was quite instantaneous about it and he kicked the door to behind him.

"'Where's the fire escape?' he asked.

"The fire escape doesn't come to any of my windows, and I told him so, but he wouldn't take my word for it. He drove me ahead of him to each of the windows; but of course he didn't find his fire escape, and he got peevish about it, as if it were my fault. I didn't like some of the things he called me, and he was such a little half-portion of a man so I tried to take him in hand. But—well, man is still the dominant animal so far as I'm concerned. In plain American, he busted me in the nose and left me where I fell. I was dazed, though not quite all the way out, and when I got up he had gone. I ran out into the corridor then, and found some policemen on the stairs. I sobbed out my pathetic little tale to them and they told me of the Toplin robbery. Two of them came back here with me and searched the apartment. I hadn't seen him actually leave, and they thought he might be foxy enough or desperate enough to jump into a closet and stay there until the coast was clear. But they didn't find him here."

"How long do you think it was after he knocked you down that you ran out into the corridor?"

"Oh, it couldn't have been five minutes. Perhaps only half that time."

"What did Mr. Robber look like?"

"Small, not quite so large as I; with a couple of days' growth of light hair on his face; dressed in shabby blue clothes, with black cloth gloves."

"How old?"

"Not very. His beard was thin, patchy, and he had a boyish face."

"Notice his eyes?"

"Blue; his hair, where it showed under the edge of his cap, was very light yellow, almost white."

"What sort of voice?"

"Very deep bass, though he may have been putting that on."

"Know him if you'd see him again?"

"Yes, indeed!" She put a gentle finger on her bandaged nose. "My nose would know, as the ads say, anyway!"

From Miss Eveleth's apartment I went down to the office on the first floor, where I found McBirney, the janitor, and his wife, who managed the apartment building. She was a scrawny little woman with the angular mouth and nose of a nagger; he was big, broad-shouldered, with sandy hair and mustache, good-humored, shiftless red face, and genial eyes of a pale and watery blue.

He drawled out what he knew of the looting.

"I was fixin' a spigot on the fourth floor when I heard the shot. I went up to see what was the matter, an' just as I got far enough up the front stairs to see the Toplins' door, the fella came out. We seen each other at the same time, an' he aims his gun at me. There's a lot o' things I might of done, but what I did do was to duck down an' get my head out o' range. I heard him run upstairs, an' I got up just in time to see him make the turn between the fifth and sixth floors.

"I didn't go after him. I didn't have a gun or nothin', an' I figured we had him cooped. A man could get out o' this buildin' to the roof of the next from the fourth floor, an' maybe from the fifth, but not from any above that; an' the Toplins' apartment is on the fifth. I figured we had this fella. I could stand in front of the elevator an' watch both the front an' back stairs; an' I rang for the elevator, an' told Ambrose, the elevator boy, to give the alarm an' run outside an' keep his eye on the fire escape until the police came.

"The missus came up with my gun in a minute or two, an' told me that Martinez—Ambrose's brother, who takes care of the switchboard an' the front door—was callin' the police. I could see both stairs plain, an' the fella didn't come down them; an' it wasn't more'n a few minutes before the police—a whole pack of 'em—came from the Richmond Station. Then we let the Toplins out of the closet where they were, an' started to search the buildin'. An' then Miss Eveleth came runnin' down the stairs, her face an' dress all bloody, an' told about him bein' in her apartment; so we were pretty sure we'd land him. But we didn't. We searched every apartment in the buildin', but didn't find hide nor hair of him."

"Of course you didn't!" Mrs. McBirney said unpleasantly. "But if you had—"

"I know," the janitor said with the indulgent air of one who has learned to take his pannings as an ordinary part of married life, "if I'd been a hero an' grabbed him, an' got myself all mussed up. Well, I ain't foolish like old man Toplin, gettin' himself plugged in the foot, or Blanche Eveleth, gettin' her nose busted. I'm a sensible man that knows when he's licked—an' I ain't jumpin' at no guns!"

"No! You're not doing anything that—"

This Mr. and Mrs. stuff wasn't getting me anywhere, so I cut in with a question to the woman. "Who is the newest tenant you have?"

"Mr. and Mrs. Jerald—they came the day before yesterday."

"What apartment?"

"704—next door to Miss Eveleth."

"Who are these Jeralds?"

"They come from Boston. He told me he came out here to open a branch of a manufacturing company. He's a man of at least fifty, thin and dyspeptic-looking."

"Just him and his wife?"

"Yes. She's poorly too—been in a sanatorium for a year or two."

"Who's the next newest tenant?"

"Mr. Heaton, in 535. He's been here a couple of weeks, but he's down in Los Angeles right now. He went away three days ago and said he would be gone for ten or twelve days."

"What does he look like and what does he do?"

"He's with a theatrical agency and he's kind of fat and red-faced."

"Who's the next newest?"

"Miss Eveleth. She's been here about a month."

"And the next?"

"The Wageners in 923. They've been here going on two months."

"What are they?"

"He's a retired real-estate agent. The others are his wife and son Jack—a boy of maybe nineteen. I see him with Phyllis Toplin a lot."

"How long have the Toplins been here?"

"It'll be two years next month."

I turned from Mrs. McBirney to her husband.

"Did the police search all these people's apartments?"

"Yeah," he said. "We went into every room, every alcove, an' every closet from cellar to roof."

"Did you get a good look at the robber?"

"Yeah. There's a light in the hall outside of the Toplins' door, an' it was shinin' full on his face when I saw him."

"Could he have been one of your tenants?"

"No, he couldn't."

"Know him if you saw him again?"

"You bet."

"What did he look like?"

"A little runt, a light-complected youngster of twenty-three or -four in an old blue suit."

"Can I get hold of Ambrose and Martinez—the elevator and door boys who were on duty last night—now?"

The janitor looked at his watch.

"Yeah. They ought to be on the job now. They come on at two."

I went out into the lobby and found them together, matching nickels.

They were brothers, slim, bright-eyed Filipino boys. They didn't add much to my dope.

Ambrose had come down to the lobby and told his brother to call the police as soon as McBirney had given him his orders, and then he had to beat it out the back door to take a plant on the fire escapes. The fire escapes ran down the back and one side wall. By standing a little off from the corner of those walls, the Filipino had been able to keep his eyes on both of them, as well as on the back door.

There was plenty of illumination, he said, and he could see both fire escapes all the way to the roof, and he had seen nobody on them.

Martinez had given the police a rap on the phone and had then watched the front door and the foot of the front stairs. He had seen nothing.

I had just finished questioning the Filipinos when the street door opened and two men came in. I knew one of them: Bill Garren, a police detective on the Pawnshop Detail. The other was a small blond youth all flossy in pleated pants, short, square-shouldered coat, and patent-leather shoes with fawn spats to match his hat and gloves. His face wore a sullen pout. He didn't seem to like being with Garren.

"What are you up to around here?" the detective hailed me.

"The Toplin doings for the insurance company," I explained.

"Getting anywhere?" he wanted to know.

"About ready to make a pinch," I said, not altogether in earnest and not altogether joking.

"The more the merrier," he grinned. "I've already made mine," nodding at the dressy youth. "Come on upstairs with us."

The three of us got into the elevator and Ambrose carried us to the fifth floor. Before pressing the Toplin bell, Garren gave me what he had.

"This lad tried to soak a ring in a Third Street shop a little while ago—an emerald and diamond ring that looks like one of the Toplin lot. He's doing the clam now; he hasn't said a word—yet. I'm going to show him to these people; then I'm going to take him down to the Hall of Justice and get words out of him—words that fit together in nice sentences and everything!"

The prisoner looked sullenly at the floor and paid no attention to this threat. Garren rang the bell and the maid Hilda opened the door. Her eyes widened when she saw the dressy boy, but she didn't say anything as she led us into the sitting-room, where Mrs. Toplin and her daughter were. They looked up at us.

"Hello, Jack!" Phyllis greeted the prisoner.

"'Lo, Phyl," he mumbled, not looking at her.

"Among friends, huh? Well, what's the answer?" Garren demanded of the girl.

She put her chin in the air and although her face turned red, she looked haughtily at the police detective.

"Would you mind removing your hat?" she asked.

Bill isn't a bad bimbo, but he hasn't any meekness. He answered her by tilting his hat over one eye and turning to her mother.

"Ever see this lad before?"

"Why, certainly!" Mrs. Toplin exclaimed. "That's Mr. Wagener who lives upstairs."

"Well," said Bill, "Mr. Wagener was picked up in a hock shop trying to get rid of this ring." He fished a gaudy green and white ring from his pocket. "Know it?"

"Certainly!" Mrs. Toplin said, looking at the ring. "It belongs to Phyllis, and the robber—" Her mouth dropped open as she began to understand. "How could Mr. Wagener—?"

"Yes, how?" Bill repeated.

The girl stepped between Garren and me, turning her back on him to face me. "I can explain everything," she announced.

That sounded too much like a movie subtitle to be very promising, but—

"Go ahead," I encouraged her.

"I found that ring in the passageway near the front door after the excitement was over. The robber must have dropped it. I didn't say anything to Papa and Mamma about it, because I thought nobody would ever know the difference, and it was insured, so I thought I might as well sell it and be in that much money. I asked Jack last night if he could sell it for me and he said he knew just how to go about it. He didn't have anything to do with it outside of that, but I did think he'd have sense enough not to try to pawn it right away!"

She looked scornfully at her accomplice.

"See what you've done!" she accused him.

He fidgeted and pouted at his feet.

"Ha! Ha! Ha!" Bill Garren said sourly. "That's a nifty! Did you ever hear the one about the two Irishmen that got in the Y.W.C.A. by mistake?"

She didn't say whether she had heard it or not.

"Mrs. Toplin," I asked, "making allowances for the different clothes and the unshaven face, could this lad have been the robber?"

She shook her head with emphasis. "No! He could not!"

"Set your prize down, Bill," I suggested, "and let's go over in a corner and whisper things at each other."

"Right."

He dragged a heavy chair to the center of the floor, sat Wagener on it, anchored him there with handcuffs—not exactly necessary, but Bill was grouchy at not getting his prisoner identified as the robber—and then he and I stepped out into the passageway. We could keep an eye on the sitting-room from there without having our low-voiced conversation overheard.

"This is simple," I whispered into his big red ear. "There are only five ways to figure the lay. First: Wagener stole the stuff for the Toplins. Second: the Toplins framed the robbery themselves and got Wagener to peddle it. Third: Wagener and the girl engineered the deal without the old folks being in on it. Fourth: Wagener pulled it on his own hook and the girl is covering him up. Fifth: she told us the truth. None of them explains why your little playmate should have been dumb enough to flash the ring downtown this morning, but that can't be explained by any system. Which of the five do you favor?"

"I like 'em all," he grumbled. "But what I like most is that I've got this baby right—got him trying to pass a hot ring. That suits me fine. You do the guessing. I don't ask for any more than I've got."

"It doesn't irritate me any either," I agreed. "The way it stands the insurance company can welsh on the policies—but I'd like to smoke it out a little further, far enough to put away anybody who has been trying to run a hooligan on the North American. We'll clean up all we can on this kid, stow him in the can, and then see what further damage we can do."

"All right," Garren said. "Suppose you get hold of the janitor and that Eveleth woman while I'm showing the boy to old man Toplin and getting the maid's opinion."

I nodded and went out into the corridor, leaving the door unlocked behind me. I took the elevator to the seventh floor and told Ambrose to get hold of McBirney and send him to the Toplins' apartment. Then I rang Blanche Eveleth's bell.

"Can you come downstairs for a minute or two?" I asked her. "We've a prize who might be your friend of last night."

"Will I?" She started toward the stairs with me. "And if he's the right one, can I pay him back for my battered beauty?"

"You can," I promised. "Go as far as you like, so you don't maul him too badly to stand trial."

I took her into the Toplins' apartment without ringing the bell, and found everybody in Frank Toplin's bedroom. A look at Garren's glum face told me that neither the old man nor the maid had given him a nod on the prisoner.

I put the finger on Jack Wagener. Disappointment came into Blanche Eveleth's eyes. "You're wrong," she said. "That's not he."

Garren scowled at her. It was a pipe that if the Toplins were tied up with young Wagener, they wouldn't identify him as the robber. Bill had been counting on that identification coming from the two outsiders—Blanche Eveleth and the janitor—and now one of them had flopped.

The other one rang the bell just then and the maid brought him in.

I pointed at Jack Wagener, who stood beside Garren staring sullenly at the floor.

"Know him, McBirney?"

"Yeah, Mr. Wagener's son, Jack."

"Is he the man who shooed you away with a gun last night?"

McBirney's watery eyes popped in surprise.

"No," he said with decision, and began to look doubtful.

"In an old suit, cap pulled down, needing a shave—could it have been him?"

"No-o-o-o," the janitor drawled, "I don't think so, though it— You know, now that I come to think about it, there was something familiar about that fella, an' maybe— By cracky, I think maybe you're right—though I couldn't exactly say for sure."

"That'll do!" Garren grunted in disgust.

An identification of the sort the janitor was giving isn't worth a damn one way or the other. Even positive and immediate identifications aren't always the goods. A lot of people who don't know any better—and some who do, or should—have given circumstantial evidence a bad name. It is misleading sometimes. But for genuine, undiluted, pre-war untrustworthiness, it can't come within gunshot of human testimony. Take any man you like— unless he is the one in a hundred thousand with a mind trained to keep things straight, and not always even then—get him excited, show him something, give him a few hours to think it over and talk it over, and then ask him about it. It's dollars to doughnuts that you'll have a hard time finding any connection between what he saw and what he says he saw. Like this McBirney—another hour and he'd be ready to gamble his life on Jack Wagener's being the robber.

Garren wrapped his fingers around the boy's arm and started for the door.

"Where to, Bill?" I asked.

"Up to talk to his people. Coming along?"

"Stick around a while," I invited. "I'm going to put on a party. But first, tell me, did the coppers who came here when the alarm was turned in do a good job?"

"I didn't see it," the police detective said. "I didn't get here until the fireworks were pretty well over, but I understand the boys did all that could be expected of them."

I turned to Frank Toplin. I did my talking to him chiefly because we—his wife and daughter, the maid, the janitor, Blanche Eveleth, Garren and his prisoner, and I—were grouped around the old man's bed and by looking at him I could get a one-eyed view of everybody else.

"Somebody has been kidding me somewhere," I began my speech. "If all the things I've been told about this job are right, then so is Prohibition. Your stories don't fit together, not even almost. Take the bird who stuck you up. He seems to have been pretty well acquainted with your affairs. It might be luck that he hit your apartment at a time when all of your jewelry was on hand, instead of another apartment, or your apartment at another time. But I don't like luck. I'd rather figure that he knew what he was doing. He nicked you for your pretties, and then he galloped up to Miss Eveleth's apartment. He may have been about to go downstairs when he ran into McBirney, or he may not. Anyway, he went upstairs, into Miss Eveleth's apartment, looking for a fire escape. Funny, huh? He knew enough about the place to make a push-over out of the stick-up, but he didn't know there were no fire escapes on Miss Eveleth's side of the building.

"He didn't speak to you or to McBirney, but he talked to Miss Eveleth, in a bass voice. A very, very deep voice. Funny, huh? From Miss Eveleth's apartment he vanished with every exit watched. The police must have been here before he left her apartment and they would have blocked the outlets first thing, whether McBirney and Ambrose had already done that or not. But he got away. Funny, huh? He wore a wrinkled suit, which might have been taken from a bundle just before he went to work, and he was a small man. Miss Eveleth isn't a small woman, but she would be a small man. A guy with a suspicious disposition would almost think Blanche Eveleth was the robber."

Frank Toplin, his wife, young Wagener, the janitor, and the maid were gaping at me. Garren was sizing up the Eveleth girl with narrowed eyes, while she glared white-hot at me. Phyllis Toplin was looking at me with a contemptuous sort of pity for my feeble-mindedness.

Bill Garren finished his inspection of the girl and nodded slowly.

"She could get away with it," he gave his opinion, "indoors and if she kept her mouth shut."

"Exactly," I said.

"Exactly, my eye!" Phyllis Toplin exploded. "Do you two correspondence-school detectives think we wouldn't know the difference between a man and a woman dressed in man's clothes? He had a day or two's growth of hair on his face—real hair, if you know what I mean. Do you think he could have fooled us with false whiskers? This happened, you know, it's not in a play!"

The others stopped gaping, and heads bobbed up and down.

"Phyllis is right." Frank Toplin backed up his offspring. "He was a man—no woman dressed like one."

His wife, the maid, and the janitor nodded vigorous endorsements.

But I'm a bull-headed sort of bird when it comes to going where the evidence leads. I spun to face Blanche Eveleth.

"Can you add anything to the occasion?" I asked her.

She smiled very sweetly at me and shook her head.

"All right, bum," I said. "You're pinched. Let's go."

Then it seemed she could add something to the occasion. She had something to say, quite a few things to say, and they were all about me. They weren't nice things. In anger her voice was shrill, and just now she was madder than you'd think anybody could get on short notice. I was sorry for that. This job had run along peacefully and gently so far, hadn't been marred by any rough stuff, had been almost ladylike in every particular; and I had hoped it would go that way to the end. But the more she screamed at me the nastier she got. She didn't have any words I hadn't heard before, but she fitted them together in combinations that were new to me. I stood as much of it as I could.

Then I knocked her over with a punch in the mouth.

"Here! Here!" Bill Garren yelled, grabbing my arm.

"Save your strength, Bill," I advised him, shaking his hand off and going over to yank the Eveleth person up from the floor. "Your gallantry does you credit, but I think you'll find Blanche's real name is Tom, Dick, or Harry."

I hauled her (or him, whichever you like) to his or her feet and asked it: "Feel like telling us about it?"

For answer I got a snarl.

"All right," I said to the others, "in the absence of authoritative information I'll give you my dope. If Blanche Eveleth could have been the robber except for the beard and the difficulty of a woman passing for a man, why couldn't the robber have been Blanche Eveleth before and after the robbery by using a—what do you call it?—strong depilatory on his face, and a wig? It's hard for a woman to masquerade as a man, but there are lots of men who can get away with the feminine role. Couldn't this bird, after renting his apartment as Blanche Eveleth and getting everything lined up, have stayed in his apartment for a couple of days letting his beard grow? Come down and knock the job over? Beat it upstairs, get the hair off his face, and get into his female rig in, say, fifteen minutes? My guess is that he could. And he had fifteen minutes. I don't know about the smashed nose. Maybe he stumbled going up the stairs and had to twist his plans to account for it—or maybe he smacked himself intentionally."

My guesses weren't far off, though his name was Fred—Frederick Agnew Rudd. He was known in Toronto, having done a stretch in the Ontario Reformatory as a boy of nineteen, caught shoplifting in his she-make-up. He wouldn't come through, and we never turned up his gun or the blue suit, cap, and black gloves, although we found a cavity in his mattress where he had stuffed them out of the police's sight until later that night, when he could get rid of them. But the Toplin sparklers came to light piece by piece when we had plumbers take apart the drains and radiators in apartment 702.

ONE
HOUR

I

This is Mr. Chrostwaite," Vance Richmond said.

Chrostwaite, wedged between the arms of one of the attorney's large chairs, grunted what was perhaps meant for an acknowledgment of the introduction. I grunted back at him, and found myself a chair.

He was a big balloon of a man—this Chrostwaite—in a green plaid suit that didn't make him look any smaller than he was. His tie was a gaudy thing, mostly of yellow, with a big diamond set in the center of it, and there were more stones on his pudgy hands. Spongy fat blurred his features, making it impossible for his round purplish face to even hold any other expression than the discontented hoggishness that was habitual to it. He reeked of gin.

"Mr. Chrostwaite is the Pacific Coast agent for the Mutual Fire Extinguisher Manufacturing Company," Vance Richmond began, as soon as I had got myself seated. "His office is on Kearny Street, near California. Yesterday, at about two forty-five in the afternoon, he went to his office, leaving his machine—a Hudson touring car—standing in front, with the engine running. Then minutes later, he came out. The car was gone."

I looked at Chrostwaite. He was looking at his fat knees, showing not the least interest in what his attorney was saying. I looked quickly back at Vance Richmond; his clean gray face and lean figure were downright beautiful beside his bloated client.

"A man named Newhouse," the lawyer was saying, "who was the proprietor of a printing establishment on California Street, just around the corner from Mr. Chrostwaite's office, was run down and killed by Mr. Chrostwaite's car at the corner of Clay and Kearny Streets, five minutes after Mr. Chrostwaite had left the car to go into his office. The police found the car shortly afterward, only a block away from the scene of the accident—on Montgomery near Clay.

"The thing is fairly obvious. Someone stole the car immediately after Mr. Chrostwaite left it; and in driving rapidly away, ran down Newhouse; and then, in fright, abandoned the car. But here is Mr. Chrostwaite's position; three nights ago, while driving perhaps a little recklessly out—"

"Drunk," Chrostwaite said, not looking up from his plaid knees; and though his voice was hoarse, husky—it was the hoarseness of a whisky-burned throat—there was no emotion in his voice.

"While driving perhaps a little recklessly out Van Ness Avenue," Vance Richmond went on, ignoring the interruption, "Mr. Chrostwaite knocked a pedestrian down. The man wasn't badly hurt, and he is being compensated very generously for his injuries. But we are to appear in court next Monday to face a charge of reckless driving, and I am afraid that this accident of yesterday, in which the printer was killed, may hurt us.

"No one thinks that Mr. Chrostwaite was in his car when it killed the printer—we have a world of evidence that he wasn't. But I am afraid that the printer's death may be made a weapon against us when we appear on the Van Ness Avenue charge. Being an attorney, I know just how much capital the prosecuting attorney—if he so chooses—can make out of the really insignificant fact that the same car that knocked down the man on Van Ness Avenue killed another man yesterday. And, being an attorney, I know how likely the prosecuting attorney is to so choose. And he can handle it in such a way that we will be given little or no opportunity to tell our side.

"The worst that can happen, of course, is that, instead of the usual fine, Mr. Chrostwaite will be sent to the city jail for thirty or sixty days. That is bad enough, however, and that is what we wish to—"

Chrostwaite spoke again, still regarding his knees.

"Damned nuisance!" he said.

"That is what we wish to avoid," the attorney continued. "We are willing to pay a stiff fine, and expect to, for the accident on Van Ness Avenue was clearly Mr. Chrostwaite's fault. But we—"

"Drunk as a lord!" Chrostwaite said.

"But we don't want to have this other accident, with which we had nothing to do, given a false weight in connection with the slighter accident. What we want then, is to find the man or men who stole the car and ran down John Newhouse. If they are apprehended before we go to court, we won't be in danger of suffering for their act. Think you can find them before Monday?"

"I'll try," I promised; "though it isn't—"

The human balloon interrupted me by heaving himself to his feet, fumbling with his fat jeweled fingers for his watch.

"Three o'clock," he said. "Got a game of golf for three-thirty." He picked up his hat and gloves from the desk. "Find 'em, will you? Damned nuisance going to jail!"

And he waddled out.

I I

From the attorney's office, I went down to the Hall of Justice, and, after hunting around a few minutes, found a policeman who had arrived at the corner of Clay and Kearny Streets a few seconds after Newhouse had been knocked down.

"I was just leaving the Hall when I seen a bus scoot around the corner at Clay Street," this patrolman—a big sandy-haired man named Coffee—told me. "Then I seen people gathering around, so I went up there and found this John Newhouse stretched out. He was already dead. Half a dozen people had seen him hit, and one of 'em had got the license number of the car that done it. We found the car standing empty just around the corner on Montgomery Street, pointing north. There was two fellows in the car when it hit Newhouse, but nobody saw what they looked like. Nobody was in it when we found it."

"In what direction was Newhouse walking?"

"North along Kearny Street, and he was about three-quarters across Clay when he was knocked. The car was coming north on Kearny, too, and turned east on Clay. It mightn't have been all the fault of the fellows in the car—according to them that seen the accident. Newhouse was walking across the street looking at a piece of paper in his hand. I found a piece of foreign money—paper money—in his hand, and I guess that's what he was looking at. The lieutenant tells me it was Dutch money—a hundred-florin note, he says."

"Found out anything about the men in the car?"

"Nothing! We lined up everybody we could find in the neighborhood of California and Kearny Streets—where the car was stolen from—and around Clay and Montgomery Streets—where it was left at. But nobody remembered seeing the fellows getting in it or getting out of it. The man that owns the car wasn't driving it—it was stole all right, I guess. At first I thought maybe there was something shady about the accident. This John Newhouse had a two- or three-day-old black eye on him. But we run that out and found that he had an attack of heart trouble or something a couple days ago, and fell, fetching his eye up against a chair. He'd been home sick for three days—just left his house half an hour or so before the accident."

"Where'd he live?"

"On Sacramento Street—way out. I got his address here somewhere."

He turned over the pages of a grimy memoranda book, and I got the dead man's house number, and the names and addresses of the witnesses to the accident that Coffee had questioned.

That exhausted the policeman's information, so I left him.

I I I

My next play was to canvass the vicinity of where the car had been stolen and where it had been deserted, and then interview the witnesses. The fact that the police had fruitlessly gone over this ground made it unlikely that I would find anything of value; but I couldn't skip these things on that account. Ninety-nine per cent of detective work is a patient collecting of details—and your details must be got as nearly first-hand as possible, regardless of who else has worked the territory before you.

Before starting on this angle, however, I decided to run around to the dead man's printing establishment—only three blocks from the Hall of Justice—and see if any of his employees had heard anything that might help me.

Newhouse's establishment occupied the ground floor of a small building on California, between Kearny and Montgomery. A small office was partitioned off in front, with a connecting doorway leading to the pressroom in the rear.

The only occupant of the small office, when I came in from the street, was a short, stocky, worried-looking blond man of forty or thereabouts, who sat at the desk in his shirt-sleeves, checking off figures in a ledger against others on a batch of papers before him.

I introduced myself, telling him that I was a Continental Detective Agency operative, interested in Newhouse's death. He told me his name was Ben Soules, and that he was Newhouse's foreman. We shook hands, and then he waved me to a chair across the desk, pushed back the papers and book upon which he had been working, and scratched his head disgustedly with the pencil in his hand.

"This is awful!" he said. "What with one thing and another, we're heels over head in work, and I got to fool with these books that I don't know anything at all about, and—"

He broke off to pick up the telephone, which had jingled.

"Yes. . . . This is Soules. . . . We're working on them now. . . . I'll give 'em to you by Monday noon at the least. . . . I know! I know! But the boss's death set us back. Explain that to Mr. Chrostwaite. And . . . And I'll promise you that we'll give them to you Monday morning, sure!"

Soules slapped the receiver irritably on its hook and looked at me.

"You'd think that since it was his own car that killed the boss, he'd have decency enough not to squawk over the delay!"

"Chrostwaite?"

"Yes—that was one of his clerks. We're printing some leaflets for him—promised to have 'em ready yesterday—but between the boss's death and having a couple new hands to break in, we're behind with everything. I've been here eight years, and this is the first time we ever fell down on an order—and every damned customer is yelling his head off. If we were like most printers they'd be used to waiting; but we've been too good to them. But this Chrostwaite! You'd think he'd have some decency, seeing that his car killed the boss!"

I nodded sympathetically, slid a cigar across the desk, and waited until it was burning in Soules's mouth before I asked:

"You said something about having a couple new hands to break in. How come?"

"Yes. Mr. Newhouse fired two of our printers last week—Fincher and Keys. He found that they belonged to the I.W.W., so he gave them their time."

"Any trouble with them or anything against them except that they were Wobblies?"

"No—they were pretty good workers."

"Any trouble with them after he fired them?" I asked.

"No real trouble, though they were pretty hot. They made red speeches all over the place before they left."

"Remember what day that was?"

"Wednesday of last week, I think. Yes, Wednesday, because I hired two new men on Thursday."

"How many men do you work?"

"Three, besides myself."

"Was Mr. Newhouse sick very often?"

"Not sick enough to stay away very often, though every now and then his heart would go back on him, and he'd have to stay in bed for a week or ten days. He wasn't what you could call real well at any time. He never did anything but the office work—I run the shop."

"When was he taken sick this last time?"

"Mrs. Newhouse called up Tuesday morning and said he had had another spell, and wouldn't be down for a few days. He came in yesterday—which was Thursday—for about ten minutes in the afternoon, and said he would be back on the job this morning. He was killed just after he left."

"How did he look—very sick?"

"Not so bad. He never looked well, of course, but I couldn't see much difference from usual yesterday. This last spell hadn't been as bad as most, I reckon—he was usually laid up for a week or more."

"Did he say where he was going when he left? The reason I ask is that, living out on Sacramento Street, he would naturally have taken a car at that street if he had been going home, whereas he was run down on Clay Street."

"He said he was going up to Portsmouth Square to sit in the sun for half an hour or so. He had been cooped up indoors for two or three days, he said, and he wanted some sunshine before he went back home."

"He had a piece of foreign money in his hand when he was hit. Know anything about it?"

"Yes. He got it here. One of our customers—a man named Van Pelt—came in to pay for some work we had done yesterday afternoon while the boss was here. When Van Pelt pulled out his wallet to pay his bill, this piece of Holland money—I don't know what you call it—was among the bills. I think he said it was worth something like thirty-eight dollars. Anyway, the boss took it, giving Van Pelt his change. The boss said he wanted to show the Holland money to his boys—and he could have it changed back into American money later."

"Who is this Van Pelt?"

"He's a Hollander—is planning to open a tobacco importing business here in a month or two. I don't know much about him outside of that."

"Where's his home, or office?"

"His office is on Bush Street, near Sansome."

"Did he know that Newhouse had been sick?"

"I don't think so. The boss didn't look much different from usual."

"What's this Van Pelt's full name?"

"Hendrik Van Pelt."

"What does he look like?"

Before Soules could answer, three evenly spaced buzzes sounded above the rattle and whirring of the presses in the back of the shop.

I slid the muzzle of my gun—I had been holding it in my lap for five minutes—far enough over the edge of the desk for Ben Soules to see it.

"Put both of your hands on top of the desk," I said.

He put them there.

The pressroom door was directly behind him, so that, facing him across the desk, I could look over his shoulder at it. His stocky body served to screen my gun from the view of whoever came through the door, in response to Soules's signal.

I didn't have long to wait.

Three men—black with ink—came to the door, and through it into the little office. They strolled in careless and casual, laughing and joking to one another.

But one of them licked his lips as he stepped through the door. Another's eyes showed white circles all around the irises. The third was the best actor—but he held his shoulders a trifle too stiffly to fit his otherwise careless carriage.

"Stop right there!" I barked at them when the last one was inside the office—and I brought my gun up where they could see it.

They stopped as if they had all been mounted on the same pair of legs.

I kicked my chair back, and stood up.

I didn't like my position at all. The office was entirely too small for me. I had a gun, true enough, and whatever weapons may have been distributed among these other men were out of sight. But these four men were too close to me; and a gun isn't a thing of miracles. It's a mechanical contraption that is capable of just so much and no more.

If these men decided to jump me, I could down just one of them before the other three were upon me. I knew it, and they knew it.

"Put your hands up," I ordered, "and turn around!"

None of them moved to obey. One of the inked men grinned wickedly; Soules shook his head slowly; the other two stood and looked at me.

I was more or less stumped. You can't shoot a man just because he refuses to obey an order—even if he is a criminal. If they had turned around for me, I could have lined them up against the wall, and, being behind them, have held them safe while I used the telephone.

But that hadn't worked.

My next thought was to back across the office to the street door, keeping them covered, and then either stand in the door and yell for help, or take them into the street, where I could handle them. But I put that thought away as quickly as it came to me.

These four men were going to jump me—there was no doubt of that. All that was needed was a spark of any sort to explode them into action. They were standing stiff-legged and tense, waiting for some move on my part. If I took a step backward—the battle would be on.

We were close enough for any of the four to have reached out and touched me. One of them I could shoot before I was smothered—one out of four. That meant that each of them had only one chance out of four of being the victim—low enough odds for any but the most cowardly of men.

I grinned what was supposed to be a confident grin—because I was up against it hard—and reached for the telephone: I had to do something! Then I cursed myself! I had merely changed the signal for the onslaught. It would come now when I picked up the receiver.

But I couldn't back down again—that, too, would be a signal—I had to go through with it.

The perspiration trickled across my temples from under my hat as I drew the phone closer with my left hand.

The street door opened! An exclamation of surprise came from behind me.

I spoke rapidly, without taking my eyes from the four men in front of me.

"Quick! The phone! The police!"

With the arrival of this unknown person—one of Newhouse's customers, probably—I figured I had the edge again. Even if he took no active part beyond calling the police in, the enemy would have to split to take care of him—and that would give me a chance to pot at least two of them before I was knocked over. Two out of four—each of them had an even chance of being dropped—which *is* enough to give even a nervy man cause for thinking a bit before he jumps.

"Hurry!" I urged the newcomer.

"Yes! Yes!" he said—and in the blurred sound of the "s" there was evidence of foreign birth.

Keyed up as I was, I didn't need any more warning than that.

I threw myself sidewise—a blind tumbling away from the spot where I stood. But I wasn't quite quick enough.

The blow that came from behind didn't hit me fairly, but I got enough of it to fold up my legs as if the knees were hinged with paper—and I slammed into a heap on the floor. . . .

Something dark crashed toward me. I caught it with both hands. It may have been a foot kicking at my face. I wrung it as a washerwoman wrings a towel.

Down my spine ran jar after jar. Perhaps somebody was beating me over the head. I don't know. My head wasn't alive. The blow that had knocked me down had numbed me all over. My eyes were no good. Shadows swam to and fro in front of them—that was all. I struck, gouged, tore at the shadows. Sometimes I found nothing. Sometimes I found things that felt like parts of bodies. Then I would hammer at them, tear at them. My gun was gone.

My hearing was no better than my sight—or not so good. There wasn't a sound in the world. I moved in a silence that was more complete than any silence I had ever known. I was a ghost fighting ghosts.

I found presently that my feet were under me again, though some squirming thing was on my back, and kept me from standing upright. A hot, damp thing like a hand was across my face.

I put my teeth into it. I snapped my head back as far as it would go. Maybe it smashed into the face it was meant for. I don't know. Anyhow the squirming thing was no longer on my back.

Dimly I realized that I was being buffeted about by blows that I was too numb to feel. Ceaselessly, with head and shoulders and elbows and fists and knees and feet, I struck at the shadows that were around me. . . .

Suddenly I could see again—not clearly—but the shadows were taking on colors; and my ears came back a little, so that grunts and growls and curses and the impact of blows sounded in them. My straining gaze rested upon a brass cuspidor six inches or so in front of my eyes. I knew then that I was down on the floor again.

As I twisted about to hurl a foot into a soft body above me, something that was like a burn, but wasn't a burn, ran down one leg—a knife. The sting of it brought consciousness back into me with a rush.

I grabbed the brass cuspidor and used it to club a way to my feet—to club a clear space in front of me. Men were hurling themselves upon me. I swung the cuspidor high and flung it over their heads through the frosted glass door into California Street.

Then we fought some more.

But you can't throw a brass cuspidor through a glass door into California Street between Montgomery and Kearny without attracting attention—it's too near the heart of daytime San Francisco. So presently—when I was on the floor again with six or eight hundred pounds of flesh hammering my face into the boards—we were pulled apart, and I was dug out of the bottom of the pile by a squad of policemen.

Big sandy-haired Coffee was one of them, but it took a lot of arguing to convince him that I was the Continental operative who had talked to him a little while before.

"Man! Man!" he said, when I finally convinced him. "Them lads sure—God!—have worked you over! You got a face like a wet geranium!"

I didn't laugh. It wasn't funny.

I looked out of the one eye which was working just now at the five men lined up across the office—Soules, the three inky printers, and the man with the blurred "s," who had started the slaughter by tapping me on the back of the head.

He was a rather tall man of thirty or so, with a round ruddy face that wore a few bruises now. He had been, apparently, rather well-dressed in expensive black clothing, but he was torn and ragged now. I knew who he was without asking—Hendrik Van Pelt.

"Well, man, what's the answer?" Coffee was asking me.

By holding one side of my jaw firmly with one hand I found that I could talk without too much pain.

"This is the crowd that ran down Newhouse," I said, "and it wasn't an accident. I wouldn't mind having a few more of the details myself, but I was jumped before I got around to all of them. Newhouse had a hundred-florin note in his hand when he was run down, and he was walking in the direction of police headquarters—was only half a block away from the Hall of Justice.

"Soules tells me that Newhouse said he was going up to Portsmouth Square to sit in the sun. But Soules didn't seem to know that Newhouse was wearing a black eye—the one you told me you had investigated. If Soules didn't see the shiner, then it's a good bet that Soules didn't see Newhouse's face that day!

"Newhouse was walking from his printing shop toward police headquarters with a piece of foreign paper money in his hand—remember that!

"He had frequent spells of sickness, which, according to friend Soules, always before kept him at home for a week or ten days at a time. This time he was laid up for only two and a half days.

"Soules tells me that the shop is three days behind with its orders, and he says that's the first time in eight years they've ever been behind. He blames Newhouse's death—which only happened yesterday. Apparently, New- house's previous sick spells never delayed things—why should this last spell?

"Two printers were fired last week, and two new ones hired the very next day—pretty quick work. The car with which Newhouse was run down was taken from just around the corner, and was deserted within quick walking distance of the shop. It was left facing north, which is pretty good evidence that its occupants went south after they got out. Ordinary car thieves wouldn't have circled back in the direction from which they came.

"Here's my guess: This Van Pelt is a Dutchman, and he had some plates for phony hundred-florin notes. He hunted around until he found a printer who would go in with him. He found Soules, the foreman of a shop whose proprietor was now and then at home for a week or more at a time with a bad heart. One of the printers under Soules was willing to go in with them. Maybe the other two turned the offer down. Maybe Soules didn't ask them at all. Anyhow, they were discharged, and two friends of Soules were given their places.

"Our friends then got everything ready, and waited for Newhouse's heart to flop again. It did—Monday night. As soon as his wife called up next morning and said he was sick, these birds started running off their counter- feits. That's why they fell behind with their regular work. But this spell of Newhouse's was lighter than usual. He was up and moving around within two days, and yesterday afternoon he came down here for a few minutes.

"He must have walked in while all of our friends were extremely busy in some far corner. He must have spotted some of the phony money, immedi- ately sized up the situation, grabbed one bill to show the police, and started out for police headquarters—no doubt thinking he had not been seen by our friends here.

"They must have got a glimpse of him as he was leaving, however. Two of them followed him out. They couldn't, afoot, safely knock him over within a block or two of the Hall of Justice. But, turning the corner, they found Chrostwaite's car standing there with idling engine. That solved their getaway problem. They got in the car and went on after Newhouse. I sup- pose the original plan was to shoot him—but he crossed Clay Street with his eyes fastened upon the phony money in his hand. That gave them a golden chance. They piled the car into him. It was sure death, they knew—

his bum heart would finish the job if the actual collision didn't kill him. Then they deserted the car and came back here.

"There are a lot of loose ends to be gathered in—but this pipe-dream I've just told you fits in with all the facts we know—and I'll bet a month's salary I'm not far off anywhere. There ought be a three-day crop of Dutch notes cached somewhere! You people—"

I suppose I'd have gone on talking forever—in the giddy, head-swimming intoxication of utter exhaustion that filled me—if the big sandy-haired patrolman hadn't shut me off by putting a big hand across my mouth.

"Be quiet, man," he said, lifting me out the chair, and spreading me flat on my back on the desk. "I'll have an ambulance here in a second for you."

The office was swirling around in front of my one open eye—the yellow ceiling swung down toward me, rose again, disappeared, came back in odd shapes. I turned my head to one side to avoid it, and my glance rested upon the white dial of a spinning clock.

Presently the dial came to rest, and I read it—four o'clock.

I remembered that Chrostwaite had broken up our conference in Vance Richmond's office at three, and I had started to work.

"One full hour!" I tried to tell Coffee before I went to sleep.

THE POLICE wound up the job while I was lying on my back in bed. In Van Pelt's office on Bush Street they found a great bale of hundred-florin notes. Van Pelt, they learned, had a considerable reputation in Europe as a high-class counterfeiter. One of the printers came through, stating that Van Pelt and Soules were the two who followed Newhouse out of the shop, and killed him.

WHO KILLED
BOB TEAL?

Teal was killed last night."

The Old Man—the Continental Detective Agency's San Francisco manager—spoke without looking at me. His voice was as mild as his smile, and gave no indication of the turmoil that was seething in his mind.

If I kept quiet, waiting for the Old Man to go on, it wasn't because the news didn't mean anything to me. I had been fond of Bob Teal—we all had. He had come to the Agency fresh from college two years before; and if ever a man had the makings of a crack detective in him, this slender, broad-shouldered lad had. Two years is little enough time in which to pick up the first principles of sleuthing, but Bob Teal, with his quick eye, cool nerve, balanced head, and whole-hearted interest in the work, was already well along the way to expertness. I had an almost fatherly interest in him, since I had given him most of his early training.

The Old Man didn't look at me as he went on. He was talking to the open window at his elbow.

"He was shot with a thirty-two, twice, through the heart. He was shot behind a row of signboards on the vacant lot on the northwest corner of Hyde and Eddy Streets, at about ten last night. His body was found by a patrolman a little after eleven. The gun was found about fifteen feet away. I have seen him and I have gone over the ground myself. The rain last night wiped out any leads the ground may have held, but from the condition of Teal's clothing and the position in which he was found, I would say that there was no struggle, and that he was shot where he was found, and not carried there afterward. He was lying behind the signboards, about thirty feet from the sidewalk, and his hands were empty. The gun was held close enough to him to singe the breast of his coat. Apparently no one either saw or heard the shooting. The rain and wind would have kept pedestrians off the street, and would have deadened the reports of a thirty-two, which are not especially loud, anyway."

The Old Man's pencil began to tap the desk, its gentle clicking setting my nerves on edge. Presently it stopped, and the Old Man went on:

"Teal was shadowing a Herbert Whitacre—had been shadowing him for three days. Whitacre is one of the partners in the firm Ogburn and Whitacre, farm-development engineers. They have options on a large area of land in several of the new irrigation districts. Ogburn handles the sales end, while Whitacre looks after the rest of the business, including the book-keeping.

"Last week Ogburn discovered that his partner had been making false entries. The books show certain payments made on the land, and Ogburn learned that these payments had not been made. He estimates that the amount of Whitacre's thefts may be anywhere from one hundred fifty to two hundred fifty thousand dollars. He came in to see me three days ago and told me all this, and wanted to have Whitacre shadowed in an endeavor to learn what he has done with the stolen money. Their firm is still a partner-ship, and a partner cannot be prosecuted for stealing from the partnership, of course. Thus, Ogburn could not have his partner arrested, but he hoped to find the money, and then recover it through civil action. Also he was afraid that Whitacre might disappear.

"I sent Teal out to shadow Whitacre, who supposedly didn't know that his partner suspected him. Now I am sending you out to find Whitacre. I'm determined to find him and convict him if I have to let all regular business go and put every man I have on this job for a year. You can get Teal's reports from the clerks. Keep in touch with me."

All that, from the Old Man, was more than an ordinary man's oath writ-ten in blood.

In the clerical office I got the two reports Bob had turned in. There was none for the last day, of course, as he would not have written that until after he had quit work for the night. The first of these two reports had already been copied and a copy sent to Ogburn; a typist was working on the other now.

In his reports Bob had described Whitacre as a man of about thirty-seven, with brown hair and eyes, a nervous manner, a smooth-shaven, medium-complexioned face, and rather small feet. He was about five feet eight inches tall, weighed about a hundred and fifty pounds, and dressed fashionably, though quietly. He lived with his wife in an apartment on Gough Street. They had no children. Ogburn had given Bob a description of Mrs. Whitacre: a short, plump, blond woman of something less than thirty.

Those who remember this affair will know that the city, the detective agency, and the people involved all had names different from the ones I have given them. But they will know also that I have kept the facts true. Names of some sort are essential to clearness, and when the use of the real names might cause embarrassment, or pain even, pseudonyms are the most satisfactory alternative.

In shadowing Whitacre, Bob had learned nothing that seemed to be of any value in finding the stolen money. Whitacre had gone about his usual business, apparently, and Bob had seen him do nothing downright suspicious. But Whitacre had seemed nervous, had often stopped to look around, obviously suspecting that he was being shadowed without being sure of it. On several occasions Bob had had to drop him to avoid being recognized. On one of these occasions, while waiting in the vicinity of Whitacre's residence for him to return, Bob had seen Mrs. Whitacre—or a woman who fit the description Ogburn had given—leave in a taxicab. Bob had not tried to follow her, but he made a memorandum of the taxi's license number.

These two reports read and practically memorized, I left the Agency and went down to Ogburn & Whitacre's suite in the Packard Building. A stenographer ushered me into a tastefully furnished office, where Ogburn sat at a desk signing mail. He offered me a chair. I introduced myself to him, a medium-sized man of perhaps thirty-five, with sleek brown hair and the cleft chin that is associated in my mind with orators, lawyers, and salesmen.

"Oh, yes!" he said, pushing aside the mail, his mobile, intelligent face lighting up. "Has Mr. Teal found anything?"

"Mr. Teal was shot and killed last night."

He looked at me blankly for a moment out of wide brown eyes, and then repeated: "Killed?"

"Yes," I replied, and told him what little I knew about it.

"You don't think—" he began when I had finished, and then stopped. "You don't think Herb would have done that?"

"What do you think?"

"I don't think Herb would commit murder! He's been jumpy the last few days, and I was beginning to think he suspected I had discovered his thefts, but I don't believe he would have gone that far, even if he knew Mr. Teal was following him. I honestly don't!"

"Suppose," I suggested, "that sometime yesterday Teal found where he had put the stolen money, and then Whitacre learned that Teal knew it. Don't you think that under those circumstances Whitacre might have killed him?"

"Perhaps," he said slowly, "but I'd hate to think so. In a moment of panic Herb might—but I really don't think he would."

"When did you see him last?"

"Yesterday. We were here in the office together most of the day. He left for home a few minutes before six. But I talked to him over the phone later. He called me up at home at a little after seven, and said he was coming down to see me, wanted to tell me something. I thought he was going to confess his dishonesty, and that maybe we would be able to straighten out this miserable affair. His wife called up at about ten. She wanted him to bring something from downtown when he went home, but of course he was not there. I stayed in all evening waiting for him, but he didn't—"

He stuttered, stopped talking, and his face drained white.

"My God, I'm wiped out!" he said faintly, as if the thought of his own position had just come to him. "Herb gone, money gone, three years' work gone for nothing! And I'm legally responsible for every cent he stole. God!"

He looked at me with eyes that pleaded for contradiction, but I couldn't do anything except assure him that everything possible would be done to find both Whitacre and the money. I left him trying frantically to get his attorney on the telephone.

From Ogburn's office I went up to Whitacre's apartment. As I turned the corner below into Gough Street I saw a big, hulking man going up the apartment house steps, and recognized him as George Dean. Hurrying to join him, I regretted that he had been assigned to the job instead of some other member of the police detective Homicide Detail. Dean isn't a bad sort, but he isn't so satisfactory to work with as some of the others; that is, you can never be sure that he isn't holding out some important detail so that George Dean would shine as the clever sleuth in the end. Working with a man of that sort, you're bound to fall into the habit—which doesn't make for teamwork.

I arrived in the vestibule as Dean pressed Whitacre's bell-button.

"Hello," I said. "You in on this?"

"Uh-huh. What d'you know?"

"Nothing. I just got it."

The front door clicked open, and we went together up to the Whitacres' apartment on the third floor. A plump, blond woman in a light blue housedress opened the apartment door. She was rather pretty in a thick-featured, stolid way.

"Mrs. Whitacre?" Dean inquired.

"Yes."

"Is Mr. Whitacre in?"

"No. He went to Los Angeles this morning," she said, and her face was truthful.

"Know where we can get in touch with him there?"

"Perhaps at the Ambassador, but I think he'll be back by to-morrow or the next day."

Dean showed her his badge.

"We want to ask you a few questions," he told her, and with no appearance of astonishment she opened the door wide for us to enter. She led us into a blue and cream living-room where we found a chair apiece. She sat facing us on a big blue settle.

"Where was your husband last night?" Dean asked.

"Home. Why?" Her round blue eyes were faintly curious.

"Home all night?"

"Yes, it was a rotten rainy night. Why?" She looked from Dean to me.

Dean's glance met mine, and I nodded an answer to the question that I read there.

"Mrs. Whitacre," he said bluntly, "I have a warrant for your husband's arrest."

"A warrant? For what?"

"Murder."

"Murder?" It was a stifled scream.

"Exactly, an' last night."

"But—but I told you he was—"

"And Ogburn told me," I interrupted, leaning forward, "that you called up his apartment last night, asking if your husband was there."

She looked at me blankly for a dozen seconds; and then she laughed, the clear laugh of one who has been the victim of some slight joke.

"You win," she said, and there was neither shame nor humiliation in either face or voice. "Now listen"—the amusement had left her—"I don't know what Herb has done, or how I stand, and I oughtn't to talk until I see a lawyer. But I like to dodge all the trouble I can. If you folks will tell me what's what, on your word of honor, I'll maybe tell you what I know, if anything. What I mean is, if talking will make things any easier for me, if you can show me it will, maybe I'll talk—provided I know anything."

That seemed fair enough, if a little surprising. Apparently this plump woman who could lie with every semblance of candor, and laugh when she was tripped up, wasn't interested in anything much beyond her own comfort.

"You tell it," Dean said to me.

I shot it out all in a lump.

"Your husband had been cooking the books for some time, and got into his partner for something like two hundred thousand dollars before Ogburn got wise to it. Then he had your husband shadowed, trying to find the money. Last night your husband took the man who was shadowing him over on a lot and shot him."

Her face puckered thoughtfully. Mechanically she reached for a package of popular-brand cigarettes that lay on a table behind the settle, and proffered them to Dean and me. We shook our heads. She put a cigarette in her mouth, scratched a match on the sole of her slipper, lit the cigarette, and stared at the burning end. Finally she shrugged, her face cleared, and she looked up at us.

"I'm going to talk," she said. "Never got any of the money, and I'd be a chump to make a goat of myself for Herb. He was all right, but if he's run out and left me flat, there's no use of me making a lot of trouble for myself over it. Here goes: I'm not Mrs. Whitacre, except on the register. My name is Mae Landis. Maybe there is a real Mrs. Whitacre, and maybe not. I don't know. Herb and I have been living together here for over a year.

"About a month ago he began to get jumpy, nervous, even worse than usual. He said he had business worries. Then a couple of days ago I discovered that his pistol was gone from the drawer where it had been kept ever since we came here, and that he was carrying it. I asked him: 'What's the idea?' He said he thought he was being followed, and asked me if I'd seen anybody hanging around the neighborhood as if watching our place. I told him no; I thought he was nutty.

"Night before last he told me that he was in trouble, and might have to go away, and that he couldn't take me with him, but would give me enough money to take care of me for a while. He seemed excited, packed his bags so they'd be ready if he needed them in a hurry, and burned up all his photos and a lot of letters and papers. His bags are still in the bedroom, if you want to go through them. When he didn't come home last night I had a hunch that he had beat it without his bags and without saying a word to me, much less giving me any money—leaving me with only twenty dollars to my name and not even much that I could hock, and with the rent due in four days."

"When did you see him last?"

"About eight o'clock last night. He told me he was going down to Mr. Ogburn's apartment to talk some business over with him, but he didn't go there. I know that. I ran out of cigarettes—I like Elixir Russians, and I can't get them uptown here—so I called up Mr. Ogburn's to ask Herb to bring some home with him when he came, and Mr. Ogburn said he hadn't been there."

"How long have you known Whitacre?" I asked.

"Couple of years, I guess. I think I met him first at one of the beach resorts."

"Has he got any people?"

"Not that I know of. I don't know a whole lot about him. Oh, yes! I do know that he served three years in prison in Oregon for forgery. He told me that one night when he was lushed up. He served them under the name of Barber, or Barbee, or something like that. He said he was walking the straight and narrow now."

Dean produced a small automatic pistol, fairly new-looking in spite of the mud that clung to it, and handed it to the woman.

"Ever see that?"

She nodded her blond head. "Yep! That's Herb's or its twin."

Dean pocketed the gun again, and we stood up.

"Where do I stand now?" she asked. "You're not going to lock me up as a witness or anything, are you?"

"Not just now," Dean assured her. "Stick around where we can find you if we want you, and you won't be bothered. Got any idea which direction Whitacre'd be likely to go in?"

"No."

"We'd like to give the place the once-over. Mind?"

"Go ahead," she invited. "Take it apart if you want to. I'm coming all the way with you people."

We very nearly did take the place apart, but we found not a thing of value. Whitacre, when he had burned the things that might have given him away, had made a clean job of it.

"Did he ever have any pictures taken by a professional photographer?" I asked just before we left.

"Not that I know of."

"Will you let us know if you hear anything or remember anything else that might help?"

"Sure," she said heartily; "sure."

Dean and I rode down in the elevator in silence, and walked out into Gough Street.

"What do you think of all that?" I asked when we were outside.

"She's a lil, huh?" He grinned. "I wonder how much she knows. She identified the gun an' gave us that dope about the forgery sentence up north, but we'd of found out them things anyway. If she was wise she'd tell us everything she knew we'd find out, an' that would make her other stuff go over stronger. Think she's dumb or wise?"

"We won't guess," I said. "We'll slap a shadow on her and cover her mail. I have the number of a taxi she used a couple days ago. We'll look that up too."

At a corner drug store I telephoned the Old Man, asking him to detail a couple of the boys to keep Mae Landis and her apartment under surveillance night and day; also to have the Post Office Department let us know if she got any mail that might have been addressed by Whitacre. I told the Old Man I would see Ogburn and get some specimens of the fugitive's writing for comparison with the woman's mail.

Then Dean and I set about tracing the taxi in which Bob Teal had seen the woman ride away. Half an hour in the taxi company's office gave us the information that she had been driven to a number on Greenwich Street. We went to the Greenwich Street address.

It was a ramshackle building, divided into apartments or flats of a dismal and dingy sort. We found the landlady in the basement: a gaunt woman in soiled gray, with a hard, thin-lipped mouth and pale, suspicious eyes. She was rocking vigorously in a creaking chair and sewing on a pair of overalls, while three dirty kids tussled with a mongrel puppy up and down the room.

Dean showed his badge, and told her that we wanted to speak to her in privacy. She got up to chase the kids and their dog out, and then stood with hands on hips facing us.

"Well, what do you want?" she demanded sourly.

"Want to get a line on your tenants," Dean said. "Tell us about them."

"Tell you about them?" She had a voice that would have been harsh enough even if she hadn't been in such a peevish mood. "What do you think I got to say about 'em? What do you think I am? I'm a woman that minds her own business! Nobody can't say that I don't run a respectable—"

This was getting us nowhere.

"Who lives in number one?" I asked.

"The Auds—two old folks and their grandchildren. If you know anything against them, it's more'n them that has lived with 'em for ten years does!"

"Who lives in number two?"

"Mrs. Codman and her boys, Frank and Fred. They been here three years, and—"

I carried her from apartment to apartment, until finally we reached a second-floor one that didn't bring quite so harsh an indictment of my stupidity for suspecting its occupants of whatever it was that I suspected them of.

"The Quirks live there." She merely glowered now, whereas she had had a snippy manner before. "And they're decent people, if you ask me!"

"How long have they been here?"

"Six months or more."

"What does he do for a living?"

"I don't know." Sullenly: "Travels, maybe."

"How many in the family?"

"Just him and her, and they're nice quiet people, too."

"What does he look like?"

"Like an ordinary man. I ain't a detective, I don't go 'round snoopin' into folks' faces to see what they look like, and prying into their business. I ain't—"

"How old a man is he?"

"Maybe between thirty-five and forty, if he ain't younger or older."

"Large or small?"

"He ain't as short as you and he ain't as tall as this feller with you," glaring scornfully from my short stoutness to Dean's big hulk, "and he ain't as fat as neither of you."

"Mustache?"

"No."

"Light hair?"

"No." Triumphantly: "Dark."

"Dark eyes, too?"

"I guess so."

Dean, standing off to one side, looked over the woman's shoulder at me. His lips framed the name "Whitacre."

"Now how about Mrs. Quirk—what does she look like?" I went on.

"She's got light hair, is short and chunky, and maybe under thirty."

Dean and I nodded our satisfaction at each other; that sounded like Mae Landis, right enough.

"Are they home much?" I continued.

"I don't know," the gaunt woman snarled sullenly, and I knew she did know, so I waited, looking at her, and presently she added grudgingly: "I think they're away a lot, but I ain't sure."

"I know," I ventured, "they are home very seldom, and then only in the daytime—and you know it."

She didn't deny it, so I asked: "Are they in now?"

"I don't think so, but they might be."

"Let's take a look at the joint," I suggested to Dean.

He nodded and told the woman: "Take us up to their apartment an' unlock the door for us."

"I won't!" she said with sharp emphasis. "You got no right goin' into folks' homes unless you got a search warrant. You got one?"

"We got nothin'." Dean grinned at her. "But we can get plenty if you want to put us to the trouble. You run this house; you can go into any of the flats any time you want, an' you can take us in. Take us up, an' we'll lay off you; but if you're going to put us to a lot of trouble, then you'll take your chances of bein' tied up with the Quirks, an' maybe sharin' a cell with 'em. Think that over."

She thought it over, and then, grumbling and growling with each step, took us up to the Quirks' apartment. She made sure they weren't at home, then admitted us.

The apartment consisted of three rooms, a bath, and a kitchen, furnished in the shabby fashion that the ramshackle exterior of the building had prepared us for. In these rooms we found a few articles of masculine and feminine clothing, toilet accessories, and so on. But the place had none of the marks of a permanent abode: there were no pictures, no cushions, none of the dozens of odds and ends of personal belongings that are usually found in homes. The kitchen had the appearance of long disuse; the interiors of the coffee, tea, spice, and flour containers were clean.

Two things we found that meant something: a handful of Elixir Russian cigarettes on a table; and a new box of .32 cartridges—ten of which were missing—in a dresser drawer.

All through our searching the landlady hovered over us, her pale eyes sharp and curious; but now we chased her out, telling her that, law or no law, we were taking charge of the apartment.

"This was or is a hide-out for Whitacre and his woman all right," Dean said when we were alone. "The only question is whether he intended to lay low here or whether it was just a place where he made preparations for his getaway. I reckon the best thing is to have the captain put a man in here night and day until we turn up Brother Whitacre."

"That's safest," I agreed, and he went to the telephone in the front room to arrange it.

After Dean was through phoning, I called up the Old Man to see if anything new had developed.

"Nothing new," he told me. "How are you coming along?"

"Nicely. Maybe I'll have news for you this evening."

"Did you get those specimens of Whitacre's writing from Ogburn? Or shall I have someone else take care of it?"

"I'll get them this evening," I promised.

I wasted ten minutes trying to reach Ogburn at his office before I looked at my watch and saw that it was after six o'clock. I found his residence listed in the telephone directory, and called him there.

"Have you anything in Whitacre's writing at home?" I asked. "I want to get a couple of samples—would like to get them this evening, though if necessary I can wait until to-morrow."

"I think I have some of his letters here. If you come over now I'll give them to you."

"Be with you in fifteen minutes," I told him.

"I'm going down to Ogburn's," I told Dean, "to get some of Whitacre's scribbling while you're waiting for your man to come from headquarters to take charge of this place. I'll meet you at the States as soon as you can get away. We'll eat there, and make our plans for the night."

"Uh-huh," he grunted, making himself comfortable in one chair, with his feet on another, as I let myself out.

Ogburn was dressing when I reached his apartment, and had his collar and tie in his hand when he came to the door to let me in.

"I found quite a few of Herb's letters," he said as we walked back to his bedroom.

I looked through the fifteen or more letters that lay on a table, selecting the ones I wanted, while Ogburn went on with his dressing.

"How are you progressing?" he asked presently.

"So-so. Heard anything that might help?"

"No, but just a few minutes ago I happened to remember that Herb used to go over to the Mills Building quite frequently. I've seen him going in and out often, but never thought anything of it. I don't know whether it is of any importance or—"

I jumped out of my chair.

"That does it!" I cried. "Can I use your phone?"

"Certainly. It's in the hallway, near the door." He looked at me in surprise. "It's a slot phone; have you a nickel in change?"

"Yes." I was going through the bedroom door.

"The switch is near the door," he called after me, "if you want a light. Do you think—"

But I didn't stop to listen to his questions. I was making for the telephone, searching my pockets for a nickel. And, fumbling hurriedly with the nickel, I muffed it—not entirely by accident, for I had a hunch that I wanted to work out. The nickel rolled away down the carpeted hallway. I switched on the light, recovered the nickel, and called the "Quirks'" number. I'm glad I played that hunch.

Dean was still there.

"That joint's dead." I sang. "Take the landlady down to headquarters, and grab the Landis woman, too. I'll meet you there—at headquarters."

"You mean it?" he rumbled.

"Almost," I said, and hung up the receiver.

I switched off the hall light and, whistling a little tune to myself, walked back to the room where I had left Ogburn. The door was not quite closed. I walked straight up to it, kicked it open with one foot, and jumped back, hugging the wall.

Two shots—so close together that they were almost one—crashed.

Flat against the wall, I pounded my feet against the floor and wainscot, and let out a medley of shrieks and groans that would have done credit to a carnival wild-man.

A moment later Ogburn appeared in the doorway, a revolver in his hand, his face wolfish. He was determined to kill me. It was my life or his, so—

I slammed my gun down on the sleek, brown top of his head.

When he opened his eyes, two policemen were lifting him into the back of a patrol wagon.

I FOUND DEAN in the detectives' assembly-room in the Hall of Justice.

"The landlady identified Mae Landis as Mrs. Quirk," he said. "Now what?"

"Where is she now?"

"One of the policewomen is holding both of them in the captain's office."

"Ogburn is over in the Pawnshop Detail office," I told him. "Let's take the landlady in for a look at him."

Ogburn sat leaning forward, holding his head in his hands and staring sullenly at the feet of the uniformed man who guarded him, when we took the gaunt landlady in to see him.

"Ever see him before?" I asked her.

"Yes"—reluctantly—"that's Mr. Quirk."

Ogburn didn't look up, and he paid not the least attention to any of us.

After we had told the landlady that she could go home, Dean led me back to a far corner of the assembly-room, where we could talk without disturbance.

"Now spill it!" he burst out. "How come all the startling developments, as the newspaper boys call 'em?"

"Well, first-off, I knew that the question 'Who killed Bob Teal?' could have only one answer. Bob wasn't a boob! He might possibly have let a man he was trailing lure him behind a row of billboards on a dark night, but he would have gone prepared for trouble. He wouldn't have died with empty hands, from a gun that was close enough to scorch his coat. The murderer had to be somebody Bob trusted, so it couldn't be Whitacre. Now Bob was a conscientious sort of lad, and he wouldn't have stopped shadowing Whitacre to go over and talk with some friend. There was only one man who could have persuaded him to drop Whitacre for a while, and that one man was the one he was working for—Ogburn.

"If I hadn't known Bob, I might have thought he had hidden behind the billboards to watch Whitacre; but Bob wasn't an amateur. He knew better than to pull any of that spectacular gumshoe stuff. So there was nothing to it but Ogburn!

"With all that to go on, the rest was duck soup. All the stuff Mae Landis gave us—identifying the gun as Whitacre's, and giving Ogburn an alibi by saying she had talked to him on the phone at ten o'clock—only convinced me that she and Ogburn were working together. When the landlady described 'Quirk' for us, I was fairly certain of it. Her description would fit either Whitacre or Ogburn, but there was no sense to Whitacre's having the apartment on Greenwich Street, while if Ogburn and the Landis woman were thick, they'd need a meeting-place of some sort. The rest of the box of cartridges there helped some too.

"Then to-night I put on a little act in Ogburn's apartment, chasing a nickel along the floor and finding traces of dried mud that had escaped the cleaning-up he no doubt gave the carpet and clothes after he came home from walking through the lot in the rain. We'll let the experts decide whether it could be mud from the lot on which Bob was killed, and the jury can decide whether it is.

"There are a few more odds and ends—like the gun. The Landis woman said Whitacre had had it for more than a year, but in spite of being muddy it looks fairly new to me. We'll send the serial number to the factory, and find when it was turned out.

"For motive, just now all I'm sure of is the woman, which should be enough. But I think that when Ogburn and Whitacre's books are audited, and their finances sifted, we'll find something there. What I'm banking on strong is that Whitacre will come in, now that he is cleared of the murder charge."

And that is exactly what happened.

Next day Herbert Whitacre walked into Police Headquarters at Sacramento and surrendered.

Neither Ogburn nor Mae Landis ever told what they knew, but with Whitacre's testimony, supported by what we were able to pick up here and there, we went into court when the time came and convinced the jury that the facts were these:

Ogburn and Whitacre had opened their farm-development business as a plain swindle. They had options on a lot of land, and they planned to sell as many shares in their enterprise as possible before the time came to exercise their options. Then they intended packing up their bags and disappearing. Whitacre hadn't much nerve, and he had a clear remembrance of the three years he had served in prison for forgery; so to bolster his courage, Ogburn had told his partner that he had a friend in the Post Office Department in Washington, D.C., who would tip him off the instant official suspicion was aroused.

The two partners made a neat little pile out of their venture, Ogburn taking charge of the money until the time came for the split-up. Meanwhile, Ogburn and Mae Landis—Whitacre's supposed wife—had become intimate, and had rented the apartment on Greenwich Street, meeting there afternoons when Whitacre was busy at the office, and when Ogburn was supposed to be out hunting fresh victims. In this apartment Ogburn and the woman had hatched their little scheme, whereby they were to get rid of Whitacre, keep all the loot, and clear Ogburn of criminal complicity in the affairs of Ogburn & Whitacre.

Ogburn had come into the Continental office and told his little tale of his partner's dishonesty, engaging Bob Teal to shadow him. Then he had told Whitacre that he had received a tip from his friend in Washington that an investigation was about to be made. The two partners planned to leave town on their separate ways the following week. The next night Mae Landis told Whitacre she had seen a man loitering in the neighborhood, apparently watching the building in which they lived. Whitacre—thinking Bob a Post Office inspector—had gone completely to pieces, and it had taken the combined efforts of the woman and his partner—apparently working separately—to keep him from bolting immediately. They persuaded him to stick it out another few days.

On the night of the murder, Ogburn, pretending skepticism of Whitacre's story about being followed, had met Whitacre for the purpose of learning if he really was being shadowed. They had walked the streets in the rain for an hour. Then Ogburn, convinced, had announced his intention of going back and talking to the supposed Post Office inspector, to see if he could be bribed. Whitacre had refused to accompany his partner, but had agreed to wait for him in a dark doorway.

Ogburn had taken Bob Teal over behind the billboards on some pretext, and had murdered him. Then he had hurried back to his partner, crying: "My God! He grabbed me and I shot him. We'll have to leave!"

Whitacre, in blind panic, had left San Francisco without stopping for his bags or even notifying Mae Landis. Ogburn was supposed to leave by another route. They were to meet in Oklahoma City ten days later, where Ogburn—after getting the loot out of the Los Angeles banks where he had deposited it under various names—was to give Whitacre his share, and then they were to part for good.

In Sacramento next day Whitacre had read the newspapers, and had understood what had been done to him. He had done all the bookkeeping; all the false entries in Ogburn & Whitacre's books were in his writing. Mae Landis had revealed his former criminal record, and had fastened the ownership of the gun—really Ogburn's—upon him. He was framed completely! He hadn't a chance of clearing himself.

He had known that his story would sound like a far-fetched and flimsy lie; he had a criminal record. For him to have surrendered and told the truth would have been merely to get himself laughed at.

As it turned out, Ogburn went to the gallows, Mae Landis is now serving a fifteen-year sentence, and Whitacre, in return for his testimony and restitution of the loot, was not prosecuted for his share in the land swindle.

A MAN
CALLED SPADE

Samuel Spade put his telephone aside and looked at his watch. It was not quite four o'clock. He called, "Yoo-hoo!"

Effie Perine came in from the outer office. She was eating a piece of chocolate cake.

"Tell Sid Wise I won't be able to keep that date this afternoon," he said.

She put the last of the cake into her mouth and licked the tips of her forefinger and thumb. "That's the third time this week."

When he smiled, the V's of his chin, mouth, and brows grew longer. "I know, but I've got to go out and save a life." He nodded at the telephone. "Somebody's scaring Max Bliss."

She laughed. "Probably somebody named John D. Conscience."

He looked up at her from the cigarette he had begun to make. "Know anything I ought to know about him?"

"Nothing you don't know. I was just thinking about the time he let his brother go to San Quentin."

Spade shrugged. "That's not the worst thing he's done." He lit his cigarette, stood up, and reached for his hat. "But he's all right now. All Samuel Spade clients are honest, God-fearing folk. If I'm not back at closing time just run along."

He went to a tall apartment building on Nob Hill, pressed a button set in the frame of a door marked 10K. The door was opened immediately by a burly dark man in wrinkled dark clothes. He was nearly bald and carried a gray hat in one hand.

The burly man said, "Hello, Sam." He smiled, but his small eyes lost none of their shrewdness. "What are you doing here?"

Spade said, "Hello, Tom." His face was wooden, his voice expressionless. "Bliss in?"

"Is he!" Tom pulled down the corners of his thick-lipped mouth. "You don't have to worry about that."

Spade's brows came together. "Well?"

A man appeared in the vestibule behind Tom. He was smaller than either Spade or Tom, but compactly built. He had a ruddy, square face and a close-trimmed, grizzled mustache. His clothes were neat. He wore a black bowler perched on the back of his head.

Spade addressed this man over Tom's shoulder. "Hello, Dundy."

Dundy nodded briefly and came to the door. His blue eyes were hard and prying.

"What is it?" he asked Tom.

"B-l-i-s-s, M-a-x," Spade spelled patiently. "I want to see him. He wants to see me. Catch on?"

Tom laughed. Dundy did not. Tom said, "Only one of you gets your wish." Then he glanced sidewise at Dundy and abruptly stopped laughing. He seemed uncomfortable.

Spade scowled. "All right," he demanded irritably; "is he dead or has he killed somebody?"

Dundy thrust his square face up at Spade and seemed to push his words out with his lower lip. "What makes you think either?"

Spade said, "Oh, sure! I come calling on Mr. Bliss and I'm stopped at the door by a couple of men from the police Homicide Detail, and I'm supposed to think I'm just interrupting a game of rummy."

"Aw, stop it, Sam," Tom grumbled, looking at neither Spade nor Dundy. "He's dead."

"Killed?"

Tom wagged his head slowly up and down. He looked at Spade now. "What've you got on it?"

Spade replied in a deliberate monotone, "He called me up this afternoon—say at five minutes to four—I looked at my watch after he hung up and there was still a minute to go—and said somebody was after his scalp. He wanted me to come over. It seemed real enough to him—it was up in his neck all right." He made a small gesture with one hand. "Well, here I am."

"Didn't say who or how?" Dundy asked.

Spade shook his head. "No. Just somebody had offered to kill him and he believed them, and would I come over right away."

"Didn't he—?" Dundy began quickly.

"He didn't say anything else," Spade said. "Don't you people tell me anything?"

Dundy said curtly, "Come in and take a look at him."

Tom said, "It's a sight."

They went across the vestibule and through a door into a green and rose living-room.

A man near the door stopped sprinkling white powder on the end of a glass-covered small table to say, "Hello, Sam."

Spade nodded, said, "How are you, Phels?" and then nodded at the two men who stood talking by a window.

The dead man lay with his mouth open. Some of his clothes had been taken off. His throat was puffy and dark. The end of his tongue showing in a corner of his mouth was bluish, swollen. On his bare chest, over the heart, a five-pointed star had been outlined in black ink and in the center of it a T.

Spade looked down at the dead man and stood for a moment silently studying him. Then he asked, "He was found like that?"

"About," Tom said. "We moved him around a little." He jerked a thumb at the shirt, undershirt, vest, and coat lying on a table. "They were spread over the floor."

Spade rubbed his chin. His yellow-gray eyes were dreamy. "When?"

Tom said, "We got it at four-twenty. His daughter gave it to us." He moved his head to indicate a closed door. "You'll see her."

"Know anything?"

"Heaven knows," Tom said wearily. "She's been kind of hard to get along with so far." He turned to Dundy. "Want to try her again now?"

Dundy nodded, then spoke to one of the men at the window. "Start sifting his papers, Mack. He's supposed to've been threatened."

Mack said, "Right." He pulled his hat down over his eyes and walked toward a green secrétaire in the far end of the room.

A man came in from the corridor, a heavy man of fifty with a deeply lined, grayish face under a broad-brimmed black hat. He said, "Hello, Sam," and then told Dundy, "He had company around half past two, stayed just about an hour. A big blond man in brown, maybe forty or forty-five. Didn't send his name up. I got it from the Filipino in the elevator that rode him both ways."

"Sure it was only an hour?" Dundy asked.

The gray-faced man shook his head. "But he's sure it wasn't more than half past three when he left. He says the afternoon papers came in then, and this man had ridden down with him before they came." He pushed his hat back to scratch his head, then pointed a thick finger at the design inked on the dead man's breast and asked somewhat plaintively, "What the deuce do you suppose that thing is?"

Nobody replied. Dundy asked, "Can the elevator boy identify him?"

"He says he could, but that ain't always the same thing. Says he never saw him before." He stopped looking at the dead man. "The girl's getting me a list of his phone calls. How you been, Sam?"

Spade said he had been all right. Then he said slowly, "His brother's big and blond and maybe forty or forty-five."

Dundy's blue eyes were hard and bright. "So what?" he asked.

"You remember the Graystone Loan swindle. They were both in on it, but Max eased the load over on Theodore and it turned out to be one to fourteen years in San Quentin."

Dundy was slowly wagging his head up and down. "I remember now. Where is he?"

Spade shrugged and began to make a cigarette.

Dundy nudged Tom with an elbow. "Find out."

Tom said, "Sure, but if he was out of here at half past three and this fellow was still alive at five to four—"

"And he broke his leg so he couldn't duck back in," the gray-faced man said jovially.

"Find out," Dundy repeated.

Tom said, "Sure, sure," and went to the telephone.

Dundy addressed the gray-faced man: "Check up on the newspapers; see what time they were actually delivered this afternoon."

The gray-faced man nodded and left the room.

The man who had been searching the secrétaire said, "Uh-huh," and turned around holding an envelope in one hand, a sheet of paper in the other.

Dundy held out his hand. "Something?"

The man said, "Uh-huh," again and gave Dundy the sheet of paper.

Spade was looking over Dundy's shoulder.

It was a small sheet of common white paper bearing a penciled message in neat, undistinguished handwriting:

> *When this reaches you I will be too close for you to escape—this time.*
> *We will balance our accounts—for good.*

The signature was a five-pointed star enclosing a T, the design on the dead man's left breast.

Dundy held out his hand again and was given the envelope. Its stamp was French. The address was typewritten:

MAX BLISS, ESQ.
AMSTERDAM APARTMENTS,
SAN FRANCISCO, CALIF.
U.S.A.

"Postmarked Paris," he said, "the second of the month." He counted swiftly on his fingers. "That would get it here to-day, all right." He folded the message slowly, put it in the envelope, put the envelope in his coat pocket. "Keep digging," he told the man who found the message.

The man nodded and returned to the secrétaire.

Dundy looked at Spade. "What do you think of it?"

Spade's brown cigarette wagged up and down with the words. "I don't like it. I don't like any of it."

Tom put down the telephone. "He got out the fifteenth of last month," he said. "I got them trying to locate him."

Spade went to the telephone, called a number, and asked for Mr. Darrell. Then: "Hello, Harry, this is Sam Spade. . . . Fine. How's Lil? . . . Yes. . . . Listen, Harry, what does a five-pointed star with a capital T in the middle mean? . . . What? How do you spell it? . . . Yes, I see. . . . And if you found it on a body? . . . Neither do I. . . . Yes, and thanks. I'll tell you about it when I see you. . . . Yes, give me a ring. . . . Thanks. . . . 'Bye."

Dundy and Tom were watching him closely when he turned from the telephone. He said, "That's a fellow who knows things sometimes. He says it's a pentagram with a Greek tau—t-a-u—in the middle; a sign magicians used to use. Maybe Rosicrucians still do."

"What's a Rosicrucian?" Tom asked.

"It could be Theodore's first initial, too," Dundy said.

Spade moved his shoulders, said carelessly, "Yes, but if he wanted to autograph the job it'd have been just as easy for him to sign his name."

He then went on more thoughtfully, "There are Rosicrucians at both San Jose and Point Loma. I don't go much for this, but maybe we ought to look them up."

Dundy nodded.

Spade looked at the dead man's clothes on the table. "Anything in his pockets?"

"Only what you'd expect to find," Dundy replied. "It's on the table there."

Spade went to the table and looked down at the little pile of watch and chain, keys, wallet, address book, money, gold pencil, handkerchief, and spectacle case beside the clothing. He did not touch them, but slowly picked up, one at a time, the dead man's shirt, undershirt, vest, and coat. A blue necktie lay on the table beneath them. He scowled irritably at it. "It hasn't been worn," he complained.

Dundy, Tom, and the coroner's deputy, who had stood silent all this while by the window—he was a small man with a slim, dark, intelligent face—came together to stare down at the unwrinkled blue silk.

Tom groaned miserably. Dundy cursed under his breath. Spade lifted the necktie to look at its back. The label was a London haberdasher's.

Spade said cheerfully, "Swell. San Francisco, Point Loma, San Jose, Paris, London."

Dundy glowered at him.

The gray-faced man came in. "The papers got here at three-thirty, all right," he said. His eyes widened a little. "What's up?" As he crossed the room toward them he said, "I can't find anybody that saw Blondy sneak back in here again." He looked uncomprehendingly at the necktie until Tom growled, "It's brand-new"; then he whistled softly.

Dundy turned to Spade. "The deuce with all this," he said bitterly. "He's got a brother with reasons for not liking him. The brother just got out of stir. Somebody who looks like his brother left here at half past three. Twenty-five minutes later he phoned you he'd been threatened. Less than half an hour after that his daughter came in and found him dead—strangled." He poked a finger at the small, dark-faced man's chest. "Right?"

"Strangled," the dark-faced man said precisely, "by a man. The hands were large."

"O.K." Dundy turned to Spade again. "We find a threatening letter. Maybe that's what he was telling you about, maybe it was something his brother said to him. Don't let's guess. Let's stick to what we know. We know he—"

The man at the secrétaire turned around and said, "Got another one." His mien was somewhat smug.

The eyes with which the five men at the table looked at him were identically cold, unsympathetic.

He, nowise disturbed by their hostility, read aloud:

"*Dear Bliss:*

I am writing this to tell you for the last time that I want my money back, and I want it back by the first of the month, all of it. If I don't get

it I am going to do something about it, and you ought to be able to guess
what I mean. And don't think I am kidding.

Yours truly,

Daniel Talbot."

He grinned. "That's another T for you." He picked up an envelope. "Post-marked San Diego, the twenty-fifth of last month." He grinned again. "And that's another city for you."

Spade shook his head. "Point Loma's down that way," he said.

He went over with Dundy to look at the letter. It was written in blue ink on white stationery of good quality, as was the address on the envelope, in a cramped, angular handwriting that seemed to have nothing in common with that of the penciled letter.

Spade said ironically, "Now we're getting somewhere."

Dundy made an impatient gesture. "Let's stick to what we know," he growled.

"Sure," Spade agreed. "What is it?"

There was no reply.

Spade took tobacco and cigarette papers from his pocket. "Didn't some-body say something about talking to a daughter?" he asked.

"We'll talk to her." Dundy turned on his heel, then suddenly frowned at the dead man on the floor. He jerked a thumb at the small, dark-faced man. "Through with it?"

"I'm through."

Dundy addressed Tom curtly: "Get rid of it." He addressed the gray-faced man: "I want to see both elevator boys when I'm finished with the girl."

He went to the closed door Tom had pointed out to Spade and knocked on it.

A slightly harsh female voice within asked, "What is it?"

"Lieutenant Dundy. I want to talk to Miss Bliss."

There was a pause; then the voice said, "Come in."

Dundy opened the door and Spade followed him into a black, gray, and silver room, where a big-boned and ugly middle-aged woman in black dress and white apron sat beside a bed on which a girl lay.

The girl lay, elbow on pillow, cheek on hand, facing the big-boned, ugly woman. She was apparently about eighteen years old. She wore a gray suit. Her hair was blond and short, her face firm-featured and remarkably sym-metrical. She did not look at the two men coming into the room.

Dundy spoke to the big-boned woman, while Spade was lighting his cigarette: "We want to ask you a couple of questions, too, Mrs. Hooper. You're Bliss's housekeeper, aren't you?"

The woman said, "I am." Her slightly harsh voice, the level gaze of her deep-set gray eyes, the stillness and size of her hands lying in her lap, all contributed to the impression she gave of resting strength.

"What do you know about this?"

"I don't know anything about it. I was let off this morning to go over to Oakland to my nephew's funeral, and when I got back you and the other gentlemen were here and—and this had happened."

Dundy nodded, asked, "What do you think about it?"

"I don't know what to think," she replied simply.

"Didn't you know he expected it to happen?"

Now the girl suddenly stopped watching Mrs. Hooper. She sat up in bed, turning wide, excited eyes on Dundy, and asked, "What do you mean?"

"I mean what I said. He'd been threatened. He called up Mr. Spade"— he indicated Spade with a nod—"and told him so just a few minutes before he was killed."

"But who—?" she began.

"That's what we're asking you," Dundy said. "Who had that much against him?"

She stared at him in astonishment. "Nobody would—"

This time Spade interrupted her, speaking with a softness that made his words seem less brutal than they were. "Somebody did." When she turned her stare on him he asked, "You don't know of any threats?"

She shook her head from side to side with emphasis.

He looked at Mrs. Hooper. "You?"

"No sir," she said.

He returned his attention to the girl. "Do you know Daniel Talbot?"

"Why, yes," she said. "He was here for dinner last night."

"Who is he?"

"I don't know, except that he lives in San Diego, and he and father had some sort of business together. I'd never met him before."

"What sort of terms were they on?"

She frowned a little, said slowly, "Friendly."

Dundy spoke: "What business was your father in?"

"He was a financier."

"You mean a promoter?"

"Yes, I suppose you could call it that."

"Where is Talbot staying, or has he gone back to San Diego?"

"I don't know."

"What does he look like?"

She frowned again, thoughtfully. "He's kind of large, with a red face and white hair and a mustache."

"Old?"

"I guess he must be sixty; fifty-five at least."

Dundy looked at Spade, who put the stub of his cigarette in a tray on the dressing table and took up the questioning. "How long since you've seen your uncle?"

Her face flushed. "You mean Uncle Ted?"

He nodded.

"Not since," she began, and bit her lip. Then she said, "Of course, you know. Not since he first got out of prison."

"He came here?"

"Yes."

"To see your father?"

"Of course."

"What sort of terms were they on?"

She opened her eyes wide. "Neither of them is very demonstrative," she said, "but they are brothers, and Father was giving him money to set him up in business again."

"Then they were on good terms?"

"Yes," she replied in the tone of one answering an unnecessary question.

"Where does he live?"

"On Post Street," she said, and gave a number.

"And you haven't seen him since?"

"No. He was shy, you know, about having been in prison—" She finished the sentence with a gesture of one hand.

Spade addressed Mrs. Hooper: "You've seen him since?"

"No, sir."

He pursed his lips, asked slowly, "Either of you know he was here this afternoon?"

They said "No" together.

"Where did—?"

Someone knocked on the door.

Dundy said, "Come in."

Tom opened the door far enough to stick his head in. "His brother's here," he said.

The girl, leaning forward, called, "Oh, Uncle Ted!"

A big blond man in brown appeared behind Tom. He was sunburned to an extent that made his teeth seem whiter, his clear eyes bluer, than they were.

He asked, "What's the matter, Miriam?"

"Father's dead," she said, and began to cry.

Dundy nodded at Tom, who stepped out of Theodore Bliss's way and let him come into the room.

A woman came in behind him, slowly, hesitantly. She was a tall woman in her late twenties, blond, not quite plump. Her features were generous, her face pleasant and intelligent. She wore a small brown hat and a mink coat.

Bliss put an arm around his niece, kissed her forehead, sat on the bed beside her. "There, there," he said awkwardly.

She saw the blond woman, stared through her tears at her for a moment, then said, "Oh, how do you do, Miss Barrow."

The blond woman said, "I'm awfully sorry to—"

Bliss cleared his throat, and said, "She's Mrs. Bliss now. We were married this afternoon."

Dundy looked angrily at Spade. Spade, making a cigarette, seemed about to laugh.

Miriam Bliss, after a moment's surprised silence, said, "Oh, I do wish you all the happiness in the world." She turned to her uncle while his wife was murmuring, "Thank you," and said, "And you too, Uncle Ted."

He patted her shoulder and squeezed her to him. He was looking questioningly at Spade and Dundy.

"Your brother died this afternoon," Dundy said. "He was murdered."

Mrs. Bliss caught her breath. Bliss's arm tightened around his niece with a little jerk, but there was not yet any change in his face. "Murdered?" he repeated uncomprehendingly.

"Yes." Dundy put his hands in his coat pockets. "You were here this afternoon."

Theodore Bliss paled a little under his sunburn, but said, "I was," steadily enough.

"How long?"

"About an hour. I got here about half-past two and—" He turned to his wife. "It was almost half-past three when I phoned you, wasn't it?"

She said, "Yes."

"Well, I left him right after that."

"Did you have a date with him?" Dundy asked.

"No. I phoned his office"—he nodded at his wife—"and was told he'd left for home, so I came on up. I wanted to see him before Elise and I left, of course, and I wanted him to come to the wedding, but he couldn't. He said he was expecting somebody. We sat here and talked longer than I had intended, so I had to phone Elise to meet me at the Municipal Building."

After a thoughtful pause, Dundy asked, "What time?"

"That we met there?" Bliss looked inquiringly at his wife, who said, "It was quarter to four." She laughed a little. "I got there first and I kept looking at my watch."

Bliss said very deliberately, "It was a few minutes after four that we were married. We had to wait for Judge Whitefield—about ten minutes, and it was a few more before we got started—to get through with the case he was hearing. You can check it up—Superior Court, Part Two, I think."

Spade whirled around and pointed at Tom. "Maybe you'd better check it up."

Tom said, "Oke," and went away from the door.

"If that's so, you're all right, Mr. Bliss," Dundy said, "but I have to ask you these things. Now, did your brother say who he was expecting?"

"No."

"Did he say anything about having been threatened?"

"No. He never talked much about his affairs to anybody, not even to me. Had he been threatened?"

Dundy's lips tightened a little. "Were you and he on intimate terms?"

"Friendly, if that's what you mean."

"Are you sure?" Dundy asked. "Are you sure neither of you held any grudge against the other?"

Theodore Bliss took his arm free from around his niece. Increasing pallor made his sunburned face yellowish. He said, "Everybody here knows about my having been in San Quentin. You can speak out, if that's what you're getting at."

"It is," Dundy said, and then, after a pause, "Well?"

Bliss stood up, "Well, what?" he asked impatiently. "Did I hold a grudge against him for that? No. Why should I? We were both in it. He could get out; I couldn't. I was sure of being convicted whether he was or not. Having him sent over with me wasn't going to make it any better for me. We talked it over and decided I'd go it alone, leaving him outside to pull things together. And he did. If you look up his bank account you'll see he gave me a check for twenty-five thousand dollars two days after I was discharged from San Quentin, and the registrar of the National Steel Corporation can tell you a thousand shares of stock have been transferred from his name to mine since then."

He smiled apologetically and sat down on the bed again. "I'm sorry. I know you have to ask things."

Dundy ignored the apology. "Do you know Daniel Talbot?" he asked.

Bliss said, "No."

His wife said, "I do; that is, I've seen him. He was in the office yesterday."

Dundy looked her up and down carefully before asking, "What office?"

"I am—I was Mr. Bliss's secretary, and—"

"Max Bliss's?"

"Yes, and a Daniel Talbot came in to see him yesterday afternoon, if it's the same one."

"What happened?"

She looked at her husband, who said, "If you know anything, for heaven's sake tell them."

She said, "But nothing really happened. I thought they were angry with each other at first, but when they left together they were laughing and talking, and before they went Mr. Bliss rang for me and told me to have Trapper—he's the bookkeeper—make out a check to Mr. Talbot's order."

"Did he?"

"Oh, yes. I took it in to him. It was for seventy-five hundred and some dollars."

"What was it for?"

She shook her head. "I don't know."

"If you were Bliss's secretary," Dundy insisted, "you must have some idea of what his business with Talbot was."

"But I haven't," she said. "I'd never even heard of him before."

Dundy looked at Spade. Spade's face was wooden. Dundy glowered at him, then put a question to the man on the bed: "What kind of necktie was your brother wearing when you saw him last?"

Bliss blinked, then stared distantly past Dundy, and finally shut his eyes. When he opened them he said, "It was green with—I'd know it if I saw it. Why?"

Mrs. Bliss said, "Narrow diagonal stripes of different shades of green. That's the one he had on at the office this morning."

"Where does he keep his neckties?" Dundy asked the housekeeper.

She rose, saying, "In a closet in his bedroom. I'll show you."

Dundy and the newly married Blisses followed her out.

Spade put his hat on the dressing table and asked Miriam Bliss, "What time did you go out?" He sat on the foot of her bed.

"To-day? About one o'clock. I had a luncheon engagement for one and I was a little late, and then I went shopping, and then—" She broke off with a shudder.

"And then you came home at what time?" His voice was friendly, matter-of-fact.

"Some time after four, I guess."

"And what happened?"

"I f-found Father lying there and I phoned—I don't know whether I phoned downstairs or the police, and then I don't know what I did. I fainted or had hysterics or something, and the first thing I remember is coming to and finding those men here and Mrs. Hooper." She looked him full in the face now.

"You didn't phone a doctor?"

She lowered her eyes again. "No, I don't think so."

"Of course you wouldn't, if you knew he was dead," he said casually.

She was silent.

"You knew he was dead?" he asked.

She raised her eyes and looked blankly at him. "But he was dead," she said.

He smiled. "Of course; but what I'm getting at is, did you make sure before you phoned?"

She put her hand to her throat. "I don't remember what I did," she said earnestly. "I think I just knew he was dead."

He nodded understandingly. "And if you phoned the police it was because you knew he had been murdered."

She worked her hands together and looked at them and said, "I suppose so. It was awful. I don't know what I thought or did."

Spade leaned forward and made his voice low and persuasive. "I'm not a police detective, Miss Bliss. I was engaged by your father—a few minutes too late to save him. I am, in a way, working for you now, so if there is anything I can do—maybe something the police wouldn't—" He broke off as Dundy, followed by the Blisses and the housekeeper, returned to the room. "What luck?"

Dundy said, "The green tie's not there." His suspicious gaze darted from Spade to the girl. "Mrs. Hooper says the blue tie we found is one of half a dozen he just got from England."

Bliss asked, "What's the importance of the tie?"

Dundy scowled at him. "He was partly undressed when we found him. The tie with his clothes had never been worn."

"Couldn't he have been changing clothes when whoever killed him came, and was killed before he had finished dressing?"

Dundy's scowl deepened. "Yes, but what did he do with the green tie? Eat it?"

Spade said, "He wasn't changing clothes. If you'll look at the shirt collar you'll see he must've had it on when he was choked."

Tom came to the door. "Checks all right," he told Dundy. "The judge and a bailiff named Kittredge say they were there from about a quarter to four till five or ten minutes after. I told Kittredge to come over and take a look at them to make sure they're the same ones."

Dundy said, "Right," without turning his head and took the penciled threat signed with the T in a star from his pocket. He folded it so only the signature was visible. Then he asked, "Anybody know what this is?"

Miriam Bliss left the bed to join the others in looking at it. From it they looked at one another blankly.

"Anybody know anything about it?" Dundy asked.

Mrs. Hooper said, "It's like what was on poor Mr. Bliss's chest, but—" The others said, "No."

"Anybody ever seen anything like it before?"

They said they had not.

Dundy said, "All right. Wait here. Maybe I'll have something else to ask you after a while."

Spade said, "Just a minute. Mr. Bliss, how long have you known Mrs. Bliss?"

Bliss looked curiously at Spade. "Since I got out of prison," he replied somewhat cautiously. "Why?"

"Just since last month," Spade said as if to himself. "Meet her through your brother?"

"Of course—in his office. Why?"

"And at the Municipal Building this afternoon, were you together all the time?"

"Yes, certainly." Bliss spoke sharply. "What are you getting at?"

Spade smiled at him, a friendly smile. "I have to ask things," he said.

Bliss smiled too. "It's all right." His smile broadened. "As a matter of fact, I'm a liar. We weren't actually together all the time. I went out into the corridor to smoke a cigarette, but I assure you every time I looked through the glass of the door I could see her still sitting in the courtroom where I had left her."

Spade's smile was as light as Bliss's. Nevertheless, he asked, "And when you weren't looking through the glass you were in sight of the door? She couldn't've left the courtroom without your seeing her?"

Bliss's smile went away. "Of course she couldn't," he said, "and I wasn't out there more than five minutes."

Spade said, "Thanks," and followed Dundy into the living-room, shutting the door behind him.

Dundy looked sidewise at Spade. "Anything to it?"

Spade shrugged.

Max Bliss's body had been removed. Besides the man at the secrétaire and the gray-faced man, two Filipino boys in plum-colored uniforms were in the room. They sat close together on the sofa.

Dundy said, "Mack, I want to find a green necktie. I want this house taken apart, this block taken apart, and the whole neighborhood taken apart till you find it. Get what men you need."

The man at the secrétaire rose, said, "Right," pulled his hat down over his eyes, and went out.

Dundy scowled at the Filipinos. "Which of you saw the man in brown?"

The smaller stood up. "Me, sir."

Dundy opened the bedroom door and said, "Bliss."

Bliss came to the door.

The Filipino's face lighted up. "Yes, sir, him."

Dundy shut the door in Bliss's face. "Sit down."

The boy sat down hastily.

Dundy stared gloomily at the boys until they began to fidget. Then, "Who else did you bring up to this apartment this afternoon?"

They shook their heads in unison from side to side. "Nobody else, sir," the smaller one said. A desperately ingratiating smile stretched his mouth wide across his face.

Dundy took a threatening step toward them. "Nuts!" he snarled. "You brought up Miss Bliss."

The larger boy's head bobbed up and down. "Yes, sir. Yes, sir. I bring them up. I think you mean other people." He too tried a smile.

Dundy was glaring at him. "Never mind what you think I mean. Tell me what I ask. Now, what do you mean by 'them'?"

The boy's smile died under the glare. He looked at the floor between his feet and said, "Miss Bliss and the gentleman."

"What gentleman? The gentleman in there?" He jerked his head toward the door he had shut on Bliss.

"No, sir. Another gentleman, not an American gentleman." He had raised his head again and now brightness came back into his face. "I think he is Armenian."

"Why?"

"Because he not like us Americans, not talk like us."

Spade laughed, asked, "Ever seen an Armenian?"

"No, sir. That is why I think—" He shut his mouth with a click as Dundy made a growling noise in his throat.

"What'd he look like?" Dundy asked.

The boy lifted his shoulders, spread his hands. "He tall, like this gentleman." He indicated Spade. "Got dark hair, dark mustache. Very"—he frowned earnestly—"very nice clothes. Very nice-looking man. Cane, gloves, spats even, and—"

"Young?" Dundy asked.

The head went up and down again. "Young, yes, sir."

"When did he leave?"

"Five minutes," the boy replied.

Dundy made a chewing motion with his jaws, then asked, "What time did they come in?"

The boy spread his hands, lifted his shoulders again. "Four o'clock—maybe ten minutes after."

"Did you bring anybody else up before we got here?"

The Filipinos shook their heads in unison once more.

Dundy spoke out the side of his mouth to Spade: "Get her."

Spade opened the bedroom door, bowed slightly, said, "Will you come out a moment, Miss Bliss?"

"What is it?" she asked wearily.

"Just for a moment," he said, holding the door open. Then he suddenly added, "And you'd better come along, too, Mr. Bliss."

Miriam Bliss came slowly into the living-room followed by her uncle, and Spade shut the door behind them. Miss Bliss's lower lip twitched a little when she saw the elevator boys. She looked apprehensively at Dundy.

He asked, "What's this fiddlededee about the man that came in with you?"

Her lower lip twitched again. "Wh-what?" She tried to put bewilderment on her face. Theodore Bliss hastily crossed the room, stood for a moment before her as if he intended to say something, and then, apparently changing his mind, took up a position behind her, his arms crossed over the back of a chair.

"The man who came in with you," Dundy said harshly, rapidly. "Who is he? Where is he? Why'd he leave? Why didn't you say anything about him?"

The girl put her hands over her face and began to cry, "He didn't have anything to do with it," she blubbered through her hands. "He didn't, and it would just make trouble for him."

"Nice boy," Dundy said. "So, to keep his name out of the newspapers, he runs off and leaves you alone with your murdered father."

She took her hands away from her face. "Oh, but he had to," she cried. "His wife is so jealous, and if she knew he had been with me again she'd certainly divorce him, and he hasn't a cent in the world of his own."

Dundy looked at Spade. Spade looked at the goggling Filipinos and jerked a thumb at the outer door. "Scram," he said. They went out quickly.

"And who is this gem?" Dundy asked the girl.

"But he didn't have any—"

"Who is he?"

Her shoulders drooped a little and she lowered her eyes. "His name is Boris Smekalov," she said wearily.

"Spell it."

She spelled it.

"Where does he live?"

"At the St. Mark Hotel."

"Does he do anything for a living except marry money?"

Anger came into her face as she raised it, but went away as quickly. "He doesn't do anything," she said.

Dundy wheeled to address the gray-faced man. "Get him."

The gray-faced man grunted and went out.

Dundy faced the girl again. "You and this Smekalov in love with each other?"

Her face became scornful. She looked at him with scornful eyes and said nothing.

He said, "Now your father's dead, will you have enough money for him to marry if his wife divorces him?"

She covered her face with her hands.

He said, "Now your father's dead, will—?"

Spade, leaning far over, caught her as she fell. He lifted her easily and carried her into the bedroom. When he came back he shut the door behind him and leaned against it. "Whatever the rest of it was," he said, "the faint's a phony."

"Everything's a phony," Dundy growled.

Spade grinned mockingly, "There ought to be a law making criminals give themselves up."

Mr. Bliss smiled and sat down at his brother's desk by the window.

Dundy's voice was disagreeable. "You got nothing to worry about," he said to Spade. "Even your client's dead and can't complain. But if I don't come across I've got to stand for riding from the captain, the chief, the newspapers, and heaven knows who all."

"Stay with it," Spade said soothingly; "you'll catch a murderer sooner or later yet." His face became serious except for the lights in his yellow-gray eyes. "I don't want to run this job up any more alleys than we have to, but don't you think we ought to check up on the funeral the housekeeper said she went to? There's something funny about that woman."

After looking suspiciously at Spade for a moment, Dundy nodded, and said, "Tom'll do it."

Spade turned about and, shaking his finger at Tom, said, "It's a ten-to-one bet there wasn't any funeral. Check on it . . . don't miss a trick."

Then he opened the bedroom door and called Mrs. Hooper. "Sergeant Polhaus wants some information from you," he told her.

While Tom was writing down names and addresses that the woman gave him, Spade sat on the sofa and made and smoked a cigarette, and Dundy walked the floor slowly, scowling at the rug. With Spade's approval, Theodore Bliss rose and rejoined his wife in the bedroom.

Presently Tom put his note book in his pocket, said, "Thank you," to the housekeeper, "Be seeing you," to Spade and Dundy, and left the apartment.

The housekeeper stood where he had left her, ugly, strong, serene, patient.

Spade twisted himself around on the sofa until he was looking into her deep-set, steady eyes. "Don't worry about that," he said, flirting a hand toward the door Tom had gone through. "Just routine." He pursed his lips, asked, "What do you honestly think of this thing, Mrs. Hooper?"

She replied calmly, in her strong, somewhat harsh voice, "I think it's the judgment of God."

Dundy stopped pacing the floor.

Spade said, "What?"

ILLUMINATIONS

There was certainty and no excitement in her voice: "The wages of sin is death."

Dundy began to advance toward Mrs. Hooper in the manner of one stalking game. Spade waved him back with a hand which the sofa hid from the woman. His face and voice showed interest, but were now as composed as the woman's. "Sin?" he asked.

She said, "'Whosoever shall offend one of these little ones that believe in me, it were better for him that a millstone were hanged around his neck, and he were cast into the sea.'" She spoke, not as if quoting, but as if saying something she believed.

Dundy barked a question at her: "What little one?"

She turned her grave gray eyes on him, then looked past him at the bedroom door.

"Her," she said; "Miriam."

Dundy frowned at her. "His daughter?"

The woman said, "Yes, his own adopted daughter."

Angry blood mottled Dundy's square face. "What the heck is this?" he demanded. He shook his head as if to free it from some clinging thing. "She's not really his daughter?"

The woman's serenity was in no way disturbed by his anger. "No. His wife was an invalid most of her life. They didn't have any children."

Dundy moved his jaws as if chewing for a moment and when he spoke again his voice was cooler. "What did he do to her?"

"I don't know," she said, "but I truly believe that when the truth's found out you'll see that the money her father—I mean her real father—left her has been—"

Spade interrupted her, taking pains to speak very clearly, moving one hand in small circles with his words. "You mean you don't actually know he's been gypping her? You just suspect it?"

She put a hand over her heart. "I know it here," she replied calmly.

Dundy looked at Spade, Spade at Dundy, and Spade's eyes were shiny with not altogether pleasant merriment. Dundy cleared his throat and addressed the woman again. "And you think this"—he waved a hand at the floor where the dead man had lain—"was the judgment of God, huh?"

"I do."

He kept all but the barest trace of craftiness out of his eyes. "Then whoever did it was just acting as the hand of God?"

"It's not for me to say," she replied.

Red began to mottle his face again.

"That'll be all right now," he said in a choking voice, but by the time she reached the bedroom door his eyes became alert again and he called, "Wait a minute." And when they were facing each other: "Listen, do you happen to be a Rosicrucian?"

"I wish to be nothing but a Christian."

He growled, "All right, all right," and turned his back on her. She went into the bedroom and shut the door. He wiped his forehead with the palm of his right hand and complained wearily, "Great Scott, what a family."

Spade shrugged. "Try investigating your own some time."

Dundy's face whitened. His lips, almost colorless, came back tight over his teeth. He balled his fists and lunged toward Spade. "What do you—?" The pleasantly surprised look on Spade's face stopped him. He averted his eyes, wet his lips with the tip of his tongue, looked at Spade again and away, essayed an embarrassed smile, and mumbled, "You mean any family. Uh-huh, I guess so." He turned hastily toward the corridor door as the doorbell rang.

The amusement twitching Spade's face accentuated his likeness to a blond satan.

An amiable, drawling voice came in through the corridor door: "I'm Jim Kittredge, Superior Court. I was told to come over here."

Dundy's voice: "Yes, come in."

Kittredge was a roly-poly ruddy man in too-tight clothes with the shine of age on them. He nodded at Spade and said, "I remember you, Mr. Spade, from the Burke-Harris suit."

Spade said, "Sure," and stood up to shake hands with him.

Dundy had gone to the bedroom door to call Theodore Bliss and his wife. Kittredge looked at them, smiled at them amiably, said, "How do you do?" and turned to Dundy. "That's them, all right." He looked around as if for a place to spit, found none, and said, "It was just about ten minutes to four that the gentleman there came in the courtroom and asked me how long His Honor would be, and I told him about ten minutes, and they waited there; and right after court adjourned at four o'clock we married them."

Dundy said, "Thanks." He sent Kittredge away, the Blisses back to the bedroom, scowled with dissatisfaction at Spade, and said, "So what?"

Spade, sitting down again, replied, "So you couldn't get from here to the Municipal Building in less than fifteen minutes on a bet, so he couldn't've ducked back here while he was waiting for the judge, and he couldn't have hustled over here to do it after the wedding and before Miriam arrived."

The dissatisfaction in Dundy's face increased. He opened his mouth, but shut it in silence when the gray-faced man came in with a tall, slender, pale young man who fitted the description the Filipino had given of Miriam Bliss's companion.

The gray-faced man said, "Lieutenant Dundy, Mr. Spade, Mr. Boris— uh—Smekalov."

Dundy nodded curtly.

Smekalov began to speak immediately. His accent was not heavy enough to trouble his hearers much, though his r's sounded more like w's. "Lieutenant, I must beg of you that you keep this confidential. If it should get out it will ruin me, Lieutenant, ruin me completely and most unjustly. I am most innocent, sir, I assure you, in heart, spirit, and deed, not only innocent, but in no way whatever connected with any part of the whole horrible matter. There is no—"

"Wait a minute." Dundy prodded Smekalov's chest with a blunt finger. "Nobody's said anything about you being mixed up in anything—but it'd have looked better if you'd stuck around."

The young man spread his arms, his palms forward, in an expansive gesture. "But what can I do? I have a wife who—" He shook his head violently. "It is impossible. I cannot do it."

The gray-faced man said to Spade in an adequately subdued voice, "Goofy, these Russians."

Dundy screwed up his eyes at Smekalov and made his voice judicial. "You've probably," he said, "put yourself in a pretty tough spot."

Smekalov seemed about to cry. "But only put yourself in my place," he begged, "and you—"

"Wouldn't want to." Dundy seemed, in his callous way, sorry for the young man. "Murder's nothing to play with in this country."

"Murder! But I tell you, Lieutenant, I happen' to enter into this situation by the merest mischance only. I am not—"

"You mean you came in here with Miss Bliss by accident?"

The young man looked as if he would like to say "Yes." He said, "No," slowly, then went on with increasing rapidity: "But that was nothing, sir, nothing at all. We had been to lunch. I escorted her home and she said, 'Will you come in for a cocktail?' and I would. That is all, I give you my word." He held out his hands, palms up. "Could it not have happened so to you?" He moved his hands in Spade's direction. "To you?"

Spade said, "A lot of things happen to me. Did Bliss know you were running around with his daughter?"

"He knew we were friends, yes."

"Did he know you had a wife?"

Smekalov said cautiously, "I do not think so."

Dundy said, "You know he didn't."

Smekalov moistened his lips and did not contradict the lieutenant.

Dundy asked, "What do you think he'd've done if he found out?"

"I do not know, sir."

Dundy stepped close to the young man and spoke through his teeth in a harsh, deliberate voice, "What *did* he do when he found out?"

The young man retreated a step, his face white and frightened.

The bedroom door opened and Miriam Bliss came into the room. "Why don't you leave him alone?" she asked indignantly. "I told you he had nothing to do with it. I told you he didn't know anything about it." She was beside Smekalov now and had one of his hands in hers. "You're simply making trouble for him without doing a bit of good. I'm awfully sorry, Boris, I tried to keep them from bothering you."

The young man mumbled unintelligibly.

"You tried, all right," Dundy agreed. He addressed Spade: "Could it've been like this, Sam? Bliss found out about the wife, knew they had the lunch date, came home early to meet them when they came in, threatened to tell the wife, and was choked to stop him." He looked sidewise at the girl. "Now, if you want to fake another faint, hop to it."

The young man screamed and flung himself at Dundy, clawing with both hands. Dundy grunted—"Uh!"—and struck him in the face with a heavy fist. The young man went backward across the room until he collided with a chair. He and the chair went down on the floor together. Dundy said to the gray-faced man, "Take him down to the Hall—material witness."

The gray-faced man said, "Oke," picked up Smekalov's hat, and went over to help pick him up.

Theodore Bliss, his wife, and the housekeeper had come to the door Miriam Bliss had left open. Miriam Bliss was crying, stamping her foot, threatening Dundy: "I'll report you, you coward. You had no right to . . ." and so on. Nobody paid much attention to her; they watched the gray-faced man help Smekalov to his feet, take him away. Smekalov's nose and mouth were red smears.

Then Dundy said, "Hush," negligently to Miriam Bliss and took a slip of paper from his pocket. "I got a list of the calls from here to-day. Sing out when you recognize them."

He read a telephone number.

Mrs. Hooper said, "That is the butcher. I phoned him before I left this morning." She said the next number Dundy read was the grocer's.

He read another.

"That's the St. Mark," Miriam Bliss said. "I called up Boris." She identified two more numbers as those of friends she had called.

The sixth number, Bliss said, was his brother's office. "Probably my call to Elise to ask her to meet me."

Spade said, "Mine," to the seventh number, and Dundy said, "That last one's police emergency." He put the slip back in his pocket.

Spade said cheerfully, "And that gets us a lot of places."

The doorbell rang.

Dundy went to the door. He and another man could be heard talking in voices too low for their words to be recognized in the living room.

The telephone rang. Spade answered it. "Hello. . . . No, this is Spade. Wait a min— All right." He listened. "Right, I'll tell him. . . . I don't know. I'll have him call you. . . . Right."

When he turned from the telephone Dundy was standing, hands behind him, in the vestibule doorway. Spade said, "O'Gar says your Russian went completely nuts on the way to the Hall. They had to shove him into a strait-jacket."

"He ought to been there long ago," Dundy growled. "Come here."

Spade followed Dundy into the vestibule. A uniformed policeman stood in the outer doorway.

Dundy brought his hands from behind him. In one was a necktie with narrow diagonal stripes in varying shades of green, in the other was a platinum scarfpin in the shape of a crescent set with small diamonds.

Spade bent over to look at three small, irregular spots on the tie. "Blood?"

"Or dirt," Dundy said. "He found them crumpled up in a newspaper in the rubbish can on the corner."

"Yes, sir," the uniformed man said proudly; "there I found them, all wadded up in—" He stopped because nobody was paying any attention to him.

"Blood's better," Spade was saying. "It gives a reason for taking the tie away. Let's go in and talk to the people."

Dundy stuffed the tie in one pocket, thrust his hand holding the pin into another. "Right—and we'll call it blood."

They went into the living-room. Dundy looked from Bliss to Bliss's wife, to Bliss's niece, to the housekeeper, as if he did not like any of them. He took his fist from his pocket, thrust it straight out in front of him, and opened it to show the crescent pin lying in his hand. "What's that?" he demanded.

Miriam Bliss was the first to speak. "Why, it's Father's pin," she said.

"So it is?" he said disagreeably. "And did he have it on to-day?"

"He always wore it." She turned to the others for confirmation.

Mrs. Bliss said, "Yes," while the others nodded.

"Where did you find it?" the girl asked.

Dundy was surveying them one by one again, as if he liked them less than ever. His face was red. "He always wore it," he said angrily, "but there wasn't one of you could say, 'Father always wore a pin. Where is it?' No, we got to wait till it turns up before we can get a word out of you about it."

Bliss said, "Be fair. How were we to know—?"

"Never mind what you were to know," Dundy said. "It's coming around to the point where I'm going to do some talking about what I know." He took the green necktie from his pocket. "This is his tie?"

Mrs. Hooper said, "Yes, sir."

Dundy said, "Well, it's got blood on it, and it's not his blood because he didn't have a scratch on him that we could see." He looked narrow-eyed from one to another of them. "Now, suppose you were trying to choke a man that wore a scarfpin and he was wresting with you, and—"

He broke off and looked at Spade.

Spade had crossed to where Mrs. Hooper was standing. Her big hands were clasped in front of her. He took her right hand, turned it over, took the wadded handkerchief from her palm, and there was a two-inch-long fresh scratch in the flesh.

She had passively allowed him to examine her hand. Her mien lost none of its tranquillity now. She said nothing.

"Well?" he asked.

"I scratched it on Miss Miriam's pin fixing her on the bed when she fainted," the housekeeper said calmly.

Dundy's laugh was brief, bitter. "It'll hang you just the same," he said.

There was no change in the woman's face. "The Lord's will be done," she replied.

Spade made a peculiar noise in his throat as he dropped her hand. "Well, let's see how we stand." He grinned at Dundy. "You don't like that star-T, do you?"

Dundy said, "Not by a long shot."

"Neither do I," Spade said. "The Talbot threat was probably on the level, but that debt seems to have been squared. Now— Wait a minute." He went to the telephone and called his office. "The tie thing looked pretty funny, too, for a while," he said while he waited, "but I guess the blood took care of that."

He spoke into the telephone: "Hello, Effie. Listen: Within half an hour or so of the time Bliss called me, did you get any call that maybe wasn't on the level? Anything that could have been a stall. . . . Yes, before. . . . Think now."

He put his hand over the mouthpiece and said to Dundy, "There's a lot of deviltry going on in this world."

He spoke into the telephone again: "Yes? . . . Yes . . . Kruger? . . . Yes. Man or woman? . . . Thanks . . . No, I'll be through in half an hour. Wait for me and I'll buy your dinner. 'Bye."

He turned away from the telephone. "About half an hour before Bliss phoned, a man called my office and asked for Mr. Kruger."

Dundy frowned. "So what?"

"Kruger wasn't there."

Dundy's frown deepened. "Who's Kruger?"

"I don't know," Spade said blandly. "I never heard of him." He took tobacco and cigarette papers from his pockets. "All right, Bliss, where's your scratch?"

Theodore Bliss said, "What?" while the others stared blankly at Spade.

"Your scratch," Spade repeated in a consciously patient tone. His attention was on the cigarette he was making. "The place where your brother's pin gouged you when you were choking him."

"Are you crazy?" Bliss demanded. "I was—"

"Uh-huh, you were being married when he was killed. You were not." Spade moistened the edge of his cigarette paper and smoothed it with his forefingers.

Mrs. Bliss spoke now, stammering a little: "But he—but Max Bliss called—"

"Who says Max Bliss called me?" Spade said. "I don't know that. I wouldn't know his voice. All I know is a man called me and said he was Max Bliss. Anybody could say that."

"But the telephone records here show the call came from here," she protested.

He shook his head and smiled. "They show I had *a* call from here, and I did, but not that one. I told you somebody called up half an hour or so before the supposed Max Bliss call and asked for Mr. Kruger." He nodded at Theodore Bliss. "He was smart enough to get a call from this apartment to my office on the record before he left to meet you."

She stared from Spade to her husband with dumbfounded blue eyes.

Her husband said lightly, "It's nonsense, my dear. You know—"

Spade did not let him finish that sentence. "You know he went out to smoke a cigarette in the corridor while waiting for the judge, and he knew there were telephone booths in the corridor. A minute would be all he needed." He lit his cigarette and returned his lighter to his pocket.

Bliss said, "Nonsense!" more sharply. "Why should I want to kill Max?" He smiled reassuringly into his wife's horrified eyes. "Don't let this disturb you, dear. Police methods are sometimes—"

"All right," Spade said, "let's look you over for scratches."

Bliss wheeled to face him more directly. "Damned if you will!" He put a hand behind him.

Spade, wooden-faced and dreamy-eyed, came forward.

SPADE AND Effie Perine sat at a small table in Julius's Castle on Telegraph Hill. Through the window beside them ferryboats could be seen carrying lights to and from the cities' lights on the other side of the bay.

". . . hadn't gone there to kill him, chances are," Spade was saying; "just to shake him down for some more money; but when the fight started, once he got his hands on his throat, I guess, his grudge was too hot in him for him to let go till Max was dead. Understand, I'm just putting together what the evidence says, and what we got out of his wife, and the not much that we got out of him."

Effie nodded. "She's a nice, loyal wife."

Spade drank coffee, shrugged. "What for? She knows now that he made his play for her only because she was Max's secretary. She knows that when he took out the marriage license a couple of weeks ago it was only to string her along so she'd get him the photostatic copies of the records that tied Max up with the Graystone Loan swindle. She knows— Well, she knows she wasn't just helping an injured innocent to clear his good name."

He took another sip of coffee. "So he calls on his brother this afternoon to hold San Quentin over his head for a price again, and there's a fight, and he kills him, and gets his wrist scratched by the pin while he's choking him. Blood on the tie, a scratch on the wrist—that won't do. He takes the tie off the corpse and hunts up another, because the absence of a tie will set the police to thinking. He gets a bad break there: Max's new ties are on the front of the rack, and he grabs the first one he comes to. All right. Now he's got to put it around the dead man's neck—or wait—he gets a better idea. Pull off some more clothes and puzzle the police. The tie'll be just as inconspicuous off as on, if the shirt's off too. Undressing him, he gets another idea. He'll give the police something else to worry about, so he draws a mystic sign he has seen somewhere on the dead man's chest."

Spade emptied his cup, set it down, and went on: "By now he's getting to be a regular master-mind at bewildering the police. A threatening letter signed with the thing on Max's chest. The afternoon mail is on the desk. One envelope's as good as another so long as it's typewritten and has no return address, but the one from France adds a touch of the foreign, so out comes the original letter and in goes the threat. He's overdoing it now; see? He's giving us so much that's wrong that we can't help suspecting things that seem all right—the phone call, for instance.

"Well, he's ready for the phone calls now—his alibi. He picks my name out of the private detectives in the phone book and does the Mr. Kruger trick; but that's after he calls the blond Elise and tells her that not only have the obstacles to their marriage been removed, but he's had an offer to go in business in New York and has to leave right away, and will she meet him in fifteen minutes and get married? There's more than just an alibi to that. He wants to make sure *she* is dead sure he didn't kill Max, because she knows he doesn't like Max, and he doesn't want her to think he was just stringing her along to get the dope on Max, because she might be able to put two and two together and get something like the right answer.

"With that taken care of, he's ready to leave. He goes out quite openly, with only one thing to worry about now—the tie and pin in his pocket. He takes the pin along because he's not sure the police mightn't find traces of blood around the setting of the stones, no matter how carefully he wipes it. On his way out he picks up a newspaper—buys one from the newsboy he meets at the street door—wads tie and pin up in a piece of it, and drops it in the rubbish can at the corner. That seems all right. No reason for the police to look for the tie. No reason for the street cleaner who empties the can to investigate a crumpled piece of newspaper, and if something does go wrong—what the deuce!—the murderer dropped it there, but he, Theodore, can't be the murderer, because he's going to have an alibi.

"Then he jumps in his car and drives to the Municipal Building. He knows there are plenty of phones there and he can always say he's got to wash his hands, but it turns out he doesn't have to. While they're waiting for the judge to get through with a case he goes out to smoke a cigarette, and there you are—'Mr. Spade, this is Max Bliss and I've been threatened.'"

Effie Perine nodded, then asked, "Why do you suppose he picked on a private detective instead of the police?"

"Playing safe. If the body had been found, meanwhile, the police might've heard of it and traced the call. A private detective wouldn't be likely to hear about it till he read it in the papers."

She laughed, then said, "And that was your luck."

"Luck? I don't know." He looked gloomily at the back of his left hand. "I hurt a knuckle stopping him and the job only lasted an afternoon. Chances are whoever's handling the estate'll raise hob if I send them a bill for any decent amount of money." He raised a hand to attract the waiter's attention. "Oh, well, better luck next time. Want to catch a movie or have you got something else to do?"

TOO MANY
HAVE LIVED

T he man's tie was as orange as a sunset. He was a large man, tall and meaty, without softness. The dark hair parted in the middle, flattened to his scalp, his firm, full cheeks, the clothes that fit him with noticeable snugness, even the small pink ears flat against the side of his head—each of these seemed but a differently colored part of one same smooth surface. His age could have been thirty-five or forty-five.

He sat beside Samuel Spade's desk, leaning forward a little over his Malacca stick, and said, "No, I want you to find out what happened to him. I hope you never find him." His protuberant green eyes stared solemnly at Spade.

Spade rocked back in his chair. His face—given a not unpleasantly satanic cast by the V's of his bony chin, mouth, nostrils, and thickish brows—was as politely interested as his voice. "Why?"

The green-eyed man spoke quietly, with assurance, "I can talk to you, Spade. You've the sort of reputation I want in a private detective. That's why I am here."

Spade's nod committed him to nothing.

The green-eyed man said, "And any fair price is all right with me."

Spade nodded as before. "And with me," he said, "but I've got to know what you want to buy. You want to find out what happened to this—uh—Eli Haven, but you don't care what it is?"

The green-eyed man lowered his voice, but there was no other change in his mien. "In a way I do. For instance, if you found him and fixed it so he stayed away for good, it might be worth more money."

"You mean even if he didn't want to stay away?"

The green-eyed man said, "Especially."

Spade smiled and shook his head. "Probably not enough more money— the way you mean it." He took his long, thick-fingered hands from the arms of his chair and turned their palms up. "Well, what's it all about, Colyer?"

Colyer's face reddened a little, but his eyes maintained their unblinking cold stare. "This man's got a wife. I like her. They had a row last week and he blew. If I can convince her he's gone for good, there's a chance she'll divorce him."

"I'd want to talk to her," Spade said. "Who is this Eli Haven?"

"He's a bad egg. He doesn't do anything. Writes poetry or something."

"What can you tell me about him that'll help?"

"Nothing Julia, his wife, can't tell you. You're going to talk to her." Colyer stood up. "I've got connections. Maybe I can get something for you through them later."

A SMALL-BONED woman of twenty-five or -six opened the apartment door. Her powder-blue dress was trimmed with silver buttons. She was full-bosomed but slim, with straight shoulders and narrow hips, and she carried herself with a pride that would have been cockiness in one less graceful.

Spade said, "Mrs. Haven?"

She hesitated before saying, "Yes."

"Gene Colyer sent me to see you. My name's Spade. I'm a private detective. He wants me to find your husband."

"And have you found him?"

"I told him I'd have to talk to you first."

Her smile went away. She studied his face gravely, feature by feature, then she said, "Certainly," and stepped back, drawing the door back with her.

When they were seated in facing chairs in a cheaply furnished room overlooking a playground where children were noisy, she asked, "Did Gene tell you why he wanted Eli found?"

"He said if you knew he was gone for good maybe you'd listen to reason." She said nothing.

"Has he ever gone off like this before?"

"Often."

"What's he like?"

"He's a swell man," she said dispassionately, "when he's sober; and when he's drinking he's all right except with women and money."

"That leaves him a lot of room to be all right in. What does he do for a living?"

"He's a poet," she replied, "but nobody makes a living at that."

"Well?"

"Oh, he pops in with a little money now and then. Poker, races, he says. I don't know."

"How long've you been married?"

"Four years, almost." She smiled mockingly.

"San Francisco all the time?"

"No, we lived in Seattle the first year and then came here."

"He from Seattle?"

She shook her head. "Some place in Delaware."

"What place?"

"I don't know."

Spade drew his thickish brows together a little. "Where are you from?"

She said sweetly, "You're not hunting for me."

"You act like it," he grumbled. "Well, who are his friends?"

"Don't ask me!"

He made an impatient grimace. "You know some of them," he insisted.

"Sure. There's a fellow named Minera and a Louis James and somebody he calls Conny."

"Who are they?"

"Men," she replied blandly. "I don't know anything about them. They phone or drop by to pick him up, or I see him around town with them. That's all I know."

"What do they do for a living? They can't all write poetry."

She laughed. "They could try. One of them, Louis James, is a—member of Gene's staff, I think. I honestly don't know any more about them than I've told you."

"Think they'd know where your husband is?"

She shrugged. "They're kidding me if they do. They still call up once in a while to see if he's turned up."

"And these women you mentioned?"

"They're not people I know."

Spade scowled thoughtfully at the floor, asked, "What'd he do before he started not making a living writing poetry?"

"Anything—sold vacuum cleaners, hoboed, went to sea, dealt blackjack, railroaded, canning houses, lumber camps, carnivals, worked on a news-paper—anything."

"Have any money when he left?"

"Three dollars he borrowed from me."

"What'd he say?"

She laughed. "Said if I used whatever influence I had with God while he was gone he'd be back at dinnertime with a surprise for me."

Spade raised his eyebrows. "You were on good terms?"

"Oh, yes. Our last fight had been patched up a couple of days before."

"When did he leave?"

"Thursday afternoon; three o'clock, I guess."

"Got any photographs of him?"

"Yes." She went to a table by one of the windows, pulled a drawer out, and turned toward Spade with a photograph in her hand.

Spade looked at the picture of a thin face with deep-set eyes, a sensual mouth, and a heavily lined forehead topped by a disorderly mop of coarse blond hair.

He put Haven's photograph in his pocket and picked up his hat. He turned toward the door, halted. "What kind of poet is he? Pretty good?"

She shrugged. "That depends on who you ask."

"Any of it around here?"

"No." She smiled. "Think he's hiding between pages?"

"You never can tell what'll lead to what. I'll be back some time. Think things over and see if you can't find some way of loosening up a little more. 'Bye."

He walked down Post Street to Mulford's book store and asked for a volume of Haven's poetry.

"I'm sorry," the girl said. "I sold my last copy last week"—she smiled—"to Mr. Haven himself. I can order it for you."

"You know him?"

"Only through selling him books."

Spade pursed his lips, asked, "What day was it?" He gave her one of his business cards. "Please. It's important."

She went to a desk, turned the pages of a red-bound sales book, and came back to him with the book open in her hand. "It was last Wednesday," she said, "and we delivered it to a Mr. Roger Ferris, 1981 Pacific Avenue."

"Thanks a lot," he said.

Outside, he hailed a taxicab and gave the driver Mr. Roger Ferris's address.

THE PACIFIC AVENUE house was a four-story graystone set behind a narrow strip of lawn. The room into which a plump-faced maid ushered Spade was large and high-ceilinged.

Spade sat down, but when the maid had gone away he rose and began to walk around the room. He halted at a table where there were three books. One of them had a salmon-colored jacket on which was printed in red an outline drawing of a bolt of lightning striking the ground between a man and a woman, and in black the words *Colored Light, by Eli Haven*.

Spade picked up the book and went back to his chair.

There was an inscription on the flyleaf—heavy, irregular characters written with blue ink:

To good old Buck, who knew his colored lights, in memory of them there days.   *Eli*

Spade turned the pages at random and idly read a verse:

STATEMENT

Too many have lived
As we live
For our lives to be
Proof of our living.
Too many have died
As we die
For their deaths to be
Proof of our dying.

He looked up from the book as a man in dinner clothes came into the room. He was not a tall man, but his erectness made him seem tall even when Spade's six feet and a fraction of an inch were standing before him. He had bright blue eyes undimmed by his fifty-some years, a sunburned face in which no muscle sagged, a smooth, broad forehead, and thick, short, nearly white hair. There was dignity in his countenance, and amiability.

He nodded at the book Spade still held. "How do you like it?"

Spade grinned, said, "I guess I'm just a mug," and put the book down. "That's what I came to see you about, though, Mr. Ferris. You know Haven?"

"Yes, certainly. Sit down, Mr. Spade." He sat in a chair not far from Spade's. "I knew him as a kid. He's not in trouble, is he?"

Spade said, "I don't know. I'm trying to find him."

Ferris spoke hesitantly, "Can I ask why?"

"You know Gene Colyer?"

"Yes." Ferris hesitated again, then said, "This is in confidence. I've a chain of motion-picture houses through northern California, you know, and a couple of years ago when I had some labor trouble I was told that Colyer was the man to get in touch with to have it straightened out. That's how I happened to meet him."

"Yes," Spade said dryly, "a lot of people happen to meet Gene that way."

"But what's he got to do with Eli?"

"Wants him found. How long since you've seen him?"

"Last Thursday he was here."

"What time did he leave?"

"Midnight—a little after. He came over in the afternoon around half-past three. We hadn't seen each other for years. I persuaded him to stay for dinner—he looked pretty seedy—and lent him some money."

"How much?"

"A hundred and fifty—all I had in the house."

"Say where he was going when he left?"

Ferris shook his head. "He said he'd phone me the next day."

"Did he phone you the next day?"

"No."

"And you've known him all his life?"

"Not exactly, but he worked for me fifteen or sixteen years ago when I had a carnival company—Great Eastern and Western Combined Shows—with a partner for a while and then by myself. I always liked the kid."

"How long before Thursday since you'd seen him?"

"Lord knows," Ferris replied. "I'd lost track of him for years. Then, Wednesday, out of a clear sky, that book came, with no address or anything, just that stuff written in the front, and the next morning he called me up. I was tickled to death to know he was still alive and doing something with himself. So he came over that afternoon and we put in about nine hours talking about old times."

"Tell you much about what he'd been doing since then?"

"Just that he'd been knocking around, doing one thing and another, taking the breaks as they came. He didn't complain much; I had to make him take the hundred and fifty."

Spade stood up. "Thanks ever so much, Mr. Ferris. I—"

Ferris interrupted him. "Not at all, and if there's anything I can do, call on me."

Spade looked at his watch. "Can I phone my office?"

"Certainly; there's a phone in the next room, to the right."

Spade said, "Thanks," and went out. When he returned he was rolling a cigarette. His face was wooden.

"Any news?" Ferris asked.

"Yes. Colyer's called the job off. He says Haven's body's been found in some bushes on the other side of San Jose, with three bullets in it." He smiled, adding mildly, "He *told* me he might be able to find out something through his connections."

MORNING SUNSHINE, coming through the curtains that screened Spade's office windows, put two fat, yellow rectangles on the floor and gave everything in the room a yellow tint.

He sat at his desk, staring meditatively at a newspaper. He did not look up when Effie Perine came in from the outer office.

She said, "Mrs. Haven is here."

He raised his head then and said, "That's better. Push her in."

Mrs. Haven came in quickly. Her face was white and she was shivering in spite of her fur coat. She came straight to Spade and asked, "Did Gene kill him?"

Spade said, "I don't know."

"I've got to know," she cried.

Spade took her hands. "Here, sit down." He led her to a chair. He asked, "Colyer tell you he'd called the job off?"

She stared at him in amazement. "He what?"

"He left word here last night that your husband had been found and he wouldn't need me any more."

She hung her head and her words were barely audible. "Then he did."

Spade shrugged. "Maybe only an innocent man could've afforded to call it off then, or maybe he was guilty but had brains enough and nerve enough to—"

She was not listening to him. She was leaning toward him, speaking earnestly, "But, Mr. Spade, you're not going to drop it like that? You're not going to let him stop now?"

While she was speaking his telephone bell rang. He said, "Excuse me," and picked up the receiver. "Yes? . . . Uh-huh. . . . So?" He pursed his lips. "I'll let you know." He pushed the telephone aside slowly and faced Mrs. Haven again. "Colyer's outside."

"Does he know I'm here?" she asked quickly.

"Couldn't say." He stood up, pretending he was not watching her closely. "Do you care?"

She pinched her lower lip between her teeth, said, "No," hesitantly.

"Fine. I'll have him in."

She raised a hand as if in protest, then let it drop, and her white face was composed. "Whatever you want," she said.

Spade opened the door, said, "Hello, Colyer. Come on in. We were just talking about you."

Colyer nodded, and came into the office holding his Malacca stick in one hand, his hat in the other. "How are you this morning, Julia? You ought to've phoned me. I'd've driven you back to town."

"I—I didn't know what I was doing."

Colyer looked at her for a moment longer, then shifted the focus of his expressionless green eyes to Spade's face. "Well, have you been able to convince her I didn't do it?"

"We hadn't got around to that," Spade said. "I was just trying to find out how much reason there was for suspecting you. Sit down."

Colyer sat down somewhat carefully, asked, "And?"

"And then you arrived."

Colyer nodded gravely. "All right, Spade," he said; "you're hired again to prove to Mrs. Haven that I didn't have anything to do with it."

"Gene," she exclaimed in a choked voice, and held her hands out toward him appealingly. "I don't think you did—I don't want to think you did—but I'm so afraid." She put her hands to her face and began to cry.

Colyer went over to the woman. "Take it easy," he said. "We'll kick it out together."

Spade went into the outer office, shutting the door behind him.

Effie Perine stopped typing a letter.

He grinned at her, said, "Somebody ought to write a book about people some time—they're peculiar," and went over to the water cooler. "You've got Wally Kellogg's number. Call him up and ask him where I can find Tom Minera."

He returned to the inner office.

Mrs. Haven had stopped crying. She said, "I'm sorry."

Spade said, "It's all right." He looked sidewise at Colyer. "I still got my job?"

"Yes." Colyer cleared his throat. "But if there's nothing special right now, I'd better take Mrs. Haven home."

"Okay, but there's one thing: according to the *Chronicle* you identified him. How come you were down there?"

"I went down when I heard they'd found a body," Colyer replied deliberately. "I told you I had connections."

Spade said, "All right; be seeing you," and opened the door for them.

When the corridor door closed behind them, Effie Perine said, "Minera's at the Buxton on Army Street."

Spade said, "Thanks." He went into the inner office to get his hat. On his way out he said, "If I'm not back in a couple of months tell them to look for my body there."

SPADE WALKED DOWN a shabby corridor to a battered green door marked *411*. The murmur of voices came through the door, but no words could be distinguished. He stopped listening and knocked.

An obviously disguised male voice asked, "What is it?"

"I want to see Tom. This is Sam Spade."

A pause, then: "Tom ain't here."

Spade put a hand on the knob and shook the frail door. "Come on, open up," he growled.

Presently the door was opened by a thin, dark man of twenty-five or -six who tried to make his beady dark eyes guileless while saying, "I didn't think it was your voice at first." The slackness of his mouth made his chin seem even smaller than it was. His green-striped shirt, open at the neck, was not clean. His gray pants were carefully pressed.

"You've got to be careful these days," Spade said solemnly, and went through the doorway into a room where two men were trying to seem uninterested in his arrival.

One of them leaned against the window-sill filing his fingernails. The other was tilted back in a chair with his feet on the edge of a table and a newspaper spread between his hands. They glanced at Spade in unison and went on with their occupations.

Spade said cheerfully, "Always glad to meet any friends of Tom Minera's."

Minera finished shutting the door and said awkwardly, "Uh—yes—Mr. Spade, meet Mr. Conrad and Mr. James."

Conrad, the man at the window, made a vaguely polite gesture with the nail file in his hand. He was a few years older than Minera, of average height, sturdily built, with a thick-featured, dull-eyed face.

James lowered his paper for an instant to look coolly, appraisingly, at Spade and say, "How'r'ye, brother?" Then he returned to his reading. He was as sturdily built as Conrad, but taller, and his face had a shrewdness the other's lacked.

"Ah," Spade said, "and friends of the late Eli Haven."

The man at the window jabbed a finger with his nail file, and cursed it bitterly. Minera moistened his lips, and then spoke rapidly, with a whining note in his voice. "But on the level, Spade, we hadn't none of us seen him for a week."

Spade seemed mildly amused by the dark man's manner.

"What do you think he was killed for?"

"All I know is what the paper says: his pockets was all turned inside out and there wasn't much as a match on him." He drew down the ends of his mouth. "But far as I know he didn't have no dough. He didn't have none Tuesday night."

Spade, speaking softly, said, "I hear he got some Thursday night."

Minera, behind Spade, caught his breath audibly.

James said, "I guess you ought to know. I don't."

"He ever work with you boys?"

James slowly put aside his newspaper and took his feet off the table. His interest in Spade's question seemed great enough, but almost impersonal. "Now, what do you mean by that?"

Spade pretended surprise, "But you boys must work at something?"

Minera came around to Spade's side. "Aw, listen, Spade," he said. "This guy Haven was just a guy we knew. We didn't have nothing to do with rubbing him out; we don't know nothing about it. You know we—"

Three deliberate knocks sounded at the door.

Minera and Conrad looked at James, who nodded, but by then Spade, moving swiftly, had reached the door and was opening it.

Roger Ferris was there.

Spade blinked at Ferris, Ferris at Spade. Then Ferris put out his hand and said, "I *am* glad to see you."

"Come on in," Spade said.

"Look at this, Mr. Spade." Ferris's hand trembled as he took a slightly soiled envelope from his pocket.

Ferris's name and address were typewritten on the envelope. There was no postage stamp on it. Spade took out the enclosure, a narrow slip of cheap white paper, and unfolded it. On it was typewritten:

You had better come to Room 411 Buxton Hotel on Army St at 5 pm this afternoon on account of Thursday night.

There was no signature.

Spade said, "It's a long time before five o'clock."

"It is," Ferris agreed with emphasis. "I came as soon as I got that. It was Thursday night Eli was at my house."

Minera was jostling Spade, asking, "What is all this?"

Spade held the note up for the dark man to read. He read it and yelled, "Honest, Spade, I don't know nothing about that letter."

"Does anybody?" Spade asked.

Conrad said, "No," hastily.

James said, "What letter?"

Spade looked dreamily at Ferris for a moment, then said, as if speaking to himself, "Of course, Haven was trying to shake you down."

Ferris's face reddened. "What?"

"Shakedown," Spade repeated patiently; "money, blackmail."

"Look here, Spade," Ferris said earnestly; "you don't really believe what you said? What would he have to blackmail me on?"

"'To good old Buck,'"—Spade quoted the dead poet's inscription— "'who knew his colored lights, in memory of them there days.'" He looked somberly at Ferris from beneath slightly raised brows. "What colored lights? What's the circus and carnival slang term for kicking a guy off a train while it's going? Red-lighting. Sure, that's it—red lights. Who'd you red-light, Ferris, that Haven knew about?"

Minera went over to a chair, sat down, put his elbows on his knees, his head between his hands, and stared blankly at the floor. Conrad was breathing as if he had been running.

Spade addressed Ferris, "Well?"

Ferris wiped his face with a handkerchief, put the handkerchief in his pocket, and said simply, "It was a shakedown."

"And you killed him."

Ferris's blue eyes, looking into Spade's yellow-gray ones, were clear and steady, as was his voice. "I did not," he said. "I swear I did not. Let me tell you what happened. He sent me the book, as I told you, and I knew right away what that joke he wrote in the front meant. So the next day, when he phoned me and said he was coming over to talk over old times and to try to borrow some money for old times' sake, I knew what he meant again, and I went down to the bank and drew out ten thousand dollars. You can check that up. It's the Seaman's National."

"I will," Spade said.

"As it turned out, I didn't need that much. He wasn't very big-time, and I talked him into taking five thousand. I put the other five back in the bank next day. You can check that up."

"I will," Spade said.

"I told him I wasn't going to stand for any more taps, this five thousand was the first and the last. I made him sign a paper saying he'd helped in the—what I'd done—and he signed it. He left some time around midnight, and that's the last I ever saw of him."

Spade tapped the envelope that Ferris had given him. "And how about this note?"

"A messenger boy brought it at noon, and I came right over. Eli had assured me he hadn't said anything to anybody, but I didn't know. I had to face it, whatever it was."

Spade turned to the others, his face wooden. "Well?"

Minera and Conrad looked at James, who made an impatient grimace and said, "Oh, sure, we sent him the letter. Why not? We was friends of Eli's and we hadn't been able to find him since he went to put the squeeze to this baby, and then he turns up dead, so we kind of like to have the gent come over and explain things."

"You knew about the squeeze?"

"Sure. We was all together when he got the idea."

"How'd he happen to get the idea?" Spade asked.

James spread the fingers of his left hand. "We'd been drinking and talk-ing—you know the way a bunch of guys will, about all they'd seen and done—and he told a yarn about once seeing a guy boot another off a train into a cañon, and he happens to mention the name of the guy that done the booting—Buck Ferris. And somebody says, 'What's this Ferris look like?' Eli tells him what he looked like then, saying he ain't seen him for fifteen years; and whoever it is whistles and says, 'I bet that's the Ferris that owns about half the movie joints in the state. I bet you he'd give something to keep that back trail covered!'

"Well, the idea kind of hit Eli. You could see that. He thought a little while and then he got cagey. He asked what this movie Ferris's first name is, and when the other guy tells him, 'Roger,' he makes out he's disappointed and says, 'No, it ain't him. His first name was Martin.' We all give him the ha-ha and he finally admits he's thinking of seeing the gent, and when he called me up Thursday around noon and says he's throwing a party at Pogey Hecker's that night, it ain't no trouble to figure out what's what."

"What was the name of the gentleman who was red-lighted?"

"He wouldn't say. He shut up tight. You couldn't blame him."

"Then nothing. He never showed up at Pogey's. We tried to get him on the phone around two o'clock in the morning, but his wife said he hadn't been home, so we stuck around till four or five and then decided he had given us a run-around, and made Pogey charge the bill to him, and beat it. I ain't seen him since—dead or alive."

Spade said mildly. "Maybe. Sure you didn't find Eli later that morning, taking him riding, swap him bullets for Ferris's five thou, dump him in the—?"

A sharp double knock sounded on the door.

Spade's face brightened. He went to the door and opened it.

A young man came in. He was very dapper, and very well proportioned. He wore a light topcoat and his hands were in its pockets. Just inside the door he stepped to the right, and stood with his back to the wall.

By that time another young man was coming in. He stepped to the left. Though they did not actually look alike, their common dapperness, the similar trimness of their bodies, and their almost identical positions—back to wall, hands in pockets, cold, bright eyes studying the occupants of the room—gave them the appearance of twins.

Then Gene Colyer came in. He nodded at Spade, but paid no attention to the others in the room, though James said, "Hello, Gene."

"Anything new?" Colyer asked Spade.

Spade nodded. "It seems this gentleman"—he jerked a thumb at Ferris—"was—"

"Any place we can talk?"

"There's a kitchen back here."

Colyer snapped a "Smear anybody that pops" over his shoulder at the two dapper young men and followed Spade into the kitchen. He sat on the one kitchen chair and stared with unblinking green eyes at Spade while Spade told him what he had learned.

When the private detective had finished, the green-eyed man asked, "Well, what do you make of it?"

Spade looked thoughtfully at the other, "You've picked up something. I'd like to know what it is."

Colyer said, "They found the gun in a stream a quarter of a mile from where they found him. It's James's—got the mark on it where it was shot out of his hand once in Vallejo."

"That's nice," Spade said.

"Listen. A kid named Thurston says James comes to him last Wednesday and gets him to tail Haven. Thurston picks him up Thursday afternoon, puts him in at Ferris's, and phones James. James tells him to take a plant on the place and let him know where Haven goes when he leaves, but some nervous woman in the neighborhood puts in a ruble about the kid hanging around, and the cops chase him along about ten o'clock."

Spade pursed his lips and stared thoughtfully at the ceiling.

Colyer's eyes were expressionless, but sweat made his round face shiny, and his voice was hoarse. "Spade," he said, "I'm going to turn him in."

Spade switched his gaze from the ceiling to the protuberant green eyes.

"I've never turned in one of my people before," Colyer said, "but this one goes. Julia's *got* to believe I hadn't anything to do with it if it's one of my people and I turn him in, hasn't she?"

Spade nodded slowly. "I think so."

Colyer suddenly averted his eyes and cleared his throat. When he spoke again it was curtly. "Well, he goes."

Minera, James, and Conrad were seated when Spade and Colyer came out of the kitchen. Ferris was walking the floor. The two dapper young men had not moved.

Colyer went over to James. "Where's your gun, Louis?" he asked.

James moved his right hand a few inches toward his left breast, stopped it, and said, "Oh, I didn't bring it."

With his gloved hand—open—Colyer struck James on the side of the face, knocking him out of his chair.

James straightened up, mumbling, "I didn't mean nothing." He put a hand to the side of his face. "I know I oughtn't've done it, Chief, but when he called up and said he didn't like to go up against Ferris without something and didn't have any of his own, I said, 'All right,' and sent it over to him."

Colyer said, "And you sent Thurston over to him, too."

"We were just kind of interested in seeing if he did go through with it," James mumbled.

"And you couldn't've gone there yourself, or sent somebody else?"

"After Thurston had stirred up the whole neighborhood?"

Colyer turned to Spade. "Want us to help you take them in, or want to call the wagon?"

"We'll do it regular," Spade said, and went to the wall telephone. When he turned away from it his face was wooden, his eyes dreamy. He made a cigarette, lit it, and said to Colyer, "I'm silly enough to think your Louis has got a lot of right answers in that story of his."

James took his hand down from his bruised cheek and stared at Spade with astonished eyes.

Colyer growled, "What's the matter with you?"

"Nothing," Spade said softly, "except I think you're a little too anxious to slam it on him." He blew smoke out. "Why, for instance, should he drop his gun there when it had marks on it that people knew?"

Colyer said, "You think he's got brains."

"If these boys killed him, knew he was dead, why do they wait till the body's found and things are stirred up before they go after Ferris again? What'd they turn his pockets inside out for if they hijacked him? That's a lot of trouble and only done by folks that kill for some other reason and want to make it look like robbery." He shook his head. "You're too anxious to slam it on him. Why should they—"

"That's not the point right now," Colyer said. "The point is, why do you keep saying I'm too anxious to slam it on him?"

Spade shrugged. "Maybe to clear yourself with Julia as soon as possible and as clear as possible, maybe even to clear yourself with the police, and then you've got clients."

Colyer said, "What?"

Spade made a careless gesture with his cigarette. "Ferris," he said blandly. "He killed him, of course."

Colyer's eyelids quivered, though he did not actually blink.

Spade said, "First, he's the last person we know of who saw Eli alive, and that's always a good bet. Second, he's the only person I talked to before Eli's body turned up who cared whether they were holding out on me or not. The rest of you just thought I was hunting for a guy who'd gone away. He knew I was hunting for a man he'd killed, so he had to put himself in the clear. He was even afraid to throw that book away, because it had been sent up by the book store and could be traced, and there might be clerks who'd seen the inscription. Third, he was the only one who thought Eli was just a sweet, clean, lovable boy—for the same reasons. Fourth, that story about a blackmailer showing up at three o'clock in the afternoon, making an easy touch for five grand, and then sticking around till midnight is just silly, no matter how good the booze was. Fifth, the story about the paper Eli signed is still worse, though a forged one could be fixed up easy enough. Sixth, he's got the best reason of anybody we know for wanting Eli dead."

Colyer nodded slowly, "Still—"

"Still nothing," Spade said. "Maybe he did the ten-thousand-out-five-thousand-back trick with his bank, but that was easy. Then he got this feeble-minded blackmailer in his house, stalled him along until the servant had gone to bed, took the borrowed gun from him, shoved him downstairs into his car, took him for a ride—maybe took him already dead, maybe shot him down there by the bushes—frisked him clean to make identification harder and to make it look like robbery, tossed the gun in the water, and came home—"

He broke off to listen to the sound of a siren in the street. He looked then, for the first time since he had begun to talk, at Ferris.

Ferris's face was ghastly white, but he held his eyes steady.

Spade said, "I've got a hunch, Ferris, that we're going to find out about that red-lighting job, too. You told me you had your carnival company with a partner for a while when Eli was working for you, and then by yourself. We oughtn't to have a lot of trouble finding out about your partner—whether he disappeared, or died a natural death, or is still alive."

Ferris had lost some of his erectness. He wet his lips and said, "I want to see my lawyer. I don't want to talk till I've seen my lawyer."

Spade said, "It's all right with me. You're up against it, but I don't like blackmailers myself. I think Eli wrote a good epitaph for them in that book back there—'Too many have lived.'"

THEY CAN ONLY
HANG YOU ONCE

Samuel Spade said: "My name is Ronald Ames. I want to see Mr. Binnett—Mr. Timothy Binnett."

"Mr. Binnett is resting now, sir," the butler replied hesitantly.

"Will you find out when I can see him? It's important." Spade cleared his throat. "I'm—uh—just back from Australia, and it's about some of his properties there."

The butler turned on his heel while saying, "I'll see, sir," and was going up the front stairs before he had finished speaking.

Spade made and lit a cigarette.

The butler came downstairs again. "I'm sorry; he can't be disturbed now, but Mr. Wallace Binnett—Mr. Timothy's nephew—will see you."

Spade said, "Thanks," and followed the butler upstairs.

Wallace Binnett was a slender, handsome, dark man of about Spade's age—thirty-eight—who rose smiling from a brocaded chair, said, "How do you do, Mr. Ames?" waved his hand at another chair, and sat down again. "You're from Australia?"

"Got in this morning."

"You're a business associate of Uncle Tim's?"

Spade smiled and shook his head. "Hardly that, but I've some information I think he ought to have—quick."

Wallace Binnett looked thoughtfully at the floor, then up at Spade. "I'll do my best to persuade him to see you, Mr. Ames, but, frankly, I don't know."

Spade seemed mildly surprised. "Why?"

Binnett shrugged. "He's peculiar sometimes. Understand, his mind seems perfectly all right, but he has the testiness and eccentricity of an old man in ill health and—well—at times he can be difficult."

Spade asked slowly: "He's already refused to see me?"

"Yes."

Spade rose from his chair. His blond satan's face was expressionless.

Binnett raised a hand quickly. "Wait, wait," he said. "I'll do what I can to make him change his mind. Perhaps if—" His dark eyes suddenly became wary. "You're not simply trying to sell him something, are you?"

"No."

The wary gleam went out of Binnett's eyes. "Well, then, I think I can—"

A young woman came in crying angrily, "Wally, that old fool has—" She broke off with a hand to her breast when she saw Spade.

Spade and Binnett had risen together. Binnett said suavely: "Joyce, this is Mr. Ames. My sister-in-law, Joyce Court."

Spade bowed.

Joyce Court uttered a short, embarrassed laugh and said: "Please excuse my whirlwind entrance." She was a tall, blue-eyed, dark woman of twenty-four or -five with good shoulders and a strong, slim body. Her features made up in warmth what they lacked in regularity. She wore wide-legged blue satin pajamas.

Binnett smiled good-naturedly at her and asked: "Now what's all the excitement?"

Anger darkened her eyes again and she started to speak. Then she looked at Spade and said: "But we shouldn't bore Mr. Ames with our stupid domestic affairs. If—" She hesitated.

Spade bowed again. "Sure," he said, "certainly."

"I won't be a minute," Binnett promised, and left the room with her.

Spade went to open the doorway through which they had vanished and, standing just inside, listened. Their footsteps became inaudible. Nothing else could be heard. Spade was standing there—his yellow-gray eyes dreamy—when he heard the scream. It was a woman's scream, high and shrill with terror. Spade was through the doorway when he heard the shot. It was a pistol shot, magnified, reverberated by walls and ceilings.

Twenty feet from the doorway Spade found a staircase, and went up it three steps at a time. He turned to the left. Halfway down the hallway a woman lay on her back on the floor.

Wallace Binnett knelt beside her, fondling one of her hands desperately, crying in a low, beseeching voice: "Darling, Molly, darling!"

Joyce Court stood behind him and wrung her hands while tears streaked her cheeks.

The woman on the floor resembled Joyce Court but was older, and her face had a hardness the younger one's had not.

"She's dead, she's been killed," Wallace Binnett said incredulously, raising his white face toward Spade. When Binnett moved his head Spade could see the round hole in the woman's tan dress over her heart and the dark stain which was rapidly spreading below it.

Spade touched Joyce Court's arm. "Police, emergency hospital— phone," he said. As she ran toward the stairs he addressed Wallace Binnett: "Who did—"

A voice groaned feebly behind Spade.

He turned swiftly. Through an open doorway he could see an old man in white pajamas lying sprawled across a rumpled bed. His head, a shoulder, an arm dangled over the edge of the bed. His other hand held his throat tightly. He groaned again and his eyelids twitched, but did not open.

Spade lifted the old man's head and shoulders and put them up on the pillows. The old man groaned again and took his hand from his throat. His throat was red with half a dozen bruises. He was a gaunt man with a seamed face that probably exaggerated his age.

A glass of water was on a table beside the bed. Spade put water on the old man's face and, when the old man's eyes twitched again, leaned down and growled softly: "Who did it?"

The twitching eyelids went up far enough to show a narrow strip of bloodshot gray eyes. The old man spoke painfully, putting a hand to his throat again: "A man—he—" He coughed.

Spade made an impatient grimace. His lips almost touched the old man's ear. "Where'd he go?" His voice was urgent.

A gaunt hand moved weakly to indicate the rear of the house and fell back on the bed.

The butler and two frightened female servants had joined Wallace Binnett beside the dead woman in the hallway.

"Who did it?" Spade asked them.

They stared at him blankly.

"Somebody look after the old man," he growled, and went down the hallway.

At the end of the hallway was a rear staircase. He descended two flights and went through a pantry into the kitchen. He saw nobody. The kitchen door was shut but, when he tried it, not locked. He crossed a narrow back yard to a gate that was shut, not locked. He opened the gate. There was nobody in the narrow alley behind it.

He sighed, shut the gate, and returned to the house.

SPADE SAT COMFORTABLY slack in a deep leather chair in a room that ran across the front second story of Wallace Binnett's house. There were shelves of books and the lights were on. The window showed outer darkness weakly diluted by a distant street lamp. Facing Spade, Detective-Sergeant Polhaus—a big, carelessly shaven, florid man in dark clothes that needed pressing—was sprawled in another leather chair; Lieutenant Dundy—smaller, compactly built, square-faced—stood with legs apart, head thrust a little forward, in the center of the room.

Spade was saying: ". . . and the doctor would only let me talk to the old man a couple of minutes. We can try it again when he's rested a little, but it doesn't look like he knows much. He was catching a nap and he woke up with somebody's hands on his throat dragging him around the bed. The best he got was a one-eyed look at the fellow choking him. A big fellow, he says, with a soft hat pulled down over his eyes, dark, needing a shave. Sounds like Tom." Spade nodded at Polhaus.

The detective-sergeant chuckled, but Dundy said, "Go on," curtly.

Spade grinned and went on: "He's pretty far gone when he hears Mrs. Binnett scream at the door. The hands go away from his throat and he hears the shot and just before passing out he gets a flash of the big fellow heading for the rear of the house and Mrs. Binnett tumbling down on the hall floor. He says he never saw the big fellow before."

"What size gun was it?" Dundy asked.

"Thirty-eight. Well, nobody in the house is much more help. Wallace and his sister-in-law, Joyce, were in her room, so they say, and didn't see anything but the dead woman when they ran out, though they think they heard something that could've been somebody running downstairs—the back stairs.

"The butler—his name's Jarboe—was in here when he heard the scream and shot, so he says. Irene Kelly, the maid, was down on the ground floor, so she says. The cook, Margaret Finn, was in her room—third floor back—and didn't even hear anything, so she says. She's deaf as a post, so everybody else says. The back door and gate were unlocked, but are supposed to be kept locked, so everybody says. Nobody says they were in or around the kitchen or yard at the time." Spade spread his hands in a gesture of finality. "That's the crop."

Dundy shook his head. "Not exactly," he said. "How come you were here?"

Spade's face brightened. "Maybe my client killed her," he said. "He's Wallace's cousin, Ira Binnett. Know him?"

Dundy shook his head. His blue eyes were hard and suspicious.

"He's a San Francisco lawyer," Spade said, "respectable and all that. A couple of days ago he came to me with a story about his uncle Timothy, a miserly old skinflint, lousy with money and pretty well broken up by hard living. He was the black sheep of the family. None of them had heard of him for years. But six or eight months ago he showed up in pretty bad shape every way except financially—he seems to have taken a lot of money out of Australia—wanting to spend his last days with his only living relatives, his nephews Wallace and Ira.

"That was all right with them. 'Only living relatives' meant 'only heirs' in their language. But by and by the nephews began to think it was better to be an heir than to be one of a couple of heirs—twice as good, in fact—and started fiddling for the inside track with the old man. At least, that's what Ira told me about Wallace, and I wouldn't be surprised if Wallace would say the same thing about Ira, though Wallace seems to be the harder up of the two. Anyhow, the nephews fell out, and then Uncle Tim, who had been staying at Ira's, came over here. That was a couple of months ago, and Ira hasn't seen Uncle Tim since, and hasn't been able to get in touch with him by phone or mail.

"That's what he wanted a private detective about. He didn't think Uncle Tim would come to any harm here—oh, no, he went to a lot of trouble to make that clear—but he thought maybe undue pressure was being brought to bear on the old boy, or he was being hornswoggled somehow, and at least being told lies about his loving nephew Ira. He wanted to know what was what. I waited until to-day, when a boat from Australia docked, and came up here as a Mr. Ames with some important information for Uncle Tim about his properties down there. All I wanted was fifteen minutes alone with him." Spade frowned thoughtfully. "Well, I didn't get them. Wallace told me the old man refused to see me. I don't know."

Suspicion had deepened in Dundy's cold blue eyes. "And where is this Ira Binnett now?" he asked.

Spade's yellow-gray eyes were as guileless as his voice. "I wish I knew. I phoned his house and office and left word for him to come right over, but I'm afraid—"

Knuckles knocked sharply twice on the other side of the room's one door. The three men in the room turned to face the door.

Dundy called, "Come in."

The door was opened by a sunburned blond policeman whose left hand held the right wrist of a plump man of forty or forty-five in well-fitting gray clothes. The policeman pushed the plump man into the room. "Found him monkeying with the kitchen door," he said.

Spade looked up and said: "Ah!" His tone expressed satisfaction. "Mr. Ira Binnett, Lieutenant Dundy, Sergeant Polhaus."

Ira Binnett said rapidly: "Mr. Spade, will you tell this man that—"

Dundy addressed the policeman: "All right. Good work. You can leave him."

The policeman moved a hand vaguely toward his cap and went away.

Dundy glowered at Ira Binnett and demanded, "Well?"

Binnett looked from Dundy to Spade. "Has something—"

Spade said: "Better tell him why you were at the back door instead of the front."

Ira Binnett suddenly blushed. He cleared his throat in embarrassment. He said: "I—uh—I should explain. It wasn't my fault, of course, but when Jarboe—he's the butler—phoned me that Uncle Tim wanted to see me he told me he'd leave the kitchen door unlocked, so Wallace wouldn't have to know I'd—"

"What'd he want to see you about?" Dundy asked.

"I don't know. He didn't say. He said it was very important."

"Didn't you get my message?" Spade asked.

Ira Binnett's eyes widened. "No. What was it? Has anything happened? What is—"

Spade was moving toward the door. "Go ahead," he said to Dundy. "I'll be right back."

He shut the door carefully behind him and went up to the third floor.

The butler Jarboe was on his knees at Timothy Binnett's door with an eye to the keyhole. On the floor beside him was a tray holding an egg in an egg-cup, toast, a pot of coffee, china, silver, and a napkin.

Spade said: "Your toast's going to get cold."

Jarboe, scrambling to his feet, almost upsetting the coffeepot in his haste, his face red and sheepish, stammered: "I—er—beg your pardon, sir. I wanted to make sure Mr. Timothy was awake before I took this in." He picked up the tray. "I didn't want to disturb his rest if—"

Spade, who had reached the door, said, "Sure, sure," and bent over to put his eye to the keyhole. When he straightened up he said in a mildly complaining tone: "You can't see the bed—only a chair and part of the window."

The butler replied quickly: "Yes, sir, I found that out."

Spade laughed.

The butler coughed, seemed about to say something, but did not. He hesitated, then knocked lightly on the door.

A tired voice said, "Come in."

Spade asked quickly in a low voice: "Where's Miss Court?"

"In her room, I think, sir, the second door on the left," the butler said.

The tired voice inside the room said petulantly: "Well, come on in."

The butler opened the door and went in. Through the door, before the butler shut it, Spade caught a glimpse of Timothy Binnett propped up on pillows in his bed.

Spade went to the second door on the left and knocked. The door was opened almost immediately by Joyce Court. She stood in the doorway, not smiling, not speaking.

He said: "Miss Court, when you came into the room where I was with your brother-in-law you said, 'Wally, that old fool has—' Meaning Timothy?"

She stared at Spade for a moment. Then: "Yes."

"Mind telling me what the rest of the sentence would have been?"

She said slowly: "I don't know who you really are or why you ask, but I don't mind telling you. It would have been 'sent for Ira.' Jarboe had just told me."

"Thanks."

She shut the door before he had turned away.

He returned to Timothy Binnett's door and knocked on it.

"Who is it now?" the old man's voice demanded.

Spade opened the door. The old man was sitting up in bed.

Spade said: "This Jarboe was peeping through your keyhole a few minutes ago," and returned to the library.

Ira Binnett, seated in the chair Spade had occupied, was saying to Dundy and Polhaus: "And Wallace got caught in the crash, like most of us, but he seems to have juggled accounts trying to save himself. He was expelled from the Stock Exchange."

Dundy waved a hand to indicate the room and its furnishings. "Pretty classy layout for a man that's busted."

"His wife has some money," Ira Binnett said, "and he always lived beyond his means."

Dundy scowled at Binnett. "And you really think he and his missus weren't on good terms?"

"I don't think it," Binnett replied evenly. "I know it."

Dundy nodded. "And you know he's got a yen for the sister-in-law, this Court?"

"I don't know that. But I've heard plenty of gossip to the same effect."

Dundy made a growling noise in his throat, then asked sharply: "How does the old man's will read?"

"I don't know. I don't know whether he's made one." He addressed Spade, now earnestly: "I've told everything I know, every single thing."

Dundy said, "It's not enough." He jerked a thumb at the door. "Show him where to wait, Tom, and let's have the widower in again."

Big Polhaus said, "Right," went out with Ira Binnett, and returned with Wallace Binnett, whose face was hard and pale.

Dundy asked: "Has your uncle made a will?"

"I don't know," Binnett replied.

Spade put the next question, softly: "Did your wife?"

Binnett's mouth tightened in a mirthless smile. He spoke deliberately: "I'm going to say some things I'd rather not have to say. My wife, properly, had no money. When I got into financial trouble some time ago I made some property over to her, to save it. She turned it into money without my knowing about it till afterward. She paid our bills—our living expenses—out of it, but she refused to return it to me and she assured me that in no event—whether she lived or died or we stayed together or were divorced—would I ever be able to get hold of a penny of it. I believed her, and still do."

"You wanted a divorce?" Dundy asked.

"Yes."

"Why?"

"It wasn't a happy marriage."

"Joyce Court?"

Binnett's face flushed. He said stiffly: "I admire Joyce Court tremendously, but I'd've wanted a divorce anyway."

Spade said: "And you're sure—still absolutely sure—you don't know anybody who fits your uncle's description of the man who choked him?"

"Absolutely sure."

The sound of the doorbell ringing came faintly into the room.

Dundy said sourly, "That'll do."

Binnett went out.

Polhaus said: "That guy's as wrong as they make them. And—"

From below came the heavy report of a pistol fired indoors.

The lights went out.

In darkness the three detectives collided with one another going through the doorway into the dark hall. Spade reached the stairs first. There was a clatter of footsteps below him, but nothing could be seen until he reached a bend in the stairs. Then enough light came from the street through the open front door to show the dark figure of a man standing with his back to the open door.

A flashlight clicked in Dundy's hand—he was at Spade's heels—and threw a glaring white beam of light on the man's face. He was Ira Binnett. He blinked in the light and pointed at something on the floor in front of him.

Dundy turned the beam of his light down on the floor. Jarboe lay there on his face, bleeding from a bullet-hole in the back of his head.

Spade grunted softly.

Tom Polhaus came blundering down the stairs, Wallace Binnett close behind him. Joyce Court's frightened voice came from farther up: "Oh, what's happened? Wally, what's happened?"

"Where's the light switch?" Dundy barked.

"Inside the cellar door, under these stairs," Wallace Binnett said. "What is it?"

Polhaus pushed past Binnett toward the cellar door.

Spade made an inarticulate sound in his throat and, pushing Wallace Binnett aside, sprang up the stairs. He brushed past Joyce Court and went on, heedless of her startled scream. He was halfway up the stairs to the third floor when the pistol went off up there.

He ran to Timothy Binnett's door. The door was open. He went in.

Something hard and angular struck him above his right ear, knocking him across the room, bringing him down on one knee. Something thumped and clattered on the floor just outside the door.

The lights came on.

On the floor, in the center of the room, Timothy Binnett lay on his back bleeding from a bullet wound in his left forearm. His pajama jacket was torn. His eyes were shut.

Spade stood up and put a hand to his head. He scowled at the old man on the floor, at the room, at the black automatic pistol lying on the hallway floor. He said: "Come on, you old cut-throat. Get up and sit on a chair and I'll see if I can stop that bleeding till the doctor gets here."

The man on the floor did not move.

There were footsteps in the hallway and Dundy came in, followed by the two younger Binnetts. Dundy's face was dark and furious. "Kitchen door wide open," he said in a choked voice. "They run in and out like—"

"Forget it," Spade said. "Uncle Tim is our meat." He paid no attention to Wallace Binnett's gasp, to the incredulous looks on Dundy's and Ira Binnett's faces. "Come on, get up," he said to the old man on the floor, "and tell us what it was the butler saw when he peeped through the keyhole."

The old man did not stir.

"He killed the butler because I told him the butler had peeped," Spade explained to Dundy. "I peeped, too, but didn't see anything except that chair and the window, though we'd made enough racket by then to scare him back to bed. Suppose you take the chair apart while I go over the window." He went to the window and began to examine it carefully. He shook his head, put a hand out behind him, and said: "Give me the flashlight."

Dundy put the flashlight in his hand.

Spade raised the window and leaned out, turning the light on the outside of the building. Presently he grunted and put his other hand out, tugging at a brick a little below the sill. Presently the brick came loose. He put it on the window-sill and stuck his hand into the hole its removal had made. Out of the opening, one at a time, he brought an empty black pistol holster, a partially filled box of cartridges, and an unsealed manila envelope.

Holding these things in his hands, he turned to face the others. Joyce Court came in with a basin of water and a roll of gauze and knelt beside Timothy Binnett. Spade put the holster and cartridges on a table and opened the manila envelope. Inside were two sheets of paper, covered on both sides with boldly penciled writing. Spade read a paragraph to himself, suddenly laughed, and began at the beginning again, reading aloud:

"'I, Timothy Kieran Binnett, being sound of mind and body, do declare this to be my last will and testament. To my dear nephews, Ira Binnett and Wallace Bourke Binnett, in recognition of the loving kindness with which they have received me into their homes and attended my declining years, I give and bequeath, share and share alike, all my worldly possessions of whatever kind, to wit, my carcass and the clothes I stand in.

"'I bequeath them, furthermore, the expense of my funeral and these memories: First, the memory of their credulity in believing that the fifteen years I spent in Sing Sing were spent in Australia; second, the memory of their optimism in supposing that those fifteen years had brought me great wealth, and that if I lived on them, borrowed from them, and never spent any of my own money, it was because I was a miser whose hoard they would inherit; and not because I had no money except what I shook them down for; third, for their hopefulness in thinking that I would leave either of them anything if I had it; and, lastly, because their painful lack of any decent sense of humor will keep them from ever seeing how funny this has all been. Signed and sealed this—'"

Spade looked up to say: "There is no date, but it's signed Timothy Kieran Binnett with flourishes."

Ira Binnett was purple with anger, Wallace's face was ghastly in its pallor and his whole body was trembling. Joyce Court had stopped working on Timothy Binnett's arm.

The old man sat up and opened his eyes. He looked at his nephews and began to laugh. There was in his laughter neither hysteria nor madness: it was sane, hearty laughter, and subsided slowly.

Spade said: "All right, now you've had your fun. Let's talk about the killings."

"I know nothing more about the first one than I've told you," the old man said, "and this one's not a killing, since I'm only—"

Wallace Binnett, still trembling violently, said painfully through his teeth: "That's a lie. You killed Molly. Joyce and I came out of her room when we heard Molly scream, and heard the shot and saw her fall out of your room, and nobody came out afterward."

The old man said calmly: "Well, I'll tell you: it was an accident. They told me there was a fellow from Australia here to see me about some of my properties there. I knew there was something funny about that some-where"—he grinned—"not ever having been there. I didn't know whether one of my dear nephews was getting suspicious and putting up a game on me or what, but I knew that if Wally wasn't in on it he'd certainly try to pump the gentleman from Australia about me and maybe I'd lose one of my free boarding houses." He chuckled.

"So I figured I'd get in touch with Ira so I could go back to his house if things worked out bad here, and I'd try to get rid of this Australian. Wally's always thought I'm half-cracked"—he leered at his nephew—"and's afraid they'll lug me off to a madhouse before I could make a will in his favor, or they'll break it if I do. You see, he's got a pretty bad reputation, what with that Stock Exchange trouble and all, and he knows no court would appoint him to handle my affairs if I went screwy—not as long as I've got another nephew"—he turned his leer on Ira—"who's a respectable lawyer. So now

I know that rather than have me kick up a row that might wind me up in the madhouse, he'll chase this visitor, and I put on a show for Molly, who happened to be the nearest one to hand. She took it too seriously, though.

"I had a gun and I did a lot of raving about being spied on by my enemies in Australia and that I was going down and shoot this fellow. But she got too excited and tried to take the gun away from me, and the first thing I knew it had gone off, and I had to make these marks on my neck and think up that story about the big dark man." He looked contemptuously at Wallace. "I didn't know he was covering me up. Little as I thought of him, I never thought he'd be low enough to cover up his wife's murderer—even if he didn't like her—just for the sake of money."

Spade said: "Never mind that. Now about the butler?"

"I don't know anything about the butler," the old man replied, looking at Spade with steady eyes.

Spade said: "You had to kill him quick, before he had time to do or say anything. So you slip down the back stairs, open the kitchen door to fool people, go to the front door, ring the bell, shut the door, and hide in the shadow of the cellar door under the front steps. When Jarboe answered the doorbell you shot him—the hole was in the back of his head—pulled the light switch just inside the cellar door, and ducked up the back stairs in the dark and shot yourself carefully in the arm. I got up there too soon for you; so you smacked me with the gun, chucked it through the door, and spread yourself on the floor while I was shaking pinwheels out of my noodle."

The old man sniffed again. "You're just—"

"Stop it," Spade said patiently. "Don't let's argue. The first killing was an accident—all right. The second couldn't be. And it ought to be easy to show that both bullets, and the one in your arm, were fired from the same gun. What difference does it make which killing we can prove first-degree murder on? They can only hang you once." He smiled pleasantly. "And they will."

A MAN NAMED
THIN

Papa was, though I may be deemed an undutiful son for saying it, in an abominable mood. His chin protruded across the desk at me in a fashion that almost justified the epithet of brutal which had once been applied to it by an unfriendly journalist; and his mustache seemed to bristle with choler of its own, though this was merely the impression I received. It would be preposterous to assume actual change in the mustache which, whatever Papa's humor, was always somewhat irregularly salient.

"So you're still fooling with this damned nonsense of yours?"

On Papa's desk, under one of his hands, lay a letter which, its odd shape and color informed me immediately, was from the editor of *The Jongleur* to whom, a few days before, I had sent a sonnet.

"If you mean my writing," I replied respectfully, but none the less staunchly; for my thirtieth birthday being some months past, I considered myself entitled to some liberty of purpose, even though that purpose might be distasteful to Papa. "If you mean my writing, Papa, I assure you I am not fooling, but am completely in earnest."

"But why in"—if now and then I garble Papa's remarks in reporting them, it is not, I beg you to believe, because he is addicted to incoherencies, but simply because he frequently saw fit to sacrifice the amenities of speech to what he considered a vigor of expression—"do you have to pick on poetry? Aren't there plenty of other things to write about? Why, Robin, you could write some good serious articles about our work, articles that would tell the public the truth about it and at the same time give us some advertising."

"One writes what one is impelled to write," I began not too hopefully, for this was by no means the first time I had begun thus. "The creative impulse is not to be coerced into—"

"Florence!"

I do not like to say Papa bellowed, but the milder synonyms are not entirely adequate to express the volume of sound he put into our stenographer's given name by which he insisted on addressing her.

Miss Queenan appeared at the door—an unfamiliar Miss Queenan who did not advance to Papa's desk with that romping mixture of flippancy and self-assurance which the press, with its propensity to exaggerate, has persuaded our generation to expect; instead, she stood there awaiting Papa's attention.

"After this, Florence, will you see that my desk is not cluttered up with correspondence dealing with my son's Mother Goose rhymes!"

"Yes, Mr. Thin," she replied in a voice surprisingly meek for someone accustomed to speak to Papa as if she were a member of his family.

"My dear Papa," I endeavored to remonstrate when Miss Queenan had retired, "I really think—"

"Don't dear Papa me! And you don't think! Nobody that thought could be such a . . ."

It would serve no purpose to repeat Papa's words in detail. They were, for the most part, quite unreasonable, and not even my deep-seated sense of filial propriety could enable me to keep my face from showing some of the resentment I felt; but I heard him through in silence and when he had underscored his last sentence by thrusting *The Jongleur's* letter at me, I withdrew to my office.

The letter, which had come to Papa's desk through the carelessness of the editor in omitting the Jr. from my name, had to do with the sonnet I have already mentioned—a sonnet entitled "Fictitious Tears." The editor's opinion was that its concluding couplet, which he quoted in his letter, was not, as he politely put it, up to my usual standard, and he requested that I rewrite it, adjusting it more exactly to the tone of the previous lines, for which it was, he thought, a trifle too serious.

> *And glisten there no less incongruously*
> *Than Christmas balls on deadly upas tree.*

I reminded myself, as I took my rhyming dictionary from behind Gross's *Kriminal Psychologie* where, in the interest of peace, I habitually concealed it, that I had not been especially pleased with those two lines; but after repeated trials I had been unable to find more suitable ones. Now, as I heard the noon whistles, I brought out my carbon copy of the sonnet and determined to devote the quiet of the luncheon hour to the creation of another simile that would express incongruity in a lighter vein.

To that task I addressed myself, submerging my consciousness to such an extent that when I heard Papa's voice calling "Robin!" with a force that fairly agitated the three intervening partitions, I roused as if from sleep, with a suspicion that the first call I had heard had not been the first Papa had uttered. This suspicion was confirmed when, putting away paper and books, I hastened into Papa's presence.

"Too busy listening to the little birdies twitter to hear me?" But this was mere perfunctory gruffness; his eyes were quite jovial so that in a measure I was prepared for his next words. "Barnable's stuck up. Get to it."

The Barnable Jewelry company's store was six blocks from our offices, and a convenient street car conveyed me there before Papa's brief order was five minutes old. The store, a small one, occupied a portion of the ground floor of the Bulwer Building, on the north side of O'Farrell Street, between Powell and Stockton Streets. The store's neighbors on the ground floor of the same building were, going east toward Stockton Street, a haberdasher (in whose window, by the way, I noticed an intriguing lavender dressing robe), a barber shop, and a tobacconist's; and going westward toward Powell Street, the main entrance and lobby of the Bulwer Building, a prescription druggist, a hatter, and a lunchroom.

At the jeweler's door a uniformed policeman was busily engaged in preventing a curious crowd, most of whom presumably out on their luncheon hours, from either blocking the sidewalk or entering the store. Passing through this throng, I nodded to the policeman, not that I was personally acquainted with him but because experience had taught me that a friendly nod will often forestall questions, and went into the store.

Detective-Sergeant Hooley and Detective Strong of the Police Department were in the store. In one hand the former held a dark gray cap and a small automatic pistol which did not seem to belong to any of the people to whom the detectives were talking: Mr. Barnable, Mr. Barnable's assistant, and two men and a woman unknown to me.

"Good morning, gentlemen," I addressed the detectives. "May I participate in the inquiry?"

"Ah, Mr. Thin!"

Sergeant Hooley was a large man whose large mouth did nothing to shape his words beyond parting to emit them, so that they issued somewhat slovenly from a formless opening in his florid face. His face held now, as when I had engaged him in conversation heretofore, an elusively derisive expression—as if, with intent to annoy, he pretended to find in me, in my least word or act, something amusing. The same impulse was noticeable in the stressed mister with which he invariably prefixed my name, notwithstanding that he called Papa Bob, a familiarity I was quite willing to be spared.

"As I was telling the boys, participating is just exactly what we need." Sergeant Hooley exercised his rather heavy wit. "Some dishonest thief has been robbing the joint. We're about through inquiring, but you look like a fellow that can keep a secret, so I don't mind letting you in on the dirt, as we used to say at dear old Harvard."

I am not privy to the quirk in Sergeant Hooley's mind which makes attendance at this particular university constitute, for him, a humorous situation; nor can I perceive why he should find so much pleasure in mentioning that famous seat of learning to me who, as I have often taken the trouble to explain to him, attended an altogether different university.

"What seems to have happened," he went on, "is that some bird come in here all by himself, put Mr. Barnable and his help under the gun, took 'em for what was in the safe, and blew out, trampling over some folks that got in his way. He then beat it up to Powell Street, jumped into a car, and what more do you want to know?"

"At what time did this occur?"

"Right after twelve o'clock, Mr. Thin—not more than a couple of minutes after, if that many," said Mr. Barnable, who had circled the others to reach my side. His brown eyes were round with excitement in his round brown face, but not especially melancholy, since he was insured against theft in the company on whose behalf I was now acting.

"He makes Julius and me lay down on the floor behind the counter while he robs the safe, and then he backs out. I tell Julius to get up and see if he's gone, but just then he shoots at me." Mr. Barnable pointed a spatulate finger at a small hole in the rear wall, near the ceiling. "So I didn't let Julius get up till I was sure he'd gone. Then I phoned the police and your office."

"Was anyone else, anyone besides you and Julius, in the store when the robber entered?"

"No. We hadn't had anyone in for maybe fifteen minutes."

"Would you be able to identify the robber if you were to see him again, Mr. Barnable?"

"Would I? Say, Mr. Thin, would Carpentier know Dempsey?"

This counter-question, which seemed utterly irrelevant, was intended, I assumed, as an affirmative.

"Kindly describe him for me, Mr. Barnable."

"He was maybe forty years old and tough-looking, a fellow just about your size and complexion." I am, in height and weight, of average size, and my complexion might best be described as medium, so there was nothing in any way peculiar about my having these points of resemblance to the robber; still I felt that the jeweler had been rather tactless in pointing them out. "His mouth was kind of pushed in, without much lips, and his nose was long and flattish, and he had a scar on one side of his face. A real tough-looking fellow!"

"Will you describe the scar in greater detail, Mr. Barnable?"

"It was back on his cheek, close to his ear, and ran all the way down from under his cap to his jawbone."

"Which cheek, Mr. Barnable?"

"The left," he said tentatively, looking at Julius, his sharp-featured young assistant. When Julius nodded, the jeweler repeated, with certainty, "The left."

"How was he dressed, Mr. Barnable?"

"A blue suit and that cap the sergeant has got. I didn't notice anything else."

"His eyes and hair, Mr. Barnable?"

"Didn't notice."

"Exactly what did he take, Mr. Barnable?"

"I haven't had time to check up yet, but he took all the unset stones that were in the safe—mostly diamonds. He must have got fifty thousand dollars' worth if he got a nickel!"

I permitted a faint smile to show on my lips while I looked coldly at the jeweler.

"In the event that we fail to recover the stones, Mr. Barnable, you are aware that the insurance company will require proof of the purchase of every missing item."

He fidgeted, screwing his round face up earnestly.

"Well, anyways, he got twenty-five thousand dollars' worth, if it's the last thing I ever say in this world, Mr. Thin, on my word of honor as a gentleman."

"Did he take anything besides the unset stones, Mr. Barnable?"

"Those and some money that was in the safe—about two hundred dollars."

"Will you please draw up a list immediately, Mr. Barnable, with as accurate a description of each missing item as possible. Now what evidence have we, Sergeant Hooley, of the robber's subsequent actions?"

"Well, first thing, he subsequently bumped into Mrs. Dolan as he was making his getaway. Seems she was—"

"Mrs. Dolan has an account here," the jeweler called from the rear of the store when he and Julius had gone to comply with my request. Sergeant Hooley jerked his thumb at the woman who stood on my left.

She was a woman of fewer years than forty, with humorous brown eyes set in a healthily pink face. Her clothes, while neat, were by no means new or stylish, and her whole appearance was such as to cause the adjective "capable" to come into one's mind, an adjective further justified by the crisp freshness of the lettuce and celery protruding from the top of the shopping-bag in her arms.

"Mrs. Dolan is manager of an apartment building on Ellis Street," the jeweler concluded his introduction, while the woman and I exchanged smiling nods.

"Thank you, Mr. Barnable. Proceed, Sergeant Hooley."

"Thank *you*, Mr. Thin. Seems she was coming in to make a payment on her watch, and just as she put a foot inside the door, this stick-up backed into her, both of them taking a tumble. Mr. Knight, here, saw the mix-up, ran in, knocked the thug loose from his cap and gun, and chased him up the street."

One of the men present laughed deprecatorily past an upraised sun-burned hand which held a pair of gloves. He was a weather-browned man of athletic structure, tall and broad-shouldered, and dressed in loose tweeds.

"My part wasn't as heroic as it sounds," he protested. "I was getting out of my car, intending to go across to the Orpheum for tickets, when I saw this lady and the man collide. Crossing the sidewalk to help her up, nothing was further from my mind than that the man was a bandit. When I finally saw his gun he was actually on the point of shooting at me. I had to hit him, and luckily succeeded in doing so just as he pulled the trigger. When I recovered from my surprise I saw he had dropped his gun and run up the street, so I set out after him. But it was too late. He was gone."

"Thank you, Mr. Knight. Now, Sergeant Hooley, you say the bandit escaped in a car?"

"Thank you, Mr. Thin," he said idiotically, "I did. Mr. Glenn here saw him."

"I was standing on the corner," said Mr. Glenn, a plump man with what might be called the air of a successful salesman.

"Pardon me, Mr. Glenn, what corner?"

"The corner of Powell and O'Farrell," he said, quite as if I should have known it without being told. "The northeast corner, if you want it exactly, close to the building line. This bandit came up the street and got into a coupé that was driving up Powell Street. I didn't pay much attention to him. If I heard the shot I took it for an automobile noise. I wouldn't have noticed the man if he hadn't been bare-headed, but he was the man Mr. Barnable described—scar, pushed-in mouth, and all."

"Do you know the make or license number of the car he entered, Mr. Glenn?"

"No, I don't. It was a black coupé, and that's all I know. I think it came from the direction of Market Street. A man was driving it, I believe, but I didn't notice whether he was young or old or anything about him."

"Did the bandit seem excited, Mr. Glenn? Did he look back?"

"No, he was as cool as you please, didn't even seem in a hurry. He just walked up the street and got into the coupé, not looking to right or left."

"Thank you, Mr. Glenn. Now can anyone amplify or amend Mr. Barnable's description of the bandit?"

"His hair was gray," Mr. Glenn said, "iron-gray."

Mrs. Dolan and Mr. Knight concurred in this, the former adding, "I think he was older than Mr. Barnable said—closer to fifty than to forty—and his teeth were brown and decayed in front."

"They were, now that you mention it," Mr. Knight agreed.

"Is there any other light on the matter, Sergeant Hooley?"

"Not a twinkle. The shotgun cars are out after the coupé, and I reckon when the papers get out we'll be hearing from more people who saw things, but you know how they are."

I did indeed. One of the most lamentable features of criminal detection is the amount of time and energy wasted investigating information supplied by people who, through sheer perversity, stupidity, or excessive imagination, insist on connecting everything they have chanced to see with whatever crime happens to be most prominent in the day's news.

Sergeant Hooley, whatever the defects of his humor, was an excellent actor: his face was bland and guileless and his voice did not vary in the least from the casual as he said, "Unless Mr. Thin has some more questions, you folks might as well run along. I have your address and can get hold of you if I need you again."

I hesitated, but the fundamental principle that Papa had instilled in me during the ten years of my service under him—the necessity of never taking anything for granted—impelled me to say, "Just a moment," and to lead Sergeant Hooley out of the others' hearing.

"You have made your arrangements, Sergeant Hooley?"

"What arrangements?"

I smiled, realizing that the police detectives were trying to conceal their knowledge from me. My immediate temptation was, naturally enough, to reciprocate in kind; but whatever the advantages of working independently on any one operation, in the long run a private detective is wiser in cooperating with the police than in competing with them.

"Really," I said, "you must harbor a poor opinion of my ability if you think I have not also taken cognizance of the fact that if Glenn were standing where he said he was standing, and if, as he says, the bandit did not turn his head, then he could not have seen the scar on the bandit's left cheek."

Despite his evident discomfiture, Sergeant Hooley acknowledged defeat without resentment.

"I might of known you'd tumble to that," he admitted, rubbing his chin with a reflective thumb. "Well, I reckon we might as well take him along now as later, unless you've got some other notion in your head."

Consulting my watch, I saw that it was now twenty-four minutes past noon: my investigation had thus far, thanks to the police detectives' having assembled all the witnesses, consumed only ten or twelve minutes.

"If Glenn were stationed at Powell Street to mislead us," I suggested, "then isn't it quite likely that the bandit did not escape in that direction at all? It occurs to me that there is a barber shop two doors from here in the opposite direction—toward Stockton Street. That barber shop, which I assume has a door opening into the Bulwer Building, as barber shops similarly located invariably do, may have served as a passageway through which the bandit could have got quickly off the street. In any event, I consider it a possibility that we should investigate."

"The barber shop it is!" Sergeant Hooley spoke to his colleague, "Wait here with these folks till we're back, Strong. We won't be long."

"Right," Detective Strong replied.

In the street we found fewer curious spectators than before.

"Might as well go inside, Tim," Sergeant Hooley said to the policeman in front as we passed him on our way to the barber shop.

The barber shop was about the same size as the jewelry store. Five of its six chairs were filled when we went in, the vacant one being that nearest the front window. Behind it stood a short swarthy man who smiled at us and said, "Next," as is the custom of barbers.

Approaching, I tendered him one of my cards, from perusal of which he looked up at me with bright interest that faded at once into rather infantile disappointment. I was not unfamiliar with this phenomenon: there are a surprising number of people who, on learning that my name is Thin, are disappointed in not finding me an emaciated skeleton or, what would doubtless be even more pleasing, grossly fat.

"You know, I assume, that Barnable's store has been robbed?"

"Sure! It's getting tough the way those babies knock 'em over in broad daylight!"

"Did you by any chance hear the report of the pistol?"

"Sure! I was shaving a fellow, Mr. Thorne, the real estate man. He always waits for me no matter how many of the other barbers are loafing. He says— Anyhow, I heard the shot and went to the door to look up there, but I couldn't keep Mr. Thorne waiting, you understand, so I didn't go up there myself."

"Did you see anyone who might have been the bandit?"

"No. Those fellows move quick, and at lunchtime, when the street's full of people, I guess he wouldn't have much trouble losing himself. It's funny the way—"

In view of the necessity of economizing on time, I risked the imputation of discourtesy by interrupting the barber's not very pertinent comments.

"Did any man pass through here, going from the street into the Bulwer Building, immediately after you heard the shot?"

"Not that I remember, though lots of men use this shop as a kind of short cut from their offices to the street."

"But you remember no one passing through shortly after you heard the shot?"

"Not going in. Going out, maybe, because it was just about lunchtime."

I considered the men the barbers were working on in the five occupied chairs. Only two of these men wore blue trousers. Of the two, one had a dark mustache between an extremely outstanding nose and chin; the other's face, pink from the shaving it had just undergone, was neither conspicuously thin nor noticeably plump, nor was his profile remarkable for either ugliness or beauty. He was a man of about thirty-five years, with fair hair and, as I saw when he smiled at something his barber said, teeth that were quite attractive in their smooth whiteness.

"When did the man in the third chair"—the one I have just described—"come in?"

"If I ain't mistaken, just before the hold-up. He was just taking off his collar when I heard the shot. I'm pretty sure of it."

"Thank you," I said, turning away.

"A tough break," Sergeant Hooley muttered in my ear.

I looked sharply at him.

"You forget or, rather, you think I have forgotten, Knight's gloves."

Sergeant Hooley laughed shortly. "I forgot 'em for a fact. I must be getting absent-minded or something."

"I know of nothing to be gained by dissembling, Sergeant Hooley. The barber will be through with our man presently." Indeed, the man rose from the chair as I spoke. "I suggest that we simply ask him to accompany us to the jeweler's."

"Fair enough," the sergeant agreed.

We waited until our man had put on his collar and tie, his blue jacket, gray coat, and gray hat. Then, exhibiting his badge, Sergeant Hooley introduced himself to the man.

"I'm Sergeant Hooley. I want you to come up the street with me."

"What?"

The man's surprise was apparently real, as it may well have been.

Word for word, the sergeant repeated his statement.

"What for?"

I answered the man's question in as few words as possible.

"You are under arrest for robbing Barnable's jewelry store."

The man protested somewhat truculently that his name was Brennan, that he was well-known in Oakland, that someone would pay for this insult, and so on. For a minute it seemed that force would be necessary to convey our prisoner to Barnable's, and Sergeant Hooley had already taken a grip on the man's wrist when Brennan finally submitted, agreeing to accompany us quietly.

Glenn's face whitened and a pronounced tremor disturbed his legs as we brought Brennan into the jewelry store, where Mrs. Dolan and Messrs. Barnable, Julius, Knight, and Strong came eagerly to group themselves around us. The uniformed man the Sergeant had called Tim remained just within the street door.

"Suppose you make the speeches," Sergeant Hooley said, offering me the center of the stage.

"Is this your bandit, Mr. Barnable?" I began.

The jeweler's brown eyes achieved astonishing width.

"No, Mr. Thin!"

I turned to the prisoner.

"Remove your hat and coat, if you please. Sergeant Hooley, have you the cap that the bandit dropped? Thank you, Sergeant Hooley." To the prisoner, "Kindly put this cap on."

"I'm damned if I will!" he roared at me.

Sergeant Hooley held a hand out toward me.

"Give it to me. Here, Strong, take a hold on this baby while I cap him."

Brennan subsided. "All right! All right! I'll put it on!"

The cap was patently too large for him, but, experimenting, I found it could be adjusted in such a manner that its lack of fit was not too conspicuous, while its size served to conceal his hair and alter the contours of his head.

"Now will you please," I said, stepping back to look at him, "take out your teeth?"

This request precipitated an extraordinary amount of turmoil. The man Knight hurled himself on Detective Strong, while Glenn dashed toward the front door, and Brennan struck Sergeant Hooley viciously with his fist. Hastening to the front door to take the place of the policeman who had left it to struggle with Glenn, I saw that Mrs. Dolan had taken refuge in the corner, while Barnable and Julius avoided being drawn into the conflict only by exercising considerable agility.

Order was at length restored, with Detective Strong and the policeman handcuffing Knight and Glenn together, while Sergeant Hooley, sitting astride Brennan, waved aloft the false teeth he had taken from his mouth.

Beckoning to the policeman to resume his place at the door, I joined Sergeant Hooley, and we assisted Brennan to his feet, restoring the cap to his head. He presented a villainous appearance: his mouth, unfilled by teeth, sank in, thinning and aging his face, causing his nose to lengthen limply and flatly.

"Is this your baby?" Sergeant Hooley asked, shaking the prisoner at the jeweler.

"It is! It is! It's the same fellow!" Triumph merged with puzzlement on the jeweler's face. "Except he's got no scar," he added slowly.

"I think we shall find his scar in his pocket."

We did—in the form of a brown-stained handkerchief still damp and smelling of alcohol. Besides the handkerchief, there were in his pockets a ring of keys, two cigars, some matches, a pocket-knife, $36, and a fountain pen.

The man submitted to our search, his face expressionless until Mr. Barnable exclaimed, "But the stones? Where are my stones?"

Brennan sneered nastily. "I hope you hold your breath till you find 'em," he said.

"Mr. Strong, will you kindly search the two men you have handcuffed together?" I requested.

He did so, finding, as I expected, nothing of importance on their persons.

"Thank you, Mr. Strong," I said, crossing to the corner in which Mrs. Dolan was standing. "Will you please permit me to examine your shopping-bag?"

Mrs. Dolan's humorous brown eyes went blank.

"Will you please permit me to examine your shopping-bag?" I repeated, extending a hand toward it.

She made a little smothered laughing sound in her throat, and handed me the bag, which I carried to a flat-topped showcase on the other side of the room. The bag's contents were the celery and lettuce I have already mentioned, a package of sliced bacon, a box of soap chips, and a paper sack of spinach, among the green leaves of which glowed, when I emptied them out on the showcase, the hard crystal facets of unset diamonds. Less conspicuous among the leaves were some banknotes.

Mrs. Dolan was, I have said, a woman who impressed me as being capable, and that adjective seemed especially apt now: she behaved herself, I must say, in the manner of one who would be capable of anything. Fortunately, Detective Strong had followed her across the store; he was now in a position to seize her arms from behind, and thus incapacitate her, except vocally—a remaining freedom of which she availed herself to the utmost, indulging in a stream of vituperation which it is by no means necessary for me to repeat.

It was a few minutes past two o'clock when I returned to our offices.

"Well, what?" Papa ceased dictating his mail to Miss Queenan to challenge me. "I've been waiting for you to phone!"

"It was not necessary," I said, not without some satisfaction. "The operation has been successfully concluded."

"Cleaned up?"

"Yes, sir. The thieves, three men and a woman, are in the city prison, and the stolen property has been completely recovered. In the detective bureau we were able to identify two of the men, 'Reader' Keely, who seems to have been the principal, and a Harry McMeehan, who seems to be well-known to the police in the East. The other man and the woman, who gave their names as George Glenn and Mrs. Mary Dolan, will doubtless be identified later."

Papa bit the end off a cigar and blew the end across the office.

"What do you think of our little sleuth, Florence?" he fairly beamed on her, for all the world as if I were a child of three who had done something precocious.

"Spiffy!" Miss Queenan replied. "I think we'll do something with the lad yet."

"Sit down, Robin, and tell us about it," Papa invited. "The mail can wait."

"The woman secured a position as manager of a small apartment house on Ellis Street," I explained, though without sitting down. "She used that as reference to open an account with Barnable, buying a watch, for which she paid in small weekly installments. Keely, whose teeth were no doubt drawn while he was serving his last sentence in Walla Walla, removed his false teeth, painted a scar on his cheek, put on an ill-fitting cap, and, threatening Barnable and his assistant with a pistol, took the unset stones and money that were in the safe.

"As he left the store he collided with Mrs. Dolan, dropping the plunder into a bag of spinach which, with other groceries, was in her shopping-bag. McMeehan, pretending to come to the woman's assistance, handed Keely a hat and coat, and perhaps his false teeth and a handkerchief with which to wipe off the scar, and took Keely's pistol.

"Keely, now scarless, and with his appearance altered by teeth and hat, hurried to a barber shop two doors away, while McMeehan, after firing a shot indoors to discourage curiosity on the part of Barnable, dropped the pistol beside the cap and pretended to chase the bandit up toward Powell Street. At Powell Street another accomplice was stationed to pretend he had seen the bandit drive away in an automobile. These three confederates attempted to mislead us further by adding fictitious details to Barnable's description of the robber."

"Neat!" Papa's appreciation was, I need hardly point out, purely academic—a professional interest in the cunning the thieves had shown and not in any way an approval of their dishonest plan as a whole. "How'd you knock it off?"

"That man on the corner couldn't have seen the scar unless the bandit had turned his head, which the man denied. McMeehan wore gloves to avoid leaving prints on the pistol when he fired it, and his hands are quite sunburned, as if he does not ordinarily wear gloves. Both men and the woman told stories that fitted together in every detail, which, as you know, would be little less than a miracle in the case of honest witnesses. But since I knew Glenn, the man on the corner, had prevaricated, it was obvious that if the others' stories agreed with his, then they too were deviating from the truth."

I thought it best not to mention to Papa that immediately prior to going to Barnable's, and perhaps subconsciously during my investigation, my mind had been occupied with finding another couplet to replace the one the editor of *The Jongleur* had disliked; incongruity, therefore, being uppermost in my brain, Mrs. Dolan's shopping-bag had seemed a quite plausible hiding place for the diamonds and money.

"Good shooting!" Papa was saying. "Pull it by yourself?"

"I cooperated with Detectives Hooley and Strong. I am sure the subterfuge was as obvious to them as to me."

But even as I spoke a doubt arose in my mind. There was, it seemed to me, a possibility, however slight, that the police detectives had not seen the solution as clearly as I had. At the time I had assumed that Sergeant Hooley was attempting to conceal his knowledge from me; but now, viewing the situation in retrospect, I suspected that what the sergeant had been concealing was his lack of knowledge.

However, that was not important. What was important was that, in the image of jewels among vegetables, I had found a figure of incongruity for my sonnet.

Excusing myself, I left Papa's office for my own, where, with rhyming dictionary, thesaurus, and carbon copy on my desk again, I lost myself in the business of clothing my new simile with suitable words, thankful indeed that the sonnet had been written in the Shakespearean rather than the Italian form, so that a change in the rhyme of the last two lines would not necessitate similar alterations in other lines.

Time passed, and then I was leaning back in my chair, experiencing that unique satisfaction that Papa felt when he had apprehended some especially elusive criminal. I could not help smiling when I reread my new concluding couplet.

> *And shining there, no less inaptly shone*
> *Than diamonds in a spinach garden sown.*

That, I fancied, would satisfy the editor of *The Jongleur*.

THE FIRST
THIN MAN

Hammett wrote these ten chapters in 1930, some three years before he wrote and published *The Thin Man*. Although the story line of these chapters bears clear similarities to that of the novel, when published the latter was a completely rewritten work. The style in this roughly first fifth of a novel is much more akin to the hard-edged work Hammett published in *Black Mask*. And Nick and Nora Charles do not appear here.

I

The train went north among the mountains. The dark man crossed tracks to the ticket-window and said: "Can you tell me how to get to Mr. Wynant's place? Mr. Walter Irving Wynant's."

The man within stopped writing on a printed form. His eyes became brightly inquisitive behind tight rimless spectacles. His voice was eager. "Are you a newspaper reporter?"

"Why?" The dark man's eyes were very blue. They looked idly at the other. "Does it make any difference?"

"Then you ain't," the ticket-agent said. He was disappointed. He looked at a clock on the wall. "Hell, I ought to've known that. You wouldn't've had time to get here." He picked up the pencil he had put down.

"Know where his place is?"

"Sure. Up there on the hill." The ticket-agent waved his pencil vaguely westward. "All the taxi drivers know it, but if it's Wynant you want to see you're out of luck."

"Why?"

The ticket-agent's mien brightened. He put his forearms on the counter, hunching his shoulders, and said: "Because the fact is he went and murdered everybody on the place and jumped in the river not more than an hour ago."

The dark man exclaimed, "No!" softly.

The ticket-agent smacked his lips. "Uh-huh—killed all three of them—the whole shooting match—chopped them up in pieces with an ax and then tied a weight around his own neck and jumped in the river."

The dark man asked solemnly: "What'd he do that for?"

A telephone bell began to ring behind the ticket-agent. "You don't know him or you wouldn't have to ask," he replied as he reached for the telephone. "Crazy as they make them and always was. The only wonder is he didn't do it long before this." He said, "Hello," into the telephone.

The dark man went through the waiting-room and downstairs to the street. The half a dozen automobiles parked near the station were apparently private cars. A large red and white sign in the next block said TAXI. The dark man walked under the sign into a small, grimy office where a bald fat man was reading a newspaper.

"Can I get a taxi?" the dark man asked.

"All out now, brother, but I'm expecting one of them back any minute. In a hurry?"

"A little bit."

The bald man brought his chair down on all its legs and lowered his newspaper. "Where do you want to go?"

"Wynant's."

The bald man dropped his newspaper and stood up, saying heartily: "Well, I'll run you up there myself." He covered his baldness with a sweat-stained brown hat.

They left the office and—after the fat man had paused at the real-estate office next door to yell, "Take care of my phone if it rings, Toby"—got into a dark sedan, took the left turn at the first crossing, and rode uphill toward the west.

When they had ridden some three hundred yards the fat man said in a tone whose casualness was belied by the shine in his eyes: "That must be a hell of a mess up there and no fooling."

The dark man was lighting a cigarette. "What happened?" he asked.

The fat man looked sharply sidewise at him. "Didn't you hear?"

"Only what the ticket-agent told me just now"—the dark man leaned forward to return the lighter to its hole in the dashboard—"that Wynant had killed three people with an ax and then drowned himself."

The fat man laughed scornfully. "Christ, you can't beat Lew," he said. "If you sprained your ankle he could get a broken back out of it. Wynant didn't kill but two of them—the Hopkins woman got away because it was her that phoned—and he choked them to death and then shot himself. I bet you if you'd go back there right now Lew'd tell you there was a cool half a dozen of them killed and likely as not with dynamite."

The dark man took his cigarette from his mouth. "Then he wasn't right about Wynant being crazy?"

"Yes," the fat man said reluctantly, "but nobody could go wrong on that."

"No?"

"Nope. Holy hell! Didn't he used to come down to town in his pajamas last summer? And then when people didn't like it and got Ray to say something to him about it didn't he get mad and stop coming in at all? Don't he make as much fuss about people trespassing on his place as if he had a gold mine there? Didn't I see him with my own eyes heave a rock at a car that had gone past him raising dust once?"

The dark man smiled meagerly. "I don't know any of the answers," he said. "I didn't know him."

BESIDE A PAINTED warning against trespass they left their graveled road for an uneven, narrow crooked one of dark earth running more steeply uphill to the right. Protruding undergrowth brushed the sedan's sides and now and then an overhanging tree-branch its top. Their speed made their ride rougher than it need have been.

"This is his place," the fat man said. He sat stiffly at the wheel fighting the road's unevenness. His eyes were shiny, expectant.

The house they presently came to was a rambling structure of gray native stone and wood needing gray paint under low Dutch roofs. Five cars stood in the clearing in front of the house. The man who sat at the wheel of one of them, and the two men standing beside it, stopped talking and watched the sedan draw up.

"Here we are," the fat man said and got out. His manner had suddenly become important. He put importance in the nod he gave the three men.

The dark man, leaving the other side of the sedan, went toward the house. The fat man hurried to walk beside him.

A man came out of the house before they reached it. He was a middle-aged giant in baggy, worn clothes. His hair was gray, his eyes small, and he chewed gum. He said, "Howdy, Fern," to the fat man and, looking steadily at the dark man, stood in the path confronting them squarely.

Fern said, "Hello, Nick," and then told the dark man: "This is Sheriff Petersen." He narrowed one eye shrewdly and addressed the sheriff again: "He came up to see Wynant."

Sheriff Nick Petersen stopped chewing. "What's the name?" he asked.

The dark man said: "John Guild."

The sheriff said: "So. Now what were you wanting to see Wynant about?"

The man who had said his name was John Guild smiled. "Does it make any difference now he's dead?"

The sheriff asked, "What?" with considerable force.

"Now that he's dead," Guild repeated patiently. He put a fresh cigarette between his lips.

"How do you know he's dead?" The sheriff emphasized "you."

Guild looked with curious blue eyes at the giant. "They told me in the village," he said carelessly. He moved his cigarette an inch to indicate the fat man. "He told me."

The sheriff frowned skeptically, but when he spoke it was to utter a vague "Oh." He chewed his gum. "Well, what was it you were wanting to see him about?"

Guild said: "Look here: is he dead or isn't he?"

"Not that I know of."

"Fine," Guild said, his eyes lighting up. "Where is he?"

"I'd like to know," the sheriff replied gloomily. "Now what is it you want with him?"

"I'm from his bank. I want to see him on business." Guild's eyes became drowsy. "It's confidential business."

"So?" Sheriff Petersen's frown seemed to hold more discomfort than annoyance. "Well, none of his business is confidential from me any more. I got a right to know anything and everything that anybody knows about him."

Guild's eyes narrowed a little. He blew smoke out.

"I have," the sheriff insisted in a tone of complaint. "Listen, Guild, you haven't got any right to hide any of his business from me. He's a murderer and I'm responsible for law and order in this county."

Guild pursed his lips. "Who'd he kill?"

"This here Columbia Forrest," Petersen said, jerking a thumb at the house, "shot her stone dead and lit out for God only knows where."

"Didn't kill anybody else?"

"My God," the sheriff asked peevishly, "ain't that enough?"

"Enough for me, but down in the village they've got it all very plural." Guild stared thoughtfully at the sheriff. "Got away clean?"

"So far," Petersen grumbled, "but we're phoning descriptions of him and his car around." He sighed, moved his big shoulders uncomfortably. "Well, come on now, let's have it. What's your business with him?" But when Guild would have replied the giant said: "Wait a minute. We might as well go in and get hold of Boyer and Ray and get it over with at one crack."

LEAVING THE fat man, Guild and the sheriff went indoors, into a pleasantly furnished tan room in the front of the house, where they were soon joined by two more men. One of these was nearly as tall as the sheriff, a rawboned blond man in his early thirties, hard of jaw and mouth, somber of eye. One was younger, shorter, with boyishly rosy cheeks, quick dark eyes, and smoothed dark hair. When the sheriff introduced them to Guild he said the taller one was Ray Callaghan, a deputy sheriff, the other District Attorney Bruce Boyer. He told them John Guild was a fellow who wanted to see Wynant.

The youthful district attorney, standing close to Guild, smiled ingratiatingly and asked: "What business are you in, Mr. Guild?"

"I came up to see Wynant about his bank account," the dark man replied slowly.

"What bank?"

"Seaman's National of San Francisco."

"I see. Now what did you want to see him about? I mean, what was there about his account that you had to come up here to see him about?"

"Call it an overdraft," Guild said with deliberate evasiveness.

The district attorney's eyes became anxious.

Guild made a small gesture with the brown hand holding his cigarette. "Look here, Boyer," he said, "if you want me to go all the way with you you ought to go all the way with me."

Boyer looked at Petersen. The sheriff met his gaze with noncommittal eyes. Boyer turned back to Guild. "We're not hiding anything from you," he said earnestly. "We've nothing to hide."

Guild nodded. "Swell. What happened here?"

"Wynant caught the Forrest girl getting ready to leave him and he shot her and jumped in his car and drove away," he said quickly. "That's all there is to it."

"Who's the Forrest girl?"

"His secretary."

Guild pursed his lips, asked: "Only that?"

The raw-boned deputy sheriff said, "None of that, now!" in a strained croaking voice. His pale eyes were bloodshot and glaring.

The sheriff growled, "Take it easy there, Ray," avoiding his deputy's eyes.

The district attorney glanced impatiently at the deputy sheriff. Guild stared gravely, attentively at him.

The deputy sheriff's face flushed a little and he shifted his feet. He spoke to the dark man again, in the same croaking voice: "She's dead and you might just as well talk decently about her."

Guild moved his shoulders a little. "I didn't know her," he said coldly. "I'm trying to find out what happened." He stared for a moment longer at the raw-boned man and then shifted his gaze to Boyer. "What was she leaving him for?"

"To get married. She told him when he caught her packing after she came back from town and—and they had a fight and when she wouldn't change her mind he shot her."

Guild's blue eyes moved sidewise to focus on the raw-boned deputy sheriff's face. "She was living with Wynant, wasn't she?" he asked bluntly.

"You son of a bitch!" the deputy sheriff cried hoarsely and struck with his right fist at Guild's face.

Guild avoided the fist by stepping back with no appearance of haste. He had begun to step back before the fist started toward his face. His eyes gravely watched the fist go past his face.

Big Petersen lurched against his deputy, wrapping his arms around him. "Cut it out, Ray," he grumbled. "Why don't you behave yourself? This is no time to be losing your head."

The deputy sheriff did not struggle against him.

"What's the matter with him?" Guild asked the district attorney. There was no resentment in his manner. "In love with her or something?"

Boyer nodded furtively, then frowned and shook his head in a warning gesture.

"That's all right," Guild said. "Where'd you get your information about what happened?"

"From the Hopkinses. They look after the place for Wynant. They were in the kitchen and heard the whole fight. They ran upstairs when they heard the shots and he stood them off with the gun and told them he'd come back and kill them if they told anybody before he'd an hour's start, but they phoned Ray as soon as he'd gone."

Guild tossed the stub of his cigarette into the fireplace and lit a fresh one.

Then he took a card from a brown case brought from an inner pocket and gave the card to Boyer.

JOHN GUILD
ASSOCIATED DETECTIVE BUREAUS, INC.
FROST BUILDING, SAN FRANCISCO

"Last week Wynant deposited a ten-thousand-dollar New York check in his account at the Seaman's National Bank," Guild said. "Yesterday the bank learned the check had been raised from one thousand to ten. The bank's nicked for six thousand on the deal."

"But in the case of an altered check," Boyer said, "I understand—"

"I know," Guild agreed, "the bank's not responsible—theoretically—but there are usually loopholes and it's— Well, we're working for the insurance company that covers the Seaman's and it's good business to go after him and recover as much as we can."

"I'm glad that's the way you feel about it," the district attorney said with enthusiasm. "I'm mighty glad you're going to work with us." He held out his hand.

"Thanks," Guild said as he took the hand. "Let's look at the Hopkinses and the body."

I I

Columbia Forrest had been a long-limbed, smoothly slender young woman. Her body, even as it lay dead in a blue sport suit, seemed supple. Her short hair was a faintly reddish brown. Her features were small and regular, appealing in their lack of strength. There were three bullet-holes in her left temple. Two of them touched. The third was down beside the eye.

Guild put the tip of his dark forefinger lightly on the edge of the lower hole. "A thirty-two," he said. "He made sure: any of the three would have done it." He turned his back on the corpse. "Let's see the Hopkinses."

"They're in the dining-room, I think," the district attorney said. He hesitated, cleared his throat. His young face was worried. He touched Guild's elbow with the back of one hand and said: "Go easy with Ray, will you? He was a little bit—or a lot, I guess—in love with her and it's·tough on him."

"The deputy?"

"Yes, Ray Callaghan."

"That's all right if he doesn't get in the way," Guild said carelessly. "What sort of person is this sheriff?"

"Oh, Petersen's all right."

Guild seemed to consider this statement critically. Then he said: "But he's not what you'd call a feverish manhunter?"

"Well, no, that's not—you know—a sheriff has other things to do most of the time, but even if he'd just as lief have somebody else do the work he won't interfere." Boyer moistened his lips and leaned close to the dark man. His face was boyishly alight. "I wish you'd—I'm glad you're going to work with me on this, Guild," he said in a low, earnest voice. "I—this is my first murder and I'd like to—well—show them"—he blushed—"that I'm not as young as some of them said."

"Fair enough. Let's see the Hopkinses—in here."

The district attorney studied Guild's dark face uneasily for a moment, started to say something, changed his mind, and left the room.

A MAN and a woman came with him when he returned. The man was probably fifty years old, of medium stature, with thin, graying hair above a round, phlegmatic face. He wore tan trousers held up by new blue suspenders and a faded blue shirt open at the neck. The woman was of about the same age, rather short, plump, and dressed neatly in gray. She wore gold-rimmed spectacles. Her eyes were round and pale and bright.

The district attorney shut the door and said: "This is Mr. and Mrs. Hopkins, Mr. Guild." He addressed them: "Mr. Guild is working with me. Please give him all the assistance you can."

The Hopkinses nodded in unison.

Guild asked: "How'd this happen?" He indicated with a small backward jerk of his head the dead young woman.

Hopkins said, "I always knew he'd do something like that some time," while his wife was saying: "It was right in this room and they were talking so loud you could hear it all over the place."

Guild shook his cigarette at them. "One at a time." He spoke to the man: "How'd you know he was going to do it?"

The woman replied quickly: "Oh, he was crazy-jealous of her all the time—if she got out of his sight for a minute—and when she came back from the city and told him she was going to leave to get married he—"

Again Guild used his cigarette to interrupt her. "What do you think? Is he really crazy?"

"He was then, sir," she said. "Why, when we ran in here when we heard the shooting and he told us to keep our mouths shut he was—his eyes—you never saw anything like them in your life—nor his voice either and he was shaking and jerking like he was going to fall apart."

"I don't mean that," Guild explained. "I mean, is he crazy?" Before the woman could reply he put another question to her. "How long have you been with him?"

"Going on about ten months, ain't it, Willie?" she asked her husband.

"Yes," he agreed, "since last fall."

"That's right," she told Guild. "It was last November."

"Then you ought to know whether he's crazy. Is he?"

"Well, I'll tell you," she said slowly, wrinkling her forehead. "He was certainly the most peculiar person you ever heard tell of, but I guess geniuses are like that and I wouldn't want to say he was out and out crazy except about her." She looked at her husband.

He said tolerantly: "Sure, all geniuses are like that. It's—it's eccentric."

"So you think he was a genius," Guild said. "Did you read the things he wrote?"

"No, sir," Mrs. Hopkins said, squirming, "though I did try sometimes, but it was too—I couldn't make heads or tails of it—much—but I ain't an educated woman and—"

"Who was she going to marry?" Guild asked.

Mrs. Hopkins shook her head vigorously. "I don't know. I didn't catch the name if she said it. It was him that was talking so loud."

"What'd she go to town for?"

Mrs. Hopkins shook her head again. "I don't know that either. She used to go in every couple of weeks and he always got mad about it."

"She drive in?"

"Mostly she did, but she didn't yesterday, but she drove out in that new blue car out there."

Guild looked questioningly at the district attorney, who said: "We're trying to trace it now. It's apparently a new one, but we ought to know whose it is soon."

Guild nodded and returned his attention to the Hopkinses. "She went to

San Francisco by train yesterday and came back in this new car at what time to-day?"

"Yes, sir. At about three o'clock, I guess it was, and she started packing." She pointed at the traveling bags and clothing scattered around the room. "And he came in and the fuss started. I could hear them downstairs and I went to the window and beckoned at Willie—Mr. Hopkins, that is—and we stood at the foot of the stairs, there by the dining-room door and listened to them."

Guild turned aside to mash his cigarette in a bronze tray on a table. "She usually stay overnight when she went to the city?"

"Mostly always."

"You must have some idea of what she went to the city for," Guild insisted.

"No, I haven't," the woman said earnestly. "We never did know, did we, Willie? Jealous like he was, I guess if she was going in to see some fellow she wouldn't be likely to tell anybody that might tell him, though the Lord knows I can keep my mouth shut as tight as anybody. I've seen the—"

Guild stopped lighting a fresh cigarette to ask: "How about her mail? You must've seen that sometimes."

"No, Mr. Gould, we never did, and that's a funny thing, because all the time we've been here I never saw any mail for her except magazines and never knew her to write any."

Guild frowned. "How long had she been here?"

"She was here when we came. I don't know how long she'd been here, but it must've been a long time."

Boyer said: "Three years. She came here in March three years ago."

"How about her relatives, friends?"

The Hopkinses shook their heads. Boyer shook his head.

"His?"

Mrs. Hopkins shook her head again. "He didn't have any. That's what he would always say, that he didn't have a relative or a friend in the world."

"Who's his lawyer?"

Mrs. Hopkins looked blank. "If he's got one I don't know it, Mr. Gould. Maybe you could find something like that in his letters and things."

"That'll do," Guild said abruptly around the cigarette in his mouth, and opened the door for the Hopkinses. They left the room.

HE SHUT THE DOOR behind them and with his back against it looked around the room, at the blanketed dead figure on the bed, at the clothing scattered here and there, at the three traveling bags, and finally at the bloodstained center of the light blue rug.

Boyer watched him expectantly.

Staring at the bloodstain, Guild asked: "You've notified the police in San Francisco?"

"Oh, yes, we've sent his description and the description and license number of his car all over—from Los Angeles to Seattle and as far east as Salt Lake."

"What is the number?" Guild took a pencil and an envelope from his pockets.

Boyer told him, adding: "It's a Buick coupé, last year's."

"What does he look like?"

"I've never seen him, but he's very tall—well over six feet—and thin. Won't weigh more than a hundred and thirty, they say. You know, he's tubercular: that's how he happened to come up here. He's about forty-five years old, sunburned, but sallow, with brown eyes and very dark brown hair and whiskers. He's got whiskers—maybe five or six inches long—thick and shaggy, and his eyebrows are thick and shaggy. There's a lot of pictures of him in his room. You can help yourself to them. He had on a baggy gray tweed suit and a soft gray hat and heavy brown shoes. His shoulders are high and straight and he walks on the balls of his feet with long steps. He doesn't smoke or drink and he has a habit of talking to himself."

Guild put away his pencil and envelope. "Had your fingerprint people go over the place yet?"

"No, I—"

"It might help in case he's picked up somewhere and we're doubtful. I suppose we can get specimens of his handwriting. Anyway we'll be able to get them from the bank. We'll try to—"

Someone knocked on the door.

"Come in," Boyer called.

The door opened to admit a man's head. He said: "They want you on the phone."

The district attorney followed the man downstairs. During his absence Guild smoked and looked somberly around the room.

The district attorney came back saying: "The car belongs to a Charles Fremont, on Guerrero Street, in San Francisco."

"What number?" Guild brought out his pencil and envelope again. Boyer told him the number and he wrote it down. "I think I'll trot back right now and see him."

The district attorney looked at his watch. "I wonder if I couldn't manage to get away to go with you," he said.

Guild pursed his lips. "I don't think you ought to. One of us ought to be here looking through his stuff, gathering up the loose ends. I haven't seen anybody else we ought to trust with it."

Though Boyer seemed disappointed he said, "Righto," readily enough. "You'll keep in touch with me?"

"Sure. Let me have that card I gave you and I'll put my home address and phone number on it." Guild's eyes became drowsy. "What do you say I drive Fremont's car in?"

The district attorney wrinkled his forehead. "I don't know," he said slowly. "It might— Oh, sure, if you want. You'll phone me as soon as you've seen him—let me know what's what?"

"Um-hmm."

I I I

A red-haired girl in white opened the door.

Guild said: "I want to see Mr. Charles Fremont."

"Yes, sir," the girl said amiably in a resonant throaty voice. "Come in."

She took him into a comfortably furnished living-room to the right of the entrance. "Sit down. I'll call my brother." She went through another doorway and her voice could be heard singing: "Charley, a gentleman to see you."

Upstairs a hard, masculine voice replied: "Be right down."

The red-haired girl came back to the room where Guild was. "He'll be down in a minute," she said.

Guild thanked her.

"Do sit down," she said, sitting on an end of the sofa. Her legs were remarkably beautiful.

He sat in a large chair facing her across the room, but got up again immediately to offer her a cigarette and to hold his lighter to hers. "What I wanted to see your brother about," he said as he sat down again, "was to ask if he knows a Miss Columbia Forrest."

The girl laughed. "He probably does," she said. "She's— They're going to be married to-morrow."

Guild said: "Well, that's—" He stopped when he heard footsteps running downstairs from the second floor.

A man came into the room. He was a man of perhaps thirty-five years, a little above medium height, trimly built, rather gaily dressed in gray with lavender shirt, tie, and protruding pocket-handkerchief. His face was lean and good-looking in a shrewd, tight-lipped fashion.

"This is my brother," the girl said.

Guild stood up. "I'm trying to get some information about Miss Columbia Forrest," he said, and gave Charles Fremont one of his cards.

The curiosity that had come into Fremont's face with Guild's words became frowning amazement when he had read Guild's card. "What—?"

Guild was saying: "There's been some trouble up at Hell Bend."

Fremont's eyes widened in his paling face. "Wynant has—?"

Guild nodded. "He shot Miss Forrest this afternoon."

The Fremonts stared at each other's blank, horrified faces. She said through the fingers of one hand, trembling so she stuttered: "I t-t-told you, Charley!"

Charles Fremont turned savagely on Guild. "How bad is she hurt? Tell me!"

The dark man said: "She's dead."

Fremont sobbed and sat down with his face in his hands. His sister knelt beside him with her arms around him. Guild stood watching them.

Presently Fremont raised his head. "Wynant?" he asked.

"Gone."

Fremont let his breath out in a low groan. He sat up straight, patting one of his sister's hands, freeing himself from her arms. "I'm going up there now," he told her, rising.

Guild had finished lighting a cigarette. He said: "That's all right, but you'll do most good by telling me some things before you go."

"Anything I can," Fremont promised readily.

"You were to be married to-morrow?"

"Yes. She was down here last night and stayed with us and I persuaded her. We were going to leave here to-morrow morning and drive up to Portland—where we wouldn't have to wait three days for the license—and then go up to Banff. I've just wired the hotel there for reservations. So she took the car—the new one we were going in—to go up to Hell Bend and get her things. I asked her not to—we both tried to persuade her—because we knew Wynant would make trouble, but—but we never thought he would do anything like this."

"You know him pretty well?"

"No, I've only seen him once—about three weeks ago—when he came to see me."

"What'd he come to see you for?"

"To quarrel with me about her—to tell me to stay away from her."

Guild seemed about to smile. "What'd you say to that?"

Fremont drew his thin lips back tight against his teeth. "Do I look like I'd tell him anything except to go to hell?" he demanded.

The dark man nodded. "All right. What do you know about him?"

"Nothing."

Guild frowned. "You must know something. She'd've talked about him."

Anger went out of Fremont's lean face, leaving it gloomy. "I didn't like her to," he said, "so she didn't."

"Why?"

"Jesus!" Fremont exclaimed. "She was living up there. I was nuts about her. I knew he was. What the hell?" He bit his lip. "Do you think that was something I liked to talk about?"

Guild stared thoughtfully at the other man for a moment and then addressed the girl: "What'd she tell you?"

"Not anything. She didn't like to talk about him any more than Charley liked to have her."

Guild drew his brows together. "What'd she stay with him for, then?"

Fremont said painfully: "She was going to leave. That's why he killed her."

THE DARK MAN put his hands in his pockets and walked down the room to the front windows and back, squinting a little in the smoke rising from his cigarette. "You don't know where he's likely to go? Who he's likely to connect with? How we're likely to find him?"

Fremont shook his head. "Don't you think I'd tell you if I knew?" he asked bitterly.

Guild did not reply to that. He asked: "Where are her people?"

"I don't know. I think she's got a father still alive in Texas somewhere. I know she's an only child and her mother's dead."

"How long have you known her?"

"Four—nearly five months."

"Where'd you meet her?"

"In a speakeasy on Powell Street, a couple of blocks beyond the Fairmont. She was in a party with some people I know—Helen Robier—I think she lives at the Cathedral—and a fellow named MacWilliams."

Guild walked to the windows again and back. "I don't like this," he said aloud, but apparently not to the Fremonts. "It doesn't make sense. It's—Look here." He halted in front of them and took some photographs from his pocket. "Are these good pictures of her?" He spread three out fanwise. "I've only seen her dead."

The Fremonts looked and nodded together. "The middle one especially," the girl said. "You have one of those, Charley."

Guild put the dead girl's photographs away and displayed two of a bearded man. "Are they good of him?"

The girl said, "I've never seen him," but her brother nodded and said: "They look like him."

Guild seemed dissatisfied with the answers he had been given. He put the photographs in his pocket again. "Then it's not that," he said, "but there's something funny somewhere." He scowled at the floor, looked up quickly. "You people aren't putting up some kind of game on me, are you?"

Charles Fremont said: "Don't be a sap."

"All right, but there's something wrong somewhere."

The girl spoke: "What? Maybe if you'd tell us what you think is wrong—"

Guild shook his head. "If I knew what was wrong I could find out for myself what made it wrong. Never mind, I'll get it. I want the names and addresses of all the friends she had, the people she knew that you know of."

"I've told you Helen Robier lives—I'm pretty sure—at the Cathedral," Fremont said. "MacWilliams works in the Russ Building, for a stockbroker, I think. That's all I know about him and I don't believe Columbia knows"— he swallowed—"knew him very well. They're the only ones I know."

"I don't believe they're all you know," Guild said.

"Please, Mr. Guild," the girl said, coming around to his side, "don't be unfair to Charley. He's trying to help you—we're both trying—but—" She stamped her foot and cried angrily, tearfully: "Can't you have some consideration for him now?"

Guild said: "Oh, all right." He reached for his hat. "I drove your car down," he told Fremont. "It's out front now."

"Thank you, Guild."

Something struck one of the front windows, knocking a triangle of glass from its lower left-hand corner in on the floor. Charles Fremont, facing the window, yelled inarticulately and threw himself down on the floor. A pistol was fired through the gap in the pane. The bullet went over Fremont's head and made a small hole in the green plastered wall there.

Guild was moving toward the street door by the time the bullet-hole appeared in the wall. A black pistol came into his right hand. Outside, that block of Guerrero Street was deserted. Guild went swiftly, though with many backward glances, to the nearest corner. From there he began to retrace his steps slowly, stopping to peer into shadowy doorways and the dark basement entrances under the high front steps.

Charles Fremont came out to join him. Windows were being raised along the street and people were looking out.

"Get inside," Guild said curtly to Fremont. "You're the one he's gunning for. Get inside and phone the police."

"Elsa's doing that now. He's shaved his whiskers off, Guild."

"That'd be the first thing he did. Go back in the house."

Fremont said, "No," and went with Guild as he searched the block. They were still at it when the police arrived. They did not find Wynant. Around a corner two blocks from the Fremonts' house they found a year-old Buick coupé bearing the license numbers Boyer had given Guild—Wynant's car.

I V

After dinner, which Guild ate alone at Solari's in Maiden Lane, he went to an apartment in Hyde Street. He was admitted by a young woman whose pale, tired face lighted up as she said: "Hello, John. We've been wondering what had become of you."

"Been away. Is Chris home?"

"I'd let you in anyhow," she said as she pushed the door farther open.

They went back to a square, bookish room where a thick-set man with rumpled sandy hair was half buried in an immense shabby chair. He put his book down, reached for the tall glass of beer at his elbow, and said jovially: "Enter the sleuth. Get some more beer, Kay. I've been wanting to see you, John. What do you say you do some detective-story reviews for my page— you know—'The Detective Looks at Detective Fiction'?"

"You asked me that before," Guild said. "Nuts."

"It's a good idea, though," the thick-set man said cheerfully. "And I've got another one. I was going to save it till I got around to writing a detective story, but you might be able to use it in your work sometime, so I'll give it to you free."

Guild took the glass of beer Kay held out to him, said, "Thanks," to her and then to the man: "Do I have to listen to it?"

"Yes. You see, this fellow's suspected of a murder that requires quite a bit of courage. All the evidence points right at him—that kind of thing. But he's a great lover of Sam Johnson—got his books all over the place—so you know he didn't do it, because only timid men—the kind that say, 'Yes, sir,' to their wives and, 'Yes, Ma'am,' to the policemen—love Johnson. You see, he's only loved for his boorishness and the boldness of his rudeness and bad manners and that's the kind of thing that appeals to—"

"So I look for a fellow named Sam Johnson and he's guilty?" the dark man said.

Kay said: "Chris has one of his nights."

Chris said: "Sneer at me and be damned to you, but there's a piece of psychology that might come in handy some day. Remember it. It's a law. Love of Doctor Johnson is the mark of the pathologically meek."

Guild made a face. "God knows I'm earning me beer," he said and drank. "If you've got to talk, talk about Walter Irving Wynant. That'll do me some good maybe."

"Why?" Chris asked. "How?"

"I'm hunting for him. He slaughtered his secretary this afternoon and lit out for parts unknown."

Kay exclaimed: "Not really!"

Chris said: "The hell he did!"

Guild nodded and drank more beer. "He only paused long enough to take a shot at the fellow his secretary was supposed to marry to-morrow."

Chris and Kay looked at each other with delighted eyes.

Chris lay back in his chair. "Can you beat that? But, you know, I'm not nearly as surprised as I ought to be. The last time I saw him I thought there was something wrong there, though he always was a bit on the goofy side. Remember I said something to you about it, Kay? And it's a cinch this magazine stuff he's been doing lately is woozy. Even parts of his last book— No, I'm being smart-alecky now. I'll stick to what I wrote about his book when it came out: in spite of occasional flaws his 'departmentalization' comes nearer to supplying an answer to Pontius Pilate's question than anything ever offered by anybody else."

"What kind of writing does he do?" Guild asked.

"This sort of thing." Chris rose grunting, went to one of his bookcases, picked out a bulky black volume entitled, in large gold letters, *Knowledge and Belief,* opened it at random, and read: "'Science is concerned with percepts. A percept is a defined, that is, a limited, difference. The scientific datum that white occurs means that white is the difference between a certain perceptual field and the rest of the perceiver. If you look at an unbroken expanse of white you perceive white because your perception of it is limited to your visual field: the surrounding, contrasting, extra-visual area of non-white gives you your percept of white. These are not scientific definitions.

They cannot be. Science cannot define, cannot limit, itself. Definitions of science must be philosophical definitions. Science cannot know what it cannot know. Science cannot know there is anything it does not know. Science deals with percepts and not with non-percepts. Thus, Einstein's theory of relativity—that the phenomena of nature will be the same, that is, not different, to two observers who move with any uniform velocity whatever relative to one another—is a philosophical, and not a scientific, hypothesis.

"'Philosophy, like science, cannot define, cannot limit, itself. Definitions of philosophy must be made from a viewpoint that will bear somewhat the same relation to philosophy that the philosophical viewpoint bears to science. These definitions may be—'"

"That'll be enough of that," Guild said.

Chris shut the book with a bang. "That's the kind of stuff he writes," he said cheerfully and went back to his chair and beer.

"What do you know about him?" Guild asked. "I mean outside his writing. Don't start that again. I want to know if he was only crazy with jealousy or has blown his top altogether—and how to catch up with him either way."

"I haven't seen him for six or seven months or maybe longer," Chris said. "He always was a little cracked and unsociable as hell. Maybe just erratic, maybe worse than that."

"What do you know about him?"

"What everybody knows," Chris said depreciatively. "Born somewhere in Devonshire. Went to Oxford. Went native in India and came out with a book on economics—a pretty good book, but visionary. Married an actress named Hana Drix—or something like that—in Paris and lived with her there for three or four years and came out of it with his second book. I think they had a couple of children. After she divorced him he went to Africa and later, I believe, to South America. Anyway he did a lot of traveling and then settled down in Berlin long enough to write his *Speculative Anthropology* and to do some lecturing. I don't know where he was during the war. He popped up over here a couple of years later with a two-volume piece of metaphysics called *Consciousness Drifting*. He's been in America ever since—the last five or six years up in the mountains here doing that *Knowledge and Belief*."

"How about relatives, friends?"

Chris shook his tousled head. "Maybe his publishers would know—Dale and Dale."

"And as a critic you think—"

"I'm no critic," Chris said. "I'm a reviewer."

"Well, as whatever you are, you think his stuff is sane?"

Chris moved his thick shoulders in a lazy shrug. "Parts of his books I know are damned fine. Other parts—maybe they're over my head. Even that's possible. But the magazine stuff he's been doing lately—since *Knowledge and Belief*—I know is tripe and worse. The paper sent a kid up to get an interview out of him a couple of weeks ago—when everybody was making the fuss over that Russian anthropologist—and he came back with something awful. We wouldn't have run it if it hadn't been for the weight Wynant's name carries and the kid's oaths that he had written it exactly as it was given to him. I'd say it was likely enough his mind's cracked up."

"Thanks," Guild said, and reached for his hat, but both the others began questioning him then, so they sat there and talked and smoked and drank beer until midnight was past.

IN HIS HOTEL ROOM Guild had his coat off when the telephone bell rang. He went to the telephone. "Hello. . . . Yes. . . . Yes. . . ." He waited. "Yes? . . . Yes, Boyer. . . . He showed up at Fremont's and took a shot at him. . . . No, no harm done except that he made a clean sneak. . . . Yes, but we found his car. . . . Where? . . . Yes, I know where it is. . . . What time? . . . Yes, I see. . . . To-morrow? What time? . . . Fine. Suppose you pick me up here at my hotel. . . . Right.

He left the telephone, started to unbutton his vest, stopped, looked at the watch on his wrist, put his coat on again, picked up his hat, and went out.

At California Street he boarded an eastbound cable car and rode over the top of the hill and down it to Chinatown, leaving the car at Grant Avenue. Rain nearly as fine as mist was beginning to blow down from the north. Guild went out beyond the curb to avoid a noisy drunken group coming out of a Chinese restaurant, walked a block, and halted across the street from another restaurant. This was a red-brick building that tried to seem oriental by means of much gilding and colored lighting, obviously pasted-on corbelled cornices and three-armed brackets marking its stories—some carrying posts above in the shape of half-pillars—and a tent-shaped terra-cotta roof surmounted by a mast bearing nine aluminumed rings. There was a huge electric sign—M A N C H U.

He stood looking at this gaudy building until he had a lit a cigarette. Then he went over to it. The girl in the cloakroom would not take his hat. "We close at one," she said.

He looked at the people getting into an elevator, at her again. "They're coming in."

"That's upstairs. Have you a card?"

He smiled. "Of course I have. I left it in my other suit."

She looked severely blank.

He said, "Oh, all right, sister," gave her a silver dollar, took his hat-check, and squeezed himself into the crowded elevator.

At the fourth floor he left the elevator with the others and went into a large, shabby, oblong room where, running out from a small stage, an oblong dance-floor was a peninsula among tables waited on by Chinese in dinner clothes. There were forty or fifty people in the place. Some of them were dancing to music furnished by a piano, a violin, and a French horn.

Guild was given a small table near a shuttered window. He ordered a sandwich and coffee.

The dance ended and a woman with a middle-aged harpy's face and beautiful satin-skinned body sang a modified version of "Christopher Colombo." There was another dance after that. Then Elsa Fremont came out to the center of the dance-floor and sang "Hollywood Papa." Her low-cut green gown set off the red of her hair and brought out the greenness of her narrowly lanceolate eyes. Guild smoked, sipped coffee, and watched her. When she was through he applauded with the others.

She came straight to his table, smiling, and said: "What are you doing here?" She sat down facing him.

He sat down again. "I didn't know you worked here."

"No?" Her smile was merry, her eyes skeptical.

"No," he said, "but maybe I should have known it. A man named Lane, who lives near Wynant in Hell Bend, saw him coming in this place this evening."

"That would be downstairs," the girl said. "We don't open up here till midnight."

"Lane didn't know about the murder till he got home late to-night. Then he phoned the district attorney and told him he'd seen Wynant and the D.A. phoned me. I thought I'd drop in just on the off-chance that I might pick up something."

Frowning a little, she asked: "Well?"

"Well, I found you here."

"But I wasn't downstairs earlier this evening," she said. "What time was it?"

"Half an hour before he took his shot at your brother."

"You see"—triumphantly—"you know I was home then talking to you."

"I know that one," Guild said.

V

At ten o'clock next morning Guild went into the Seaman's National Bank, to a desk marked MR. COLER, ASSISTANT CASHIER. The sunburned blond man who sat there greeted Guild eagerly.

Guild sat down and said: "Saw the papers this morning, I suppose."

"Yes. Thank the Lord for insurance."

"We ought to get him in time to get some of it back," Guild said. "I'd like to get a look at his account and whatever canceled checks are on hand."

"Surely." Coler got up from his desk and went away. When he came back he was carrying a thin pack of checks in one hand, a sheet of typed paper in the other. Sitting down, he looked at the sheet and said: "This is what happened: on the second of the month Wynant deposited that ten-thousand-dollar check on—"

"Bring it in himself?"

"No. He always mailed his deposits. It was a Modern Publishing Company check on the Madison Trust Company of New York. He had a balance of eleven hundred sixty-two dollars and fifty-five cents: the check brought it up to eleven thousand and so on. On the fifth a check"—he took one from the thin pack—"for nine thousand dollars to the order of Laura Porter came through the clearing house." He looked at the check. "Dated the third, the day after he deposited his check." He turned the check over. "It was deposited in the Golden Gate Trust Company." He passed it across the desk to Guild. "Well, that left him with a balance of twenty-one hundred sixty-two dollars and fifty-five cents. Yesterday we received a wire telling us the New York check had been raised from one thousand to ten."

"Do you let your customers draw against out-of-town checks like that before they've had time to go through?"

Coler raised his eyebrows. "Old accounts of the standing of Mr. Wynant—yes."

"He's got a swell standing now," Guild said. "What other checks are there in there?"

Coler looked through them. His eyes brightened. He said: "There are two more Laura Porter ones—a thousand and a seven hundred and fifty. The rest seem to be simply salaries and household expenses." He passed them to Guild.

Guild examined the checks slowly one by one. Then he said: "See if you can find out how long this has been going on and how much of it."

Coler willingly rose and went away. He was gone half an hour. When he returned he said: "As near as I can learn, she's been getting checks for several months at least and has been getting about all he deposited, with not much more than enough left over to cover his ordinary expenses."

Guild said, "Thanks," softly through cigarette smoke.

FROM THE Seaman's National Bank, Guild went to the Golden Gate Trust Company in Montgomery Street. A girl stopped typewriting to carry his card into the cashier's office and presently ushered him into the office. There he shook hands with a round, white-haired man who said: "Glad to see you, Mr. Guild. Which of us criminals are you looking for now?"

"I don't know whether I'm looking for any this time. You've got a depositer named Laura Porter. I'd like to get her address."

The cashier's smile set. "Now, now, I'm always willing to do all I can to help you chaps, but—"

Guild said: "She may have had something to do with gypping the Seaman's National out of eight thou."

Curiosity took some of the stiffness from the cashier's smile.

Guild said: "I don't know that she had a finger in it, but it's because I think she might that I'm here. All I want's her address—now—and I won't want anything else unless I'm sure."

The cashier rubbed his lips together, frowned, cleared his throat, finally said: "Well, if I give it to you you'll understand it's—"

"Strictly confidential," Guild said, "just like the information that the Seaman's has been nicked."

Five minutes later he was leaving the Golden Gate Trust Company carrying, in a pocket, a slip of paper on which was written *Laura Porter, 1157 Leavenworth*.

HE CAUGHT a cable car and rode up California Street. When his car passed the Cathedral Apartments he stood up suddenly and he left the car at the next corner, walking back to the apartment building.

At the desk he said: "Miss Helen Robier."

The man on the other side of the counter shook his head. "We've nobody by that name—unless she's visiting someone."

"Can you tell me if she lived here—say—five months ago?"

"I'll try." He went back and spoke to another man. The other man came over to Guild. "Yes," he said, "Miss Robier did live here, but she's dead."

"Dead?"

"She was killed in an automobile accident the Fourth of July."

Guild pursed his lips. "Have you had a MacWilliams here?"

"No."

"Ever have one?"

"I don't think so. I'll look it up." When he came back he was positive. "No."

Outside the Cathedral, Guild looked at his watch. It was a quarter to twelve. He walked over to his hotel. Boyer rose from a chair in the lobby and came to meet him, saying: "Good morning. How are you? Anything new?"

Guild shrugged. "Some things that might mean something. Let's do our talking over a lunch-table." He turned beside the district attorney and guided him into the hotel grill.

When they were seated and had given their orders he told Boyer about his conversation with the Fremonts, the shot that had interrupted them, and their search for Wynant that had resulted in their finding his car; about his conversation with Chris—"Christopher Maxim," he said, "book critic on the *Dispatch*"; about his visit to the Manchu and his meeting Elsa Fremont there; and about his visits that morning to the two banks and the apartment house. He spoke rapidly, wasting few words, missing no salient point.

"Do you suppose Wynant went to that Chinese restaurant, knowing the girl worked there, to find out where she and her brother lived?" Boyer asked when Guild had finished.

"Not if he'd been at Fremont's house raising hell a couple of weeks ago."

Boyer's face flushed. "That's right. Well, do you—?"

"Let me know what's doing on your end," Guild said, "and maybe we can do our supposing together. Wait till this waiter gets out of the way."

When their food had been put in front of them and they were alone again the district attorney said: "I told you about Lane seeing Wynant going in this Chinese place."

Guild said, "Yes. How about the fingerprints?" and put some food in his mouth.

"I had the place gone over and we took the prints of everybody we knew had been there, but the matching-up hadn't been done when I left early this morning."

"Didn't forget to take the dead girl's?"

"Oh, no. And you were in there: you can send us yours."

"All right, though I made a point of not touching anything. Any reports from the general alarm?"

"None."

"Anyway, we know he came to San Francisco. How about the circulars?"

"They're being printed now—photo, description, handwriting specimens. We'll get out a new batch when we've got his fingerprints: I wanted to get something out quick."

"Fine. I asked the police here to get us some of his prints off the car. What else happened on your end?"

"That's about all."

"Didn't get anything out of his papers?"

"Nothing. Outside of what seemed to be notes for his work there wasn't a handful of papers. You can look at them yourself when you come up."

Guild, eating, nodded as if he were thoroughly satisfied. "We'll go up for a look at Miss Porter first thing this afternoon," he said, "and maybe something'll come of that."

"Do you suppose she was blackmailing him?"

"People have blackmailed people," Guild admitted.

"I'm just talking at random," the district attorney said a bit sheepishly, "letting whatever pops into my mind come out."

"Keep it up," Guild said encouragingly.

"Do you suppose she could be a daughter he had by that actress wife in Paris?"

"We can try to find out what happened to her and the children. Maybe Columbia Forrest was his daughter."

"But you know what the situation was up there," Boyer protested. "That would be incest."

"It's happened before," Guild said gravely. "That's why they've got a name for it."

GUILD PUSHED the button beside Laura Porter's name in the vestibule of a small brownstone apartment building at 1157 Leavenworth Street. Boyer, breathing heavily, stood beside him. There was no response. There was no response the second and third times he pushed the button, but when he touched the one labeled M A N A G E R the door-lock buzzed.

They opened the door and went into a dim lobby. A door straight ahead of them opened and a woman said: "Yes? What is it?" She was small and sharp-featured, gray-haired, hook-nosed, bright-eyed.

Guild advanced toward her saying, "We wanted to see Miss Laura Porter—310—but she doesn't answer the bell."

"I don't think she's in," the gray-haired woman said. "She's not in much. Can I take a message?"

"When do you expect her back?"

"I don't know, I'm sure."

"Do you know when she went out?"

"No, sir. Sometimes I see my people when they come in and go out and sometimes I don't. I don't watch them and Miss Porter I see less than any."

"Oh, she's not here most of the time?"

"I don't know, mister. So long as they pay their rent and don't make too much noise I don't bother them."

"Them? Does she live with somebody?"

"No. I meant them—all my people here."

Guild turned to the district attorney. "Here. One of your cards."

Boyer fumbled for his cards, got one of them out, and handed it to Guild, who gave it to the woman.

"We want a little information about her," the dark man said in a low, confidential voice while she was squinting at the card in the dim light. "She's all right as far as we know, but—"

The woman's eyes, when she raised them, were wide and inquisitive. "What is it?" she asked.

Guild leaned down toward her impressively. "How long has she been here?" he asked in a stage whisper.

"Almost six months," she replied. "It is six months."

"Does she have many visitors?"

"I don't know. I don't remember ever seeing any, but I don't pay much attention and when I see people coming in here I don't know what apartment they're going to."

Guild straightened, put his left hand out, and pressed an electric-light button, illuminating the lobby. He put his right hand to his inner coat-pocket and brought out pictures of Wynant and his dead secretary. He gave them to the woman. "Ever see either of these?"

She looked at the man's picture and shook her head. "No," she said, "and that ain't a man I'd ever forget if I'd once seen him." She looked at Columbia Forrest's picture. "That!" she cried. "That *is* Miss Porter!"

VI

Boyer looked round-eyed at Guild.

The dark man, after a little pause, spoke to the woman. "That's Columbia Forrest," he said, "the girl who was killed up in Hell Bend yesterday."

The woman's eyes became round as the district attorney's. "Well!" she exclaimed, looking at the photograph again, "I never would've thought she was a thief. Why, she was such a pleasant, mild-looking little thing—"

"A thief?" Boyer asked incredulously.

"Why, yes." She raised puzzled eyes from the photograph. "At least that's what the paper says, about her going—"

"What paper?"

"The afternoon paper." Her face became bright, eager. "Didn't you see it?"

"No. Have you—?"

"Yes. I'll show you." She turned quickly and went through the doorway open behind her.

Guild, pursing his lips a little, raising his eyebrows, looked at Boyer.

The district attorney whispered loudly: "She wasn't blackmailing him? She was stealing from him?"

Guild shook his head. "We don't know anything yet," he said.

The woman hurried back to them carrying a newspaper. She turned the newspaper around and thrust it into Guild's hand, leaning over it, tapping the paper with a forefinger. "There it is." Her voice was metallic with excitement. "That's it. You read that."

Boyer went around behind the dark man to his other side, where he stood close to him, almost hanging on his arm, craning for a better view of the paper.

They read:

MURDERED SECRETARY KNOWN
TO N.Y. POLICE

NEW YORK, Sept. 8 (A.P.)—Columbia Forrest, in connection with whose murder at Hell Bend, Calif., yesterday the police are now searching for Walter Irving Wynant, famous scientist, philosopher and author, was convicted of shoplifting in New York City three years ago, according to former police magistrate Erle Gardner.

Ex-magistrate Gardner stated that the girl pleaded guilty to a charge brought against her by two department stores and was given a six-month sentence by him, but that the sentence was suspended due to the intervention of Walter Irving Wynant, who offered to reimburse the stores and to give her employment as his secretary. The girl had formerly been a typist in the employ of a Wall St. brokerage firm.

Boyer began to speak, but Guild forestalled him by addressing the woman crisply: "That's interesting. Thanks a lot. Now we'd like a look at her room."

The woman, chattering with the utmost animation, took them upstairs and unlocked the door of apartment 310. She went into the apartment ahead of them, but the dark man, holding the corridor door open, said pointedly: "We'll see you again before we leave." She went away reluctantly and Guild shut the door.

"Now we're getting somewhere," Boyer said.

"Maybe we are," Guild agreed.

Words ran swiftly from the district attorney's mouth. "Do you suppose she handled the details of his banking and forged those Laura Porter checks and juggled his books to cover them? The chances are he didn't spend much and thought he had a fat balance. Then when she had his account drained she raised the last check, drew against it, and was running away?"

"Maybe, but—" Guild stared thoughtfully at the district attorney's feet.

"But what?"

Guild raised his eyes. "Why didn't she run away while she was away instead of driving back there in another man's car to tell him she was going away with another man?"

Boyer had a ready answer. "Thieves are funny and women are funny and when you get a woman thief there's no telling what she'll do or why. She could've had a quarrel with him and wanted to rub it in that she was going. She could have forgotten something up there. She might've had some idea of throwing suspicion away from the bank-account juggling for a while. She could've had any number of reasons, they need not've been sensible ones. She could've—"

Guild smiled politely. "Let's see what the place'll tell us."

On a table in the living-room they found a flat brass key that unlocked the corridor door. Nothing else they found anywhere except in the bathroom seemed to interest them. In the bathroom, on a table, they found an obviously new razor holding a blade freshly spotted with rust, an open tube of shaving-cream from which very little had been squeezed, a new shaving-brush that had been used and not rinsed, and a pair of scissors. Hanging over the edge of the tub beside the table was a face-towel on which smears of lather had dried.

Guild blew cigarette smoke at these things and said: "Looks like our thin man came here to get rid of his whiskers."

Boyer, frowning in perplexity, asked: "But how would he know?"

"Maybe he got it out of her before he killed her and let himself in with the key on the table—hers." Guild pointed his cigarette at the scissors. "They make it look like him and not—well—Fremont for instance. He'd need them for the whiskers, and the things are new, as if he'd bought them on his way here." He bent over to examine the table, the inside of the tub, the floor. "Though I don't see any hairs."

"What does it mean, then—his coming here?" the district attorney asked anxiously.

The dark man smiled a little. "Something or other, maybe," he said. He straightened up from his examination of the floor. "He could've been careful not to drop any of his whiskers when he hacked them off, though God knows why he'd try." He looked thoughtfully at the shaving-tools on the table. "We ought to do some more talking to her boyfriend."

DOWNSTAIRS they found the manager waiting in the lobby for them. She stood in front of them using a bright smile to invite speech.

Guild said: "Thanks a lot. How far ahead is her rent paid?"

"Up to the fifteenth of the month it's paid."

"Then it won't cost you anything to let nobody in there till then. Don't, and if you go in don't touch anything. There'll be some policemen up. Sure you didn't see a man in there early last night?"

"Yes, sir, I'm sure I didn't see anybody go in there or come out of there, though the Lord knows they could if they had a key without me—"

"How many keys did she have?"

"I only gave her one, but she could've had them made, all she wanted to, and likely enough did if she was— What'd she do, mister?"

"I don't know. She get much mail?"

"Well, not so very much and most of that looked like ads and things."

"Remember where any of it was from?"

The woman's face colored. "That I don't. I don't look at my people's mail like that. I was always one to mind my own business as long as they paid their rent and don't make so much noise that other people—"

"That's right," Guild said. "Thanks a lot." He gave her one of his cards. "I'll probably be back, but if anything happens—anything that looks like it might have anything to do with her—will you call me up? If I'm not there leave the message."

"Yes, sir, I certainly will," she promised. "Is there—?"

"Thanks a lot," Guild said once more, and he and the district attorney went out.

They were sitting in the district attorney's automobile when Boyer asked: "What do you suppose Wynant left the key there for, if it was hers and he used it?"

"Why not? He only went there to shave and maybe frisk the place. He wouldn't take a chance on going there again and leaving it there was easier than throwing it away."

Boyer nodded dubiously and put the automobile in motion. Guild directed him to the vicinity of the Golden Gate Trust Company, where they parked the automobile. After a few minutes' wait they were shown into the white-haired cashier's office.

He rose from his chair as they entered. Neither his smile nor his bantering "You are shadowing me" concealed his uneasy curiosity.

Guild said: "Mr. Bliss, this is Mr. Boyer, district attorney of Whitfield County."

Boyer and Bliss shook hands. The cashier motioned his visitors into chairs.

Guild said: "Our Laura Porter is the Columbia Forrest that was murdered up at Hell Bend yesterday."

Bliss's face reddened. There was something akin to indignation in the voice with which he said: "That's preposterous, Guild."

The dark man's smile was small with malice. "You mean as soon as anybody becomes one of your depositors they're sure of a long and happy life?"

The cashier smiled then. "No, but—" He stopped smiling. "Did she have any part in the Seaman's National swindle?"

"She did," Guild replied, and added, still with smiling malice, "unless you're sure none of your clients could possibly touch anybody else's nickels."

The cashier, paying no attention to the latter part of Guild's speech, squirmed in his chair and looked uneasily at the door.

The dark man said: "We'd like to get a transcript of her account and I want to send a handwriting man down for a look at her checks, but we're in a hurry now. We'd like to know when she opened her account, what references she gave, and how much she's got in it."

Bliss pressed one of the buttons on his desk, but before anyone came into the room he rose with a muttered, "Excuse me," and went out.

Guild smiled after him. "He'll be ten pounds lighter before he learns whether he's been gypped or not and twenty if he finds he has."

When the cashier returned he shut the door, leaned back against it, and spoke as if he had rehearsed the words. "Miss Porter's account shows a balance of thirty-eight dollars and fifty cents. She drew out twelve thousand dollars in cash yesterday morning."

"Herself?"

"Yes."

Guild addressed Boyer: "We'll show the teller her photo on the way out just to be doubly sure." He turned to the cashier again: "And about the date she opened it and the references she gave?"

The white-haired man consulted a card in his hand. "She opened her account on November the eighth, last year," he said. "The references she gave were Francis X. Kearny, proprietor of the Manchu Restaurant on Grant Avenue, and Walter Irving Wynant."

VII

"The Manchu's only five or six blocks from here," Guild told Boyer as they left the Golden Gate Trust Company. "We might as well stop in now and see what we can get out of Francis Xavier Kearny."

"Do you know him?"

"Uh-uh, except by rep. He's in solid with the police here and is supposed to be plenty tough."

The district attorney nodded. He chewed his lips in frowning silence until they reached his automobile. Then he said: "What we've learned to-day seems to tie him, her, the Fremonts, and Wynant all up together."

"Yes," Guild agreed, "it seems to."

"Or do you suppose she could have given Wynant's name because she knew, being his secretary, she could catch the bank's letter of inquiry and answer it without his knowing anything about it?"

"That sounds reasonable enough," the dark man said, "but there's Wynant's visit to the Manchu yesterday."

The district attorney's frown deepened. "What do you suppose Wynant was up to—if he was in it with them?"

"I don't know. I know somebody's got the twelve thousand she drew out yesterday. I know I want six of it for the Seaman's National. Turn left at the next corner."

THEY WENT INTO the Manchu Restaurant together. A smiling Chinese waiter told them Mr. Kearny was not in, was not expected until nine o'clock that night. They could not learn where he might be found before nine o'clock. They left the restaurant and got into Boyer's automobile again.

"Guerrero Street," Guild said, "though we ought to stop first at a booth where I can phone the police about the Leavenworth Street place and the office to pick up canceled checks from both banks, so we'll know if any of them are forgeries." He cupped his hands around the cigarette he was lighting. "This'll do. Pull in here."

The district attorney turned the automobile in at the Mark Hopkins.

Guild, saying, "I'll hurry," jumped out and went indoors. When he came out ten minutes later his face was thoughtful. "The police didn't find any fingerprints on Wynant's car," he said. "I wonder why."

"He could've taken the trouble to—"

"Uh-huh," the dark man agreed, "but I'm wondering why he did. Well, on to Guerrero Street. If Fremont's not back from Hell Bend we'll see what we can shake the girl down for. She ought to know where Kearny hangs out in the daytime."

A FILIPINO MAID opened the Fremonts' door.

"Is Mr. Charles Fremont in?" Guild asked.

"No, sir."

"Miss Fremont?"

"I'll see if she's up yet."

The maid took them into the living-room and went upstairs.

Guild pointed at the broken window-pane. "That's where the shot was taken at him." He pointed at the hole in the green wall. "That's where it hit." He took a misshapen bullet from his vest-pocket and showed it to Boyer. "It."

Boyer's face had become animated. He moved close to Guild and began to talk in a low, excited voice. "Do you suppose they could all have been in some game together and Wynant discovered that his secretary was double-crossing him besides getting ready to go off with—"

Guild jerked his head at the hall-door. "Sh-h-h."

Light footsteps ran down the stairs and Elsa Fremont in a brightly figured blue *haori* coat over light-green silk pajamas entered the room. "Good morning," she said, holding a hand out to Guild. "It is for me anyway." She used her other hand to partly cover a yawn. "We didn't close the jernt till nearly eight this morning."

Guild introduced the district attorney to her, then asked: "Your brother go up to Hell Bend?"

"Yes. He was leaving when I got home." She dropped down on the sofa with a foot drawn up under her. Her feet were stockingless in blue embroidered slippers. "Do sit down."

The district attorney sat in a chair facing her. The dark man went over to the sofa to sit beside her. "We've just come from the Manchu," he said.

Her lanceolate eyes became a little narrower. "Have a nice lunch?" she asked.

Guild smiled and said: "We didn't go there for that."

She said: "Oh." Her eyes were clear and unwary now.

Guild said: "We went to see Frank Kearny."

"Did you?"

"See him? No."

"There's not much chance of finding him there during the day," she said carelessly, "but he's there every night."

"So we were told." Guild took cigarettes from his pocket and held them out to her. "Where do you think we could find him now?"

The girl shook her red head as she took a cigarette. "You can search me. He used to live in Sea Cliff, but I don't know where he moved to." She leaned forward as Guild held his lighter to her cigarette. "Won't whatever you want to see him about wait till night?" she asked when her cigarette was burning.

Guild offered his cigarettes to the district attorney, who shook his head and murmured: "No, thanks."

The dark man put a cigarette between his lips and set fire to it before he answered the girl's question. Then he said: "We wanted to find out what he knows about Columbia Forrest."

Elsa Fremont said evenly: "I don't think Frank knew her at all."

"Yes, he did, at least as Laura Porter."

Her surprise seemed genuine. She leaned toward Guild. "Say that again."

"Columbia Forrest," Guild said in a deliberately monotonous voice, "had an apartment on Leavenworth Street where she was known as Laura Porter and Frank Kearny knew her."

The girl, frowning, said earnestly: "If you didn't seem to know what you're talking about I wouldn't believe it."

"But you do believe it?"

She hesitated, finally said: "Well, knowing Frank, I'll say it's possible."

"You didn't know about the Leavenworth Street place?"

She shook her head, meeting his gaze with candid eyes. "I didn't."

"Did you know she'd ever gone as Laura Porter?"

"No."

"Ever hear of Laura Porter?"

"No."

Guild drew smoke in and breathed it out. "I think I believe you," he said in a casual tone. "But your brother must have known about it."

She frowned at the cigarette in her hand, at the foot she was not sitting on, and then at Guild's dark face. "You don't have to believe me," she said slowly, "but I honestly don't think he did."

Guild smiled politely. "I can believe you and still think you're wrong," he said.

"I wish," she said naively, "you'd believe me and think I'm right."

Guild moved his cigarette in a vague gesture. "What does your brother do, Miss Fremont?" he asked. "For a living, I mean?"

"He's managing a couple of fighters now," she said, "only one of them isn't. The other's Sammy Deep."

Guild nodded. "The Chinese bantam."

"Yes. Charley thinks he's got a champ in him."

"He's a good boy. Who's the other?"

"A stumble-bum named Terry Moore. If you go to fights much you're sure to've seen him knocked out."

Boyer spoke for the first time since he had declined a cigarette. "Miss Fremont, where were you born?"

"Right here in San Francisco, up on Pacific Avenue."

Boyer seemed disappointed. He asked: "And your brother?"

"Here in San Francisco too."

Disappointment deepened in the district attorney's young face and there was little hopefulness in his voice asking: "Was your mother also an actress, an entertainer?"

The girl shook her head with emphasis. "She was a school-teacher. Why?"

Boyer's explanation was given more directly to Guild. "I was thinking of Wynant's marriage in Paris."

The dark man nodded. "Fremont's too old. He's only ten or twelve years younger than Wynant." He smiled guilelessly. "Want another idea to play with? Fremont and the dead girl have the same initials—C.F."

Elsa Fremont laughed. "More than that," she said, "they had the same birthdays—May twenty-seventh—though of course Charley is older."

Guild smiled carelessly at this information while the district attorney's eyes took on a troubled stare.

The dark man looked at his watch. "Did your brother say how long he was going to stay in Hell Bend?" he asked.

"No."

Guild spoke to Boyer. "Why don't you call up and see if he's there. If he is, ask him to wait for us. If he's left, we'll wait here for him."

The district attorney rose from his chair, but before he could speak the girl was asking anxiously: "Is there anything special you want to see Charley about? Anything I could tell you?"

"You said you didn't know," Guild said. "It's the Laura Porter angle we want to find out about."

"Oh." Some of her anxiety went away.

"Your brother knows Frank Kearny, doesn't he?" Guild asked.

"Oh, yes. That's how I happened to go to work here."

"Is there a phone here we can use?"

"Certainly." She jumped up and, saying, "Back here," opened a door into an adjoining room. When the district attorney had passed through she shut the door behind him and returned to her place on the sofa beside Guild. "Have you learned anything else?" she asked. "Anything besides about her being known as Laura Porter and having the apartment?"

"Some odds and ends," he said, "but it's too early to say what they'll add up to when they're sorted. I didn't ask you whether Kearny and Wynant know each other, did I?"

She shook her head from side to side. "If they do I don't know it. I don't. I'm telling you the truth, Mr. Guild."

"All right, but Wynant was seen going into the Manchu."

"I know, but—" She finished the sentence with a jerk of her shoulders. She moved closer to Guild on the sofa. "You don't think Charley has done anything he oughtn't've done, do you?"

Guild's face was placid. "I won't lie to you," he said. "I think everybody connected with the job has done things they oughtn't've done."

She made an impatient grimace. "I believe you're just trying to make things confusing, to make work for yourself," she said, "so you'll be looking like you're doing something even if you can't find Wynant. Why don't you find him?" Her voice was rising. "That's all you've got to do. Why don't you find him instead of trying to make trouble for everybody else? He's the only one that did anything. He killed her and tried to kill Charley and he's the one you want—not Charley, not me, not Frank. Wynant's the one you want."

Guild laughed indulgently. "You make it sound simple as hell," he told her. "I wish you were right."

Her indignation faded. She put a hand on his hand. Her eyes held a frightened gleam. "There isn't anything else, is there?" she asked, "something we don't know about?"

Guild put his other hand over to pat the back of hers. "There is," he assured her pleasantly. "There's a lot none of us knows and what we do know don't make sense."

"Then—"

The district attorney opened the door and stood in the doorway. He was pale and he was sweating. "Fremont isn't up there," he said blankly. "He didn't go up there."

Elsa Fremont said, "Jesus Christ!" under her breath.

V I I I

Night was settling between the mountains when Guild and Boyer arrived at Hell Bend. The district attorney drove into the village, saying: "We'll go to Ray's. We can come back to Wynant's later if you want to."

"All right," Guild said, "unless Fremont might be there."

"He won't if he came up to see the body. She's at Schumach's funeral parlor."

"Inquest to-morrow?"

"Yes, unless there's some reason for putting it off."

"There's none that I know of," Guild said. He looked sidewise at Boyer. "You'll see that as little as possible comes out at the inquest?"

"Oh, yes!"

They were in Hell Bend now, running between irregularly spaced cottages toward lights that glittered up along the railroad, but before they reached the railroad they turned off to the right and stopped before a small square house where softer lights burned behind yellow blinds.

Callaghan, the raw-boned blond deputy sheriff, opened the door for them. He said, "Hello, Bruce," to the district attorney and nodded politely if without warmth at Guild.

They went indoors, into an inexpensively furnished room where three men sat at a table playing stud poker and a huge German sheep dog lay attentive in a corner. Boyer spoke to the three men and introduced Guild while the deputy sheriff sat down at the table and picked up his cards.

One of the men—thin, bent, old, white-haired, white-mustached—was Callaghan's father. Another—stocky, broad-browed over wide-spaced clear eyes, sunburned almost as dark as Guild—was Ross Lane. The third—small, pale, painfully neat—was Schumach, the undertaker.

Boyer turned from the introductions to Callaghan. "You're sure Fremont didn't show up?"

The deputy sheriff replied without looking up from his cards. "He didn't show up at Wynant's place. King's been there all day. And he didn't show up at Ben's to—to see her. Where else'd he go if he came up here?" He pushed a chip out on the table. "I'll crack it." He had two kings in his hand.

Schumach pushed a clip out and said: "No, sir, he didn't show up to look at the *corpus delicti*."

Lane dropped his cards face-down on the table. The elder Callaghan put in a chip and picked up the rest of the deck.

His son said, "Three cards," and then to Boyer: "You can phone King if you want." He moved his head to indicate the telephone by the door.

Boyer looked questioningly at Guild, who said: "Might as well."

Guild addressed a question to Lane while the other three men at the table were making their bets and Boyer was using the telephone. "You're the man who saw Wynant going into the Manchu?"

"Yes." Lane's voice was a quiet bass.

"Was anybody with him?"

Lane said, "No," with certainty, then hesitated thoughtfully and added: "unless they went in ahead of him. I don't think so, but it's possible. He was just going in when I saw him and it could've happened that he'd stopped to shut his car-door or take his key out or something and whoever was with him had gone on ahead."

"Did you see enough of him to make sure it was him?"

"I couldn't go wrong on that, even if I did see only his back. My place being next to his, I guess I've seen a lot more of him than most people around here, and then, tall and skinny, with those high shoulders and that funny walk, you couldn't miss him. Besides, his car was there."

"Had he cut his whiskers off, or was he still wearing them?"

Lane opened his eyes wide and laughed. "By God, I don't know," he said. "I heard he shaved them, but I never thought of that. You've got me there. His back was to me and I wouldn't've seen them unless they happened to be sticking out sideways or I got a slanting look at him. I don't remember seeing them, yet I might've and thought nothing of it. If I'd seen his face without them it's a cinch I'd've noticed, but— You've got me there, brother."

"Know him pretty well?"

Lane picked up the cards the younger Callaghan dealt him and smiled. "Well, I don't guess anybody could say they know him pretty well." He spread his cards apart to look at them.

"Did you know the Forrest girl pretty well?"

The deputy sheriff's face began to redden. He said somewhat sharply to the undertaker: "Can you do it?"

The undertaker rapped the table with his knuckles to say he could not.

Lane had a pair of sixes and a pair of fours. He said, "I'll do it," pushed out a chip, and replied to the dark man's question: "I don't know just what you mean by that. I knew her. She used to come over sometimes and watch me work the dogs when I had them over in the field near their place."

Boyer had finished telephoning and had come to stand beside Guild. He explained: "Ross raises and trains police dogs."

The elder Callaghan said: "I hope she didn't have you going around talking to yourself like she had Ray." His voice was a nasal whine.

His son slammed his cards down on the table. His face was red and swollen. In a loud, accusing tone he began: "I guess I ought to go around chasing after—"

"Ray! Ray!" A stringy white-haired woman in faded blue had come a step in from the next room. Her voice was chiding. "You oughtn't to—"

"Well, make him stop jawing about her, then," the deputy sheriff said. "She was as good as anybody else and a lot better than most I know." He glowered at the table in front of him.

In the uncomfortable silence that followed, Boyer said: "Good evening, Mrs. Callaghan. How are you?"

"Just fine," she said. "How's Lucy?"

"She's always well, thanks. This is Mr. Guild, Mrs. Callaghan."

Guild bowed, murmuring something polite. The woman ducked her head at him and took a backward step. "If you can't play cards without rowing I wish you'd stop," she told her son and husband as she withdrew.

Boyer addressed Guild: "King, the deputy stationed at Wynant's place, says he hasn't seen anything of Fremont all day."

Guild looked at his watch. "He's had eleven hours to make it in," he said. He smiled pleasantly. "Or eleven hours' start if he headed in another direction."

The undertaker leaned over the table. "You think—?"

"I don't know," Guild said. "I don't know anything. That's the hell of it. We don't know anything."

"There's nothing to know," the deputy sheriff said querulously, "except that Wynant was jealous and killed her and ran away and you haven't been able to find him."

Guild, staring bleakly at the younger Callaghan, said nothing.

Boyer cleared his throat. "Well, Ray," he began, "Mr. Guild and I have found quite a bit of confusing evidence in the—"

The elder Callaghan prodded his son with a gnarled forefinger. "Did you tell them about that Smoot boy?"

The deputy sheriff pulled irritably away from his father's finger. "That don't amount to nothing," he said, "and, besides, what chance've I got to tell anything with all the talking you've been doing?"

"What was it?" Boyer asked eagerly.

"It don't amount to nothing. Just that this kid—maybe you know him, Pete Smoot's boy—had a telegram for Wynant and took it up to his house. He got there at five minutes after two. He wrote down the time because nobody answered the door and he had to poke the telegram under the door."

"This was yesterday afternoon?" Guild asked.

"Yes," the deputy sheriff said gruffly. "Well, the kid says the blue car, the one she drove out from the city in, was there then, and Wynant's wasn't."

"He knew Wynant's car?" Guild asked.

Pointedly ignoring Guild, the deputy sheriff said: "He says there wasn't any other car there, either in the shed or outside. He'd've seen it if there was. So he put the telegram under the door, got on his bike, and rode back to the telegraph office. Coming back along the road he says he saw the Hopkinses cutting across the field. They'd been down at Hooper's buying Hopkins a suit. The kid says they didn't see him and they were too far from the road for him to holler at them about the telegram." The deputy sheriff's face began to redden again. "So if that's right, and I guess it is, they'd've got back to the house, I reckon, around twenty past two—not before that, anyway." He picked up the cards and began to shuffle them, though he had dealt the last hand. "You see, that—well—it don't mean anything or help us any."

Guild had finished lighting a cigarette. He asked Callaghan, before Boyer could speak: "What do you figure? She was alone in the house and didn't answer the kid's knock because she was hurrying to get her packing done before Wynant came home? Or because she was already dead?"

Boyer began in a tone of complete amazement: "But the Hopkinses said—"

Guild said: "Wait. Let Callaghan answer."

Callaghan said in a voice hoarse with anger: "Let Callaghan answer if he wants to, but he don't happen to want to, and what do you think of that?" He glared at Guild. "I got nothing to do with you." He glared at Boyer. "You got nothing to do with me. I'm a deputy sheriff and Petersen's my boss. Go to him for anything you want. Understand that?"

Guild's dark face was impassive. His voice was even. "You're not the first deputy sheriff that ever tried to make a name for himself by holding back information." He started to put his cigarette in his mouth, lowered it, and said: "You got the Hopkinses' call. You were first on the scene, weren't you? What'd you find there that you've kept to yourself?"

Callaghan stood up. Lane and the undertaker rose hastily from their places at the table.

Boyer said: "Now, wait, gentlemen, there's no use of our quarreling."

Guild, smiling, addressed the deputy sheriff blandly: "You're not in such a pretty spot, Callaghan. You had a yen for the girl. You were likely to be just as jealous as Wynant when you heard she was going off with Fremont. You've got a childish sort of hot temper. Where were you around two o'clock yesterday afternoon?"

Callaghan, snarling unintelligible curses, lunged at Guild.

Lane and the undertaker sprang between the two men, struggling with the deputy sheriff. Lane turned his head to give the growling dog in the corner a quieting command. The elder Callaghan did not get up, but leaned over the table whining remonstrances at his son's back. Mrs. Callaghan came in and began to scold her son.

Boyer said nervously to Guild: "I think we'd better go."

Guild shrugged. "Whatever you say, though I would like to know where he spent the early part of yesterday afternoon." He glanced calmly around the room and followed Boyer to the front door.

Outside, the district attorney exclaimed: "Good God! You don't think Ray killed her!"

"Why not?" Guild snapped the remainder of his cigarette to the middle of the roadbed in a long red arc. "I don't know. Somebody did and I'll tell you a secret. I'm damned if I think Wynant did."

I X

Hopkins and a tall younger man with a reddish mustache came out of Wynant's house when Boyer stopped his automobile in front of it.

The district attorney got down on the ground, saying: "Good evening, gentlemen." Indicating the red-mustached man, he said to Guild: "This is deputy sheriff King, Mr. Guild. Mr. Guild," he explained, "is working with me."

The deputy sheriff nodded, looking the dark man up and down. "Yes," he said, "I been hearing about him. Howdy, Mr. Guild."

Guild's nod included Hopkins and King.

"No sign of Fremont yet?" Boyer asked.

"No."

Guild spoke: "Is Mrs. Hopkins still up?"

"Yes, sir," her husband said, "she's doing some sewing."

The four men went indoors.

Mrs. Hopkins, sitting in a rocking-chair hemming an unbleached linen handkerchief, started to rise, but sank back in her chair with a "How do you do" when Boyer said: "Don't get up. We'll find chairs."

Guild did not sit down. Standing by the door, he lit a cigarette while the others were finding seats. Then he addressed the Hopkinses: "You told us it was around three o'clock yesterday afternoon that Columbia Forrest got back from the city."

"Oh, no, sir!" The woman dropped her sewing on her knees. "Or at least we never meant to say anything like that. We meant to say it was around three o'clock when we heard them—him—quarreling. You can ask Mr. Callaghan what time it was when I called him up and—"

"I'm asking you," Guild said in a pleasant tone. "Was she here when you got back from the village—from buying the suit—at two-twenty?"

The woman peered nervously through her spectacles at him. "Well, yes, sir, she was, if that's what time it was. I thought it was later, Mr. Gould, but if you say that's what time it was I guess you know, but she'd only just got home."

"How do you know that?"

"She said so. She called downstairs to know if it was us coming in and she said she'd just that minute got home."

"Was there a telegram under the door when you came in?"

The Hopkinses looked at each other in surprise and shook their heads. "No, there was not," the man said.

"Was he here?"

"Mr. Wynant?"

"Yes. Was he here when you got home?"

"Yes. I—I think he was."

"Do you know?"

"Well, it"—she looked appealingly at her husband—"he was here when we heard them fighting not much after that, so he must've been—"

"Or did he come in after you got back?"

"Not—we didn't see him come in."

"Hear him?"

She shook her head certainly. "No, sir."

"Was his car here when you got back?"

The woman started to say yes, stopped midway, and looked questioningly at her husband. His round face was uncomfortably confused. "We—we didn't notice," she stammered.

"Would you have heard him if he'd driven up while you were here?"

"I don't know, Mr. Gould. I think—I don't know. If I was in the kitchen with the water running and Willie—Mr. Hopkins that is—don't hear any too good anyway. Maybe we—"

Guild turned his back to her and addressed the district attorney. "There's no sense to their story. If I were you I'd throw them in the can and charge them with the murder."

Boyer gaped. Hopkins's face went yellow. His wife leaned over her sewing and began to cry. King stared at the dark man as at some curio seen for the first time.

The district attorney was the first to speak. "But—but why?"

"You don't believe them, do you?" Guild asked in an amused tone.

"I don't know. I—"

"If it was up to me I'd do it," Guild said good-naturedly, "but if you want to wait till we locate Wynant, all right. I want to get some more specimens of Wynant's and the girl's handwriting." He turned back to the Hopkinses and asked casually: "Who was Laura Porter?"

The name seemed to mean nothing to them. Hopkins shook his head dumbly. His wife did not stop crying.

"I didn't think you knew," Guild said. "Let's go up and get those scratch samples, Boyer."

The district attorney's face, as he went upstairs with Guild, was a theater where anxiety played. He stared at the dark man with troubled, pleading eyes. "I—I wish you'd tell me why you think Wynant didn't do it," he said in a wheedling voice, "and why you think Ray and the Hopkinses are mixed up in it." He made a despairing gesture with his hands. "What do you really think, Guild? Do you really suspect these people or are you—?" His face flushed under the dark man's steady, unreadable gaze and he lowered his eyes.

"I suspect everybody," Guild said in a voice that was devoid of feeling. "Where were you between two and three o'clock yesterday afternoon?"

Boyer jumped and a look of fear came into his young face. Then he laughed sheepishly and said: "Well, I suppose you're right. I want you to understand, Guild, that I keep asking you things not because I think you're off on the wrong track, but because I think you know so much more about this kind of thing than I do."

GUILD WAS in San Francisco by two o'clock in the morning. He went straight to the Manchu.

Elsa Fremont was singing when he stepped out of the elevator. She was wearing a taffeta gown—snug of bodice, billowy of skirt—whereon great red roses were printed against a chalky blue background, with two rhinestone buckles holding a puffy sash in place. The song she sang had a recurring line, "Boom, chisel, chisel!"

When she finished her second encore she started toward Guild's table, but two men and a woman at an intervening table stopped her, and it was then ten minutes or more before she joined him. Her eyes were dark, her face and voice nervous. "Did you find Charley?"

Guild, on his feet, said: "No. He didn't go up to Hell Bend."

She sat down twisting her wrist-scarf, nibbling her lip, frowning.

The dark man sat down, asking: "Did you think he'd gone there?"

She jerked her head up indignantly. "I told you I did. Don't you ever believe anything that anybody tells you?"

"Sometimes I do and am wrong," Guild said. He tapped a cigarette on the table. "Wherever he's gone, he's got a new car and an all-day start."

She put her hands on the table suddenly, palms up in a suppliant gesture. "But why should he want to go anywhere else?"

Guild was looking at her hands. "I don't know, but he did." He bent his head further over her hands as if studying their lines. "Is Frank Kearny here now and can I talk to him?"

She uttered a brief throaty laugh. "Yes." Letting her hands lie as they were on the table, she turned her head and caught a passing waiter's attention. "Lee, ask Frank to come here." She looked at the dark man again, somewhat curiously. "I told him you wanted to see him. Was that all right?"

He was still studying her palms. "Oh, yes, sure," he said good-naturedly. "That would give him time to think."

She laughed again and took her hands off the table.

A man came to the table. He was a full six feet tall, but the width of his shoulders made him seem less than that. His face was broad and flat, his eyes small, his lips wide and thick, and when he smiled he displayed crooked teeth set apart. His age could have been anything between thirty-five and forty-five.

"Frank, this is Mr. Guild," Elsa Fremont said.

Kearny threw his right hand out with practiced heartiness. "Glad to know you, Guild."

They shook hands and Kearny sat down with them. The orchestra was playing "Love Is Like That" for dancers.

"Do you know Laura Porter?" Guild asked Kearny.

The proprietor shook his ugly head. "Never heard of her. Elsa asked me."

"Did you know Columbia Forrest?"

"No. All I know is she's the girl that got clipped up there in Whitfield County and I only know that from the papers and from Elsa."

"Know Wynant?"

"No, and if somebody saw him coming in here all I got to say is that if lots of people I don't know didn't come in here I couldn't stay in business."

"That's all right," Guild said pleasantly, "but here's the thing: when Columbia Forrest opened a bank-account seven months ago under the name of Laura Porter you were one of the references she gave the bank."

Kearny's grin was undisturbed. "That might be, right enough," he said, "but that still don't mean I know her." He put out a long arm and stopped a waiter. "Tell Sing to give you that bottle and bring ginger ale set-ups." He turned his attention to Guild again. "Look it, Guild. I'm running a joint. Suppose some guy from the Hall or the Municipal Building that can do me good or bad, or some guy that spends with me, comes to me and says he's got a friend—or a broad—that's hunting a job or wants to open some kind of account or get a bond, and can they use my name? Well, what the hell! It happens all the time."

Guild nodded. "Sure. Well, who asked you to O.K. Laura Porter?"

"Seven months ago?" Kearny scoffed. "A swell chance I got of remembering! Maybe I didn't even hear her name then."

"Maybe you did. Try to remember."

"No good," Kearny insisted. "I tried when Elsa first told me about you wanting to see me."

Guild said: "The other name she gave was Wynant's. Does that help?"

"No. I don't know him, don't know anybody that knows him."

"Charley Fremont knows him."

Kearny moved his wide shoulders carelessly. "I didn't know that," he said.

The waiter came, gave the proprietor a dark quart bottle, put glasses of cracked ice on the table, and began to open bottles of ginger ale.

Elsa Fremont said: "I told you I didn't think Frank knew anything about any of them."

"You did," the dark man said, "and now he's told me." He made his face solemnly thoughtful. "I'm glad he didn't contradict you."

Elsa stared at him while Kearny put whisky and the waiter ginger ale into the glasses.

The proprietor, patting the stopper into the bottle again, asked: "Is it your idea this fellow Wynant's still hanging around San Francisco?"

Elsa said in a low, hoarse voice: "I'm scared! He tried to shoot Charley before. Where"—she put a hand on the dark man's wrist—"where is Charley?"

Before Guild could reply Kearny was saying to her: "It might help if you'd do some singing now and then for all that dough you're getting." He watched her walk out on the dance-floor and said to Guild: "The kid's worried. Think anything happened to Charley? Or did he have reasons to scram?"

"You people should ask me things," Guild said and drank.

The proprietor picked up his glass. "People can waste a lot of time," he said reflectively, "once they get the idea that people that don't know anything do." He tilted his glass abruptly, emptying most of its contents into his throat, set the glass down, and wiped his mouth with the back of his hand. "You sent a friend of mine over a couple of months ago—Deep Ying."

"I remember," Guild said. "He was the fattest of the three *boo how doy* who tried to spread their tong war out to include sticking up a Japanese bank."

"There was likely a tong angle to it, guns stashed there or something."

The dark man said, "Maybe," indifferently and drank again.

Kearny said: "His brother's here now."

Some of Guild's indifference went away. "Was he in on the job too?"

The proprietor laughed. "No," he said, "but you never can tell how close brothers are and I thought you'd like to know."

The dark man seemed to weigh this statement carefully. Then he said: "In that case maybe you ought to point him out to me."

"Sure." Kearny stood up grinning, raised a hand, and sat down.

Elsa Fremont was singing "Kitty From Kansas City."

A plump Chinese with a round, smooth, merry face came between tables to their table. He was perhaps forty years old, of less than medium stature, and though his gray suit was of good quality it did not fit him. He halted beside Kearny and said: "How you do, Frank."

The proprietor said: "Mr. Guild, I want you to meet a friend of mine, Deep Kee."

"I'm your friend, you bet you." The Chinese, smiling broadly, ducked his head vigorously at both men.

Guild said: "Kearny tells me you're Deep Ying's brother."

"You bet you." Deep Kee's eyes twinkled merrily. "I hear about you, Mr. Guild. Number-one detective. You catch 'em my brother. You play trick on 'em. You bet you."

Guild nodded and said solemnly: "No play trick on 'em, no catch 'em. You bet you."

The Chinese laughed heartily.

Kearny said: "Sit down and have a drink."

Deep Kee sat down beaming on Guild, who was lighting a cigarette, while the proprietor brought his bottle from beneath the table.

A woman at the next table, behind Guild, was saying oratorically: "I can always tell when I'm getting swacked because the skin gets tight across my forehead, but it don't ever do me any good because by that time I'm too swacked to care whether I'm getting swacked or not."

Elsa Fremont was finishing her song.

Guild asked Deep Kee: "You know Wynant?"

"Please, no."

"A thin man, tall, used to have whiskers before he cut them off," Guild went on. "Killed a woman up at Hell Bend."

The Chinese, smiling, shook his head from side to side.

"Ever been in Hell Bend?"

The smiling Chinese head continued to move from side to side.

Kearny said humorously: "He's a high-class murderer, Guild. He wouldn't take a job in the country."

Deep Kee laughed delightedly.

Elsa Fremont came to the table and sat down. She seemed tired and drank thirstily from her glass.

The Chinese, smiling, bowing, leaving his drink barely tasted, went away. Kearny, looking after him, told Guild: "That's a good guy to have liking you."

"Tong gunman?"

"I don't know. I know him pretty well, but I don't know that. You know how they are."

"I don't know," Guild said.

A quarrel had started in the other end of the room. Two men were standing cursing each other over a table. Kearny screwed himself around in his chair to stare at them for a moment. Then, grumbling, "Where do these bums think they are?" he got up and went over to them.

Elsa Fremont stared moodily at her glass. Guild watched Kearny go to the table where the two men were cursing, quiet them, and sit down with them.

The woman who had talked about the skin tightening on her forehead was now saying in the same tone: "Character actress—that's the old stall. She's just exactly the same kind of character actress I was. She's doing bits—when she can get them."

Elsa Fremont, still staring at her glass, whispered: "I'm scared."

"Of what?" Guild asked as if only moderately interested.

"Of Wynant, of what he might—" She raised her eyes, dark and harried. "Has he done anything to Charley, Mr. Guild?"

"I don't know."

She put a tight fist on the table and cried angrily: "Why don't you do something? Why don't you find Wynant? Why don't you find Charley? Haven't you got any blood, any heart, any guts? Can't you do anything but sit there like a—" She broke off with a sob. Anger went out of her face and the fingers that had been clenched opened in appeal. "I—I'm sorry. I didn't mean—But, oh, Mr. Guild, I'm so—" She put her head down and bit her lower lip.

Guild, impassive, said: "That's all right."

A man rose drunkenly from a nearby table and came up behind Elsa's chair. He put a fat hand on her shoulder and said: "There, there, darling." He said to Guild: "You cannot annoy this girl in this way. You cannot. You ought to be ashamed of yourself, a man of your complexion." He leaned forward sharply, peering into Guild's face. "By Jesus, I believe you're a mulatto. I really do."

Elsa, squirming from under the fat drunken hand, flung a "Let me alone" up at the man. Guild said nothing. The fat man looked uncertainly from one to the other of them until a hardly less drunken man, mumbling unintelligible apologies, came and led him away.

Elsa looked humbly at the dark man. "I'm going to tell Frank I'm going," she said in a small tired voice. "Will you take me home?"

"Sure."

They rose and moved toward the door. Kearny was standing by the elevator.

"I don't feel like working to-night, Frank," the girl told him. "I'm going to knock off."

"Oke," he said. "Give yourself a hot drink and some aspirin." He held his hand out to Guild. "Glad I met you. Drop in any time. Anything I can ever do for you, let me know. You going to take the kid home? Swell! Be good."

X

Elsa Fremont was a dusky figure beside Guild in a taxicab riding west up Nob Hill. Her eyes glittered in a splash of light from a street-lamp. She drew breath in and asked: "You think Charley's run away, don't you?"

"It's likely," Guild said, "but maybe he'll be home when we get there."

"I hope so," she said earnestly. "I do hope so, but—I'm afraid."

He looked obliquely at her. "You've said that before. Mean you're afraid something's happened to him or will happen to you?"

She shivered. "I don't know. I'm just afraid." She put a hand in his, asking plaintively: "Aren't you ever going to catch Wynant?"

"Your hand's cold," he said.

She pulled her hand away. Her voice was not loud: intensity made it shrill. "Aren't you ever human?" she demanded. "Are you always like this? Or is it a pose?" She drew herself far back in a corner of the taxicab. "Are you a damned corpse?"

"I don't know," the dark man said. He seemed mildly puzzled. "I don't know what you mean."

She did not speak again, but sulked in her corner until they reached her house. Guild sat at ease and smoked until the taxicab stopped. Then he got out, saying: "I'll stop long enough to see if he's home."

The girl crossed the sidewalk and unlocked the door while he was paying the chauffeur. She had gone indoors leaving the door open when he mounted the front steps. He followed her in. She had turned on ground-floor lights and was calling upstairs: "Charley!" There was no answer.

She uttered an impatient exclamation and ran upstairs. When she came down again she moved wearily. "He's not in," she said. "He hasn't come."

Guild nodded without apparent disappointment. "I'll give you a ring when I wake up," he said, stepping back toward the street door, "or if I get any news of him."

She said quickly: "Don't go yet, please, unless you have to. I don't—I wish you'd stay a little while."

He said, "Sure," and they went into the living-room.

When she had taken off her coat she left him for a few minutes, going into the kitchen, returning with Scotch whisky, ice, lemons, glasses, and a siphon of water. They sat on the sofa with drinks in their hands.

Presently, looking inquisitively at him, she said: "I really meant what I said in the cab. Aren't you actually human? Isn't there any way anybody can get to you, get to the real inside you? I think you're the most"—she frowned, selecting words—"most untouchable, unreal person I've ever known. Trying to—to really come in contact with you is just like trying to hold a handful of smoke."

Guild, who had listened attentively, now nodded. "I think I know what you're trying to say. It's an advantage when I'm working."

"I didn't ask you that," she protested, moving the glass in her hand impatiently. "I asked you if that's the way you really are or if you just do it."

He smiled and shook his head noncommittally.

"That isn't a smile," she said. "It's painted on." She leaned to him swiftly and kissed him, holding her mouth to his mouth for an appreciable time. When she took her mouth from his her narrow green eyes examined his face carefully. She made a moue. "You're not even a corpse—you're a ghost."

Guild said pleasantly, "I'm working," and drank from his glass.

Her face flushed. "Do you think I'm trying to make you?" she asked hotly.

He laughed at her. "I'd like it if you were, but I didn't mean it that way."

"You wouldn't like it," she said. "You'd be scared."

"Uh-uh," he explained blandly. "I'm working. It'd make you easier for me to handle."

Nothing in her face responded to his bantering. She said, with patient earnestness: "If you'd only listen to me and believe me when I tell you I don't know any more what it's all about than you do, if that much. You're just wasting your time when you ought to be finding Wynant. I don't know anything. Charley doesn't. We'd both tell you if we did. We've both already told you all we know. Why can't you believe me when I tell you that?"

"Sorry," Guild said lightly. "It don't make sense." He looked at his watch. "It's after five. I'd better run along."

She put a hand out to detain him, but instead of speaking she stared thoughtfully at her dangling wrist-scarf and worked her lips together.

Guild lit another cigarette and waited with no appearance of impatience.

Presently she shrugged her bare shoulders and said: "It doesn't make any difference." She turned her head to look uneasily behind her. "But will you—will you do something for me before you go? Go through the house and see that everything is all right. I'm—I'm nervous, upset."

"Sure," he said readily, and then, suggestively: "If you've got anything to tell me, the sooner the better for both of us."

"No, no, there's nothing," she said. "I've told you everything."

"All right. Have you got a flashlight?"

She nodded and brought him one from the next room.

WHEN GUILD RETURNED to the living-room Elsa Fremont was standing where he had left her. She looked at his face and anxiety went out of her eyes. "It was silly of me," she said, "but I do thank you."

He put the flashlight on the table and felt for his cigarettes. "Why'd you ask me to look?"

She smiled in embarrassment and murmured: "It was a silly notion."

"Why'd you bring me home with you?" he asked.

She stared at him with eyes in which fear was awakening. "Wh-what do you mean? Is there—?"

He nodded.

"What is it?" she cried. "What did you find?"

He said: "I found something wrong down in the cellar."

Her hand went to her mouth.

"Your brother," he said.

She screamed: "What?"

"Dead."

The hand over her mouth muffled her voice: "K-killed?"

He nodded. "Suicide, from the looks of it. The gun could be the one the girl was killed with. The—" He broke off and caught her arm as she tried to run past him toward the door. "Wait. There's plenty of time for you to look at him. I want to talk to you."

She stood motionless, staring at him with open, blank eyes.

He said: "And I want you to talk to me."

She did not show she had heard him.

He said: "Your brother did kill Columbia Forrest, didn't he?"

Her eyes held their blank stare. Her lips barely moved. "You fool, you fool," she muttered in a tired, flat voice.

He was still holding her arm. He ran the tip of his tongue over his lips and asked in a low, persuasive tone: "How do you know he didn't?"

She began to tremble. "He couldn't've," she cried. Life had come back to her voice and face now. "He couldn't've."

"Why?"

She jerked her arm out of his hand and thrust her face up toward his. "He couldn't've, you idiot. He wasn't there. You can find out where he was easily enough. You'd've found out long before this if you'd had any brains. He was at a meeting of the Boxing Commission that afternoon, seeing about a permit or something for Sammy. They'll tell you that. They'll have a record of it."

The dark man did not seem surprised. His blue eyes were meditative under brows drawn a little together. "He didn't kill her, but he committed suicide," he said slowly and with an air of listening to himself say it. "That don't make sense too."

ACKNOWLEDGMENTS

The book has been a long time in making its way to publication, and much is owed to the kindness and encouragement of friends and colleagues: Glenn Lord, Walker Martin, Robert Weinberg, Gordon R. Dickson, David Drake, T. E. D. Klein, Judy Zelazny, Isidore Haiblum, Richard Layman, Otto Penzler, Larry Segriff, William F. Nolan, and Kay McCauley.

We are also grateful to our good and patient agents, Kassandra Duane and Joy Harris; and to New York bookseller Jon White for his knowledgeable assistance in locating individual stories in rare old magazines and books.

We are indebted as well to Martin Asher of Vintage Books and Sonny Mehta of Alfred A. Knopf for their continued support of this book over the rather lengthy period of time from agreement to publication. Edward Kastenmeier gave the best kind of editing one could ask for: exacting, insightful, and replete with good critiques and suggestions.

Finally, a salute to Ellery Queen is very much in order. He was a great connoisseur of the art of the mystery and the detective short story, and his belief in and publishing of Dashiell Hammett's short works for almost twenty years is a lasting achievement.

THE EDITORS

A NOTE ABOUT THE AUTHOR

Dashiell Hammett was born in St. Marys County, Maryland, in 1894. He grew up in Philadelphia and Baltimore. He left school at the age of fourteen and held several jobs thereafter— messenger boy, newsboy, clerk, timekeeper, yardman, machine operator, and stevedore. He finally became an operative for the Pinkerton Detective Agency.

World War I, in which he served as a sergeant, interrupted his sleuthing and injured his health. When he was finally discharged from the last of several hospitals, he resumed detective work. Subsequently, he turned to writing, and in the late 1920s he became the unquestioned master of detective-story fiction in America. During World War II, Mr. Hammett again served in the army, this time for more than two years, most of which he spent in the Aleutians. He died in 1961.